MARILYN K.

"You've heard the story a dozen tir
the lips of hundreds of liars. This guy is driving down a lonely road, all by himself, bored, indifferent, not really going any place in particular. Nothing to do. Then, suddenly, there at the side of the road is this beautiful, young, helpless girl. No one else in sight, nothing but the girl and the lonesome road and she standing there waiting for a ride..."

The indifferent guy is Sam Russell, who soon finds he gets more than he bargains for when he stops for the girl by the side of the road. Lying in a ditch is the remains of her crashed vehicle. And at the wheel, a very dead guy who looks suspiciously like famed mobster, Aurelio Marcus. And sitting nearby, a suitcase...filled with greenbacks. Russell has just met Marilyn K. She needs his help. What's a guy to do....?

THE HOUSE NEXT DOOR

Tomlinson has figured out the perfect heist. But it begins to unravel when a passer-by sees the gun, screams, causing Tomlinson to flinch before he can make the snatch. After that, it's one problem after another. First Arbuckle is shot. After Tomlinson brings his accomplice back to the house, a drunk neighbor accidentally climbs into the wrong window and discovers Arbuckle in the bed. The Swansons are having one of their wild parties that night, so of course no one can hear much over the noise, least of all the gun shots.

The next morning, it's not Arbuckle who is found dead under Mrs. Kitteridges juniper bush, but young Louisa Julio, who had been babysitting for the McNallys. And who do the police suspect of the murder? Why, young Len Neilsen, of course, the poor drunk neighbor who climbed into the wrong window and now has only this preposterous tale to tell in his defense. There may be hope for Tomlinson's scheme yet.

LIONEL WHITE BIBLIOGRAPHY
(1905-1985)

The Snatchers (1953)
To Find a Killer (1954; reprinted as Before I Die, 1964)
Clean Break (1955; reprinted as The Killing, 1956)
Flight Into Terror (1955)
Love Trap (1955)
The Big Caper (1955)
Operation—Murder (1956)
The House Next Door (1956)
Right for Murder (1957)
Hostage to a Hood (1957)
Death Takes the Bus (1957)
Invitation to Violence (1958)
Too Young to Die (1958)
Coffin for a Hood (1958)
Rafferty (1959)
Run, Killer, Run! (1959; orig mag version as Seven Hungry Men, 1952)
The Merriweather File (1959)
Lament for a Virgin (1960)
Marilyn K. (1960)
Steal Big (1960)
The Time of Terror (1960)
A Death at Sea (1961)
A Grave Undertaking (1961)
Obsession (1962) [screenplay pub as Pierrot le Fou: A Film, 1969]
The Money Trap (1963)
The Ransomed Madonna (1964)
The House on K Street (1965)
A Party to Murder (1966)
The Mind Poisoners (1966; as Nick Carter, written with Valerie Moolman)
The Crimshaw Memorandum (1967)
The Night of the Rape (1967; reprinted as Death of a City, 1970)
Hijack (1969)
A Rich and Dangerous Game (1974)
Mexico Run (1974)
Jailbreak (1976; reprinted as The Walled Yard, 1978)

As L. W. Blanco

Spykill (1966)

Non-Fiction

Protect Yourself, Your Family, and Your Property in an Unsafe World (1974)

MARILYN K.

THE HOUSE NEXT DOOR

Lionel White

Introduction by Brian Greene

Stark House Press • Eureka California

MARILYN K. / THE HOUSE NEXT DOOR

Published by Stark House Press
1315 H Street
Eureka, CA 95501, USA
griffinskye3@sbcglobal.net
www.starkhousepress.com

ISBN: 1-933586-87-7
ISBN: 978-1-933586-87-8

Book design by Mark Shepard, shepgraphics.com
Cover illustration by James Heimer, jamesheimer.com

First Stark House Press Edition: November 2015

Table of Contents

Lionel White and the Movies

By Brian Greene

Lionel White (1905-1985) never worked in Hollywood but there are strong ties between White and the movies. Two of the most influential filmmakers of all time – Stanley Kubrick and Jean-Luc Godard – made movies based on novels by White. Kubrick's film noir classic from 1956, *The Killing*, works from White's '55 heist novel *Clean Break*, while Godard's avant-garde 1965 title *Pierrot Le Fou* is loosely based on White's book *Obsession*, from '62. And while these next-named films are not as critically lauded as those two, there's much to be said for *The Big Caper* (1957), *The Money Trap* (1965), and *The Night of the Following Day* (1968), which are based, respectively, on White's novels *The Big Caper* (1955), *The Money Trap* (1963), and *The Snatchers* (1953). The list of stars who acted in those various films is staggering: Sterling Hayden, Jean-Paul Belmondo, Anna Karina, Marlon Brando, Glenn Ford, Rita Hayworth, Richard Boone, Rita Moreno, Rory Calhoun, Marie Windsor, Timothy Carey, Elke Sommer, Joseph Cotten, et al. If all of that isn't an impressive enough set of connections between White and the movies, take in the fact that Quentin Tarantino name-checked White as an inspiration on *Reservoir Dogs*.

The two White novels in this collection have never been made into movies, but it's interesting to consider what might be done in adapting them to big screen features. The likely reason that Tarantino cited White in reference to *Reservoir Dogs* is that White was a master of the heist (gone wrong) novel, as evidenced by *Clean Break* and *The Big Caper*, both of which concern, as Tarantino's film does, criminal outfits who carefully plan large-scale thefts, only to see their schemes go horribly and violently wrong. *The House Next Door*, one of the two stories you're about to read, is that kind of tale. But what's interesting about this heist novel is that it is mostly concerned with the aftereffects of a robbery, rather than the planning and attempted execution of the crime.

The heist in *The House Next Door* occurs right at the opening of the book. A disgraced former cop named Gerald Tomlinson, with the aid of a thug named Danny Arbuckle, has plotted out the following scheme: they are going to head off a private detective who's about to make a large cash deposit for a horse racing syndicate, before the detective can get the money into a particular New York bank's overnight depository. The two will then take the money and run to a safe house Tomlinson has established in the suburbs, roughly forty miles away from the city, this home part of a planned community and inhabited by Tomlinson's widowed sister-in-law and her child.

Their heist goes wrong after it is carried out, for reasons best discovered by the reader. And what White's novel really explores is all that goes down as a result of the botched escape plan of the robbers. People who don't know Tomlinson or Arbuckle, and who have nothing to do with the life of crime, become inadvertently involved in their cycle of mayhem. Some die, one is accused of a murder he didn't commit, others lose their children and one is threatened with losing her spouse, others' marriages become strained to the breaking point ... and much of this tragedy and chaos comes about simply because of the fact that Tomlinson chose a planned community, with its cookie-cutter houses, as his and Arbuckle's initial hiding spot after the job. White's omniscient narrator nicely sums up the domino effect of the aftermath of the initial crime:

"It is an established fact that all too frequently violence seems to set off a sort of chain reaction; as though the very fact of an initial act of violence were to spark a veritable epidemic which travels from one person to another, in greater or lesser forms, so that before long people who have had no connection with the first event are involved in all sorts of odd situations which could not be foreseen and to which they react in various fashions."

The House Next Door is ripe for film adaptation. And, if a movie made from it stuck to the sequence of events as depicted in White's novel, what would make such a film unique from the movies *The Killing* and *The Big Caper* is that it would follow the events that are consequences of a crime. If that setup sounds like it might be lacking in the kind of suspense one would hope for in such cinematic fare, that's misleading; because White's novel is filled with bracing tension, this effect coming from circumstances such as how the police come to tag a particular, innocent man as being responsible for one of the deaths, and that man's wife's efforts to save him from the electric chair. Other facets of the story that bring out excited anticipation in the reader, and that could do the same for a film viewer, include all that goes on in the homes of the handful or so of families who live in the planned community and whose lives are affected, in one way or another, by the madness that erupts after Tomlinson and Arbuckle make their theft and flee to the neighborhood. Just as White's novel does, this hypothetical movie could go into each of those homes and show scenes that make clear how the inhabitants' lives have been shaken up by the pandemonium.

While he was a master at the heist novel, that's not the only type of story White crafted. Using his experience both as a police reporter and an editor of true crime publications for reference, he authored many different types of crime stories. The above-mentioned *The Snatchers* is a thriller that revolves around a kidnapping. *Marilyn K.*, the other White novel you're soon to encounter, is from another classic subgenre of suspense fiction: the femme fatale story. Similar to the superb film noir *Detour*, *Marilyn K.* involves a hapless guy who picks up a troublesome dame on the open road. Sam Russell, the fella who narrates the tale, is driving through a part of Maryland, on his way home to New York by way of Florida, after having done a stint working in Havana. He comes across a beautiful young woman who is standing on the road and he can't help himself but pull over and talk to her. Sam very quickly learns that there is trouble surrounding this woman. She takes him to the car she'd been riding in before their meeting, this vehicle now overturned in a culvert, and shows him the dead man who is in that car. Soon enough it comes out that the deceased is a key player in the syndicate, and that he and the woman had been traveling with a large amount of cash.

The titular character of *Marilyn K.*, Marilyn Kelley, is pure femme fatale. She's a desirable young woman who's part of a popular singing duo with her twin sister. And she's involved with the mob, by way of her past association with the dead man with whom she'd just been traveling. She wants Sam Russell to help her flee the scene of what she says was a car accident, but what Russell suspects involved some kind of foul play. And Russell knows something is amiss when she insists that they simply leave the scene of the dead man without involving the police in any way. Russell makes the decision to do as the beguiling beauty asks of him, and the story takes off from there.

Marilyn K. has more in common with the femme fatale movies *Gun Crazy* or *Double Indemnity* than with the afore-mentioned *Detour*, since the guy who is victimized by the toxic lady in *Detour* meets his femme fatale by chance and gets saddled with her against his will; while in *Marilyn K.*, as in the other two stories just mentioned, the guy knows he shouldn't be doing what he's doing with the dangerous but irresistible woman with whom he gets involved, but he can't help himself. Russell is like *Gun Crazy's* Barton Tare and *Double Indemnity's* Walter Neff, in that as he gets more and more entangled in a femme fatale's web of both passion and peril, he is aware that he is quite possibly sinking into existential quicksand, but all that's happening to him as he slips into the deathly stuff feels so good that he is powerless to pull himself out. As Russell so neatly states in the early part of *Marilyn K.*:

"You think that sort of decision is easy? You think it is simple just to reason it out? To get in a car and forget that a girl like Marilyn K. is waiting for you in a motel bedroom a few miles down the road? That several hundred thousand dollars are waiting in a bedroom a few miles down the road? Would you follow the dictates of your intelligence and drive on back to New York and ignore the fact that you would be passing up something most guys would give their lives to have?

"And that was the key to the whole thing. I would be very likely giving my own life if I did take a crack at it. I think I am probably as smart as the next cookie, but I will tell you something. As I started to open the door of the convertible, I had already made my decision. I was going back to that motel and I wasn't going to spare the horses. That's the kind of idiot I am."

Marilyn K. could be the makings of an excellent film, an addition to the long list of worthwhile femme fatale movies. Marilyn's desirability, combined with the trouble that clearly surrounds her, juxtaposed with Russell's inability to resist her even when he knows his surrender to her is putting his life on the line, is vintage film fodder. And the story has plenty of other characters and facets that would be easily convertible to the big screen. There's a sadistic law enforcement official, a "good girl" who becomes another potential love interest of Russell's and who offsets the "bad girl" qualities of Marilyn K., sinister mob characters who are after Marilyn and the money, Marilyn's enigmatic twin sister whose presence lurks about the story throughout but who only becomes actively involved in the proceedings near the end, etc. There's fisticuffs, gun play, and other raw violence, steamy love scenes, police interrogations ... there's a lot of exhilaration involved in the tale, and all of it is sitting there ready for some filmmaker to adapt it all to a celluloid version.

In sum, what's between these covers are two novels by an under-appreciated master of crime fiction. And what's nice about the pairing is that one of the stories is an example of the kind of tale the author is mostly known for, while the other shows him working in a different vein. Enjoy both, and as you do, imagine what could be done with each if they were made into films that would add to the already impressive legacy of Lionel White's connection to the cinema.

—Durham, NC
June 2015

Brian Greene is a writer of short stories, personal essays, and articles and reviews on books, music, and film. His is a regular contributor to the crime fiction web sites *Criminal Element* and *The Life Sentence*, and has written about crime fiction for *Crime Time, Paperback Parade,* Mulholland Books, *Noir Originals*, and *Crimeculture*.

MARILYN K.

Lionel White

For
Shirley and Dick

Chapter One

You've heard the story a dozen times; a hundred times. From the lips of a hundred liars.

This guy is driving down a lonely road, all by himself, bored, indifferent, not really going any place in particular. Nothing to do. Then, suddenly, there at the side of the road is this beautiful, young, helpless girl. No one else in sight, nothing but the girl and the lonesome road and she standing there waiting for a ride.

So he pulls over to stop and she smiles, beautifully and with that old invitation in her deep, green-blue eyes. She gets into this car, a convertible of course, but with a nice soft six foot wide seat and a top which flips up in a matter of seconds with the push of a button. Of course she takes the cigarette and drink he offers her. And naturally...

Oh well, who can blame them: Those legions of liars and dreamers. Every man would like it to happen, hopes that some day it will.

Maybe we can improve on it a little. Let's say the girl is standing there at the side of this lonely road and she has a small suitcase and inside of this suitcase is two hundred and fifty thousand dollars. Let's go on and say that this girl is in need of help and wants nothing better than to check into the nearest motel, along with her money and her fair young body and her gratitude.

Some dream, eh? And of course it couldn't actually happen. Things like that never really happen. Incredible. Impossible.

But it isn't impossible. Incredible yes, but not impossible. Because it did happen. It happened to me!

And if you think that it's a lie, another in the endless chain of lies that men are always telling each other, then just listen to this. Not only did it happen, all of it, the whole bit including the suitcase with the two hundred and fifty thousand dollars and the motel and the drink and the cigarette and a hell of a lot more—it not only happened, but I would give ten years off the end of my life if it hadn't!

That's right. I would give anything not to have had it happen, anything I own or ever will own, not to have been on U.S. Route 301 on that early Tuesday morning in late April. Never to have seen the slender, silhouetted figure of Marilyn Kelley, standing there in the false dawn beside the lonely, deserted highway, infinitely pathetic and helpless and with the suitcase sitting in the dust beside her.

Route 301 runs on almost endlessly, passing through Georgia, South Carolina, North Carolina, Virginia, a bit of Maryland and Delaware, to end up meeting the Jersey Turnpike.

The part we are interested in is that segment which runs from the Chesapeake Bay Bridge, northeast through Maryland until, after some sixty-five or seventy miles, it crosses the state border into Delaware. It is a particularly lonely ribbon of new two-lane highway, passing through neither towns nor hamlets. It is a relatively new road, which accounts for the lack of commercial establishments along its lop-lolly pine length.

There are few hills and almost no turns. This, combined with a certain lack of vigilance by the local speed cops, makes it possible to rattle along at eighty and ninety miles an hour in comparative safety.

I was doing just that on Tuesday morning, April twenty-first, and I had passed no car in either direction for more than fifteen minutes, when I first saw her. She was standing there, as I have said, just off the side of the road, a slender, appealing figure in the thin false dawn. The minute I spotted her, my foot instinctively reached for the brake. I knew at once what I would do. I would...

But let me explain who I am and what I was doing on U.S. Route 301 on that particular morning.

My name is Russell. Samuel James Russell. Twenty-eight years old, born in Brooklyn, New York and graduate of P.S. 47, four years at Townsend Harris High School, two years at Columbia University, four years in the United States Marines (still in reserve) and two years as a croupier in a gambling casino in Havana.

I left Columbia when I pulled a ligament in my right ankle and couldn't make the varsity football squad; I left the Marines when my enlistment period was up, and I left Havana when Castro took over and kicked out the Americans. I had recently left Florida. I was on my way back home to New York.

I was driving a Pontiac convertible and I carried my worldly possessions in the tonneau in two Gladstones. A sheaf of American Express money orders in the inside breast pocket of my sports jacket established that I was worth something under two thousand dollars in hard cash and I had my health and a clean record.

I had an overriding sense of ennui, a lot of soiled linen, a couple of dozen books and a portable phonograph. I had an illegal .38 automatic which I had taken away from a drunken Cuban in a brawl in a dockside brothel in Key West, a slightly twisted nose which had not been broken playing football, but was the result of a sassy remark to a Havana cop, and I had a tremendous desire to do something to break the streak of utter boredom which had engulfed me during the last three months of loafing.

I had a hangover which I had picked up the previous night in a dismal after-hours ginmill in Alexandria, Virginia, which had made my sleep so restless that I'd gotten on the road around three-thirty in the morning. Four cups of black coffee on the outskirts of Washington had done something for the hangover, but it hadn't done much for a state of chronic depression and so I was driving along, just at daybreak, some thirty miles north of the Bay Bridge, when I first saw her.

She was on the right hand side of the road, standing there all alone, the suitcase beside her. It was one of the few high points in the road, where the ribbon of asphalt crossed over a small ravine.

At first I thought it was a child, but as I instinctively slowed down and the figure grew larger, I could see that it was a girl or a woman.

She wore a small turban on her head and dark chestnut hair escaped around its edges. She wore a light suit, severely cut from something which was probably raw silk, a knee-high skirt and sheer stockings above tiny shoes with Cuban heels. There was a silk scarf around her throat. One white gloved hand was partly raised, tentatively, as though not quite sure of itself.

I was driving almost due east at the moment and the sun, just peeking above the horizon, was behind her so as to silhouette her tiny figure. The details were not clear, but the fact that she was young and attractive and beautifully built, was quite clear.

There was no sign of a car, there hadn't been a house in miles. She was utterly and completely alone.

The Pontiac's tires screamed and even before I had pulled to a stop some fifty yards ahead of her, I had already lost my overwhelming sense of ennui. I backed up fast and made my second stop opposite her. Reaching for the door handle, I knew I had seen her before; was sure I had seen those heavy lashed, gray-green eyes somewhere. They were eyes no man would ever forget.

She took a tentative step toward the car, looking at me with a peculiar, almost frightened expression. Her face was dead white and even as I started to smile and speak, I realized that something had happened. Something terrible.

She made a tiny gesture, sort of half nodding, and then spoke in a low, barely audible voice.

"I've had an accident," she said. "Please help me."

She stood there, making no move to get into the car, and so I got out.

"A lift?" I asked, pointlessly.

"Yes," she said, her voice soft, husky. "Yes, please, I need help."

I started to reach for her arm, to help her into the car, but she stepped back and sort of half nodded with her head, looking over at the culvert.

"The car," she said. "You had better look at the car. He might still be living."

My eyes opened wide. I had seen no car.

"Over there," she said, pointing.

I didn't wait for her to show me, but stepped to the side of the road and looked down into the culvert. I saw it at once.

A large, midnight-blue Cadillac Eldorado. It had apparently skidded off the side of the road and crashed down the bank, ending up against the concrete of the culvert. It was well out of sight of anyone driving along the road.

I could see the still figure of the man between the wheel and the dashboard, his head hanging at an odd angle. When I clambered down the bank, the shattered glass of the windshield told me what had happened. He must have hit the glass with his head and had probably broken his neck. I didn't have to examine him to know that he was dead. He looked dead.

The door at the side opposite him had been sprung open and she must have been sitting next to him and been thrown out. She'd been lucky; she seemed neither bruised nor were her clothes torn or rumpled.

I held his wrist in my hand, feeling for a pulse that wasn't there. But the wrist was still warm. The accident couldn't have happened more than a few minutes previously.

It took only a moment to realize that the Caddie was pretty badly smashed. He must have been doing about sixty or better when he had skidded and gone off the road.

I circled the car, saw that it carried New York license plates.

There didn't seem to be much I could do about the dead man behind the steering wheel and there was certainly nothing I could do about the car itself. So I climbed back up to the road.

She was sitting quietly in the front seat of the Pontiac, holding a small fragment of handkerchief to her mouth.

"Good God," I said, "What happened?"

She looked over to me, lifting her large, blue-green eyes and staring, a sort of odd, dazed expression on her face.

"I don't know," she said. "I must have dozed off. All I know is that I was in the car and then suddenly I seemed to be rolling on the ground. When I came to I was lying in the soft grass down in the ditch and the car was next to me, all smashed up. I got up and brushed myself off and went to the car and he was in it and he looked dead."

She sort of half sobbed as she finished speaking.

"He is dead," I said.

"Oh!"

"Must have hit his head on the windshield. It is shattered, but it didn't give and I guess he broke his neck. Who was he?"

She blinked her eyes several times and gave an odd little shrug.

"His name is Marcus," she said. "He..." she stopped and started to sob.

I got the pint flask out of the glove compartment and poured her a stiff shot in a paper cup. I held it out and she looked at it for a moment and then took it without a word and downed it, making a face and shuddering.

"Sorry," I said. "No chaser. But try a cigarette."

I lighted it for her and held it out and she took it. She still seemed badly shaken.

"Please take me somewhere," she said. "I feel sick."

"I'll get you to a doctor," I said. "I guess the best bet would be to turn back. Head for—"

But she quickly shook her head, reached for my sleeve with her hand.

"No," she said. "No. I'm not hurt. Really I'm not. I just want to go some place where I can lie down and rest and collect myself."

"You sure—"

"Please," she said, looking full into my eyes. "Please."

She didn't have to add the second please. I knew, the minute she looked at me like that, that I would take her any place she would ever want to go. That I'd take her through hell, if she asked me to, kicking the flames out of the way with my bare feet.

I gestured toward the culvert.

"I better get to a phone," I said. "Call the police. They want to know about these things as soon as possible."

The small, almost transparent hand holding my coat sleeve suddenly tightened on my arm and she shook her head violently.

"Do you have to report it?" she asked. "Can't you just take me some place, a motel or somewhere? Can't we just go. I don't want to—"

"Good Lord," I said, "don't you understand? You've been in an auto accident and your friend has been killed."

"I know," she said. "He's dead. No one can help him now."

"But the police..." I began.

"I don't want to see the police," she said. "There is nothing at all I can tell them. He was driving and I guess he skidded or something and he's dead now and there is nothing..."

"Where were you coming from?" I asked, trying to collect myself and just talking to gain a little time while I tried to figure it out. "Where were you headed and where—"

"Marcus," she said, interrupting me. "His name was Marcus, and we were coming from Miami and going to New York."

"Well, Mrs. Marcus," I began, but again she interrupted me.

"Marilyn," she said. "You can call me Marilyn K. Mrs. Marcus lives in Hollis—that's on Long Island."

"Oh."

I was begging to understand.

"Please," she said. "Someone will be along and I..."

I circled the Pontiac and climbed behind the wheel, reaching for the starter key.

"If you turn around and go back," she said. "I think you will find a motel just before the bridge."

"I was heading for New York," I said.

"It would be better to go back," she said, again turning those lustrous eyes on me. "I really should lie down. I feel very faint. I guess I must have..."

I made a U-turn, returning southwest. I remembered having passed a fancy new motel some twenty odd miles down the road.

She wasn't the sort of girl who needed to ask me twice to take her to a motel.

"I feel just a little faint myself," I said. "I wonder if you would mind pouring me a shot of that stuff. I put the flask in the glove compartment and you'll find a paper cup..."

She nodded, saying nothing, but reaching for the glove compartment.

I took my eyes off the road long enough to look at her for a second. I saw that she had placed the small suitcase on the floor of the car, between her feet. I was suddenly remembering something.

I was remembering that there had been no signs of skid marks on the highway. I was remembering that the road was bone dry and I was wondering how in the world he had managed to drive off a perfectly smooth, straight highway and wreck his car. I really needed that drink.

Of course, he could have fallen asleep at the wheel.

I was remembering something else. I was remembering where I had once before seen this girl who called herself Marilyn K.

And I suddenly knew exactly why she was so anxious that I didn't call the state police and report the accident.

She handed me the paper cup, half filled with Scotch, and I took it in my right hand, holding the wheel with my left and slowing down slightly while I put the rim of the cup to my lips.

If I'd had a brain in my head I would have slowed down all the way: pulled on the brake and opened the door of the car and dragged her out and left her there at the side of the road while I got out of Maryland and as far as I could drive, without stopping.

I would have left her, asking no questions, and I would promptly have forgotten that I had ever seen her or seen a wrecked Caddie Eldorado with a dead man behind the shattered windshield, piled up against a stone culvert off a lonely stretch of Highway 301. I would have forgotten that such a man as Aurelio Marcus ever existed, or that I had ever seen him or even knew who he was.

Because by now I knew exactly who Marcus was and I had a pretty fair idea of why he was on his way from Florida to New York. Anyone who ever read a newspaper or listened to a radio or watched television knew who Marcus was.

But I didn't want to think about Aurelio Marcus. I wanted to think about this girl, this Marilyn who was sitting hunched down in the seat of the car beside me. This girl who had seemed familiar and whom I now remembered from that one time I had seen her.

It was the day before I was to leave Florida to start back to New York. I had been standing out on the dock at Baker's Haulover, in north Miami, waiting for the charter boats to come in from the day's deep-sea fishing. I didn't have anything else to do.

I always liked to watch the boats come in, watch the mates take the catch out of the fish boxes and hang the dolphins and the big sails and bonitas on the hooks of the frame at the end of the dock while the fishermen stood proudly beside them and had their pictures taken to show to the folks back home.

The first half dozen boats were already in and it had been a pretty disappointing day. No flags up indicating sailfish; no big ones at all. Just a few bottom grouper and trash fish, a stray sand shark.

And then the *IDA* pulled up and the mate tossed a line to the dockmaster. She was an old Mathews, about fortyeight feet, and she carried twin engines and a pulpit and outriggers. I had often watched and admired her.

She carried three small flags in her rigging, showing she'd taken three sailfish aboard. She only carried one fisherman. One was all she needed.

I guess everyone on the dock that afternoon turned to stare at the girl in the Bermuda shorts, barefooted and with her breasts covered only by a twisted, polka dot bandanna, stepping over the rail, still holding her heavy fishing rod. No one really noticed the rod.

She stood just a little over five feet two and she had the sort of figure that made you instinctively lean forward. She was blonde and her skin was tanned a sort of golden rust color, evenly and beautifully. Just looking at her, a man would suddenly get ideas that he could be arrested for. No one feature really stood out, but you were vaguely aware of perfect, dazzling white teeth, small upturned nose, a firm little chin and broad forehead under the curly, chestnut hair. But it was the eyes which were really arresting. Great blue-green eyes shaded by the longest black lashes I had ever seen.

God, she was something. Miami is a town where you often see beautiful women and spectacular women, but this girl made them all look sick by comparison.

She was grinning, facing into the late afternoon sun and with her eyes squinted as the mate tried to help her ashore. She ignored his outstretched hand and leaped sure-footed, laughing as she landed.

She was the fisherman all right and she had really turned the trick. Three sailfish, all good-sized, a half dozen dolphin, a bonita and four or five great amberjack.

She didn't look a day over eighteen, but she had a face and a figure that any woman of any age would have given her right arm to have and any man would have given both arms to hold.

She laughed aloud when the mate began to hang up the fish and you could see how proud she was of the catch.

She wore no lipstick or make-up and she needed none. She didn't need anything.

It was about the prettiest picture I had ever seen, even without the fish, and I am a guy who likes my fishing.

I knew just what she would look like in a cocktail dress and I could see what she would look like in a Bikini. She was ravishing.

She was Marilyn K.

Chapter Two

I spoke, keeping my eyes on the road, wanting to look at her but hardly daring to.

"Do you want to tell me about, it?" I asked.

She turned and was watching me closely.

"Tell you about it?"

"About the accident."

She hesitated for several moments and then spoke very slowly, her voice showing her inner tension.

"It is like I said. We were driving up to New York. Marcus was going pretty fast. Maybe he fell asleep, or maybe he had a sudden heart attack or a stroke or something. Anyway, I was dozing and then the next thing I knew was when the car hit the culvert and I fell out of the opened door and came to lying on the grass. I got up and went to the car. He was still inside and I could see that he was probably dead."

She stopped talking and I didn't say anything for several minutes.

"And then you came along," she said.

"And then I came along. And now you want me to take you to a hotel and not say anything to the police."

"To a motel," she said, again searching my face.

"To a motel. But perhaps you would like to tell me why I shouldn't get in touch with—"

"I want you to help me."

"I want to help you," I said, and, at the moment, I meant it; I wanted to help her more than anything else in the world.

"I want to help you, but don't you think maybe, if we just reported the accident..."

She reached over, again taking my arm by the sleeve.

"You don't understand," she said. "I don't feel well; I'm not really hurt, but the shock and all..."

"I understand," I said, "but sooner or later..."

"I have to have time to think," she said. "You see, Marcus—Aurelio Marcus..."

"That's who I thought he was," I said.

She again stared at me for several moments before going on.

"You know about him?"

"Yes, I know about him; or at least what I read. Big-time gambler, supposed to be connected with the Syndicate, supposed to be the contact man between the important money and the front men who ran the Cuban casinos. Ex-mobster, ex-union racketeer, ex-professional killer. You came up from Florida with him, you were saying?" I couldn't help the note of sarcasm. You don't expect a girl like that to take up with a guy like Marcus.

"Yes," she said simply. "I came up from Florida with him."

I thought for a second she was going to cry and I felt like a murderer. Instinctively I took one hand off the wheel and patted her small, soft hand.

"You don't have to explain to me," I said. "It's O.K. I can see why you might not want to go to the—"

Her hand turned under mine and I felt the pressure as she squeezed.

"I can explain everything," she said. "But I don't want to have to do it to the police. The publicity. You know what the papers would say; what people would think."

I nodded. I knew all right.

"So if you really want to help me," she said, "please do what I ask you. Take me to a motel. I could be Mrs.—"

Again she squeezed my hand and giggled a little.

"I don't even know your name," she said shyly.

"Sam Russell," I said. "Samuel James Russell. You mean, you want me to register you as Mrs. Sam Russell?"

She looked up at me and this time I did take my eyes off the road. I swear I never saw a more completely naive and innocent expression on anyone's face. A look of sheer guilelessness. A look of pure faith in my own goodness and generosity.

"Yes," she said. "That is what I want. That is, if you don't think your wife would object. Anyway, maybe we shouldn't use your real name."

I was quick to tell her that she would be the one and original Mrs. Sam Russell.

"But I still don't understand why—"

"I have to have time to think," she said. "Just trust me and take care of me. I must rest and I must think and then I have to get in touch with Suzy, you know."

I didn't know.

"Suzy?"

"Suzy is my sister and she always takes care of me and tells me what to do. We can check into the motel and then I'll have Suzy come down from New York after I have rested and then you won't have to worry about me any more."

"I don't mind at all—worrying about you," I said. "And if that is what you want, that's what we'll do. We'll be coming to the motel any minute now. You're sure—"

"Oh yes, I'm sure."

It was a full ten minutes before we came to the sprawling, newly built motel and during those ten minutes I had plenty of time to think.

It didn't make any sense at all.

I tried to remember what I knew of Aurelio Marcus. As I mentioned earlier, I had spent some time working for one of the big gambling outfits in Havana. A famous hotel was the location of the gambling operation, but the hotel merely leased out the gambling rights. I had no idea who actually ran the operation, but one thing I did know: It was controlled by mobs and the mobs, in turn, were controlled by the Syndicate.

Marcus worked for the Syndicate, was rumored to be one of its top men. He had a reputation as a bagman—the guy who carts the dough around, collecting and making the pay-offs.

If you crossed up Marcus, you were crossing up the Syndicate itself and that was just about the same thing as signing your own death warrant. Marcus was rumored to be plenty tough himself, but that didn't worry me. Marcus was dead. I had seen him and there was no doubt in my mind about that. And this girl, who looked like a college kid or the spoiled daughter of a rich family, had been Marcus' traveling companion. Coming up from Florida with him.

There was just about only one conclusion I could draw. She certainly wasn't any run-of-the-mill hooker. But she must have been his mistress. And yet, somehow, looking at her and listening to her, I simply couldn't believe it. It just didn't make sense.

For a second I vaguely wondered if she might be his daughter, using another name to avoid notoriety. But this theory made even less sense than the first one. A guy like Marcus simply couldn't have had a daughter like Marilyn K.

Then who—and what—was she? Why had she been traveling with him and why was she so anxious to avoid any connection with him now that he was dead?

I shrugged helplessly.

Anyway, what the hell was the difference? What did it matter? Who cared?

After all, the important thing was that I had come along when I did, that I had stopped and that she had asked me to help her. That she wanted me to take her to the motel and register her as my wife.

It made less and less sense. Things like this just plain don't happen. That's what I started out by saying and that is what I still—

Once more she cut in, interrupting my thoughts.

"You won't leave me until Suzy comes, will you?" she asked.

I gulped, blushing because of what was just then going through my mind.

"No," I said, "I won't leave you. I promise."

"I knew the minute you stopped back there on the road for me, and I saw your face, that I could trust you to help me," she said.

Common decency made me blush. Seeing the long low silhouette of the motel looming up, I began to slow down to turn into the curving driveway leading past the outdoor heated swimming pool. I remember thinking that tourist spots sure had changed in the last ten years. The owners of this one must have laid out a cool million, building and landscaping their little roadside rest. They had named it the Whispering Willows.

A colored boy showed as I pulled the Pontiac to a stop in front of the office. I got out and opened the trunk, taking out a bag. I helped her out of the car and started to reach for her small suitcase, but she shook her head, smiling. She wanted to carry it herself.

The kid on the desk was about twenty and he had wide, knowing eyes and a rather snotty leer.

I signed the register Mr. and Mrs. George Mason and added New York City after the name.

The clerk said, speaking with a phony Harvard accent, "Twin beds, I suppose."

"You have something with a sitting room?"

"We have two-room suites. Twenty dollars," he said.

It would be worth it, every cent of it.

"There's a carport in back of your suite," he volunteered.

She still carried her bag as the colored boy took a key from the room clerk, who stared after us. My God, you would have thought we were the first couple ever to register before breakfast. I could see the wheels turning in his head. About four hours out of New York, he was thinking. He probably figured we had driven right on through after closing up some night club or other. I knew what was going through his mind all right. And I'll admit something of the same idea was going through my own.

It was a nice suite, even at twenty bucks a day.

I saw that she gave a quick glance at the large couch in the living room as we passed through to the bedroom.

I waited until the colored boy had fumbled around opening the window a crack, putting the bags on stands and sort of patting the bed as he passed. I handed him a dollar bill and asked if he could bring some ice and soda.

He said he could.

"Would you like me to order some breakfast, dear?" I asked, turning to Marilyn K.

She looked just a little surprised at the "dear" and then, catching on, smiled sweetly and said no.

"I think a cold drink," she said.

"Is there a place to get a bottle of Scotch," I asked, as the boy was about to turn away. I didn't think I had more than a couple of ounces or so left in the flask.

"No, sir," he said. "You'd have to go into town. However," he hesitated, smiling and showing a set of the prettiest teeth this side of a museum, "however, I just happen to have a fifth of Haig and Haig, if you can drink that brand."

"I just happen to have a ten-dollar bill," I said, handing it to him.

He wasn't gone three minutes and while he was out of the room, Marilyn walked over and sat on the edge of one of the twin beds and then suddenly fell back, stretching out and opening her mouth wide in a yawn. She had her long slender arms above her head and lay back with her knees bent and her feet on the floor and I swear to God as I looked at her breasts, rising up in twin peaks as she yawned, I could understand why men commit rape.

I shook my head and deliberately turned away, reaching for a cigarette with a shaking hand.

The colored boy came back with the bottle and the ice and the soda and asked if there was anything else. I could tell by the way he asked that he knew damned well I had everything right there that I could ever possibly want.

I snapped the lock on the outside door after him and turned back into the room.

She was on her feet now, standing by the dressing table and looking at the bottle.

"I want you to make me a pretty strong one," she said. "But something else, before you do."

I stopped a foot away from her.

"Yes?"

"Just this," she said, "for being so nice to me."

And before I even guessed what she was going to do she stepped forward and her arms came out and went around my waist and she leaned against me, lifting her head. Her eyes closed and her lips half opened.

I have kissed at least a couple of hundred girls in my day. Every kind and every description. But none of them, none at all, were anything like this.

I could feel her lips against mine, sweet and tasting like wild strawberries.

Her body contoured into my own, pressing hard against me; it was soft and as pliable as a baby's. I could feel the hard nipples of her breasts pressing into my shirt, felt the quiver go through her slender frame as her delicate tongue forced its way into my mouth.

I damned near swooned and if she hadn't pulled away when she did, pushing her tiny hands against my chest and leaning her head far back, I think I would have flipped right then.

"No," she said, as I tried to hold her and pull her back. "No, please, not just now."

I could see suddenly how she had managed to fight those great fish to a standstill and land them. She was surprisingly, almost unbelievably, strong.

I released her, reluctantly. She smiled up at me.

"You kiss nice," she said.

I reached for the whiskey bottle. I needed a drink, myself, now.

"Strong," she said. "Plenty of ice, little soda."

I mixed two drinks. As I did, she crossed the room and took the bag which she had carried in, laid it on the bed and snapped open the twin latches.

"Give me a drink," she said, "and then I will show you something."

I handed her the drink, watching her curiously.

She took about half of it and put the glass down.

"Drink yours," she said.

I drank mine.

"Look!"

I looked.

I swear to God I never saw so much money before in my life. And remember, I'd been working in a gambling casino.

That suitcase was jam-packed full of greenbacks. All in nice, neat bundles, fitted in perfectly, as though the bag had been made for the sole purpose of holding them, which it probably had.

I shook my head a couple of times to clear it.

"Holy Jesus!"

"Please don't swear," she said.

I stared at that money and then I stared at her.

"Holy Je—. Good Lord," I said. "Good God Almighty! Where did you ever—"

She stood up and walked over and put her finger against my lips, shaking her head a little.

"I don't like swearing," she said. Then she turned and went back to the bed and almost carelessly flipped the lid closed.

"If you are nice to me and help me," she said, "I will give you some of it. You will help me, won't you?"

I swallowed about half of the air in the room before I was able to open my mouth.

"Baby," I said. "Baby, I'll help you. I'll be nice to you and I will help you and I will be your complete slave if you want me to be."

"I don't want you to be my slave," she said. "I just want you to be nice to me."

She reached for her drink and finished it and then sat on the bed beside the suitcase.

"You go into the other room now for a while," she said. "I want to just lie down and rest for a few minutes. You go into the other room and sit and have another drink."

I pointed to the suitcase, fumbling for words.

"But that," I said. "That money. Where..."

"Do what I say, Sam," she said. "Please. Just let me rest for a few minutes and then we can talk and I will tell you all about it. Later we can have some breakfast and I will call my sister. But right now all I want is a few minutes rest."

I nodded.

"Please," she said. "Just for a little while." She hesitated a moment, probably seeing the look on my face. She smiled just slightly and said, "After all, we may be here for several days. We'll have a lot of time."

I staggered into the other room, still in a fog.

I hoped that she meant what I hope she meant.

I sat on the edge of the couch in the living room of the suite and I tried to put my thoughts together. The more I thought about things, the surer I was that the smartest move I could possibly make was to quietly open the door, walk out into the sunshine, and get in my car, turn on the ignition, put the

Pontiac into gear and start going. Keep right on going.

Instead, I waited about twenty minutes and then, walking softly, went to the bedroom door. I put my ear to the door and heard nothing. My hand reached for the knob and I slowly turned it. I moved the door in and waited.

Nothing happened.

I opened the door about halfway and put my head inside the room.

She was lying on the bed, fully dressed, the suitcase held in her arms.

She was sound asleep!

Carefully I closed the door. Two minutes later I left the motel. The desk clerk was standing outside, watching a yard man moving garbage cans, and he looked at me but said nothing.

I got into the car and started west. I had decided it was time I made a telephone call. And I didn't want to make it from the Whispering Willows.

I found the glass-enclosed booth about four miles down the road, in front of a broken-down tourist camp. This place was a far cry from the spot where I had checked in with Marilyn K.; a ten-room cabin affair, dying on its feet. I parked and entered the outside, glass-enclosed phone booth.

I didn't find Mel Mitchell at the newspaper but fortunately I still had his private number in my little blue book.

Mel Mitchell is one of those bright young men around Manhattan who, even in his early thirties, was a dead cinch to be a success. When he got out of the Marines, he took a job on a New York tabloid and within a year or so had been moved up from the police beat to doing a column on night life.

He sounded sleepy and a little irritated when I finally reached him. It took him a second or so to realize who I was.

"Why Sam, you old bastard," he said, when I ultimately got through. "Sam, where are you? What's up? And what the hell are you getting me out of bed at this time of night for?"

"It's not night," I said. "It's morning. Anyway I am in a phone booth some damned place in Maryland and I'm paying cash for this call so I don't want to waste time chattering. I'll write and let you know the latest jazz. In the meantime, a favor, if you will?"

"A favor, boy? Sure. How much and where do I wire it?"

"Not money, Mel," I said. "But God bless you anyway for the thought. What I need is a little private info. I want to know something about a girl named Marilyn K. Ever hear of her? A good-looking dish with—"

"Are you kidding?" he cut in.

"Hell no," I said. "I just want to know."

"Boy you really have been out in the woods," Mel said. "Marilyn K., eh? You mean Marilyn Kelley. Are you trying to tell me you've never heard of the Kelley sisters?"

"Right. I never have."

"You better catch up on your rock 'n' roll," Mel said. "Although I still think you are kidding. Why the Kelley sisters are the biggest thing on the platters. They have recently cut *Dream Song* and it will go over a million for sure. The girls are really red hot. What's the pitch?"

"Just curious," I said. "I'm sorry I'm so square. Ran into Marilyn and got sort of curious."

"Listen, Sam," Mel said, his voice suddenly serious. "Don't get curious. There's something you should know. The story around town is that mob money is in back of the girls. That the juke-box combine is personally interested and that is one reason they have come up so fast. The idea seems to be that Marilyn is Aurelio Marcus' private stock, and brother, if it is true, you want no part of any of that."

"Aurelio Marcus?"

"Right," Mel said. "Aurelio Marcus, the bagman for the Syndicate. He's supposed to be down in either Miami or Havana now picking up the loot which was on hand when Castro closed up the casinos. Marilyn is probably with him. She's his traveling piece."

"Well, I just was curious—"

"Listen, Sam," Mel interrupted me, quick alarm in his voice. "Don't tell me you are mixed up—"

"Forget it, Mel," I said. "I just happened to run into her and sort of wondered."

"Stop wondering," Mel said. "If you have to wonder about anyone, wonder about her sister, Suzy. Suzy is safe. Or at least so far as anyone knows, she isn't tied in with any of the racket boys. But Marilyn—brother, watch your step. She's dynamite. And so is Marcus, keed. Dynamite."

"He's exploded dynamite," I said, without thinking.

"What did you say, Sam?" Mel yelled. "What are you trying to tell me about Aurelio Marcus? Have you run across something I should—"

"I can't talk now, Mel," I quickly interrupted. "But thanks for the tip anyway. I'll contact you as soon as I hit town. Again, thanks."

I hung up as he was sputtering over the wire.

Chapter Three

I had the picture.

What Mel had told me really wasn't news. Instinctively I had known the setup. It was easy enough to fill in the blank spots.

Marilyn K. had been Marcus' girl and she was driving back to New York with him. The suitcase? There was only one way to add it up. The money represented the boodle which Marcus had been able to get out of Cuba. His money or the Syndicate's money—it didn't matter. It sure as hell wasn't Marilyn K.'s money. But she had it.

I could see why she wanted a little time to think, as she put it. And I knew what she was thinking about. She was thinking about how she was going to manage to hang on to that money.

Yes, it was easy to figure.

They had been riding along and then the accident had taken place. Marcus was killed and there she was, alone at the side of that road, holding what was probably the best part of a half million dollars, and not knowing quite what to do. The police would find the car, find his body. And his friends would know. They would know that he had been bringing the money back and that she was with him

They would know the money was missing.

I could see why she needed a little time to gather herself. Even why she might like to have a patsy. And I was the patsy.

I slammed the door of the phone booth and I started over to the Pontiac. I walked slowly. I needed a little time myself. I needed quite a lot of time. I had a few decisions of my own to make.

You think that sort of decision is easy? You think it is simple just to reason it out? To get in a car and forget that a girl like Marilyn K. is waiting for you in a motel bedroom a few miles down the road? That several hundred thousand dollars are waiting in a bedroom a few miles down the road? Would you follow the dictates of your intelligence and drive on back to New York and ignore the fact that you would be passing up something most guys would give their lives to have?

And that was the key to the whole thing. I would be very likely giving my own life if I did take a crack at it. I think I am probably as smart as the next cookie, but I will tell you something. As I started to open the door of the convertible, I had already made my decision. I was going back to that motel and I wasn't going to spare the horses. That's the kind of idiot I am.

It was just about then that I became aware of the noise coming from the direction of the shabby little tourist camp outside of which I had found the telephone.

There was a sudden series of high-pitched cries followed by a crash. I swung quickly to face a row of some ten or twelve attached cabins. The sign over the screen door read CUTTER'S CABINS, and underneath it was the small shingle with the single word, OFFICE.

I was no more than fifteen yards away and as I hesitated, staring at the door which was partly opened, the sound of a scuffle reached me and then there was a second, muffled cry. Just outside the door, parked in the driveway, was a beaten up station wagon with Maryland plates. The two things which made it unusual were the red spotlights and the two-way radio antenna.

I moved toward the building. It was my day for butting into other people's business.

I don't know what I expected to find; perhaps a couple of young punks taking over the place, perhaps someone...

But it didn't matter. Whoever had cried out sounded as though they needed help. It sounded like the voice of a child or a young girl. I jerked the door open and entered.

I was right on two accounts. The cry had come from a young girl and someone was trying to take over. Only it wasn't a couple of young punks. It was a big beefy man, about six foot two and weighing a good two hundred and thirty pounds. He made a good match for the car parked in front of the place.

His violent red hair needed cutting and he could have used a shave. His face and his body had run to fat and he had a dirty, uncared-for look about him. He wore a T-shirt which was sweat stained, a dirty pair of tan slacks and a vicious greedy expression on his fat, pug-nosed face. He was grunting as he went about his work.

The little dark-haired girl he had pressed back against the desk wasn't bothering to cry any more and she was giving him a good fight of it, pound for pound. The trouble was that she was outweighed. She stood about five feet two and dripping wet, her slender, well-formed little body wouldn't have tipped the scales at more than a hundred and five.

A couple of deck chairs had been kicked over and a vase of flowers that must have been on the office desk had been knocked to the floor. A framed motto hung cockeyed on the wall and the floor itself was strewn with papers and what had been a desk set. A card index made confetti around the tiny room.

She had put up a good fight, but the fight was over. The only damage he showed was a scratch along one side of his face which was bleeding a little and a torn T-shirt, but from the looks of him, the shirt could have been that way for a long time. The girl, however, wasn't doing as well.

He held both of her slender wrists in one hairy paw and his gross body pinned her down to the scarred desk as he bent her over backwards. His free hand was grasping the thin cotton shirt she wore and as I started across the room, he jerked and the whole front of it came away, along with a strip of fabric which must have been her brassiere. He had his face buried in her neck and he was rapidly getting where he wanted to get. But he never made it.

I may be the careless, heroic type, but I am not a complete damned fool. I took time to pick up the ceramic flower vase from the floor as I crossed the room. I didn't care whether the vase or his skull would shatter when I hit him.

If I expected the big man to suddenly relax and drop neatly at my feet, I was in for a shock. He did, however, pay me the compliment of recognizing a new force in the room and he relaxed his hold on the girl. He straightened up, shaking his head and rapidly blinking his eyes. He turned slowly around. He grunted, but it was a new sort of grunt, inspired by shock and surprise rather than by sex. He grunted again. He had quite a repertoire of grunts. The last one was inspired by anger.

His little red eyes became pinpoints and his flabby mouth opened to show a set of broken teeth. He stuck out a bull-dog chin and moved an arm as big around as a piano leg, pushing the girl aside.

He led with his right, which was a mistake, and I landed my own right full to that bull-dog chin. It bothered him, but it didn't do what it was supposed to do. He kept right on coming in and I knew that if he ever got his hands on me I was gone. But I know something about boxing and I hit him twice more and his nose started to bleed.

That was when he decided boxing wasn't his forte.

The blackjack came out of his back pocket and he got my left arm at the wrist, on the first swing. It didn't break it, but it put it out of working order.

He wasn't satisfied with the handicap. He swung again. He might not have known a great deal about boxing, but he knew how to use a blackjack. I backed toward the door realizing that in just about one more half minute, I'd be lying on the floor with my head split open.

But he was clever. He circled me, cutting off escape.

The girl had spunk. She picked up a heavy brass wastebasket and swinging it, clouted him on the side of the head. But it wasn't going to help.

He had his hand on my throat and his knee in my groin and had backed me to the wall. I saw the blackjack going back for a full swing and there was nothing at all I could do. He was too close for me to use my right. It was then that the voice came from the doorway. A thin, high, slightly effeminate voice which pronounced the words sharp and clear. I didn't have much confidence in the voice, but I should have. It stopped him cold.

"All right, Battle," the voice said. "That will be enough. Drop your weapon."

I felt the hand on my throat tighten for a second and then it relaxed. His other hand, the one with the blackjack, slowly fell to his side. He turned slowly, staring at the little man who stood in the doorway, his mouth opening and his jaw dropping. He looked, very suddenly, like a whipped dog.

"Deputy sheriffs don't beat up their prisoners—not in my county," the voice said, and Battle moved aside and I could see the man who was speaking.

He was about five feet one inch tall, thin as a toothpick. He didn't look more than twenty-six or -seven and he was dressed in a neat blue serge suit, a white shirt and conservative tie. He was as immaculate as his voice. He looked prissy and smug, but I was never happier in my life to see someone and I wasn't going to be critical.

"Was this man causing you trouble, Miss Cutter?" the little man asked.

I thought at first he was talking about the big redhead, but he wasn't. He was talking about me. "You are to arrest troublemakers, Battle," he went on before anyone else could speak. "Arrest them, not beat them up."

The girl cut in before I could say a word.

"Martin," she said, "I have asked you to keep your ape away from me. He came here again and he was the one who was making trouble. This other one—"

But she didn't get to finish.

The little man stepped into the room and he moved so fast I barely saw it happen. His arm shot out and his hand slapped the redheaded man across the face, back and forth, a half dozen times. He hit as hard as he could and I was surprised to see the big man stagger under the blows. For a lightweight, Martin carried a lot of muscle.

"You were told to stay away from here," he said, and his voice was more vicious than his hand. "There won't be any more warnings. Understand? No more warnings."

He shoved past the other man and went to the girl, who was making an attempt to cover herself with her torn shirt.

"I am sorry, Sarah," he said. "It won't happen again. You may be sure of that."

"You should keep your animal chained," she said, her young voice furious. Her hazel eyes were blazing and she was shaking, but I don't know whether it was anger or the reaction to what had happened. It wasn't fear. She was no more afraid of the little man than she had been of the one called Battle.

"If an assistant district attorney can't protect—" she started, but he quickly interrupted her.

"I am sorry," he said. "I promise, Miss Cutter, that he will stay away from now on."

He sounded as afraid of her as the big man had been afraid of him. I didn't get it at all.

"Who is he?" he asked, nodding his head toward me.

"He heard me cry out and he came in and tried to help me," the girl said. "I guess he was stopping to get a room."

She turned and looked at me, making a small smile, and the little man stared at me. His eyes were cold and curious. He was waiting for me to say something.

It was then that Battle interrupted. He had time to collect himself and do a little thinking.

"I was here trying to check the registrations, Mr. Fleming," he said. "That's my duty an' I'm supposed to do it. This girl wouldn't let me see 'em and I was tryin' to and this guy come in and hit me over the head with that flower pot."

The girl swung around, her eyes blazing.

"Flower vase," she said. "And you are lying. When this man came in you were trying to—"

But Fleming cut it short.

"You are both a liar and a fool, Battle," he said, his thin voice like the edge of a razor. "And I have told you to stay away from here. Understand? Stay away. As for you," he swung back to me, "it isn't a good idea to strike an officer of the law. If you want a room, just check in and let it go at that. I assume that was what you were here for?"

I don't know why I did it, but I guess I was still in a fog. But before I had a chance to really think, I spoke.

"I want a room," I said.

The look of gratitude the girl gave me almost made up for the sudden sense of stupidity which overcame me the moment the words left my mouth.

He nodded his small head and again turned to the other man.

"As for you," he said, "it might be a good idea to listen to your radio once in a while. I have been trying to get you for the last half hour. There's been a bad accident up the road several miles. A dead man in a Cadillac in that culvert just before you come to Kilski's broiler farm. Now get on up there. We don't want the state police taking this one over. I'll be along and I want you there. Don't let anyone touch anything until I arrive."

The redhead edged out of the door and the little man again turned to the girl.

"Miss Cutter," he said, "I am very sorry that Battle—"

But she wasn't having any of his apologies.

"You should keep him chained," she said. "I have enough troubles without your pet gorilla coming around here and making more. Some day he's going to—"

"Please," he said. "I have told you. He won't be back. If there was any damage—" his eyes went around the room.

"The damage is personal—to my feelings," she said. She leaned down and picked up a registration book from the floor. "You can sign right here," she continued, ignoring him and smiling at me. "Cabin with private bath is five dollars a day."

I signed, aware of the little man staring into my back. He started to speak again, but once more the girl cut his words short.

"You better get up and see to your dead man," she said icily, and then added, "before your ape steals his wrist watch."

I thought that would get him but it didn't. He just turned and walked out, closing the door behind himself.

"That will be five dollars and you may pay now if you will," she said. "Take cabin six. And thanks for coming in. The Lord knows I can use the business."

She had crossed the tiny office and taken a jacket from a hook on the wall and slipped into it.

"I hope he didn't hurt you," she said. "Is your wrist—"

"It isn't in the best shape in the world," I said, moving my fingers painfully, "but at least it isn't broken. Are you all right? Is there anything—"

"I'm all right," she said. "And you don't have to worry—he won't be back. Martin Fleming will see to that." She was starting to pick up some of the junk which had been scattered to the floor. "As though I don't have enough trouble making a go of this place since Dad died," she said, half speaking to herself and shaking her head and beginning to look mad. She looked up at me again.

"If you don't like number six," she said, "you can have one of the others. They are all empty."

"Number six will do fine," I said. "I just want to wash up a little and then I will be going out for a while. I'll be back later to catch a little sleep."

I started for the door, but her voice stopped me.

"You have forgotten your key," she said. And then, with a certain hesitancy, "I want to thank you. Thank you first for trying to stop Battle and thank you secondly for taking a room which I don't believe you need at all. I need the five dollars but I don't need charity. And even if you did want the room, I think I should advise you to be on your way. Battle isn't the sort to forget what happened. And he carries weight in this county."

She started to hand me back the five-dollar bill.

"If he will make trouble for me," I said, "how about you?"

She smiled without humor.

"Fleming will keep him away from me from now on," she said, her voice filled with irony. "This time he went too far."

I began to get the picture. The assistant D. A. was in love with her and Battle was his boy. I thought it quite possible that Fleming had put Battle up to bothering her in the first place so that he might time his arrival so as to appear to be a knight in shining armor. I dropped the key back on the desk and took the five dollars from her. I had her pretty well figured. She was running the place herself and having a tough time of it, but she wasn't asking for, or accepting, favors.

She must have been reading my mind.

"Martin Fleming wants to marry me," she said. "He doesn't think I can make a go of the cabins, now that Dad is gone. He wants to take care of me."

"And you?"

"I can take care of myself," she said.

"I think you can. And I wish you luck."

She was back straightening out the office as I left.

The thought of Sarah Cutter and her personal problems quickly faded from my mind as I got back into the Pontiac and headed for the Whispering Willows. It had been an unpleasant interlude, but it was over and done with and I had more important things to think about. I had Marilyn K. and a suitcase full of money to think about.

And I had reached a decision.

I would stop at the motel, but I wanted to put as many miles as I could between that dead man up the road, crouched down behind the wheel of his wrecked Caddie, and myself. I would pick up the girl and her suitcase—and also my own suitcase which I had left at the tourist camp—and we would get out of Maryland as fast as we could. It would be dangerous enough to be with her, but it would be doubly dangerous to be anywhere in this neighborhood.

The boys from New York would be on their way down in no time at all; even without them, I wanted nothing to do with Martin Fleming's private territory. I would be having troubles enough without him and his stooge, Battle.

An hour later I realized I could have saved myself considerable mental and emotional energy if I hadn't bothered making decisions. The decisions which were to vitally effect my immediate future were already made. They were made by the girl who was waiting for me at Whispering Willows and her decisions were a lot stronger and a lot more binding than any I might formulate.

Marilyn K. knew exactly what she planned to do and she also knew what she wanted me to do. It wasn't that she was stronger than I am or any more stubborn; it was merely that she was a hell of a lot more persuasive. And she was endowed with exactly the proper weapons and the right ammunition to win all her points.

I parked the Pontiac in the driveway and walked down the path which led to the lobby of the motel. There was no one at the desk when I passed on my way to the rooms we had checked into.

I keyed the door open, walked through the living room of the suite and carefully opened the door of the bedroom. I didn't want to alarm her if she was still sleeping.

I was wasting my time being quiet about it.

One of the prettiest pictures in the world is a really beautiful girl sitting cross-legged on a double bed, her hair rumpled and down over one eye, dressed in nothing but a brassiere and panties and with her stockings rolled down just below her knees. It is especially fetching if the girl happens to be smiling when she looks up at you.

There is only one thing which can improve this picture and Marilyn K. had managed it.

She was sitting there counting money.

The smile, which was a seemingly impossible blend of childish delight, wickedness and invitation, turned into a tingling laugh.

"Three hundred and thirty-five thousand dollars," she said. "And I called Suzy."

I didn't say anything. I just stood there in the doorway with my mouth open.

"Where did you go?" she asked. "I missed you."

I made it all the way into the room.

"Phone call," I said. "You were sleeping."

The words were automatic; my mind was on other things. My mind was on the staggering pile of greenbacks. My mind was on the small, slender, beautifully formed body of the girl who sat there with her tiny hands still leafing them. The money lost out to the girl, which merely goes to prove that whereas money may be the root of all evil, it sure as hell isn't the root of all desire.

"Give me the suitcase, Sam," she said, "and I'll put it back. While I am doing it, you can make me a drink. A small one."

I had a little trouble taking my eyes away from her long enough to pick up the bag from where she had dropped it on the floor.

"I'll make us both a drink," I stuttered. "And get that stuff put away. We have to get out of here."

I found it hard to be convincing. If there was one thing in the world I didn't want to do at that moment, it was to leave that particular room. But some lingering fragment of common sense remained and my words were making more sense than my intentions.

"We have to get as far away from here as soon as we can." I said. "The police have found Marcus," I added. "The story will be on the wires any minute now, if it already isn't. So put that money away and get into your clothes. We're moving."

She didn't say anything and I turned away to pour the drinks. There was still a little ice left in the bucket and I made them straight, on the rocks. I needed a strong drink. My hand was shaking a little and it could have been from the blow which Battle had struck on my wrist or it could have been something else, but in any case I spilled the first drink and had to spend a few extra moments wiping up the mess and repouring. By the time I had turned back, ready to hand her the drink, I expected she would be dressing.

But she hadn't moved.

"I told you I called Suzy," she said, her mouth petulant. "We can't leave until Suzy comes. Suzy said she couldn't start before noon."

For a second I forgot she was a hundred and ten pounds of sheer, unadulterated sex, that she was sitting cross-legged on a double bed almost naked and that she wanted to stay on that bed.

"Listen, kid," I said, walking over and handing her the drink. "I don't think you understand. Marcus has been found. The police will identify him and the second they do, you can bet the story will get out. It will probably make the radio newscasts. It will be heard in New York. There will be people coming down here. I don't have to draw a diagram, do I, baby?"

She looked at me with a hurt expression.

"They won't know where I am," she said. "Anyway they won't even be sure I was with him."

"They'll guess," I said. "They'll guess about you and they'll damn soon find out about the money. So forget about Suzy. Suzy can't help you. No one is going to help you—so long as you have that suitcase."

"But Suzy will help," she said, frowning. "Anyway, I promised her I would wait here."

"So leave her a message."

But even as I said it, I realized that would be impossible. Any message which reached Suzy could be traced. Mentally I damned this Suzy. I didn't want any sisters butting in, in any case. And I didn't want to hang around waiting for sure trouble. I looked at my watch. It was just half past eleven.

"Listen," I said, "I don't know why you feel you have to have your sister, but if you say you do it's O.K. with me. But we can't wait around here for her and we can't leave any messages for her. You said she was leaving at noon. Call her back then and get her before she does leave. Tell her—well, tell her to go to Baltimore. Check into a hotel under a phony name and we will contact her."

For a moment she looked doubtful and then once more she looked up at me and smiled, nodding. She started to reach for the telephone.

"Not from here," I said quickly. "That goes through a switchboard in the office. There's a phone booth at a little tourist place called *Cutter's Cabins*, about three or four miles down the road, toward the bridge. We'll leave and you can make the call from there."

She could move when she wanted to. Even before I was through speaking, she was off the bed and had grabbed her clothes from the chair where she had tossed them.

"I'll go and you stay here and get washed up. It will make you feel better," she said. "I can take your car—"

"But we both might just as well—" I began.

"No," she said. "You stay and wait. After all, if I can't get Suzy, we will both have to wait here. If I do reach her in time, well, I'll come right back. You get washed up and be ready to leave."

She had a quick mind and she saw the sudden look I gave to the suitcase which held the money. She made a face and laughed.

"I'll leave the money with you while I am gone, Sam," she said. "You can trust me."

I was ashamed of what I had been thinking. That's probably why I wasn't thinking quite straight.

She had got into her clothes quicker than a strip-teaser could get out of them and she stepped over in front of me and looked up into my face and then stood on her toes and quickly kissed me on the lips.

"Let me have the keys to the car, Sam," she said. "I won't be more than fifteen minutes. You said about four miles down the road?"

I nodded and handed her the keys.

"Make it fast, kid," I said. "I'll be ready by the time you get back."

She kissed me again and my arms started to go around her slender waist, but she dodged away with the dexterity of a ballet dancer and a second later she was closing the door behind her. She had my keys in her hand and her heavy leather pocketbook slung from a strap over her shoulder.

I am normally not a sneaky type and I don't usually read other people's mail or poke through their private possessions, but within two minutes from the time she had left the room, I wasn't in the bathroom washing up. I was looking into an open suitcase and making a rapid mental calculation.

She would have made a darned good bank teller. My estimate was that three hundred and thirty-five thousand dollars would just about hit it on the head.

For a moment I was just slightly bewildered that she would have taken off as she did, even for fifteen minutes, and trust me with that much money. And then, of course, it occurred to me that although I might have the money, she had my car.

And anyway, she was no fool. She knew that I would be a damned sight more interested in the money with her, than I would be without her.

I just prayed that she would get hold of her Suzy quickly and return.

The Whispering Willows was beginning to whisper things I didn't want to hear.

Chapter Four

I began to worry the moment she left the room. It occurred to me, after what seemed like an endless wait, that she might have decided to get in my car and just keep on going. Perhaps she had come to her senses, had realized the danger of attempting to keep Marcus' money.

But I didn't entertain that thought for very long. I had only known her a very short time, but I felt that I knew her well enough to realize she had no intention of abandoning more than a quarter of a million dollars. She would be back all right.

The next thought I had was that perhaps it wasn't Sister Suzy she had gone out to telephone to. There was a sister Suzy all right; of that I had made sure when I had called Mel in New York. But this obsession about getting her down to Maryland? There was something very odd about it. Very odd indeed.

Speculation was futile. I had no way of figuring what was in her mind, no way of knowing what she planned. I was having enough difficulty straightening out what was in my own mind. But at least, without her disturbing personal presence, I was beginning to think a little more clearly. I knew exactly what I would say and what I would do the moment she returned. No more uncertainty for me.

If she wanted me to play along with her, she was going to have to do it my way. She was going to listen to reason. I'd risk my neck for her but I wasn't going to stack the deck against myself.

The wind had tossed her chestnut hair and her azure eyes had apparently absorbed the cerulean blue of the spring skies and when she opened the door and again entered the room, she looked more than ever like a seventeen-year-old schoolgirl. She was smiling that secret smile—she always seemed to be smiling when she wasn't pouting—and the moment she came in she crossed over and again stood on her toes and lifted her face and kissed me.

I should have known by this time what it meant.

"Suzy wasn't there," she said. "I couldn't reach her. We'll just have to wait."

I took her by the arms, careful not to bruise her soft flesh, and picked her up and carried her over and sat her on the edge of the bed. She started to say something, but I put my hand over her soft lips.

"You are going to sit right there and listen," I began.

The lips puckered and she kissed the palm of my hand, and then the lips opened and her tongue, hot as a flame, licked me like a cat would lick me. I almost stopped talking, but I didn't.

I said, "Listen. We are not going to wait for Suzy. We are not going to wait for anyone at all. Understand? We are leaving. Right now."

"But, Sam," she said, moving her mouth away from my hand.

"No buts, baby," I said. "You listen. We don't have any more time to play games. Understand? No games. Marcus is dead. This money here belonged to him, or rather, it belonged to the boys higher up. You want the money and maybe you are entitled to it and maybe you are not. I don't care. If you want it, and you think it should go to you, I'll help you take it. Although I'll tell you this, sweetheart, I think you are crazy to try to get away with it."

"You think I am stealing it," she said. It wasn't a question.

"I don't care," I said.

She shook her head and the pout was back.

"You listen to me, Sam," she said. "I have a right to the money. You seem to know about Marcus, so you probably have heard about me. You probably have ideas about me—me and Marcus. Well, I don't care what you think. That money is mine. I gave a lot to Marcus. Gave him everything. And that money isn't half of what he promised me in return. But now he's dead. Once that is known, I'm through. Understand? Through."

"Don't be stupid," I said. "You still have your voice. Still have your rep. Why you and your sister can go on now and—"

"You *are* naive," she said, her voice suddenly angry. "I guess you just don't understand. It was Marcus—Marcus and his connections—which put Suzy and me across. He owned the record company which made our platters. He owned the distributors which released them. He had the connections with the juke box boys who played them. Sure, we were going places and if he hadn't killed himself, we would have made it. But now he's dead. His connections don't care about me and Suzy. And his wife, who will get his record business, hates us. Once the newspapers get hold of the story about his death, I'm washed up. Do you think any legitimate outfit wants to take on the ex-mistress of a racketeer? Do you think—"

She stopped suddenly and for the first time since I had met her, I realized she had spoken in complete sincerity. Sincerity and bitterness.

"Marcus owes me that money," she said, "and I mean to keep it. If you want to help me, I'll share it with you. That is, of course," she added, hesitating, "I'll share it with you and Suzy. Suzy has to have her share."

"And what makes you think that sister Suzy will go along?" I began, but again she interrupted me.

"Suzy always handles things," she said. "And Suzy will do what I ask her to do. Suzy loves me."

"And so we just wait here for Suzy?"

"We wait."

I stepped back. It was an effort, but I stepped back and I leaned down and picked up the suitcase.

"And you insist on keeping this money?"

"Yes," she said.

"And waiting for Suzy right here?"

"Yes."

"All right, baby," I said. "I have told you what I think. Now I will tell you what I am going to do. I am going to take this suitcase and go out and get into the car. If you want to come with me, come right now and get out of this trap. I'll go along with you and I'll do everything I can to see that you make a clean getaway—with the money. If you don't—"

"If I don't?"

"I'll still take the money. And I'll turn it over to the nearest cop I can find."

For a moment she stared at me, neither anger nor fear nor surprise on her lovely, childlike face.

"You wouldn't, Sam," she said.

"I would, baby."

I didn't think she was going to go along with it. I didn't think she really believed me. I don't even know myself if I was telling the truth. But she didn't give me the chance to find out.

The smile was suddenly back—a little pathetic and making her look like a slightly recalcitrant and slightly hurt child. She shrugged, started to get to her feet.

"All right, Sam," she said. "All right, honey. You're the boss."

I couldn't help the surge of masculine pride.

"Then let's get with it." I lifted the suitcase from the floor and moved over to pick up my own bag.

"Just let me pour one more drink," she said.

"Sure, baby," I said. I could afford to be generous. I'd just proven who was the stronger.

I had to drop the suitcase with the money to the floor while I leaned over to latch my own Gladstone. I had my back to her and I could hear the gurgle of the liquor as she poured from the bottle of Scotch.

"We'll each have a drink," she said.

"Sure," I said.

I could hear her step toward me.

"Here's yours, Sam," she said.

And then it hit me.

I guess I must have known, at the last split second, what she was going to do, because I remember thinking *I hope to God the bottle breaks, otherwise I won't have a head left.*

I didn't have time for any more idle thoughts. I was too busy observing a galaxy of northern lights and discovering a whole new private world of constellations. First the lights and the stars and then the sense of my head leaving my shoulders and then just nothing.

I was either loaded with luck or else she was an expert, because the bottle didn't break and it didn't fracture my skull. It just knocked me out cold as a neglected mackerel.

I don't know exactly at what moment the realization came to me that I was still alive. I only know that when it did, for the next several minutes, I was sorry. It seemed that someone was slowly beating my brains out with a baseball bat while an evil confederate was tearing my eyeballs from their sockets. I have had headaches before, but never one which could quite equal that one in vicious intensity.

But gradually I knew that I was living and breathing and gradually I came to understand that no one was batting my brains out—that I just had a headache to end all headaches.

I forced one eye open and then the other one and I started to move my head, but I quickly saw the silliness of that. So I just lay there, trying not to move and increase what was obviously a pain which had already reached the limits of my endurance. It took a moment to even realize where I was or what had happened.

I remembered what had happened first. But where I was came a little harder.

I thought at first that the blow had probably blinded me and that that was why everything seemed dark. But then I understood that the venetian blinds had been drawn and the heavy drapes pulled over the windows and the lights turned out. I could, however, make out the outlines of the motel bedroom.

What confused me was that I wasn't lying on the floor. There was a mattress under me and a sheet over me. I lifted a hand, reaching for my throbbing forehead, but the hand didn't make it. It stopped somewhere on my chest and it was then I realized that I was stark naked. Lying on the bed, between white cotton sheets, without a stitch of clothes on my body.

I didn't know how I had gotten there and I didn't really care. I was too busy at the moment trying to figure out if there was anything left of my skull.

It may have been five minutes or it may have been an hour, but gradually the horrible shooting pains began to recede. Gradually I had a little room for considering something besides the agony of my aching head.

So she had conked me with the whiskey bottle. I hadn't wanted to play it her way and she'd taken the matter in her own hands. And I had naively thought that I was going to be the one to take care of her.

If the effort hadn't been so great I would have laughed.

Well, she was gone now and so was the money. The money I didn't regret. It wasn't mine and I had never had it. But I had almost had her and in spite of the king-sized headache, I was able to regret that.

It was about then that I became aware of a movement in the room.

Someone was quietly crossing the floor, approaching the bed. Someone was probably going to finish the job she had started.

I told myself I should get up and do something about it, although for the life of me, in my present condition I couldn't imagine what. I did the one thing which at the time seemed to make the most sense. I closed my eyes and tried to comfort myself with the thought that nothing which could happen could be more painful than that which already had.

I felt the sheet over me move.

The bedsprings sagged gently.

And then a small, soft hand lingered for a moment on my cheek and in another moment she had slid in under the sheet beside me and I could feel her soft flesh as her lithe, slender body pressed close to me.

I lay for a moment breathless, afraid to move. It was a dream I didn't care to disturb.

I was lying sprawled on my back and she snuggled close with her head over my outstretched right arm. She moved and her lips suddenly touched my head just behind my ear. I could feel her fine gossamer hair as it caressed my cheek like a wanton spider web. She pressed a little closer and her lips moved, slowly traveling down from my ear to my neck. Her hand was across my chest and it moved slowly down my side. I could feel the hard acorn of her erect nipples as they pressed against my side.

Her body tautened and moved closer and her lips were under my chin and on my neck and then she suddenly moved and raised herself and her lips found my own.

I almost went out again and I don't know how long we held the kiss. At last she moaned and she pulled me, turning a little away.

She had found my left hand and guided it and when she was satisfied with that, her own hands had again moved down. And then I too turned and now she was breathing as deeply as I was breathing.

I felt the blood in my veins surge and churn and the northern lights and the constellations and the unchartered stars were back, but I no longer cared about them.

The bed had found a life of its own.

The tiny hands were on my shoulders now, the nails digging into my flesh and my own two hands had at last discovered the soft natural curves below and behind. Her mouth was wide on my own as she drew me in, moaning and writhing.

There was no longer any headache, no longer any suitcase filled with thousands of dollars, no longer any room in a motel. There was only herself and myself, the single ecstatic unit into which we had blended. Only the rhythmic, tossing surge of our passion.

Her nails suddenly dug deep into my flesh and this time she cried out and her small white teeth bit sharply into my neck and the moment had arrived when the whole world ended.

We must have lain there, side by side, for a full ten minutes before she finally stirred and spoke.

"I am sorry I had to hit you with the bottle, Sam," she said.

I was breathing like a wounded stag, but I managed an answer. It wasn't bright, but I meant every word of it.

"You can hit me any time you like, baby," I said.

She laughed and then, before I knew what she was going to do, she leaped up, tossing the sheet from the bed. I heard the pitter-patter of her steps across the room and suddenly the light went on, half blinding me.

"I put the cork in the bottle before I hit you," she said, facing me coolly and serenely in all her exciting nakedness, "so it wouldn't spill. I'll make you a drink."

She thought of everything.

She sat on the edge of the bed, holding her own glass as I sat up and swallowed my drink.

"You'll be nice, won't you, Sam, and wait for Suzy?" she said. "It is really best."

"If you put that glass down and turn that light off," I said, "I'll wait for Suzy. I'll wait for Marcus' ghost or any damned thing in or out of this world you want me to wait for."

She leaned over and patted my cheek. "You are sweet," she said. "And you won't be sorry, either. You'll like Suzy. I know you will."

"I like you," I said. "And that's enough for any one man. Put down the drink. Turn out the light."

She carefully set the glass on the floor.

"I can see, my boy," she said, "that you are a glutton for punishment. But we'll leave the light on. I like the light to be on."

I started to reach for her but she moved off the bed.

"You just lie and rest for a few minutes," she said. "We have a lot of time. Suzy won't be here for at least another couple of hours."

She was reaching for her clothes and I guess she saw the look on my face.

"I'll only be a minute," she said. "I'm going to have that bellboy find another bottle of Scotch. Suzy will want a drink when she gets here and we will, probably, be all out. But I'll be right back. How is your head? I was careful to hit you on the side of it so I wouldn't really hurt you."

"My head is fine," I said. "It isn't my head that is bothering me. It's my—"

She laughed and tossed her clothes back on the chair. "I'll just slip into your shirt and trousers while I send for the liquor," she said. "It's quicker."

She was facing me as she stretched out her slender arms to put them into the sleeves of my shirt and I was lost in admiration at the perfection of her beautifully rounded body. Her skin was a delicate ivory, as smooth as satin and without a blemish. There wasn't an ounce of surplus flesh on her, and yet every bone was softly concealed.

My eyes traveled down her lovely figure, lingering on the satin-smooth slopes of her breasts. I noticed, too, the odd, heart-shaped birthmark on her hip, just below the bone where the curve began.

Somehow it enhanced her loveliness. It could have been painted on by an artist to accentuate the sweetness of her curving, voluptuous thigh.

"The hell with the whiskey," I began, but she moved quickly across the room, again doing the trick, with her hand over my lips.

"I told you, darling, that I'll only be a minute," she said. The hand moved down to caress me.

"You can wait for a couple of minutes, can't you, sweet?"

"I'm not sure that I can," I said, and I really meant it.

It was more like fifteen minutes than one before she was back, holding a fresh bottle of unopened Scotch in her hand. She set it on the dresser and began to unbutton my white shirt, slipping her arms out of the sleeves.

The trousers fell to the floor and she stretched, lifting her hand to stifle a tiny yawn.

"See," she said, "I told you I would be right back." She moved toward the bed, her naked body gliding forward with a soft, liquid grace.

"And now, until Suzy gets here," she said, "we won't think about anything at all but just us."

She was right as usual. For the next two hours, nothing in this world existed except the two of us. There was no suitcase full of money, there was no Suzy, there was no dead racketeer named Marcus. There was no problem and no future and no past. Just the wildly delicious, ecstatic, intoxicating, overpowering present.

Two hours that proved everything man has learned since Adam and Eve took a bite of that apple has been pretty much a waste of time and energy.

Chapter Five

I didn't wait for the weather report, but reached over and switched off the television set as soon as the newscaster was through speaking and the commercial started to come on.

We were sitting in the living room and I was in my shorts and Marilyn was fully dressed. I drew a long puff from the cigarette I held in my hand and looked at my wrist watch, which was a wasted gesture as I had just heard the announcer give the time. I started to get up.

"She still isn't here, kid," I said. "We're crazy to hang around any longer. You heard the broadcast. Everybody in America knows that Marcus was killed up the road in that car accident."

"You promised, Sam," Marilyn said.

"I know, baby. But how long do we wait? Can't you understand? Marcus' friends—"

"She'll be here, Sam. And don't forget, Marcus' friends don't know where we are. They won't even be sure that I was with him."

"You know better than that," I said.

"All right. They'll know. But we have to wait, anyway. Oh, honey, don't worry. Think about the future. Just you and me and Suzy and all this money."

She looked over to the table where the suitcase lay, still opened where we had left it when we had recounted the money a few minutes ago.

"Just the three of us. In South America where we'll be safe. And, honey, you'll love Suzy. You'll love her as much as you'll love me. Just be patient."

"Sure," I said. "Sure. But I don't need Suzy, honey. One of you is plenty. Plenty for any man. Anyway, what will Suzy think? After all, you say she takes care of you and so forth. Maybe she won't care so much to have me along on the party."

Marilyn quickly crossed over and stretched up and kissed me lightly.

"Sam," she said, "you'll have to meet Suzy to understand about us. Why, do you know we are identical? Absolutely identical. You won't be able to tell us apart, I'll bet. And Suzy is just like I am. She'll like you as much as I do. She's bound to."

"Did she like Marcus as much?" I couldn't help saying.

She didn't get sore.

"Marcus was different," she said. "I never loved him and Suzy knew it. Suzy couldn't stand him and neither could I. But she'll like you."

"In the same way you like me?"

She looked at me and smiled wickedly.

"We'll see," she said. "We'll see when she gets here. Just be patient. I'll tell you what. I'll go in and bring you the rest of your clothes and we can get all ready."

She turned quickly and entered the bedroom. I started to follow and it was then I heard the sound at the door.

I turned swiftly, staring, and I saw the knob move. I heard the key turning and as I took a step forward the door suddenly slammed open.

It wasn't the gun he held in his ugly fist that stopped me cold in my tracks, although I must admit that would have been enough to do so. No, it wasn't the gun. It was the man who held it. I couldn't have been more surprised seeing him there, his wide beefy shoulders filling the doorway and his short-cropped red hair almost reaching to the top of it. Nothing was changed but his shirt. He'd traded the torn dirty T-shirt for a turtle-neck sweater. He hadn't been able to change the purple bruise on his jaw where my right hand reached him, however.

He was smiling and it failed to improve his face in the slightest.

Battle, the demon deputy, was back in action.

He lifted a tufted eyebrow over one small piglike eye and his crooked mouth twisted into what he probably fancied was a sinister smile. It just made him look more then ever like a pig with indigestion.

"My, my," he said, "you do like to check into tourist camps, don't you?"

He moved forward, closing the door behind him with one hand but keeping the other one very steady on the gun. I almost felt complimented. This time he seemed to think a gun was necessary.

"Saw your car and remembered it," he said. His tiny eyes quickly took in the room, passing hurriedly over the opened suitcase. I guess he didn't see the money or if he did, it didn't register.

"You seem to have as many names as you have tourist rooms, Mr. Russell," he said, accenting my name and looking very smug at his own brightness. He reached out with a foot as big as a small steam shovel, catching his toe under the rung of a straight backed chair to pull it up and sit. I thought the seat would go under his vast bulk, but it held.

"You are supposed to knock before you bust into private rooms," I said, "or hasn't your boss told you about that yet?"

The sarcasm was lost on him.

"You're supposed to register under your own name," he said, taking my gambit and neatly cornering me. "Furthermore, in this state, it is illegal to register in a public hotel or lodging house with a woman other than your own wife—or didn't you know?"

"I didn't know," I said, playing it for laughs.

"Don't be unhappy. You'll learn fast from now on in, Mr. Russell."

"Did the car tell you my name?" I asked, stalling for time. I was listening for sounds from the other room. I wanted a second to catch my breath.

"The license plates told me," he said, "after I checked with New York. They told me several things, or at least a farmer a few miles down the road who saw them early this morning, told me several things."

"Never believe a farmer," I said. It wasn't very witty, but at the moment I didn't know quite what to say. I got part of the picture. But I didn't get it all. And I knew that it was a whole canvas.

He had, without doubt, spotted my car at *Cutter's Cabins* and taken the number down. He'd seen the same car sitting in front of the Whispering Willows and had known I'd checked in. He'd found out that I was there under a false name and had registered with a woman who was not my wife.

But why the gun—why the sinister, sly mannerism? Sure, he didn't like me and there certainly was no reason he should and he probably would do everything he could to give me a hard time. He undoubtedly felt he had that right after my butting into his little act up the road earlier in the day. But why the gun? You don't use a gun to arrest a man on a charge of checking into a tourist camp under an alias with a woman.

His crack about the farmer up the road came through then and I began to sweat gently under the armpits. He may have looked stupid, but he had the instinctive sense of an animal. He seemed to smell my sudden fear.

What passed for a smile came back.

"The farmer's name is Kilski. He runs a broiler spread. Maybe you remember the place? It's just before you come to a culvert, on Route 301. Funny thing about that culvert. Seems some guy missed the road and flipped over into it and got himself killed this morning. Does that mean anything to you?"

"It means you should be very careful to drive with caution. The life you save may be your own."

I was still the life of the party. Just one little *bon mot* after the next. It went right over his head, but it didn't matter. It wasn't a very good crack, anyway.

"This chicken farmer, this guy Kilski who saw your car, he said you were headed toward New York. You're an odd man, Mr. Russell. You were going to New York and then suddenly you changed your mind and started back toward the Chesapeake Bay Bridge. Just about the time a guy piles up his Caddie and gets himself killed. But I guess I shouldn't be surprised. You always seem to be changing your mind. Like checking into one tourist camp under one name and then turning around and checking into another one under another name. What's the matter, fellow—can't you ever make up your mind?"

He was getting ahead of me in the joke department. I decided humor wasn't my forte after all.

"All right, Battle," I said. "So I've checked into a public establishment, as you put it, under a false name. So it's a misdemeanor at best. What's with the gun? You don't need it to serve a summons."

If I thought he was going to put the gun away and apologize, I was very far out in left field.

"You look at television?" he asked. His eyes went to the set.

"Can't stand it," I said. "I read books."

"Too bad. You see, that guy I was talking about—it was on the air and in all the late afternoon newspapers. Seems he was pretty important. Guy named Marcus. Big time racketeer. Supposed to be the money man for the mobs. He was on his way from Florida and the news commentators seemed to feel that he had been down there for other reasons than getting a suntan."

"A lot of people go to Florida."

"Not like this guy Marcus. They say be went down to pick up the money which the Cuban gamblers were able to get out of the country after those anarchists with the beards took over. Poor fella—just think of it—probably bringing all that dough back to his pals and he has to go and get himself killed."

"I'm bleeding for him," I said.

"You'll be bleeding all right, Mr. Russell," Battle said, and I didn't like the look on his face when he said it. He started to say something else, but I missed the words. I was listening again to the slight sound coming from the bedroom. I don't know how Battle himself missed hearing it unless he was so fascinated by the sound of his own voice.

I looked quickly back at him and again listened. I wanted him to keep on talking.

"Yes," he said. "This day has just been chuck-full of coincidences. First let's take you. You just happen to be driving north on Route 301 about the time this guy Marcus gets himself killed. That chicken farmer just happened to be out in the field and saw you go by and remembered your car 'cause he saw you slow down and pull to a stop near that culvert I was telling you about. Then I just happen to run into you while I am on my way to check into the accident.

"A day of coincidences, all right. I just happen to drive by here and remember your car from earlier. And poor Marcus. He just happens to get killed while he is driving around with a car full of money. You know what the final and funniest coincidence of all is?"

"Don't tell me," I said. "I can't bear too many surprises in one day."

"Comes the jokes again," he said. "But I'll tell you, anyway. I can take jokes. The final coincidence is that when we searched the car after we got to the accident scene, there wasn't any money. Not one little bit. Just the couple of hundred bucks Marcus had in his wallet along with his credit cards and identification."

"Maybe that chicken farmer—Kilski you said his name was didn't you?—maybe he wanted to see why I stopped."

"Oh, he saw all right," Battle said. "But if you can stand it, I'll tell you about the last and the strangest coincidence of all. Want to hear it?"

"Sure," I said. "I'm a captive audience."

"Always jokes. Oh well, I'll tell you anyway. The final coincidence is that poor Marcus didn't really get himself killed by driving off the road and hitting a culvert."

"No?" I said. He was beginning to get a little ahead of me. "You mean the news commentators were wrong? There was still a spark of life...?"

"Oh, no, nothing like that. He was killed all right. But it wasn't the accident. The Cadillac wasn't the weapon. The weapon was a blunt instrument, Mr. Russell. An iron pipe or a blackjack or something along those lines. Applied expertly to the base of his skull."

I looked up sharply. I was remembering something. And the words came out without my really thinking about them.

"I seem to remember that you are pretty handy with—"

He leaned forward and the hand which was free swung and the blow caught me alongside the face, leaving my cheek feeling as though someone had just removed the flesh. He hadn't even stood up to reach me.

The joking hour was over.

He stood up.

"You in the bedroom," he said. "You can come in now." He was looking at the bedroom door but the gun was still looking at me. There was no sound from the other room.

"Call your broad in," Battle said.

I didn't move and he began to raise that left fist again.

"Come on in, kid," I said loudly. "We got company."

Nothing happened.

"She must be shy," he said. "Come on, we'll get her. Maybe she wants an escort."

He reached out, grabbing me by the hair and swinging me around. The gun prodded me in the back. We started marching into the bedroom. I was just about at the door when I felt the gun muzzle leave my back and sensed that he had stopped. There was a long low whistle. Mr. Battle had finally found what he had come looking for.

"Well, twist my dirty—" he said, using an expression I hadn't heard in twenty-five years. He whistled again and I half turned around.

His eyes went from the suitcase full of money to my face and he slowly shook his head.

"You really are the most careless man I have ever known," he said. "Leaving this loot just lying around like so much hay in a hopper. Tish, tish."

Almost reverently he reached over and flipped the lid of the suitcase shut. "Let's see if the girl is one half as pretty," he said.

But Battle was disappointed and his disappointment was only matched by my own surprise. Because Marilyn K. was no longer in the bedroom. She wasn't in the bedroom and she wasn't in the bathroom. In fact, she wasn't any place in the suite at all. The moment I saw that the venetian blind was pulled up and the window open a crack at the bottom I realized what had happened. I understood the noises I had heard.

I don't know whether Battle realized that she had been there and had sneaked out while we had been talking or not. But in any case, her absence didn't seem to bother him.

"So the chick is gone," he said. "Too bad, but after all, a man can't have everything." He pulled the window tight and dropped the blind.

I had finished up with all the jokes and now I was getting a little desperate for something to say. And I was getting a little tired of playing charades.

"So you have me and you have the money," I said. "That doesn't prove it is Marcus' money and even if it is, it doesn't prove that I took it from him. But you are an officer of the law. I suggest you take me in and book me—on any charge you like. I'll do my explaining in front of the proper authorities."

I had decided to play it serious from now on, but so, unfortunately, had he. He slapped me again and froze the other side of my face.

"Right now I am the proper authority," he said. "And let's stop with the wise-guy stuff. I know all the answers. You killed Marcus and you took his dough."

"Sure," I said. "So book me."

My face had only the two sides so he decided to start on my abdomen. This time he used his fist and I doubled up and went down on the bed. I was still trying to get my breath as he outlined it for me.

"We don't need no higher authority," he said. "I got you and I got the evidence. You, I don't care about; the evidence, I do. I'm not even going to bother to take you in."

"But you are going to take the evidence?"

"Yeah—I'm going to take the evidence."

I'm a great one for talking before I think what I am going to say and I did it again.

"Great," I said. "I can't think of a quicker way for you to commit suicide. Those friends of Mister Marcus are going to be around soon, looking—"

I should have saved my breath.

"That's where you fit in, buddy," Battle said. "They'll find you. And—

don't interrupt me now—they'll find the money. Some of it. Say maybe a few grand. That I can spare."

The canvas was complete at last. He had finished his diagram.

"And of course I am going to tell them that I just swallowed the remainder of the money," I said, "and they will believe me."

"I don't think they would believe you," Battle said, "but that doesn't really matter. You see, Russell, you are not going to be in any position to talk. When they find you—or later—or ever."

It hit me then—full in the face. I knew exactly what he had planned from the second he keyed that door open. If he found the money—and he fully expected to—I was to be set up as the patsy. But not a live patsy. A dead patsy.

I was no longer afraid of the gun in his hand.

He'd kill me—he had to kill me—but he couldn't do it with the gun. The sound of the shot would bring people and people were the one thing in the world he couldn't stand to have around. Not until he had knocked me out and gotten me and the suitcase away from the motel.

Oh, he was going to murder me all right. There wasn't the slightest doubt about that. But not with a gun and not until he had me safely away.

I opened my mouth to yell.

The hand is faster than the eye and it is certainly faster than the larynx. His hand was over my mouth and his knee buried itself in my groin. I would have bent double in agony but I couldn't. He had already slammed me to the bed and with his knee still in my lower stomach, he was holding me now by the throat, cutting off my breath. I knew he wanted to get me out of the place alive if he could.

I could feel the blood throbbing in my temples and the room began to grow dim. I couldn't retain consciousness for more than another couple of seconds and I was completely powerless to move. My eyes were popping and I could barely see when suddenly it seemed that a shadow drifted over his shoulder. I was dimly wondering if I was seeing some sort of optical illusion when there was the sudden unmistakable sound of a hard object smacking against solid flesh.

I blanked out for a matter of seconds and when I opened my eyes, the pressure at the throat was gone. The knee was still in my groin but again there was no pressure. I was in agony but I heaved and he rolled off me.

I shook my head, pulling myself to a sitting position on the bed as his body slid to the floor. It took me another few seconds to focus.

Marilyn slowly came to life out of the fog which surrounded her and she looked just as sweet and young and adorable as she always looked. Even standing there with the tire iron in her hand and the tiny frown between her azure blue eyes.

"A very nasty man," Marilyn K. said. "Did he hurt you bad, baby?"

"He damn near killed me," I said, choking out the words. I looked down at Battle, surprised to see him lying there at my feet with his nasty mouth opened wide and the gurgling sounds coming from his throat. He was out like an exploded flash bulb. I hadn't believed that even a tire iron could make an impression on that anthropoid skull. I had to hand it to Marilyn—whiskey bottle or tire iron, she was a genius.

"I heard everything he said," she said. "Everything. And Suzy still hasn't showed up."

She was also a genius with the non sequiturs.

Chapter Six

I started to stand up, but fell back to the bed and my hands went to where his knee had been. The pain was excruciating.

"He's a filthy man," Marilyn said, looking at me with eyes filled with sympathy. "If he has injured you I'll kill him. And the language he used. Have you got a pocketknife with you, honey?"

I looked up at her in quick alarm.

"He didn't do anything permanent," I said. "And for God's sake, I'm not going to—"

"Silly," she said. "I just want the knife to cut the cords from the venetian blinds. We have to tie him up."

"He doesn't look like he'll be moving around for some time," I said. I managed to reach down and get the gun which had fallen to the carpet.

"We'll tie him up anyway," Marilyn said.

I had a knife and while she cut the cords from the blinds, she explained how, while we had been talking, she'd climbed out the window and gone around and gotten the tire iron from the trunk of my car. She came back through the door he'd left open and she'd come just in time.

"Who is he, anyway?" she asked. "And how did he know you?"

"His name's Battle and he's a deputy sheriff. The private stooge of an assistant D.A. named Fleming. I met him this morning down the road when I went out for a breath of air."

She looked at me curiously.

"Well, he was right about one thing. You do manage to get around. Here," she said, handing me a length of cord. "Tie him."

"It will be a pleasure," I said. "And then, honey, we are leaving. We are leaving just as fast as we can get out of here. Suzy or no Suzy, you and I are blowing. This place is getting hotter than the hinges of hell."

"Please don't swear, Sam," Marilyn said. "And we are not leaving. We can't leave now."

"We can't leave?" I guess I must have raised my voice to a near scream. "Dear God, don't you realize that this guy is a deputy sheriff? You said you overheard what he had to say. That someone spotted my car when I stopped to pick you up. Honey, we have to get out of here. Right this minute."

She shook her head, looking stubborn.

"I don't care about Suzy," I yelled. "I tell you—"

"But it isn't Suzy any longer," she said.

I opened my eyes wide.

"Well, if it isn't Suzy then just why—?"

"Socks," she said.

"Socks?"

"Socks. Socks Leopold. He's outside. In the cocktail lounge. I saw him when I was coming in with the tire iron. He has Binge and Hymie with him."

I sank back on the bed.

"Give it to me slow," I said. "I'm still a little punchy. I've been through a lot today. Who is Socks and who is Binge and who is Hymie?"

She sighed and spoke slowly, as though she were explaining the facts of life to a not too bright thirteen-year-old.

"Socks is Marcus' boss. He's the one who really runs things—both in New York and Florida and in Cuba. Aurelio—Mr. Marcus—was just really a sort of front for him.

"Great," I said. "Just great! And who are Binge and Hymie?"

"Well, I don't really know. Except Mr. Marcus always called them in when someone gave him trouble. Binge and Hymie took care of the trouble."

"So Binge and Hymie are the muscle and your Socks is the brain," I said. "God, this is just great. Here we are, with a half-dead deputy sheriff on our hands and outside we have a little reception committee. Tell me, did they see you? Do they know you are here?"

"I'm sure they don't," Marilyn said. "I saw them first and I am sure they didn't see me."

"Then why did they come here?"

"It's simple, silly," she said. "Don't you see? They heard about what happened to Mister Marcus and they drove down here. They went to find out what happened to the—well, they just want to find out what happened. So they had to stay some place and this is the only decent place around."

"And so they just accidentally came here and checked in," I said, my voice a little desperate.

"But they didn't check in. They just stopped by to have dinner. Maybe they will check in, but they haven't yet."

"How can you tell?"

"There was no one in the lobby and I looked in the registration book. They weren't checked in."

"Under other names?"

"No. I saw Socks' car outside and checked the license number. The book has the license numbers of the cars which check in. They will go away after a while, but in the meantime we have to stay here."

I shook my head.

"Honey," I said. "You are not thinking very clearly. Suzy is due any minute now. Remember? When she comes, and they see her—"

"That's all the more reason why we have to stay," Marilyn said. She saw the expression on my face and hurried on. "Please," she said. "Please, I have it all figured out."

"You have what figured out?" I guess I sounded a little hysterical.

"Everything," she said. "I overheard just about all that this horrible man said to you."

She was beginning to lose me again.

"Don't you see his plan?' she asked, shaking her head sadly.

"His plan?"

"Yes. Like he was going to do to you. Only we will do it to him. You go out and get the car and drive around to the carport in back. We'll gag him if he comes to and then you just take him in the car and you leave him somewhere. With some of the money on him. I hate to give up any of the money," she continued, rather sadly, "but it will be best. A whole package of hundred-dollar bills. They have the Havana bank wrappers still around them.

"Well, wherever you leave him, you have to make it look like it was an accident. Like he was hit by a car or something. And then you get right to a phone and you call the state police and you tip them off to where he is. Then they find him and the money and put two and two together."

"And your pal Socks will figure he was the first one at the scene of the accident and got away with the loot," I finished for her. "And in the meantime, those apes will see your sister and will case this joint and turn up the real loot and—"

"Please," Marilyn said. "Please, honey. Listen. Of course Suzy will come and they may see her. But they won't dare actually do anything as long as Suzy and I stay here at the motel. They are much too smart for that. And I want them to come in. I want them to look for the money. But they won't find it."

"Why not?"

"Because you will have the money with you. Don't you see, honey? They search the room and they don't find the money. And then the story is out that this Battle is found unconscious with some of the money on him. They won't be bothering me anymore. They'll be trying to get to him to see who was in it with him when he found Marcus' body. While they are doing that, well, that's when Suzy and I will duck out to meet you."

I drew a long sigh and shook my head. She was good. She was very, very good.

"And you trust me to take the money?" I said.

She gave me that almost sly look from under her eyelids. A look that suddenly wanted me to forget the pain in my groin and forget just about everything but the hours we had spent together that afternoon.

"Of course I trust you, honey."

I nodded. She could make a guy feel wonderful.

"There's just one flaw," I said. "I'll have the money and Socks can't, or his boys can't, know about that. But one guy will know. Battle. And sooner or later, after he is found, he is going to—"

I didn't like the way she was looking at me.

"I'm not going to kill him," I said. "Baby, I love you a great deal and I love money, but I am not—"

"Sam," she interrupted in shocked surprise, "who ever suggested anything like that? Of course you aren't going to kill him. Who ever suggested that you should? There will be no reason to. By the time he does come to and tells his story—which I don't think he would even dare tell—why, by then you won't have the money if they do pick you up and it will just be his word against yours."

"I won't have the money? I thought you said—"

She sucked in her lips and shook her head.

"After you drop Battle," she said, "you must drive straight into Baltimore. I don't think it is very far and as I remember you pass an airport on the way. Friendship Airport, I think it is called. Well, cut in and go to the waiting room. You will find a whole lot of lockers where passengers on the airlines check luggage while they are waiting between planes. So you just check the suitcase with the money."

"And then?"

"And then you put the key in an envelope, but be sure to wrap it well in a couple of pieces of paper. Address it to General Delivery. But not to yourself. Just in case you are picked up for questioning, which I don't think you will be. Address it to, well, say Mr. and Mrs. Harold O. Southern, General Delivery, Baltimore."

"Why Mr. and Mrs.?"

"Why so either one of us can pick it up if the other one can't make it. And then, whichever one does, takes a train and goes to Washington. Checks into the Statler and waits and the other one comes as soon as he can. Either you—or Suzy and me."

Boy, I had to hand it to her. She had it figured. I began to wonder why she had ever wanted me around in the first place, except to drive her to the nearest telephone after she had been stymied there at the side of the road.

For the first time I really began to look forward to meeting sister Suzy. She had said Suzy was the bright one and took care of her. Suzy must really be something in the mental department.

One thing, however, I was quite sure about. No one in this world could top Marilyn K. in what was a far more important female activity.

Battle began to stir and his mouth opened and closed as he gasped. He reminded me, with his snaggled teeth, of a dying barracuda gasping for air.

Again she was faster than I was. She tore the pillow case in two and jammed in into his mouth, telling me to cut another piece from the venetian blind cords. While I was cutting it, I heard a dull thwack and I turned just in time to see her again hitting him with the tire iron.

She looked up at me, shaking her head defensively.

"I really didn't hurt him," she said childishly. "I know how to hit so it just knocks them out and doesn't fracture anything. Marcus' bodyguard taught me. He used to be a policeman."

"Did he use a tire iron, too?" I couldn't help asking.

"Don't be mean to me, Sam," she said. "And hurry up now. It's dark out and you better get the car around to the back. But be very careful. Don't let anyone notice you."

"I'll be very, very careful," I promised. "You don't mind if I have a drink first, though, do you. I can use one."

"You really should eat something before you drink any more," she said.

I agreed with her. I needed to build up my strength. Watching her, as I poured the drink, I knew I would want every ounce of strength I could possibly get, once we were alone again. I was already dreaming about that small safe little place somewhere in South America, as I left the motel suite and went out in front to get the car.

I was tempted to stop in at the cocktail lounge on the way and see if I could pick out Marcus' boy friends, but I resisted the temptation. I didn't want Battle staying in that room a second longer than necessary, even if he was gagged and had his hands tied behind him. I had a lot of confidence in Battle's resistance and his eventual capacity for making trouble, even with his hands tied.

There was a new man behind the desk in the lobby but he ignored me as I passed through. Outside were a couple of dozen cars, most of which probably belonged to the crowd that had come in for dinner. The cars which belonged to the transients were around in the carports behind the individual suites, where I wished that Marilyn had had the sense to leave mine.

Battle's old station wagon was parked at an angle two or three slots down from the entrance. He'd left his door open and as I passed, I gave it a shove, slamming it shut. As I did I caught a movement out of the corner of my eye and I looked up.

The long black Imperial limousine was parked next to it and leaning against the front fender was a short, broad-shouldered man with a broken nose and wearing a Brooks Brothers suit. The tip-off was the shoes. They were Harlem yellow. He had "racket" written all over him.

He was watching me casually but missing nothing. No special interest; he was the kind who watched everything. I saw that the plates on the Imperial were New York. Broken-nose would be either Binge or Hymie.

She had left the keys in the Pontiac and I hit the starter button. The motor turned over and nothing happened. I goosed the gas pedal a couple of times and tried again. I guess I must have been nervous. I managed to flood the engine. I tried twice more and still nothing happened.

I swore. The battery was a little old and I was afraid of drawing too much juice so I just waited for a minute or so.

The joker who had been leaning against the Imperial walked over. He shook his head a little sadly. "Flooded her," he said.

"I know."

"You gotta be careful with these old heaps," he said. "You flood 'em and they're hell. When you try again, keep your gas pedal all the way down to the floor."

I said thanks and I put the gas pedal on the floor, which I knew all along I should do. I pushed the starter and the engine caught.

"You should trade that iron in," Broken-nose said. "I see you are from New York."

"Right," I said.

"Been down to Florida? You got a nice tan."

He was leaning against the door and the only way I could get rid of him was to either take off and leave him hanging on air, or answer him. I answered him, without enthusiasm.

"Nope—Baltimore," I said. "I got a sun lamp."

He nodded, thought about it for a second or two and decided there wasn't anything more to say and took his arm off the door and went back to lean on the fender of the black Imperial. I pulled out of the parking spot, circled the motel and drew up behind the suite where Marilyn K. was waiting. She opened the back door the moment I knocked.

"Cut off that overhead light," I said, "and then just stand here and see that no one comes by. I'll go in and get him."

She nodded and switched the light as I stepped into the living room of the suite.

He was exactly where I had left him. Lying flat on his back. There was only one thing different. The area between his little pig eyes and the line where the wiry red crew-cut began was no longer convex. It was concave. And the short, tortured gasps were no longer coming from his barracuda mouth. His chest wasn't slowly rising and falling.

I leaned over him quickly, but it wasn't necessary to listen to his heart or feel his pulse. He was dead. He had to be dead. No man could live with his entire forehead bashed in.

There was surprisingly little blood.

I didn't touch him. Instead I stood up and slowly went toward the door where Marilyn stood looking out. I took her gently by the arm and pulled her into the room, closing the door after her.

"You'd better hurry," she said. "Hurry and get him into the car."

"Why did you do it?" I tried hard to keep the anger out of my voice.

"You are hurting my arm, Sam," she said. "Why did I do what?"

"Why did you kill him?"

She looked up at me, wide-eyed.

"Kill him? Kill who?"

"Don't be cute, kitten," I said. "I asked you a question. Why did you kill him? Why did you beat that deputy's head in with the tire iron as soon as I left the room."

"Oh Sam," she said. "I didn't kill him. Of course I hit him. I had to. The minute you left to get the car he came to. I guess he was just acting all along. Anyway, he reared up and started for me."

"He was tied," I said, coldly.

"Of course he was tied. But he got up and he's a big man. He started for me and he was between me and the door. And so I reached for the tire iron and I had to hit him again."

"You hit him again all right," I said through clenched teeth. "I thought you said you knew how to do it—that one of Mister Marcus' boys had taught you."

"Don't be mean to me, Sam," she said. "I didn't have time to do anything but just swing. Otherwise he would have been on top of me. Anyway, he probably isn't really dead. He's probably just—"

"He's dead," I said bitterly.

"Well then, you should certainly hurry and get him out of here. And don't look at me like that, Sam. I told you it was an accident. Self-defense. Anyway, it solves one problem. When you call the state police and they find him, you won't have to worry about what he will say."

I didn't answer her. I was afraid that if I did, I'd lose my temper completely.

Wordlessly I went back and got my arms under his shoulders. I didn't try to lift him, but just dragged him along the floor. The tire iron was lying where it had fallen and I kicked it out of my way, suddenly sick to my stomach.

She held the door open for me and then circled and opened the trunk of the Pontiac. It was a job getting him in and closing the lid. I was sweating when I went back inside. I didn't say anything, but just went over and poured a water glass full of Scotch and took it without a chaser.

She had gone in and got the bags and was carrying them with her when she came back. She was panting a little and dropped them to the floor. She went back and returned a moment later with a package of money, tightly wrapped in a printed bank band.

"Here," she said. "You had better put it in his pocket after you get him out of the car. Now don't forget."

I reached for the money, saying nothing, and I guess she read the expression on my face.

"Darling," she said. "Darling, I told you I didn't do it on purpose." She leaned forward on her toes and her arms went out and around my waist and she pulled herself tight against me. "Honey."

I guess it was then I realized for the first time that lust is even stronger than revulsion.

The money fell from my hand to the floor and as our lips met, my own arms went around her and my hands dropped down her back and as she strained against me, they found their favorite hold. Nature had designed her buttocks exactly the right size and shape to fit into a man's palms.

She started to moan a little and her tongue was forcing my lips apart. I didn't care then, for the next few minutes, whether she had murdered Battle or whether she had murdered a dozen men. I didn't care about the pain in my groin where Battle had kneed me; I didn't care about anything on this God's green earth but just one simple thing.

I started to move, with her clinging to me, toward the bed.

But she twisted suddenly and I was made aware once more of her fantastic strength. She twisted and pushed against me with her own two small hands, pulling her lips away.

"No—no, not now," she said. "Suzy will be here any minute and you have to get started."

I groaned.

"Suzy!" I said. "Jesus Christ!"

"Sam," she said. "Please don't swear."

I released her, staring at her.

"Hurry now, Sam," she urged. "And don't forget. Mr. and Mrs. John Southern, General Delivery, Baltimore. And we'll meet at the Washington Statler."

I picked up the money as I left the room. I also picked up the half-empty bottle of Scotch.

Chapter Seven

Life is filled with new experiences, but this was one I could have gotten along without. Two dead men in one day is a little hard on the system at best; it makes it sort of rough, when you end up with one of them in the trunk of your car.

I remembered the broken-down station wagon with the red spotlight still sitting parked in front of the Whispering Willows and I decided that I would get rid of my passenger at the first opportunity. I knew that station wagon would be spotted pretty quickly and that someone would be looking for him. Every second I had his body with me increased my chances of trouble.

I found the place about a mile before I came to *Cutter's Cabins*. A vacant, broken-down roadside stand and gas station which I had vaguely remembered from the morning's drive. As I approached I looked first ahead and then into the rear vision mirror to be sure no cars were coming from either direction. The road was clear. Not a car in sight.

I cut into the curved drive which led into the gas station and pulled up beside it. I punched out my lights and swallowed the lump in my throat. Then I got out of the convertible, circled it and opened the trunk.

Thank the Lord, it was too early for rigor mortis or I never would have gotten his body out of that small compartment. I just let it lay where it fell. I was reaching down to put the money into his trouser pocket when I saw the headlights coming.

My first instinct was to run for the car and get going, but I realized that if I did, whoever was in the oncoming car would see me leaving the place. So I just kneeled down and waited. The twin headlights were beating up the road at about eighty miles an hour and the driver didn't slow down as he passed.

A half minute later and I was back behind the wheel of the Pontiac. This time I didn't take any chances on its flooding and stalling out.

When I passed *Cutter's Cabins*, I noticed the sign, *Vacancies*, pathetically lighted outside the small office. There were only two cars parked in front of the place, a small pickup truck and an ancient two-toned sedan.

Sarah Cutter was having her problems in making a go of the establishment her Dad had left her when he died. But I didn't have any extra energy to waste on considering her problems. I had plenty of problems of my own.

I guess it was during the drive into the outskirts of Baltimore, with the wind blowing into my face from the open windows of the car, that for the first time I really began to think clearly. It was a funny thing, but while I had been with Marilyn K.—even while I had been away from her but was waiting to get back to her—it was almost as though someone had drugged me. My mind simply hadn't functioned. It was easy enough to understand. Marilyn, in her own way, was a lot more powerful than any drug I could imagine.

Anyway, as I say, I really started using my brain for something besides holding up the top of my cranium. Did I say I had a problem? It was an understatement.

The first problem was the simple one. Three hundred and some odd thousand dollars in mob money, laying in a suitcase on the seat next to me. That was a problem I had to solve and solve quickly. Well, I was solving it. I was on my way to a locker at Friendship Airport in Baltimore.

The next problem was a gentleman named Socks Leopold and his two muscle boys, looking for this suitcase full of money. I didn't sell them short. Sooner or later they were going to know that Marilyn K. was checked into the Whispering Willows. They weren't going to have to be geniuses to discover that she had not checked in alone. I had used a phony name, but that wasn't going to be a bit of help. The motel had taken down my car license number and it would be simple enough to trace it to me.

They would know that I had checked in with her.

And then, of course, there was a deputy sheriff named Battle, lying back at the deserted roadside stand with his head bashed in. When young Mr. Fleming learned about that he was going to remember something. He was going to remember me. He was going to remember the fight we had had at *Cutter's Cabins*. He was going to remember that Battle's car would be found in front of the Whispering Willows, where I had been registered. Because he, like Brother Leopold, would find out soon enough that I had been there. And he was going to put two and two together and come up with an answer. The answer might not necessarily be right, but that was just my own tough luck.

There was only one single thing in this world I could think to do to change that answer. I had to get to a phone booth as soon as I possibly could and put in that anonymous call to the state police and let them know where to find Mr. Fleming's dead deputy. Find Battle and the money from Marcus' loot. It might just possibly work out the way Marilyn had planned it. Take the heat off of me so far as Leopold and company were concerned.

It wouldn't clear me when it came to Battle, but at least it would establish a motive for someone else having knocked him off. He would be found with some of the money and Fleming would soon enough learn that money was being sought by the Syndicate boys from New York.

Yes, Marilyn had figured the answers all right. The trouble was, she had figured an extra answer and it was an answer that I didn't like at all. No matter how Fleming worked it out, one thing was sure. The alarm would be out and I would be picked up for questioning. And where would they pick me up? Why they would pick me up while I was obviously trying to make a getaway!

It was then that something else came back to me. Something that, because of the stress of current events, had completely escaped my memory during the last couple of hours. Something which Battle had said.

Marcus had not been killed in the car accident. He had been murdered!

Maybe the deputy had been lying—trying to trap me. Maybe. Certainly nothing had been said about it in the news broadcasts. But then, maybe again he hadn't been. There was, in any case, a certain chicken farmer who had seen me when I had pulled to a stop to pick up Marilyn K.

So suppose Marcus had been murdered, and they picked me up while I was very obviously trying to make a getaway. Well, one thing was sure. I didn't want to be in Washington at the Statler. I didn't want to be getting any mail at the General Delivery window in Baltimore.

Marilyn and Sister Suzy could be counted upon to take care of that chore.

I should have taken some comfort in the knowledge that I hadn't killed Marcus and I hadn't killed Battle. And if the police picked up Marilyn later on?

I could just visualize us telling our separate stories. I could visualize us in front of twelve honest men and true—our peers. Facing a jury, me with my hands clean and my heart pure and the moral conviction that I was innocent.

And I knew just what that jury would do. They would listen to me and they would look at Marilyn K.

And I would be given a one-way ticket directly to the gas chamber or whatever they use to dispatch multiple murderers in the state of Maryland.

Yes, the kid really had a head on those beautiful, desirable shoulders. Marilyn K. was something all right.

I saw the sign saying telephone booth, one mile, and I automatically began to slow down. This is one thing I will hand Maryland; they may not have a particularly neat gas chamber or whatever it is they use, but they do have damned fine roads and they put up glass enclosed phone booths every few miles, just in case some passing tourist may feel like getting a little social.

I was lucky. It was a booth beside a roadside picnic area and there was nothing in sight. I pulled over and stopped, got out and stepped into the booth, not closing the door completely as I didn't want the light to go on inside. I reached into my pants pocket for a coin and had a momentary fainting spell. I went into my other pocket and I still didn't find a coin.

I cursed myself for a damned fool and went through the rest of my pockets. No coins.

For a moment I almost panicked and then I remembered the glove compartment of the Pontiac. I always throw loose change into it so I'll have a convenient nickel or dime for a parking meter. It only took me a second to find the dime and to dial the operator.

"Let me have the state police," I said, when she answered. "It's an emergency, so please hurry. There has been an accident."

It was probably one of the greatest understatements of my career.

I wasn't familiar with the road after passing over the Chesapeake Bay Bridge, but I had no trouble. I found Friendship Airport and driving into it was somewhat like coming into the civilized world after a long, hard safari across the Gobi Desert. Bright lights never looked so good.

I left my own bag in the car and didn't even bother to lock the door. I was anxious to get the suitcase full of money into that locker.

There were two banks of lockers in the corridor off the main lobby. One was for people who just wanted to leave something overnight and the other was for customers who needed a place for their surplus luggage for several days. These cost half a dollar but the hell with expense. I put the bag inside of the top one at the end and extracted the key.

A pretty brunette at the American Airlines desk loaned me an envelope and several sheets of paper and a stamp machine spewed out six four-cent stamps for a quarter.

There was a fountain pen attached to a chain on the desk supplied by Western Union for potential customers.

I didn't bother with a return address. But I did think about Marilyn K. while I addressed the envelope.

I wrote it out in a nice Spencerian hand. Over in the left hand corner I added: *Please hold until called for.*

I dropped it into the mailbox in the lobby and I didn't bother to check when it would be picked up. I wasn't in any hurry to have it delivered. The key wouldn't rust.

What I did next will probably convince you that I am completely insane. Maybe I was. Certainly, within the next few hours I had good enough reason to think so.

Anyway, I left the waiting room of the airport and I went back and climbed into my car. I left the airport. I didn't get back on 301 and head south for Washington. I didn't drive into Baltimore proper. I didn't head out at random for far away places.

I turned the car around and started back up Route 301 toward Whispering

Willows.

I wasn't planning on actually going to Whispering Willows, but I wanted to be near it. I wanted to be very close. Because I knew one thing. I knew that sooner or later I would be arrested and questioned and I didn't want anyone to get the idea I was running away. I also figured that when the alarm went out to pick me up, about the last place the police would look would be in the neighborhood of the place where I had recently checked in and departed from. And I wanted to have all the free time I could get. I was going to need every minute of it.

I was no longer interested in the three hundred and some odd thousand dollars. I was no longer even interested in meeting Marilyn K. in the bedroom of a Washington D.C. hotel; I was only interested in one thing. I was interested in clearing myself on a charge of murdering a deputy sheriff and possibly murdering a gentleman named Marcus, who had excellent taste in girls, but a very poor sense of self-preservation.

I knew exactly where I was going to spend the rest of the night. I was dead tired and I needed rest and sleep. I had had a very busy day. I'd been beaten over the head and I had had quite a few thrilling experiences. And I had spent those two or three hours locked in Marilyn K's arms and that was an experience which alone would have called for a week's convalescence on the part of a heavy weight discus thrower.

I was heading for *Cutter's Cabins*, a quiet little unsuccessful tourist camp where the units rented for five dollars a night and the little dark-eyed owner was too proud to take charity.

The vacancy sign was still burning up electricity when I pulled up in front of the place, but the office was dark. I left the car around at the side, where it wouldn't be noticed from the road, and walked back and found the doorbell. There was a dim light over the door and a small, typewritten sign: *Please Ring for Rooms.*

I rang.

She must have been lying down somewhere in a room behind the office, because I didn't have to wait for more than a minute at the most. A light went on inside and then the door opened and she was standing there, a faded dressing gown wrapped around her tiny figure, her bare feet thrust in a pair of sandals. She might have been sleeping, but her hair was neat and combed and her face was clean and clear-eyed and she looked wide-awake and as cute as a button. She recognized me at once.

"Why Mister—Mister—I guess I have forgotten your name. You've come back."

"I have come back," I said.

She stepped to one side, inviting me in. I entered and closed the door.

"Decided I would take that room after all, Miss Cutter," I said.

She looked at me curiously, a little doubtfully.

"You came back," she said, a little aimlessly, as though she couldn't quite get over her surprise.

"I need some sleep," I said.

She cocked her head and stretched her chin and still looked at me oddly and then she shrugged and smiled.

"I can always use the business," she said. She reached for the registration book and swung it around toward me. She had cleaned up the office and although it still looked shabby, it was neat and she had done the best she could with what she had to work with.

I signed the register and took out my wallet and counted out some singles.

"Still five bucks?"

"Still five bucks. And number six is still empty."

She took the money and opened the dressing gown and put it in the side pocket of the tailored suit she was wearing under the gown. I looked at the clock on the wall and saw that it was well after midnight.

"Don't you sleep yourself?" I asked, for no particular reason.

She smiled again.

"Well, I just sort of lie down and doze. I wait until about two and then I really get into bed. I don't want to miss any cars that might stop and I hate to get up after I have really turned in for the night. Nothing ever happens after two around here."

She handed me the key.

I was about to turn away when she spoke again.

"I guess you didn't hear about it," she said.

"Hear about it?"

I swung back to face her. She wasn't smiling any more.

"That man. Battle. The one who was here this morning when you came in."

I tried to make my expression blank.

"Don't tell me he's been back again," I said. I wanted to keep it on a light plane. But she wasn't in a mood for fun and laughter.

"He's dead."

"Good Lord!" I raised my voice in shocked surprise. "Dead? What do you mean? How—"

"An accident. State police were here. The ambulance passed by a few minutes ago. He was struck by a hit-and-run driver, a bit down the highway. He was killed. Whoever did it, pulled off to the side of the road and just left him there. The police found him."

I looked shocked but I was unable to look sorry. I wanted to say something but I didn't have to. She took the play away from me and expressed exactly my own sentiments.

"I feel bad because I can't honestly say that I am sorry about it. He was a terrible man. But I just can't stand the thought of anyone being murdered. And that's what it is when someone kills someone else and just goes off callously and leaves them lying there. It's really murder, even if it was an accident."

"I agree with you," I said. "I can't say I feel any deep sense of personal loss, but I don't condone murder."

She nodded, sagely and again looked up at me curiously.

"Why did you come back here?" she asked.

At first I thought there was a double meaning to her question, but one look into her frank open face, and I knew she was incapable of double meanings. If there had been anything but simple curiosity in her mind, she would have come out with it. She had neither guile nor fear.

"Let's just say I came back because I am tired and I want to get some sleep," I said.

"But why here?" she asked, still curious. "Nobody ever stops here unless every other place is closed. Except maybe a truck driver or someone with almost no money. You look like you have plenty of money. So why did you come back? Not of course," she quickly added, smiling, "that I am not very glad you did."

"Let's just say it is because you are very pretty and a very sweet girl and I like you," I said.

"Well—I like you, too," she said. She looked up at me, still smiling. I could see why Martin Fleming had flipped for her. I could see why any man would flip for her. And it was a funny thing about the way she said it, "—and I like you, too." Coming from the lips of most women, it would sound like an invitation. But coming from her, the remark was simple and direct. She said it the way a child would say it and you knew at once that the words meant exactly what they said. She liked me—no more and no less.

"I'm glad you do," I said. "And now, if you will excuse me, I'll say good night. Good night and sweet dreams and I am on my way to number six and, I hope, a solid eight hours of undisturbed and dreamless slumber."

"The mattress is soft and clean but not very fancy, I am afraid. The shower may be a little lukewarm, but it will be hot when you get up. Good night."

She smiled again and it almost made the day worthwhile. It suddenly seemed awfully important to have someone like me rather than love me.

I found cabin number six and fifteen minutes later, stripped to my shorts, I had verified her statement that the mattress was comfortable. But it wouldn't have mattered if it had been a slab of concrete. I was so dead on my feet that I was asleep before my head had made a dent in the pillow. I was so dead beat that I didn't think anything in this world including the second coming of our Savior could have awakened me for the next eight or ten hours.

But I was wrong. I was very wrong.

I didn't sleep ten hours and I didn't sleep eight hours. I didn't even sleep one hour. I slept eight minutes.

And it wasn't the Second Coming which brought me wide-awake and leaping from the bed.

It was the beam of a flashlight held not more than ten inches from my face. It was the heavy gauntleted hand of a state trooper, banging back and forth across my cheeks.

Chapter Eight

I said: "Go away. Whoever you are, go away."

The hand which had been slapping my face closed into a fist and I knew that talk wasn't going to solve my problems. I had only been sleeping, as I have said, a matter of eight or ten minutes, but it was like waking from an overdose of Miltowns. The spotlight hitting my face blinded me and the fist began to be painful. I didn't want a broken nose so I woke up. And then the overhead light snapped on.

It took a minute or so for me to get my eyes back into focus. There were two of them, big six-footers, leather-belted with wide-brimmed hats. Holsters at their sides. Behind them, barely visible, was an old friend—Martin Fleming, the assistant D. A. Fleming had the floor.

"On your feet, mister," he said. "Quick."

I started to twist and get out of bed and then I noticed Sarah Cutter standing over by the door. I don't know why, but I was overcome by modesty. I got up, but I held the sheet around me.

"You are a fool as well as a criminal," Fleming said.

I looked at the girl and I felt a surge of bitterness.

"It didn't take you long to call them," I said.

"Shut up," Fleming said. "Get into your clothes. Sarah, you had better leave."

"I won't leave," she said. "This is my place and nobody, especially you, can order me around." She turned toward me. "I didn't call them," she said. "They were checking and—"

"I asked you to be quiet, Sarah," Fleming said.

"I won't be quiet," the girl snapped. "I want him to know that it wasn't I who called the police. And anyway, you have no right barging in here and disturbing my clients. I'll—"

It was the bigger of the two state troopers who interrupted. He had a soft deep voice and a Southern accent.

"Just take the lady outside while we get him into his clothes, Mr. Fleming," he said. You could tell from the way he said it that he didn't like the little man, but also that he didn't want any trouble with him.

Fleming muttered under his breath and turned to the door.

"Be careful, men," he cautioned. "He's dangerous. You're dealing with a killer."

The big one who had spoken grunted. He reached down and swooped up my clothes and tossed them to me.

"Get into them, Buster," he said.

"Now look here," I began. "Just what the hell—"

His partner doubled his fist and I let it go at that. I got into my clothes. I tried to talk but they didn't want any of my conversation. When I asked what the charge was, they said Fleming would do all the talking that would be necessary.

But I didn't really have to ask any questions. I pretty much figured I already had the answers.

I was just about ready to leave when Fleming returned. He was holding a flashlight in one hand and the tire iron under his arm. In his other hand was a wicked-looking, lead-weighted blackjack.

"Found them in his car," he said laconically. "He's our boy, all right."

The tire iron really threw me. It was mine, all right. There was no question about that. I had been looking at it only a few hours before after Marilyn K. had finished using it. I remembered kicking it out of the way when I had left the motel. But I had definitely not put it in the car.

"You bastard," I said. "You planted that tire iron."

He looked at me pityingly, slowly shaking his head.

"I didn't have to plant it, Russell," he said. "The name is Russell, isn't it? It was in your car, all right. Miss Cutter was with me when I found it."

I didn't like him and I wouldn't have taken his word if he told me the sun was shining at high noon, but somehow I did believe him. I could only guess that Marilyn had managed to drop it in the car when I hadn't been looking.

"I suppose you are going to tell me you found that blackjack in my car, too," I said.

"That's right. I did. Which one did you use for the job? Or did you use both of them?" His voice was sarcastic.

"Damn you," I said, "I never saw that blackjack before in my life. Never. Now you just tell me—"

"I'll tell you nothing," he snapped. "You are going to tell me. All right, men," he added, turning to the troopers. "Let's get moving."

It was the big man who spoke again.

"You want us to take him in to be booked first?"

Fleming shook his head.

"No. I want to stop by the funeral parlor. I want to see his face when he looks at his handiwork."

A fist in my back pushed me out through the door and the state patrol car was parked there. I got in the back with one of the troopers and Fleming got in front with the other one. He spoke to the driver as the car started.

"Stop at the Whispering Willows for a moment first," he said. "I want the girl to get a good look at him. She says she don't know him and has never seen him, but I want to be sure."

This one really had me baffled. The girl had to be Marilyn and I couldn't imagine what sort of story she had given them. I couldn't even begin to guess. I wondered how she was going to justify having checked into the place with me if she had never seen me before. The clerk had seen us together and so had the bellboy. I had a lot of respect for her sense of intrigue, but this time I figured she'd overplayed her hand. This time she'd got herself in a box.

One thing I was determined to do, however. Play along with her, at least until I knew what the score was. She might be double-crossing me—there was every chance in the world that she was. But I couldn't be sure and I wouldn't know what to do in any case. So if she wanted to take this line, then I'd go along with her. At least until I knew where I stood.

Of course I was pretty sure where I stood. That remark about a killer had not exactly passed over my head. Even if it had, the sight of the tire iron was enough to give me the outline.

There wasn't another word spoken until we pulled up in front of the Whispering Willows. I was surprised to see the number of cars in front of the place. Hell, there was even a truck which looked like it was from a television station.

There was a large crowd of people hovering around and they surged toward us as the trooper's car came to a halt.

I heard someone say, "They've got him. They've got the dirty murderer."

And then a couple of other troopers pushed the crowds back and Fleming got out.

"I'll get the girl," he said.

He turned and entered the lobby. I didn't get it at all. I couldn't figure what all these people were doing at the motel. It didn't make sense. Battle wasn't that big a story.

I saw her for only a second as Fleming escorted her out the door and toward the car. Just one quick look before the bright spotlight hit me full in the face and blinded me. But one second was enough. It was Marilyn K. all right.

Her hair seemed different, but I guess it was the light. And somehow or other she'd managed to find a neatly tailored tweed suit.

Fleming walked her to the car and said something to her I didn't understand. I could only make out her silhouette and couldn't see her features, but I was aware that she didn't answer him. That she only turned away, crying.

"I'm sorry, Miss Kelley," Fleming said. "I'll take you back inside."

He was gone several minutes this time and when he returned he was alone again.

"All right, boys," he said. "We'll go to the funeral parlor now. I was sure she was telling the truth."

He wasn't as smart as I had figured him. As nasty, but not as smart.

The funeral parlor which they took me to was in the county seat and it took us the best part of a half hour to get there.

There was a light on over the front porch and the windows were all lighted up and I guess we were expected.

They took me by the arms, a trooper at each side, as we went up the path and climbed the steps. A fat man in a black suit opened the door wordlessly, not looking at me at all, and led us through several rooms. He opened a door and held it but I knew what it was. It was the room they keep in undertaking establishments to lay out the bodies and do whatever it is they have to do. Cold, whitewashed, bare. Nothing but a long table on large casters and a glass and chrome medical cabinet with a lot of odd-looking instruments.

We walked over to the sheeted figure on the table and I should have known right then what to expect. But I didn't. I was listening to Fleming

"You filthy bastard," he said. "I want you to have a good look. I want you to see what an animal like you is willing to do for money."

Even as he reached for the corner of the sheet, I knew what he knew and how he had it figured. They had found Battle and they had found the money. They knew about Marcus and his reputation. They figured that either I had rolled him while he lay there dead in the Caddie and had stolen his dough, and Battle had found out about it and tried to shake me down and I had killed him. Or they figured Battle had found the money when he was the first to arrive on the scene and had taken the money and that then I had caught up with the deputy and murdered him. Either way I was a dead duck. Either way.

"Take a good look, killer," Fleming said.

He jerked back the sheet.

For just a second, I thought I was going to faint. I didn't have to fake it, didn't have to pretend shock and surprise.

My hand went up to my face and I rubbed my eyes and staggered and then I looked again.

I hope that never in my life will I ever see anything like it again.

I guess I had looked first for the face, because I was remembering that tire iron and I wanted to see just how bad the blow had actually been which had caved in the front of the skull. But what I saw wasn't a caved in skull. It wasn't even a face.

But what there was of it had never belonged to Battle, that redheaded anthropoid whose body I had taken out of the trunk of the Pontiac. No, the face wasn't his and the long blood-soaked red hair wasn't his and the slender, naked, bruised and beaten body wasn't his.

I was looking down at what was left of Marilyn K. after someone had beaten and flayed her until she had died—and then gone right on beating the corpse.

I suddenly began to vomit.

I knew then, even as I turned away, that the girl at the motel had been telling the truth a half-hour before. She had never seen me before. She couldn't have. Because that girl was Suzy. Yes, Sister Suzy had finally arrived.

Fleming must have been reading my mind.

"Sweet, isn't it, killer? A nice thing to leave on a bed for her sister to find. I'm surprised you didn't start chewing on her after you got through. That's what some of them do, you know."

I vomited again.

A fist hit me in the back of the neck and then I was once more outside of the lab room. They had me back in the car now and it was a relief that no one said anything. I had no desire for small conversation. I didn't want to think, but I had to think. And what I thought about was a man named Socks Leopold and two filthy sadists named Binge and Hymie. I had to think about Marilyn K. and how I had finally figured her wrong at the end. I had to think of the price that she herself had paid for being wrong. For guessing wrong. And in thinking about her, I forgot for a moment to worry about myself.

Fleming brought me back to reality soon enough, however.

They left me alone for a few minutes in the cell, after first stripping me to my short and socks. There was a bed in the cell and a small, straight-backed chair under which was an old-fashioned china pot. No water or sink. Nothing.

I must have been there for about ten minutes with the single, wire-guarded bulb burning overhead, when they returned. This time there were four of them; the two troopers, Fleming and another man. The last one looked familiar somehow. I knew why right away.

"This is the man," Fleming said, pointing at me. "He and your brother had an argument this morning, or rather yesterday morning. You want to talk to him, Georgie."

"Yeah, I wanna talk to him."

The minute he spoke I knew why he seemed familiar. He had a voice which was a dead ringer for Battle's voice. He had the same red hair, except it wasn't crew-cut. He was a little cleaner, but he wasn't any prettier. He was probably a few years older and he was also bigger. Maybe no taller, but even wider in the shoulders. He had a gut on him which could have held a half barrel of beer.

"Well, as soon as we get his statement, you can have him," Fleming said.

"I want him now."

He had a key in his hand and he started to put it in the cell lock. It was the bigger of the troopers who stopped him.

"Until this man is indicted," he said, "he is, still in the technical custody of the state police. It is your privilege to question him, Mr. Fleming, but he is not to be touched until he is technically out of our hands. It that understood?"

Battle's brother looked at him in disgust.

"State police!" he snorted. "What will you guys do? Pin a rose on him and kiss him good night?"

The trooper looked at him coldly.

"After seeing that girl," he said, "I would personally like to kick his knockers off and then slowly take him apart. Except I wouldn't dirty my hands. But that isn't the point. We have found out that we get more convictions when we get a statement while the prisoner is still able to pass an examination by his own doctor. Mr. Fleming knows that."

Fleming nodded coldly.

"I'll have a statement while he is still in one piece," he said. He turned to Battle's brother. "You'll have your turn, Georgie," he said. "Go on up and get a stenographer."

It was time I said something.

"You won't need a stenographer," I said. "There isn't going to be any statement."

"Why you—" Georgie began, but Fleming cut him short. "Just go upstairs and wait," he said. "I'll have a talk with the prisoner. There'll be a statement, all right."

"Should I tell the stenographer to come down?"

"I'll tell you when." He took the keys from Georgie. He started to unlock the door.

The second trooper spoke for the first time.

"I think you shouldn't go in there with him until maybe we soften him up a little first, Mr. Fleming," he said.

Fleming looked at him angrily.

"I won't need you men any more," he said. "I can handle things from now on."

They both started to protest but Fleming insisted. After a minute the two turned and left.

The door opened and Fleming came in and sat down on the straight-backed chair.

There were only four cells in the room and the one we were in was the only one occupied. I had to give the little man credit. He had plenty of guts, considering what he was thinking about me.

He sat on the edge of the chair, his trousers neatly pulled up so that they wouldn't wrinkle. His small hands rested on his knees and he stared at me out of eves which were coal black and as chilly as twin icicles.

He was an immaculate little man, a neat little man. And I suddenly understood that I had completely misunderstood him all along. He was a man with an angle.

"You don't care to make a statement, Mr. Russell," he said in his high, precise voice, "so I will make a statement to you. The statement is this.

"I have three bodies on my hands. There is Mr. Marcus, who was supposed to have been killed when his car went off the road. I think he was murdered.

"There is Herman Battle, my deputy sheriff, who could have been killed by a hit-and-run driver. I think he was murdered. And there is a girl named Marilyn K. and there is no doubt about her. She was brutally and sadistically beaten to death. There is something else. There is a lot of money which we are positive Mr. Marcus had with him when he was killed. That money is missing."

He hesitated, still staring at me.

"And there is you," he said.

"And there is me."

He smiled thinly.

"Yes. There is you. Let me tell you what we know about you, so that you won't have to bother to lie. We know who you are. We know almost everything you have done during the past twenty-four hours. We know that you were driving north on Route 301 early yesterday morning at the same time Mr. Marcus was driving on 301. We know that you stopped along the roadside, at just about the spot where his car was wrecked, before the police arrived on the scene. We know that you met Battle at the *Cutter Cabins* and fought with him.

"We know that you checked into the hotel with the Kelley girl. We know that you spent the day and part of the evening with her. We know that Battle returned to Whispering Willows and we are morally certain it was because he knew you were there. We know that Marcus had a lot of money with him and that the money was gone before the police arrived. Now would you like to take it from there? Just sort of informally?"

This time I studied him for a long time before answering. I hadn't figured him out completely, but I knew that I had been wrong in thinking he might be a stupid, pompous little jerk.

"All right," I said at last. "I'll take it from there. I'll take it under just one condition. I'll tell you exactly what I did and what I know. But you have to tell me one thing first. You have to tell me exactly what your own interest is."

He looked at me slightly shocked, an expression I hadn't thought him capable of showing.

"My interest? Why I'm the assistant district attorney. And right now, while the boss is sick, I am in charge."

"I understand that," I said. "But I still want to know something. I want to know this. I want to know where you yourself are headed. Are you looking for the murderers of the three people you have mentioned, assuming they were all murdered? Or are you merely looking for convictions? And exactly what is your interest in the money? Assuming again that there was any money."

If I expected him to get mad, I was disappointed. "There was money," he said thinly "I know that for sure. Battle knew it, too, and it cost him his life."

"You still haven't answered me," I said.

"And if I do answer you?"

"Then I will do as you want me to do. I'll give you a statement."

Again he was silent for a long time. At last he looked up at me again and the look was no more friendly and no warmer than it had been before.

"I want to find out who killed those three people and I want to see that whoever did is convicted of first degree murder and sentenced to die. I want to find that money because it will be vital evidence in obtaining a conviction."

This time I was the one who remained silent for a long time.

He was a funny little man, an odd, supercilious and slightly ridiculous figure. But for some strange reason, I suddenly realized that he was deadly serious. That he was being completely honest. That the one thing he really wanted was to perform to perfection the job to which he had been appointed.

"All right," I said at last, "I'll tell you my story. But no stenographer. Not yet. Not until you have heard me out."

He took a pack of cigarettes from his pocket and put one in his mouth and lighted it, and then he looked at me as he was putting the pack back. He hesitated and held the pack out. I took a cigarette but he didn't hold the match for me. He handed me the pack.

"Start talking," he said.

Chapter Nine

So I told him my story. I started right from the beginning and I told him the way it happened. I told him almost everything and I only lied twice. I lied twice and I left out a few minor details, but I told it almost straight. He only interrupted me two or three times.

I started when I had been driving up Route 301 and had seen Marilyn K. standing there beside the highway. I got us as far back as the Whispering Willows when the first interruption came.

"And you had no idea of what might be in that suitcase?" he asked.

"I had no idea," I said, happy that I wasn't taking a lie detector test.

"Go on," he said.

"I found out who she was when I called my friend in New York," I continued. "That was how I happened to be at the *Cutter Cabins* when I butted in on your deputy pal. I went there to call because I didn't want to telephone from the room in front of the girl."

He looked annoyed when I mentioned Battle and the scene at the cabins. Again he interrupted.

"Herman Battle was going to have to answer for that," he said. "It was only because of his brother, Georgie, who is a good man and an honest officer, that we carried Battle as long as we did."

He didn't have to apologize to me. Anyway, I went on talking.

"So I returned to Whispering Willows, even after I found out who she was," I explained. "All I knew is that she was lovely and she was in trouble. Maybe it was a protective instinct or maybe it was pure lust. But I returned."

I went on from there. I didn't give him a blow-by-blow description of that wonderful afternoon we had spent together. I didn't think he would either appreciate it or even understand. I just said we sat around and made love and got half tight. I brought the story up to the point when Battle knocked on the door. I figured I had to mention it. It was more than likely someone had heard him asking about me.

"The girl answered and he identified himself. I remembered his name," I explained. "I didn't want trouble. So I went into the shower and she let him in. I don't know what she said or he said. I had the shower door closed and the bedroom door was shut and I could only hear them muttering to each other. Anyway, he stayed for about a half an hour. And then he left."

"Why did he leave without seeing you if it was you he came to see?" Fleming asked.

"She said that she gave him something so that he would go away," I answered. I knew the answer would hold up. I was remembering the sheaf of bills I had stuffed in Battle's pants pocket when I had left him.

He nodded, but I couldn't tell whether he believed me or not.

"And then she saw the three men," I said.

"The three men?"

"Three mobsters from New York. A man named Socks Leopold and two hoods called Binge and Hymie. They were in the cocktail lounge. They had arrived in a black Chrysler Imperial. They were associates of the dead man, Marcus."

"No one named Leopold checked into Whispering Willows last night," he said.

"I can't help that. They were there. In the cocktail lounge. She saw them and later, when I left, I talked to one of them outside by the car. A big, beefy, ugly man with a broken nose."

"And they saw her?"

"No. Not then at least. Or so she said. But she did say that she was frightened to death of them and that they were there looking for her."

"So you left her then, is that it?" he asked, his voice sarcastic. "What happened to that protective instinct?"

I could see that I had lost him.

"Yes, I left her. I left because she insisted I leave. She told me she had telephoned her sister to come down and meet her. She said once her sister arrived she wouldn't be afraid any more. She didn't want me to be there when her sister showed up."

"Then you waited for the sister to arrive and left?"

I shook my head.

"I left soon after Battle left. Maybe I am a coward and certainly I am a fool, but you want the truth and I am giving it to you. She told me she was afraid of Socks Leopold and his hoodlums, but she also said that she could handle any situation which might come up. She asked me to leave; she insisted I leave. So I did. I packed my bag and left."

"But you didn't check out?"

"No. I just went out the back door to the carport and got in my car and left."

"With both suitcases? Hers and your own?"

"With only my own."

"Hers was gone when her sister came in and found her dead."

"Listen," I said, "I didn't kill her. I didn't kill her and I didn't take that suitcase. I don't even know what was in it. Whether it was full of money, as you seem to think it was, or not."

I don't really know why I lied about it. I wanted to tell him the truth. I felt that my only hope lay in telling the truth. But I did lie. Somehow or other, in the back of my mind was the thought that as long as the money was missing and as long as I was the sole living person who knew where it was, I still had something left to bargain with. The idea wasn't completely stupid, either. I had Leopold pegged as her murderer and Leopold wanted only one thing. He wanted that money. And so, sooner or later, the money was going to be the means of my contacting him. He was a man I very much wanted to see.

In short, I lied.

"All right," he said, "go on with the rest of it."

And that is where he had me. Up to this point I had been doing fine. Even with an occasional omission and an occasional perversion of the facts. But now it was different. I had three hours to account for. He may not have known when I left the motel, but he did know when I checked into *Cutter's Cabins*. And I didn't want to keep myself in that motel one second longer than I had actually stayed there.

Someone had killed Marilyn K. at the Whispering Willows, sometime during the period when I was driving to Baltimore airport and back and it was essential that I establish an alibi. But I just didn't have an alibi. Not unless I wanted to tell him about the money and I wasn't ready to play my trump card yet.

"I drove to Baltimore," I said. "And then I drove back to *Cutter's Cabins* and checked in."

"You drove to Baltimore? Why?"

"I can't tell you that."

"Did you see anyone in Baltimore? Talk to anyone who could identify you?"

"I talked to a couple of people. I had never seen them before but I feel sure that they could identify me. When and if it is necessary."

"It is going to be very necessary. Who were they?"

"I can't tell you that, either. Not just yet."

"You mean you won't. And you won't tell me why you drove to Baltimore?"

Hell, I wanted to tell him. I knew that sooner or later I would probably have to tell him. But if I told him now, told him about going to the airport, he'd quickly enough put two and two together. And I still needed that money for bait. I just had to take a chance on his getting mad. Although his getting mad was a sort of silly anticlimax to worry about at this stage of the game.

He got up from his chair and still stared at me.

"You are either the world's biggest liar or the world's God damndest fool," he said. "Probably both."

He didn't know how heartily I agreed with him.

He was opening the cell door when the man in the uniform of a county patrolman poked his head down the stairwell. He beckoned and Fleming went out and the two of them whispered for several moments, looking over at me in the meantime. Fleming came back and the other one disappeared.

He had a nasty expression on his face when he spoke.

"Your lawyer is upstairs," he said. "He has come to see you. And I have decided I was right. You are both a fool and a liar."

He swung on his heel and left.

I was surprised that they let him see me. But I guess even in Maryland a lawyer can see his client.

He was a thin, scrawny man in a rumpled suit and a pair of nose glasses which he wore on a ribbon. He had gray hair, what there was of it, a tall narrow forehead and a pair of the most guileless eyes I had ever seen. His nose and his mouth were large and there was no chin at all. He looked local.

The turnkey opened the cell door and he came in but didn't sit down. He waited until we were alone before he spoke.

"Hardie's the name," he said. "From down on the Eastern Shore. I handle work for Moore and Moore, New York attorneys, when they have something down this way."

"Do they have something?"

"They have you."

"They do? Well, that's news," I said. "Just who gave me to them?"

He looked very knowing.

"I guess we won't mention names," he said, smiling. "The kind of connections you have, Mr. Russell, well—"

"Well, nuts," I said. "I don't have connections. And right at this moment I don't need a lawyer."

He shook his head sadly.

"You need a lawyer, all right," he said. "You need one bad if what they tell me is true. That's why I am here. To try and get you out on bail."

"Look," I said. "You are wasting your time. Nobody is going to get me out on anything."

"Mr. Russell," he said, "I have been instructed to go as high as fifty thousand dollars if I have to. Down here that is all the money in the world. And I know this part of the world. I'm here to protect your interests and to get you out on bail until you can have a fair and unprejudiced—"

"Who did you say sent you?" I cut in.

Again he shook his head, looking at me as though I wasn't quite bright.

"Why, Moore and Moore—as I explained."

"And Moore and Moore were hired by?"

"Hired by your friends, Mr. Russell. You see, your friends feel that you have something they want and they have something you want."

"What do I want?"

"You want to get out of this cell."

"And they want?"

"They will discuss that with you when we get your release," he said. "Now—"

"Tell me, Mr. Hardie," I interrupted. "These people who want to get me out. They sort of have interests around. Like say gambling casinos, slots, juke boxes?"

He nodded sagaciously.

"Many interests," he said.

"All right, Mr. Hardie," I said. "I'll tell you what to do. You get in touch with your principals, Moore and Moore in New York. Tell them to tell their clients that I don't want to get out. I have no intention of getting out. That I would much rather stay alive inside than be dead outside. Understand?"

"Oh, now see here—"

"And Mr. Hardie," I went on, "one other thing. You seem like a nice, simple, honest country boy. Sort of a modern Abe Lincoln, I might even say. I advise you to seek new associates in New York. Give up Moore and Moore. Otherwise, one of these days, you may find yourself facing a charge of conspiracy to commit murder."

Well, it was my day for misjudging character. Mr. Hardie wasn't quite the dull-witted oaf he had made himself out to be.

He stepped back and called for the turnkey. While he was waiting he spoke again and they were the last words he bothered to waste on me.

"The boys are going to get that money, brother," he said. "Understand? They are going to get it. And what these local clowns will do to you will be a day in the country compared to what the boys will do if you don't cough up."

Mr. Hardie left and I thought my day was complete. But it wasn't. I had one more little surprise in store.

The light went out over my head and I fell back on the bunk. I tried to make my mind a blank. I was so dead tired that I ached all over. I was completely beat.

But I didn't sleep. I couldn't sleep.

In spite of myself, I laughed. I had to laugh. There was something screamingly funny about it.

Within the last twelve hours I had been in bed with what was probably the most luscious and the most expert bit of female flesh in the Western Hemisphere. I had experienced thrills that most men don't even have the knowledge to dream about. I had better than three hundred thousand dollars in cash money waiting for me not sixty miles away. I should close my eyes and smile with delight at my memories and my expectancies.

I laughed—and then I damned near cried.

All I was facing was three murder charges and a nice friendly lawyer was even trying to get me free of them—so that a man named Socks Leopold could do to me what he had done to Marilyn K.

I didn't want to think about it, but I couldn't seem to close my eyes. It wouldn't have mattered if I had. The light came back on.

The heavy footsteps coming down the stairs followed the turning on of the lights and I sighed and again pulled myself up so that I was sitting on the edge of the cot.

George Battle was wearing his hat, but he had taken off his coat and his shirt and pulled his suspenders back up over his woolen underwear. He was carrying a pad of paper and a fountain pen and he had a dead cigar hanging out of the corner of his mouth.

I changed my mind; he was fully as repulsive as his brother had been. Just in a different way.

He stood in front of the cell and took out the old-fashioned gold watch from his watch pocket and looked at it and then at me.

"Five-thirty," he said. "We got just one hour. One hour to get that confession."

"There isn't going to be any confession," I said. "Go away and let me sleep. I've already talked with your boss."

He went on talking, ignoring my words.

"You murdered my brother, fella," he said. "I know just what happened and I'll tell you, to refresh your memory. Herm told me about the fight at Cutters. He might have been in the wrong, but it wasn't none of your business. Later on, I was with him and he told me he saw your car at the Whispering Willows and was going back to take you. So I know what happened. He went there and you killed him.

"I don't know how you did it because Herm was strong. Guess you tricked him. Anyway, you killed him. Then you took his body out and planted that stolen money on him. Ain't no use lying about it. None at all. I know Herm. Herm had his good points and he had his bad. If Herm had come across that money Marcus was supposed to have, he wouldn't have taken just a little bit of it; he'd have taken it all. So you killed him and planted the money and made him out a thief."

He spoke calmly and without passion and I was surprised at how close he was to the truth. He was smarter than I had figured. And I didn't like that calmness of his at all.

"I'd like to kill you for that," he said. "I loved Herm and I always took care of him. But I ain't going to kill you, Mr. Russell. I'm going to let the state do that. If they do it, then Herm's reputation will be cleared and you'll still pay for your crime. So we got just an hour."

He was taking off the heavy leather belt which circled his waist and assisted the suspenders in holding up his trousers.

"You want to sign this confession here now, or do you want to do it the hard way?" he said.

"Listen, mister," I said. "I've told you. I didn't kill your brother. I didn't kill anyone. Now get out of here. Get out of here before I start yelling. You heard what Fleming said."

"Martin Fleming's gone home," he said. "Go ahead and yell. Ain't no one here to hear you but me, and it is going to do me good to hear you yell. I want to hear you yell."

The leather belt supported his holster and his billy was hung to it on a hook and he carefully laid them on the floor, well away from the door. He took the key to the cell out of his pocket.

"You aren't going to hit me with that belt," I said. "If you come in here, bring your gun or bring your blackjack. You aren't going to get any confession and you aren't going to beat me. If you do anything, you are going to have to kill me. You aren't going to use that belt."

I might just as well have been talking to a blank wall. He opened the door and I got set. He was a big man and he was fat and although I was dead on my feet, I figured I had speed on him.

But I was wrong.

I guess he'd done it so often before that he had the technique down pat. Before he had even finished opening the cell door, the belt lashed out like a bullwhip. The first blow was a strike and the cruel end of it caught me across the nose and almost blinded me. It stopped me cold.

I don't like to even think about those next few minutes. I never had a chance; couldn't even get close to him. His technique was perfect. He knew just how to inflict the punishment so that it hurt the worst and still didn't knock me out. The leather strap snapped and curled and flayed and he used it like a lion trainer handling a cage full of cats.

I didn't think I'd scream but I did. I didn't go down, but I screamed. Time stopped, but the screams went on.

I knew I couldn't last. I had to do something. He was sweating like a pig when he finally stepped back, puffing, to catch his breath.

"Ready to sign?" he said.

I couldn't speak, there was too much blood in my mouth. But I nodded my head up and down.

He stepped outside and picked up the pad of paper and the pen he had carried in with him. It took the last ounce of strength I had, but I made my play. I dove out of the door after him, hitting him in the kidneys with my head.

He turned like a cat, off balance but still on his feet. The belt again lashed out and this time he really scored. But it was his one mistake. He had forgotten that he was holding the belt by the wrong end and the heavy brass buckle got me across the side of the head. I went to the floor, out cold, and there was nothing he could do during the few minutes which were left of his hour. There was nothing that anyone could have done, including the Mayo brothers. I was unconscious and I was going to stay that way for some time.

Chapter Ten

I knew it was a dream because I didn't feel any pain. I didn't want to disturb the dream, so I didn't open my eyes, but my hand moved and I could feel the sheet under me. Something small and soft and cool was on my forehead. I smelled a faint perfume. It had to be a dream.

The voice said, "He's coming out of it."

The soft, cool hand left my forehead and someone leaned over me and the perfume was a little stronger. I moved my head. No pain. I opened my eyes and she emerged gradually out of the fog. A small, piquant face surrounded by dark, curly hair. I closed my eyes. It was a dream, after all.

Sarah Cutter said, "Will he be all right, doctor?"

"The morphine will wear off in about an hour," a man's voice said. "He'll start feeling the pain, but he'll be all right. He won't look very well for some time and he won't be comfortable, but he's lucky. He must have the constitution of an ox. He'll be all right. You better go on home yourself, Sarah, or you'll be sick, too. You have been hanging around here all day now."

"I want to stay until I am sure," she said.

"I have to leave now, but I'll look in later tonight," the man's voice said. "You can't stay here alone with him, Sarah. He'll be conscious in a few more minutes. Fleming says he's a killer and although he won't be able to do much, you shouldn't stay here alone with him."

"I don't think he killed anybody," she said. "Anyway, I don't care. All I know is that he helped me when I needed help and he didn't have to. He needs help now. I pay my debts. Anyway, I don't think he killed anybody. I just think he got in trouble because he goes around helping people. He picked up that girl who got killed and got in trouble. He helped me and got into trouble. After what these animals have done to him, he needs someone."

"As you like," then the other voice said. "At least the guard is outside if you need him. But get some rest. You haven't slept for twenty-four hours."

A moment later I heard a door close. I opened my eyes. She was still there. But it was another ten minutes before my mind was really clear and I could make sense or understand what was happening. Unfortunately, along with mental clarity came the pain.

"Where am I and what has happened?" I finally managed. I could see that I was in a small, whitewashed room. Bare walls, but clean. A sink in the corner. No bars on the door. Bars on the window. Nighttime. Sarah Cutter beside the bed, on which I lay between clean sheets.

"Martin Fleming says you killed three people and stole a whole lot of money that belonged to some gangster. Did you kill three people, Mr. Russell?"

"I didn't kill anyone," I said. "I have never killed anyone and I never will kill anyone."

That was a lie. I would kill someone. I would kill the person who beat a girl to death in a room at the Whispering Willows. But she didn't question me. She just nodded her head and said, "Martin Fleming has never been right about anything in his whole life."

"Now tell me what has happened," I said.

"You were badly hurt," she said. "That man, Battle, almost killed you. I came to visit you with Martin and we found you unconscious in your cell. Even Martin was frightened. Martin is stiff and stubborn, but he is fair. He doesn't want his prisoners beaten, even if they are murderers."

She blushed, but I told her not to mind my feelings, just tell me.

"Anyway, Martin had you brought up here. He doesn't want any scandal because he hopes to be district attorney someday and the thought that a man could die while in his care, scared him so much he almost became human. So they brought you here. This is the room they reserve for women prisoners. He had a doctor come in and take care of you. You have been here for almost thirty hours.

"It is," she looked down at her watch, "it is six o'clock, Thursday evening."

I started to move, to sit up, but the pain came and I found it easier to lie back.

"The doctor gave you something so you would sleep. And everyone has been here to see you. The girl is still downstairs. She has been here for over two hours. The lawyer is still here. But Martin says I am the only one, outside of the doctor, who can see you."

"I don't have a lawyer and I don't want a lawyer. And what girl is here to see me? I don't know any girl."

"The girl whose sister they say you killed. Kelley. Suzy Kelley."

"What does she want?" I asked. "I should think I'd be the last person in the world she would want to see."

"I talked to her and she is very sweet. She doesn't think you killed her sister and that is one of the reasons I don't think so either. She says her sister talked to her over the telephone about you. Before she was killed."

I made the effort again and this time I managed to raise myself and twist around so that I was sitting on the edge of the bed. They had put an old-fashioned flannel nightgown on me and I felt like a fool, but at least I was covered. I was also beginning to ache in every muscle of my body.

I sat there and I looked at Sarah Cutter; I looked into her open, sweet face, her serious eyes. And I made my decision. I had to gamble and I had to gamble on somebody. She was my only hope.

"Sarah Cutter," I said, "I want you to listen to me. I have to make this short because it would take too long to explain everything. But I was telling you the truth. I killed no one. I'm being framed. I am being framed for three murders."

She shook her head.

"Martin Fleming has his faults," she said, "but he wouldn't frame anybody."

"Fleming isn't framing me. Someone else is. You said you would help me if you could. Well, I need help. I need your help."

She stared back at me, a frank, almost disconcerting stare.

"What can I do?"

"Just how much would Martin Fleming do for you? How much influence do you have with him?"

"Martin would do anything for me," she replied simply. "Anything, unless it interfered with his job."

"Good," I said. "Then this is what I want you to do. I want you to see that I get some clothes. I want a bucket of hot, black coffee. I want a package of cigarettes. And I want to see that girl downstairs. Suzy Kelley."

"I think I can arrange that," she said. "But you shouldn't have your clothes. You should stay in bed. You have been—"

"I know," I interrupted. "I have been sick. But unless I do what I have to do, I am going to be a lot sicker. I have to have the clothes. And there is one more thing I want you to do. After you leave here I want you to go back home and I want you to stay there. That is very important. Go back to the cabins and stay there. Do you have a phone inside?"

She looked at me curiously.

"Why yes, I have a phone."

"Then do as I say. Just stay home. But first see that I get my clothes, that I get the coffee and cigarettes and that I am allowed to see Suzy Kelley. Will you do this for me?"

"But why should I go home and what has my phone to do with it?"

"Do you trust me?"

"Yes. I trust you."

"Then, Sarah, do what I ask you to do."

It is fantastic what three cups of black coffee and a couple of cigarettes can do for a man. Twenty-five minutes after Sarah left the room, I was sitting in the chair she had vacated. I was sore all over and I ached in muscles I didn't even know I had. My nose was probably broken and my head felt like a muskmelon, but I was whole and I was functioning in all departments.

There was a rattle at the door and I looked up and the turnkey poked his head in.

"Lady to see you, mister," he said. "She's got exactly ten minutes."

He took his head away and Suzy Kelley walked into the room.

I had prepared myself, but I had not prepared enough.

You should never see someone whom you have loved laying stiff and cold on a marble slab, her chestnut hair a shade redder with dried blood, her beautiful face smashed almost beyond recognition, her body all torn and bruised—and then, a few hours later, have her walk into a room looking more lovely and desirable than ever.

The turnkey had said Suzy Kelley and I had asked to see Suzy Kelley, but it was just as though Marilyn K. herself was standing there, looking at me through serious azure eyes. The same small, exquisite figure—although this girl had done everything she could to conceal it with the harsh outlines of a tweed skirt and jacket—the same lovely contours and the same heart-shaped face. The same eyes, although plain and clear and without make-up. Hair different, a soft, ash blond; manner different, subjected, almost mousy.

Marilyn K. had been right, though. Sister Suzy was a dead ringer for her.

"Mr. Russell?" she said.

A different voice also. Not small and helpless. But a strong, determined, honest voice. With just those two words I knew what Marilyn had meant when she said that Suzy always knew what to do. Just the way she spoke, you understood at once that this girl might be a little provincial, a little subdued, but that she had superb confidence, complete control.

"How are you, Suzy Kelley?" I said.

She held out her hand like a man. A strong, firm grip. She sat down in the seat I had gotten out of. She came right to the point.

"I know that you didn't kill my sister, Mr. Russell," she said. "I know, because I talked with her over the telephone five minutes after you left the motel. My car broke down and I called her."

"I am glad you know," I said.

"But someone killed her, Mr. Russell. I always knew she was going to be killed someday. I had told her as much, right from the beginning when she started taking up with those gangsters. I knew it must happen. I loved my sister, Mr. Russell."

"I loved her, too," I said. "After my fashion."

She wasn't listening to me. She went right on talking. "I know why they killed her. She told me, indirectly, when we talked on the telephone. She was killed because she took the money. The money you took away from the motel when you left. She told me about that also. This afternoon a man found me. A Mr. Leopold. He says it was really his money. He knows I don't have it and he knows you do. He wants that money."

"Mr. Leopold will never get that money," I said. "I rather suspect Mr. Leopold killed your sister because of that money. Tell me, Suzy, why did you come here?"

She looked into my face. She was like Marilyn but then again she wasn't. She had a hardness, but it was of a different kind. She was a girl who would never ask anyone to help her. Would never have to.

"I will be frank with you, Mr. Russell," she said. "I came to get the money. There is nothing I can do for you or I would do it. But you can do something for me. You can see that I get that money. Marilyn paid with her life for it and I mean to see that her life wasn't wasted."

"Marilyn is dead," I said.

"Yes, Marilyn is dead. But I am alive. I want to say something to you. I always loved Marilyn but she really thought I was a fool and I think, perhaps, she may even have hated me. I understood what would happen to her some day and now it has happened. She paid with her life for a suitcase full of cash. Her life is not going to be spent in vain."

"You want the money," I said, "and I want to get out of here."

Again she stared at me.

"I can't help you, Mr. Russell. You know that. And you know the money can't help you. They will never let you keep it. They wouldn't let Marilyn and they won't let you. But if I get the money, I might be able to help you. They have already talked with me. They know all about me. They have always known about me. The money will only be safe when it is in my hands."

"Marilyn said you were a strong person," I said.

"I am a strong person, Mr. Russell. And I know what I am talking about."

"So you want the money?"

"Yes."

I stood up and tossed the cigarette butt on the floor. "You can have the money," I said. "There is only one little thing."

"And what is that?"

"I am the only person in this world who will be able to get it for you. I can't do it while I am in this jailhouse."

"You could tell me where—"

"I have told you that you can have the money. I will give you my solemn word. But you must do something for me. If you agree, then I will do the thing which you want me to do for you."

"And what must I do for you?"

I walked over to the door and held my ear against it. I could hear no one. I came back and I faced her. I spoke as low as I could.

"You must come back within an hour. You must bring a loaded gun in your handbag. You can say you are going out to get me something to eat. They won't suspect anything. And you must have a fast car downstairs on the street."

If I had expected to shock her, I was disappointed.

"You want me to do this? To commit a criminal act?"

"You want the money?"

She didn't say anything so I went on talking.

"A fast car," I said. "And you must be with me when I leave. It is a chance, but less than the chance you are taking with our Mr. Leopold. Now tell me, what is the setup here? How many people are around? Where is this place located? Where is the nearest main road? How far are we from Route 301?"

I am making it sound a lot easier than it really was. She was hard and determined and direct, but she was also very difficult to convince. She knew a hundred reasons why my plan wouldn't work. But I had the final convincer. I knew where the money was and I wasn't going to tell her, or anyone else. Not until I was out of jail.

But I was going to keep my word. I was going to give her the money.

And as I talked to her I learned one thing.

This girl Suzy was, in her own subdued and mousy, conventional fashion, a lot tougher than her sister had been. She was retiring and probably unimaginative and naive. But she had the toughness that only comes with complete determination. With a one-track, undeviating mentality...

The break itself was easier than I had hoped for. Almost undramatic in its simplicity.

She was back within less than an hour. How she managed to get the gun I will never know, but she got it. Anyone can buy a gun in Maryland. The car was no problem. She merely took the rented car she had driven down from New York to a garage. Said she wanted to have certain repairs made, a partial engine overhaul, and borrowed a car to use while they worked on her own. It was a Merc and it was fast.

I didn't stick the gun under the turnkey's chin when he came to let her out on her second visit. I slapped him on the side of the head with it and pulled him into the room and tied him up and gagged him. We ran into a cleaning woman on the way out, and I tied her up. We had to pass the room off the main lobby where a half dozen men, probably deputies and hangers on, were sitting shooting the breeze, but they never even saw us. I figured we would have a good half-hour before the alarm was out.

She had thought of something which even I had missed up on. She had a county map.

We took back roads and fifteen minutes after we were on our way, I found an isolated phone booth. I left her in the car while I made the call.

Sarah Cutter must have been keeping her word literally. She picked up the receiver at the first ring.

For the second time within the last two hours I was trusting everything to my faith in someone I didn't even know.

"Don't say anything until I finish speaking," I said. "Are you alone and do you know who this is?"

The silence lasted so long that I thought she had gone off and left the phone. Perhaps gone to call for help. I knew that when she spoke I would know. I would know if my gamble was going to work out. And at last she spoke, in a small, frightened voice.

"I know," she said. "And I am alone."

"You said you would help me," I said. "Will you still help me? You don't have to; there is no reason you should. But I am asking you to. Will you?"

Again that long, tortuous silence. At last she spoke, the words very far away. "What do you want me to do?"

"I want you to get a room ready. That same cabin, number six. I will be there within the next twenty minutes. I don't want to see you or check in. I just want to use the room. Perhaps for several hours. And I will have a car with me. The keys will be in the car. I want you to get in it and take it somewhere. Get it out of sight. That is all I will ask of you."

"That is plenty," she said, her voice not at all far away. I thought she was going to refuse; I was almost sure then that she would. But she surprised me. She waited a long time again and then, at last, she said, "You know what you are doing?"

"I know," I said.

"The room will be ready," she said. "Don't worry about the car. I'll put it in the barn in back of the place. No one will see it there."

"As long as there is a barn, I'll take care of it," I said. "Will I be able to find it all right?"

"There will be a light over the doors and they will be unlocked," she said.

I didn't bother to thank her when I hung up. Thanks would be superfluous. You don't just thank someone for saving your life.

Chapter Eleven

At ten minutes to ten, on Wednesday night, I pulled shut the door of cabin number six, Cutter's tourist court, and turned the key in the lock. I checked to see that the shades were drawn, and then I turned on the overhead light.

"Take a look around," I said. "Get yourself oriented. You have exactly one minute and then the light goes out and it stays out."

Suzy stared at me.

"What are we doing here?" she said. "You promised you would get me the money. You must keep your promise. Is the money—?"

"Do what I tell you. Now. Look around. Get oriented. You will get the money. I have promised and I'll keep that promise. But we have to stay here. We have to stay here until morning."

Her expression changed and for a moment it was just as though I were looking again into the face of her dead sister.

"Until morning? Alone here with you?"

"Alone. With me," I said. "Now quick. The light is going out."

She looked around and she saw the same things I saw. Two small, fairly comfortable chairs, a dresser, a washstand behind a screen, an open door leading to a tiny bathroom. A faded rug on the floor. An electric heater. A clothes tree. A large, beaten-up double bed.

I pulled the light cord.

"Take off your jacket and make yourself comfortable," I said. "We have a long wait. Until daybreak."

She was moving around and stumbled against me and I took her arms and I could feel her grow taut. I moved her and when I came to the edge of the bed, I said. "Sit here."

I could hear her breathing heavily. I don't know whether she was frightened or not. If she was, her next remark certainly didn't indicate it.

"You promised me the money," she said. "I want it."

"Until dawn," I repeated.

"You can at least tell me."

I sat down next to her and I was surprised when she didn't move.

"Listen, Suzy," I said. "You might just as well be patient. We are going to stay here, right here, until morning. We aren't going to move and we aren't going to have a light and if we talk at all, we are going to whisper. And in the morning I will get you the money."

She hesitated several minutes and then she spoke again. "Just what are we going to do?"

"Well, if you have any sense, you'll get out of your jacket, slip off your shoes and lie back on the bed and get some rest. That's what I am going to do." I started to kick my shoes off.

For several seconds she didn't move and then she spoke in a tiny voice.

"I have never been on a bed with a man," she said.

"You'll have your clothes on."

Again she didn't say anything and finally I heard a small shoe drop to the floor. Then the second shoe. I could hear her removing the jacket.

I didn't stop with my shoes and jacket. I stripped down to my shorts, undershirt and socks. I lay back on the bed, moving carefully to one side. A moment later I felt the spring sag and I knew that she was beside me.

I reached out my hand and I found hers. She didn't take it away.

She said, "Did you bring me here on purpose?"

"I brought you here because this is where I had to come if I want to get the money for you. Now forget the money and forget everything else. There is absolutely nothing that I can do until morning."

She was silent for a long time, but she left her small hand in mine. And then at last she spoke again.

"I have never been with a man," she said.

I turned on my side and I reached over and I put my arm across her breasts and I pulled her around so that she faced me. She didn't say a word.

I put my hand in back of her head and then I found her lips. I had force her mouth open. She didn't try to stop me. Her hands were against my chest, her elbows doubled up. I leaned far over her, half covering her with my body, and the hands moved and went up under my T-shirt and around the bare flesh of my back.

I moved my own hands then. She had taken off the jacket but she still wore the starched white shirt. There was no brassiere under it.

Her breasts were firm and she didn't flinch when my palms caressed them. She cried out a little when I pressed too hard and I took one hand away. I reached down and I found the snap of the tweed skirt.

She struggled under me when I pulled it off and then she cried out and moaned as my hand explored the loveliness of her thighs and finally discovered its destiny.

She said: "Please—oh, please!"

I don't know whether she meant "please don't" or whether she just meant "please." It wouldn't have mattered anyway. I had suddenly lost all control and I was tearing the last of her clothes off and she was clinging to me and her mouth was wide on mine. Her hands were tearing at me but her body was pressed close.

I had to take my mouth away to breathe and she whispered something that

I didn't hear. I pressed harder and she cried out and said, "Don't hurt me. Please don't hurt me."

And again I moved and the old beaten-up bed cracked and then rose and fell and she suddenly screamed and the arms around me tightened until I thought that she would break my ribs.

She was her sister's twin. She was everything that Marilyn K. had been and then a hundred things more.

She didn't cry out after that first scream; she lay there, her body a mound of flame, and the desire came again and again as we moved and struggled and found each other's innermost secret places.

It ended finally. It had to end.

I fell back, spent and empty and exhausted and later I heard her get up and she crossed the room.

When I finally sat up on the edge of the bed and found my cigarette lighter and looked at my watch, the time was five-thirty. I could see a tiny ribbon of light just beginning to peek through the crack behind the window shade.

She was back on the bed beside me now and I knew that she was stark naked, lying there breathing heavily. I thought that she must be sleeping.

I got up and put on some clothes and then I reached up and pulled the light cord and the light went on.

She wasn't sleeping.

She jumped as though someone had doused her with a bucket of cold water. She was reaching wildly for the sheet.

"Please," she said. "Turn it off."

I laughed and pulled the light cord again.

"Get dressed," I said. "It's time to get the money."

She was off the bed in a flash and she was asking questions again as she dressed.

"Within the hour," I said. "Now here is what you must do. Just be ready to leave. I am going out. I will be gone anywhere from ten minutes to an hour. But I will be back. And when I get back—"

She stopped me and I could tell by the tone of her voice that she still didn't trust me.

"I'll come with you," she said. "You can't leave me here alone. You must take me."

"You must stay right in this room," I said. "I am not going far. I am going into the office. There is something I have to do and I have to do it alone. I shall not be more than a hundred or two hundred feet from you."

"I'm coming with you."

I turned and took her by the arms, digging my fingers into her soft flesh.

"Unless you do exactly as I say—to the letter—you will never see that money. Understand? Exactly as I say. You stay in this room and be quiet. I will be back within an hour. Perhaps within fifteen minutes. But you are not to move."

I didn't give her a chance to argue. I dropped her arms and quickly opened the door and slipped out and quietly closed it.

The dawn was just breaking in the east. I had the gun Suzy had brought me, in the band of my trousers.

There was a Plymouth coupe parked directly in front of the office and I could see that the lights were on inside. Miss Sarah was having an early morning visitor and I hesitated, cursing my bad luck. But I didn't stop. I couldn't stop. Time was running out.

I took a few quick steps, put my hand on the door and shoved. I stepped into the tiny office, the gun in my fist.

For a second then, I don't know which one of us was the most surprised, the little man who jumped to his feet and whose eyes went wide as he saw and recognized me, or myself.

But Martin Fleming was the first one to speak.

"Russell!" he said. "Put down that gun!"

He started for me. I didn't have time to say anything. I have to give him credit. I outweighed him two to one. I stood there with a loaded gun in my hand and he thought I was a triple murderer. But he kept right on coming.

Sarah stayed frozen in the chair in which she sat.

I didn't want to hit him, but I had to. I didn't use the gun, I used my left and because the wrist was still swollen and sore, I didn't hit him hard enough to knock him out. But he landed halfway across the room on his knees.

"Now stay there—both of you," I said. I pointed the gun at them again.

She looked at me. She wasn't frightened. She knew that I wouldn't use the gun. She knew that I knew she knew. But she played along. I could have kissed her for it.

"Don't be a fool, Martin," she said. "Do what he says."

"Yes, Martin, do," I said.

He was looking at me with absolute hatred.

"Do you know an attorney named Hardie?" I asked. Neither of them answered.

"You, Fleming, quick. Do you know Hardie?"

This time he nodded his head, his mouth a grim, tight line.

"All right, get him on the phone. Sarah, look up his number."

"He lives in Denton," Fleming said.

Sarah picked up the phone book and a moment later she read off the number.

"When you get him," I said, "don't say anything. Just hand me the phone."

Fleming stood up and moved over beside Sarah. He dialed the number and I could hear it ring. It rang three times and then stopped. I heard a voice at the other end.

Silently he handed the instrument to me.

I took it, being careful to keep the gun on him. I knew he was a hero-type. I didn't trust him.

"Hardie?" I said.

There was a yes at the other end.

"This is Sam Russell. Listen to me carefully. I want you to get hold of your contact. I want you to tell them that I am at *Cutter's Cabins* on Route 301, just before you come to the Chesapeake Bay Bridge. I am in cabin number six. I have what they want. Do you understand me?"

There was a long silence and finally he spoke.

"I understand you."

"Can you do it at once? I will be here for not more than an hour. An hour at the most. Do you follow me?"

"What do you have for them, Russell?" he countered.

"I have the money," I said. "The money. But only for an hour."

"Stay where you are," he said. There was a click at the other end of the line.

Fleming was staring at me. Suddenly he spoke.

"You are a bigger fool than I took you to be, Russell," he said. "I guess the state won't have to kill you after all."

"Nobody will kill me," I said.

"No? Well it happens I know who Hardie represents. What do you think you can do? Just ask them here and turn the money over to them? That they will thank you? You damned idiot, they'll take the money and gun you down. They'll kill you and they'll kill us, too."

"They won't kill me, Mr. Fleming," I said. "And if you will just shut up for a few minutes and do what I tell you to do, they won't kill you, either. They have no reason to kill you."

He turned to Sarah. "The man is insane," he said.

I could tell by the way she was looking at me that she agreed.

"All right," I said, "we have nothing to do but wait. So just sit there and make yourselves—"

He started to argue again but I finally shut him up and at last the three of us were just standing there in the room, waiting. Sarah had gotten out of the chair and she and Fleming were back against the wall. I stood just inside the door, where I could watch the road from the window.

I had figured it would take at least a half an hour. I was wrong by a full fifteen minutes.

The first car to pass was the black Chrysler sedan. A heavy-set man was driving and I figured it was Leopold. He must have been shacked up very close by. He was alone in the car. A couple of hundred yards behind him was a second car. A green station wagon. Four men were in it. Neither car slowed up or hesitated as they passed. But I could see the occupants carefully eying the cabins.

I turned quickly to Fleming.

"If you want to be alive in time for breakfast, do exactly what I say," I said. "How long will it take to get the state police here?"

He hesitated, looking at me as though I wasn't making good sense.

"How long?" I yelled. "Quick!"

"About eight minutes," he said. "Why—?"

"Shut up," I said. "Get on that phone. Call them. Tell them not to spare the horses and tell them to bring riot guns. You," I turned to Sarah, "duck out of the back door and head for the barn. Get inside and don't stir. Fleming, as soon as you get that call through, follow her. Unless you see a car coming. If you do, just stay where you are. Understand?"

He lifted his head from the phone which he had just finished dialing and nodded. But I could see that he didn't understand. He still thought I had blown my stack.

"All right, Sarah," I said. "Now." I opened the door and I ran for cabin number six.

I thought eight minutes would do it. That it would be just about right.

I was wrong.

Even as I slammed the door of number six, out of the corner of my eye I saw two cars screaming back down the road toward *Cutter's Cabins.*

Suzy started to say something but I didn't have time for casual conversation.

"On the floor!" I yelled. "Under that bed!"

She started to protest, but I didn't have time to join any discussion group. I hated to hit a woman who had recently finished giving me one of the greatest thrills a man can have in this life, but I had no option.

My right caught her on the point of the jaw and her slight, small-boned body fell back on the bed.

I pulled her and the mattress off together and I half rolled her up in it and shoved it behind the bed. I wasn't going to take a chance on a stray shot getting her if there was any possible way to avoid it.

And then I shifted the gun back to my right hand. I went to the window then and knelt down so that I could see out of the crack between the shade and the window, which faced the road.

Chapter Twelve

I got one break and it probably saved my life.

The Chrysler screeched to a stop in front of the cabin, but the station wagon went on and didn't stop until it as fifty yards up the road.

The fat man got out of the front seat. He looked around for a moment and then he walked slowly to the door. He wasn't three feet from where I was squatting when he softly knocked.

"Mr. Russell?" he whispered, his voice a hoarse, nervous croak.

He rattled the knob. The door was open but he didn't come in.

"Mr. Leopold?" I asked. "Come right in."

But he wasn't having any.

"This is Leopold," he said. "I understand you have something for me. Do you want to give it to me? If you do, please come out."

"I have your money, Mr. Leopold," I called through the door. "Or at least I understand it is yours. But you will have to come in for it."

He hesitated for several moments. I could see what was going through his mind. He felt it would be a mistake to open that door. It would have been.

"The money is mine," he said at last. "I suggest if you are telling the truth, you come outside. And bring it with you."

"You come in, Mr. Leopold."

He waited again for a moment and I saw the knob begin to turn. But then he must have changed his mind. The knob stopped turning and the next thing I saw was his big meaty shoulders as he slowly walked back to the Chrysler.

He must have made some sort of signal that I didn't see. The next moment I heard the sound of a motor as someone stepped on a throttle and an engine suddenly roared. There was the scream of tires spinning in a torturous start on the cement pavement.

I knew what was going to happen next. So did Mr. Leopold. But he made one mistake. He figured that because he didn't have a gun, that because he was just simply walking away and getting back into his car, he was safe.

I only waited until the crack of the first shot and even that was risky. But I took the chance. Mr. Leopold had no chance at all.

The single shot I was able to get off before I flattened out on the floor, caught him just in back of his right ear, a little to the left.

And then all hell broke loose.

If Fleming's estimate was right, I had two and a half minutes to go.

Their strategy would have done credit to a brigadier general, but unfortunately, it wasn't correct for the current target. They drove past, firing everything they had at the cabin and they went up the road a hundred yards or so and braked and came back and tried it all over again. I just lay there, not moving.

They did it once more, and then, on the last trip back, the wagon screeched to a stop. I heard the doors open.

I didn't get up but just raised the gun and fired blindly out of the window. I didn't care if I hit anyone or not. I just wanted them to know that I still had firepower. I knew if I could stall them for another half minute, I would have it made.

A couple of them must have had Tommy guns, because the woodwork just above my head began to open up as though a buzz saw was going through it.

I rolled over, past the door and fired through the other window.

The Tommies opened up again and I started to change my mind about guessing right. And then I heard the sirens.

For the next three or four minutes it sounded like a busy morning on the Western Front. And then suddenly it was over.

The cabin looked like a sieve.

I stood up, went over to the iron bed. I reached under it and pulled out the mattress.

Suzy slowly got to her feet. She was as white as a sheet and I truly believe it was the only time in her entire life that she was really frightened.

A half-hour later seven of us were crowded together in the tiny office of *Cutter's Cabins*. Sarah Cutter, Fleming, Suzy, myself and three husky state troopers. One trooper had a notebook in his hand and Fleming, as usual, was popping off.

Outside were a half dozen state police cars. An ambulance had just left with the last of the dead and a couple of troopers were hurrying traffic past.

"All right, Russell, you have proved your point," Fleming said. "You almost got us all shot down by that gang of killers, but you proved your point. You have only made one mistake. You haven't proved anything which changes my mind. Officer," he turned to one of the troopers, "put the handcuffs on that man. I am holding him for murder."

I sighed.

"Will you listen to me for just one minute," I said. "Just one minute, please."

He hesitated and the trooper hesitated. I hurried it up. He wasn't going to give me anything.

"Just which murder are you talking about now?" I asked. "The prisoner should have the right to know."

"The murder of a woman named Marilyn Kelley will do as well as the next," he said.

I laughed.

"You have the evidence?" I asked.

"I have the corpse."

It was the time for the gambit.

"You have a corpse Mr. Fleming, but you have the wrong corpse." I said.

There was a sudden gasp and I looked quickly over at Suzy. I went on quickly.

"Fingerprints don't lie," I said. "This girl here is Marilyn Kelley, or as she likes to be known, 'Marilyn K.'!"

There was a sudden din of voices and then Fleming yelled for silence.

"Let him finish," he said. "It's pathetic, but let him finish."

"Thanks," I said. "Thanks a lot. As far as identity is concerned, that's easy. The Kelley sisters were entertainers. In New York. They would have had to have been fingerprinted, according to municipal regulations. The fingerprints of this girl here—" I looked over to where the girl who had been calling herself Suzy stood—"of this girl and the corpse can be checked. You could save time by not bothering with any denials."

They all looked at her then. She didn't move; her expression remained cold and unchanged. She just stood there, saying nothing. I looked back at Fleming. I could see that for the first time I was beginning to reach him.

"Now can I have a couple of minutes?" I asked.

He nodded.

"This is Marilyn K." I said. "The dead girl is Suzy, her twin sister, whom she murdered. And here is exactly what happened. I will start with Marcus."

No one said a word. I took a deep breath and went on.

"It was the way I told it to you, Fleming," I said. "I stopped when I saw her at the side of the road and picked her up. There was just one thing that I didn't understand. I didn't understand that she had just finished murdering a man named Aurelio Marcus. She got him with a blackjack, at the root of the neck. She's an expert with that sort of thing. I know. I have witnessed her at work."

This time is was Marilyn who interrupted.

"You louse," she said. "You dirty louse. You can't prove a thing. Not a thing. Nobody can prove that Marcus—"

"You'll have your turn to talk," Fleming said. "Let him finish."

"She killed Marcus. I didn't know that at the time but I know it now. I know because she planted the blackjack in my car. The one you found. But I did know she had the money. She told me, right away.

"The second time she murdered she killed Herman Battle, your deputy. Battle was more or less an accident. He smelled something and moved in, planning to shake us down. It cost him his life. And it was deliberate murder. Battle was tied up; I had tied him up myself. And then, for a moment, I stepped out of the room. When I came back, his forehead was caved in and he was dead. She used the tire iron from my car for that one."

Again she interrupted, her voice a harsh croak. "Proof," she said. "Where's the proof?"

"I'm the proof," I said. "I saw you do it. But let's go on. As I say, Battle was a sort of innocent bystander. But her twin sister, the girl who lies in the marble slab, was not just a casual little piece of homicide. That was the real murder. The one she had planned all along. The one she has probably been planning for years. Because sister Suzy was the only person in the world who could give her something that she absolutely had to have."

Her voice was sarcastic now. And she wasn't bothering to deny her identity any longer.

"And what could Suzy ever give me that I needed or wanted?" she asked.

"Her identity," I said. "Her identity, baby. Your sister was clean, she had a decent reputation, she didn't fool around with mobs. She had talent, although God knows you have your share of that, too, in a slightly different field. But you knew one thing. That the only way you would ever get away from your Mob friends was to lose your identity—or trade it for your sister's. This would be especially true if you stole money from them.

"And so you planned it. Planned it beautifully. The one thing you lacked, I came along and supplied. You lacked a patsy. If there was to be a murder, there had to be a murderer. Leopold might fit the bill, but that would be a calculated risk. I was a perfect setup and I played right into your hands. You arranged to have Suzy arrive at the motel after I left. When she walked into that room, you killed her. And then you did the kind of job on her that no one would ever believe a woman would do. But I know you, sweetie. I know what you are capable of. Your trouble is you made one big mistake."

"Yes—and what was that?" The voice was bitter with sarcasm.

"You didn't sucker me completely. You didn't get the money. And so you had to come back and try all over again!"

"You dirty louse," she said. "You promised!"

I really had to laugh at that one. I promised!

"Sure I promised." I said. "I'll keep that promise, too. The money is still in the locker at the airport where I told you I would stash it. The key is at the General Delivery window in Baltimore, just like I said."

"You're a liar!" she screamed. "There was no key."

"Yes, there was and there is, toots," I said. "The trouble with you is you aren't used to using your own name. You see, I wanted to make doubly sure you got that money. I mailed the key under your name—I mailed it to Marilyn Kelley!"

That was the one that finally got her. It took all three troopers to hold her. After about six minutes they finally got her calmed down and they put the cuffs on her.

They were starting to take her out when she balked. She turned to me.

"Tell me something," she asked and her voice was as calm as a summer's breeze. "Tell me something. How did you know? You couldn't have checked fingerprints. I am a good actress and my sister and I were absolutely identical. So how could you tell?"

"I couldn't—at first," I said. "You did a great job with the hair bleach and the lack of make-up was a disguise in itself. You are a great actress—you don't know how great, baby. But there is one thing you couldn't change. You couldn't change that birthmark on your leg. And the chance of twins having identical birthmarks just doesn't exist. But don't feel bad about it. I knew, even before I switched on the light early this morning and saw that heart-shaped mark."

"You're a liar," she said. "You couldn't have known."

I shook my head sadly.

"I knew," I said. "I knew, all right. You see, baby, there is one thing a woman can never lie about successfully and one thing which a woman can never forget."

"And they are?" she asked, still sardonic.

"She can't lie about being a virgin," I said, "and she can't forget her technique in a bed—not if she really has a technique. And you do, Marilyn K.—you do!"

They took her away then and I felt sick about it. No matter what she was or what she had done, it made me sick to see her go out of that room.

But I was glad about one thing. I was glad I had kept my promise and that she would get the three hundred thousand dollars.

A woman like Marilyn K., with her talents and three hundred grand, can do amazing things with a jury.

THE END

THE HOUSE NEXT DOOR

Lionel White

This book is for
Helene
My wife
Whom I Love

Chapter One

A man not reticent in accepting credit when credit was due, Gerald Tomlinson was particularly proud of his wisdom in selecting Fairlawn Acres as a base of operations.

The choice of Fairlawn, of course, was just another of the endless details in Tomlinson's overall planning; a mere cypher, but in a sense, symptomatic of the extreme care and vivid imagination Tomlinson exercised in laying the groundwork. Tomlinson, a tall, thin man with a complexion like aging newsprint, had been at one time a policeman, a second grade detective in fact, before the scandal broke and he'd been forced to leave the department in disgrace.

That early training had come in handy more than once and it was largely responsible for the slightly unorthodox, but rather brilliant arrangements which the ex-policeman made before embarking on the venture.

As Tomlinson had explained it to Arbuckle, there were several essential factors which must be present to insure success.

"The first thing," he'd said, in his ridiculously high-pitched voice, "the first thing is to have a place to go after we leave. The place must be not too far away; it should be readily approachable from a number of different routes, it should be in a nice, middle-class residential neighborhood. A neighborhood of small homes, young married couples with children, run-of-the-mill working people. A neighborhood where our arrival, by car if we're lucky, or by taxi or even walking if we're not, won't seem at all unusual."

He had been equally conservative in other details, details like the time that it was to take place, the business of switching cars, the securing of maps of the surrounding streets and the checking of the routine habits of everyone in the immediate neighborhood. He had also checked on the location of traffic policemen, the availability of public telephones in the vicinity, and a hundred and one other details which anyone else, contemplating such a maneuver, might easily overlook.

Even his selection of Arbuckle, Danny Arbuckle, an ex-con whom he'd known from the old days, and his limiting the operation to only the two of them, had shown foresight.

"The two of us can handle it without help," he'd said to Arbuckle. "We don't want a gang walking in on this. More than two, at that hour and place, would arouse suspicion. Anyway, this is a job which takes brains, not muscles."

Arbuckle was inclined to be skeptical, but quick reflection that a two-way split was a lot more attractive than a three- or four-way split, was sufficient to set his mind at rest. In any case, he had a lot of confidence in Tomlinson. When the whole thing had been satisfactorily outlined for him, he was forced to agree with the other man, that barring a miracle, it was foolproof.

If Arbuckle had any worries at all, they were not concerned with the job itself; they were, strangely enough, concerned with the place out at Fairlawn which Tomlinson had rented. Several times during the last two weeks, while they had been busy making the arrangements, he'd brought up the matter. Each time Tomlinson had reassured him.

"Don't worry about it," he'd say. "I've told you. A dozen times now I've told you. She's my brother's widow and she doesn't even know what the score is. All she knows is that she's being paid, well paid, to stay there in the house with the kid. If anyone gets nosy, I'm supposed to be her husband and I'm a salesman. She isn't likely to do any crabbing. She understands what would happen—to her and the kid, too—if she talks. Anyway, I've been keeping her since George died and she's grateful."

"But how about the kid? Hell, a nine-year-old girl must..."

"I said don't worry. The girl thinks we're married. Marian and I have been together for some time now. I've used them both before for this kind of thing."

And so, naturally, Arbuckle didn't worry about the woman and the child. After a while, as the time approached, he stopped worrying about anything, even the possibility of a miracle. Arbuckle didn't believe in miracles, either good or bad.

Certainly no one in this world could possibly have considered old Mrs. Manheimer—Mrs. Isidore Manheimer, the woman who ran the newsstand in the kiosk on the street by the subway station out in Jamaica—in any sense a miracle. Nor would they have considered a certain very pretty fifteen-year-old girl, hysterically running from the embraces of a middle-aged pursuer, a miracle; at least in any sense other than that each and every living human being is to a certain extent a rather miraculous thing, when you come to think of it.

The fact remains, nevertheless, that if it hadn't been first for Mrs. Manheimer, and then later for that certain fifteen-year-old girl, Tomlinson's plans would have been without flaw and nothing in particular would have happened except the loss of some forty-eight thousand dollars in deposits by the South Shore National Bank.

The bank, however, could have suffered the loss with considerably less discomfort than the discomfort suffered by Allie Neilsen and her husband, Len, two normal young persons who were to be vitally affected because of what was to happen.

Tomlinson and his partner, Arbuckle, having finally checked every small detail and allowed for every possible contingency, made the first move in putting their plans into execution around four o'clock on the second Friday in January.

The day itself was a little overcast, but it was not particularly cold or unpleasant for the time of year.

Arbuckle alone took the initial step. He stole a Checker Cab from its parking spot near a barroom in Long Island City.

It wasn't a difficult theft in as much as Arbuckle had invited the driver into the bar earlier in the afternoon and had spent a considerable sum of money in getting the man drunk. He had stood the cabbie to drinks several times before and he knew his man. It hadn't even been necessary to drink along with him. After two hours of knocking over boiler makers, the cab driver had been helped into a booth where he drooped over black coffee, carefully spiked with brandy. Arbuckle departed when the cabbie's head began to nod.

He'd had no difficulty starting the cab as the driver had left the key in the lock. Arbuckle was sure that the cab wouldn't be missed for at least two hours and two hours was all that they needed.

At four-thirty, wearing a chauffeur's cap and a leather jacket, Arbuckle, by prearrangement, picked up Tomlinson in downtown Jamaica. Tomlinson himself was dressed as usual except that he wore a yellow rubber slicker over his topcoat and had on dark glasses. He said nothing at all as he got into the back of the taxi and Arbuckle immediately pulled the flag down and started toward their destination.

It was necessary to kill a half hour as Tomlinson had arranged things so as to give them a little leeway in case there was any trouble in getting the taxi. Consequently, they drove at a normal speed, but around a rather circuitous route which had previously been mapped. They arrived in front of the South Shore Bank at exactly five o'clock.

The bank itself had closed for the business day at two o'clock. That is to say, at two o'clock the bank's doors were no longer open for regular business with the public. By two-twenty, all monies had been taken from the tellers' cages and placed in the burglar-proof safe, the door closed and the time lock set, so that it couldn't possibly he opened again until the following Monday morning.

At three-thirty the two guards who worked on the floor during banking hours had finished certain extra curricular chores, punched the time clock, and were leaving the building by a side entrance. One of them proceeded immediately to a nearby tavern where he ordered a shot of straight whiskey and drank it slowly as he looked over a scratch sheet. The other, a family man, picked up his car in an adjacent parking lot and went home.

At four o'clock the last employee had left by the same side door and the bank was deserted.

The South Shore Bank is, like thousands of similar institutions about the country, a rather phenomenal institution. In spite of the fact that its doors were closed and locked, that the employees had gone their diverse ways and all activities within its sterile confines had ceased, the South Shore Bank continued absorbing money into its greedy maw.

It accomplished this singular feat by the use of a very simple device; a device which consisted of a large brass roller drawer imbedded in its granite face, some three and a half feet up from the sidewalk and next to the main entrance. It had been placed there to accommodate depositors who, finding themselves with large amounts of cash on hand after banking hours, wished to deposit those sums in a safe and secure sanctuary.

Among the several hundred persons who periodically found the device at the South Shore Bank a convenience was a man by the name of Angelo Bertolli.

Bertolli was a private detective, but a very special kind of private detective. He didn't dabble with divorce cases, or investigate bad credit risks or handle the usual type of work which occupied his brethren in the profession. He had but a single customer. The customer wasn't an individual; the customer was a syndicate. To be exact, a horse betting syndicate which used Mr. Bertolli's services for only one reason. It used him each afternoon for the safe conduct of a large sum of money, which had been collected by its various runners from bookies who made "layoff" bets. Bertolli carried the money from a certain central office to the South Shore Bank.

The fact that this money wasn't gathered until fairly late in the afternoon was responsible for the using of Mr. Bertolli to guarantee that it reached ultimate safety in the night depository of the bank. Mr. Bertolli, as a private detective, was licensed to carry a gun. The syndicate, whenever possible, preferred to use legal methods in the conduct of its business.

One of the few persons outside of the inner circle of syndicate members who was aware of Bertolli's daily chore was Gerald Tomlinson. How he happened to know about this is relatively unimportant; the thing is that he did know and that on this particular Friday afternoon, at five minutes after five, he was sitting in a cab opposite the front door of the bank as Angelo Bertolli drove up and parked.

Each man stepped to the sidewalk at the same moment. Bertolli had been driving his own car, a Cadillac convertible, and Arbuckle was in the driver's seat of Tomlinson's car, the stolen taxi.

Bertolli carried a large yellow manila envelope under his left arm and as he approached the bank, he pulled the depository key from his right-hand trouser pocket. Tomlinson was not two feet away, in his own left hand a somewhat similar envelope.

Bertolli saw Tomlinson out of the corner of his eye and he also noticed the envelope he carried. He paid him no further attention.

The street was comparatively busy at this moment as the bank was at a busy corner and a number of neighborhood offices were emptying. A half dozen persons were within fifty or sixty feet, but each was intent only on reaching his own destination and no one noticed as Tomlinson suddenly took a quick step forward. At the same moment he tore the end off the envelope he carried. He had raised the gun and was bringing it down on Bertolli's skull even as the other man started to swing around.

It was at this precise moment that Mrs. Manheimer rounded the corner.

Bertolli knew that something was happening; perhaps he felt the swift rush of air as Tomlinson swung or perhaps it was only instinct. But he knew there was something wrong and he started to duck. He would never, however, have escaped the full force of that vicious blow, if it hadn't been for Mrs. Manheimer.

Less than ten minutes before, Mrs. Manheimer had left her newsstand where she had been on duty since seven o'clock that morning. She had been relieved by her oldest son, but before she had left, she had collected the day's receipts, tallied them up and made out a deposit slip. As usual she had gone directly to the bank to leave the money in the night depository.

The odd thing was that Mrs. Manheimer, when she saw the gun in Tomlinson's hand about to descend on the head of Bertolli, hadn't the slightest idea of what was happening or what was about to happen. One thought and one thought alone occurred to her. In front of her, not five feet distant, was a man with a gun. And in the large cloth bag which she carried was her day's receipts.

Mrs. Manheimer screamed.

The scream didn't act as an additional warning to Bertolli. It was too late for that. But what it did was to halt, for just the fraction of a second, the action of Tomlinson's arm as he brought the gun crashing down.

That sudden high-pitched cry, coming from less than two yards distance, was one of the few things which Tomlinson had not allowed for in making his plans.

The split-second lapse in timing was enough to cause the damage. Instead of the pistol butt crashing into Bertolli's skull, it slashed down the side of his face leaving a long brutal gash and almost dismembering an ear.

Bertolli sunk to the sidewalk, but he didn't lose consciousness. For a moment he was powerless, the moment it took Tomlinson to grab the yellow manila envelope and turn and leap into the cab. And then, while Mrs. Manheimer was still screaming as though it were she herself who had been assaulted, Bertolli pulled out the thirty-eight cal. revolver for which he had a license.

He managed to fire twice as the cab screeched away from the curb.

It wasn't until the taxi had turned the second corner that Tomlinson realized something was wrong. Until that time he had been busy stripping off the yellow raincoat and changing his homburg for a soft felt hat he'd rolled up and stuffed into his pocket. Also, he'd been watching behind to see if by any chance they were being followed.

Assuring himself that at least for the time being they had made a clean break, he finally leaned forward in his seat to speak to Arbuckle. He was about to warn him to slow down when he saw the blood welling from the side of his partner's neck.

"Jesus!" He pushed his head through the opened window separating himself from the other man as he made the exclamation. "He got you, Dan!" Tomlinson said. "How bad is it?"

The other man spoke in a low, choking voice, not turning his head and barely moving his lips.

"I can make the car," he said. "But I'll never get up the steps. There's something wrong with my stomach."

Tomlinson could see that except for the place where the channel of blood ran down his neck and soaked into the collar of the leather jacket, Arbuckle's face was deathly white. He knew he was badly hurt. He understood at once about the steps.

"The hell with the steps," he said. "Go right to the car. Stop anywhere near it."

It was the first change he had to make in his blueprint. Until that moment, he had planned that they should drive the half dozen blocks to the Long Island Railroad station in Jamaica.

They would be there, if things went according to schedule, at just about five-fifteen. At this hour, the neighborhood would be jammed with commuters, literally thousands of whom drove into Jamaica and parked their cars and then took the train on into New York. Five-fifteen would see the first big batches of them returning.

This particular station had another advantage. A large percentage of all trains coming from New York stopped at Jamaica, and passengers destined for points on the eastern end of Long Island were forced to change trains. As a result the station at this hour was a maelstrom of confusion, overrun by rushing commuters. Tomlinson's plans called for ducking out of the cab, running upstairs to the station, crossing over among the crowds to the far platform and going back on down the stairs to the street.

He had parked his own Chevrolet sedan not two blocks from the station.

He was confident, that even if they should be followed, this technique would be bound to shake off any pursuers. Arbuckle was to discard the leather jacket and the chauffeur's cap as they deserted the cab. Once in the Chevvie, he knew that they'd be safe.

If the police were looking for anything by that time, it would be for a Checker Cab. No one who saw them leave the cab could possibly see them entering Tomlinson's own car.

But now this plan was out. Arbuckle was bleeding badly. He'd never be able to run up and down those long flights of stairs; never be able to fight his way through the crowds. And even if he could, a man with a stream of blood running down his neck would attract far too much attention.

Tomlinson leaned forward again in the seat.

"Directly to the car, Dan," he said again. "Wait in the cab until I get the Chevvie. I'll drive alongside and pick you up. You sure you can make it?"

Arbuckle didn't answer. It was taking every ounce of his will power and his rapidly flagging strength to drive the car. As it was, he ran through the next stop light, never seeing it at all. Fortunately, there was no police officer around.

They were hitting heavy traffic now and Tomlinson leaned forward again. He took a handkerchief out of his back pocket and padding it, he tucked it into the top of Arbuckle's leather collar so that it partly covered the blood.

It was one hell of a break. But he didn't panic. When the cab pulled into the street on which he'd left his car an hour before, Tomlinson drew a long breath of relief.

Three cars down from where the Chevvie stood, on the same side of the street, was a fire plug. Arbuckle swung the cab into the empty space and cut the ignition. As Tomlinson leaped out of the back of the taxi, Arbuckle slowly leaned over the steering wheel until his head was resting on its rim.

A minute later and the Chevvie was parallel with him. Tomlinson had to get out and run around the car and open the door in order to help him out. Arbuckle's eyes were half closed and he was groaning as Tomlinson got him into the front seat and closed the door.

Several persons had stopped and were watching curiously as the Chevrolet pulled away.

A half mile from the business section of the town, Tomlinson found a dark, narrow alley. He pulled into it long enough to transfer Arbuckle from the front seat to the back of the car, where he laid him on the floor. Arbuckle, by now, was unconscious.

It was dark by the time Tomlinson cut into Northern State Parkway. Traffic was extremely heavy, as was only normal for that hour on a Friday evening. He knew that he was safe. Once or twice as he drove east in the endless stream of cars, he heard muffled groans from the back. He would have liked to have been able to stop to see if there was anything he could do for Arbuckle, but he didn't dare. He knew that the parkway was well patrolled and pulling off the road, even for a minute or two, would invite trouble.

The possibility of dumping the other man entered his mind for a moment but he quickly discarded it. It wasn't that he had any scruples as far as loyalty to Arbuckle went. Arbuckle had to take his chances; it was unfortunate that things had gone wrong, but such things were a calculated risk. Tomlinson would have gotten rid of him in a second if it were the practical thing to do. But Tomlinson was well aware of Arbuckle's criminal record and he knew that, dead or alive, the other man would be found. He'd be fingerprinted and identified and once the police had his identity, they would be quick to trace the connection to himself.

No, he had to hang on to Arbuckle, even though the other man had become an albatross around his own neck. The trick would be getting him out of the car and into the house unobserved. Once in the house, things would be all right.

It was going to be too bad if Arbuckle needed a doctor. A doctor would be out of the question.

Tomlinson found himself considering the possibility that Arbuckle might die—if he were not already dead. He'd heard no sound for several miles now. Arbuckle, dead, was worth a lot more than Arbuckle alive. His death would mean that everything in the envelope would be his, Tomlinson's. No split would be necessary. There would, of course, be the matter of disposing of the body. Given time, however, this shouldn't prove too difficult. Time, enough time, was of the essence.

Tomlinson turned off the parkway at the exit marked thirty-six. He headed south for a mile or two and then turned once more and entered Fairlawn Acres. The street lights were on, but there was almost no traffic.

A couple of minutes later he again turned and drove slowly up the driveway next to the house. The garage doors had been left open. He drove in, got out of the car, and closed and locked the overhead door from the inside. He then opened the back door of the car and looked in. Arbuckle lay still, a crumpled, formless mass. Carefully, Tomlinson closed the car door. He would do what he had to do after the child was safely asleep in bed. Almost unconsciously he caressed the revolver he was carrying in the outside pocket of his jacket.

Marian, his brother's widow, was standing at the kitchen sink as he came through the back door. She stood there, her back to the sink and stared at him, her eyes wide and curious.

"Patsy?" Tomlinson said.

"In the living room, looking at television."

"Get her to bed."

He went to the cupboard over the drainboard and opened the cabinet door. He took out the bottle of bourbon, reached for a water glass and filled it a third full. He drank it straight.

"Get dinner," he said.

It was the proper hour for serving dinner among the six or seven hundred residents of Fairlawn Acres.

Chapter Two

Len Neilsen put the first call through at exactly five minutes after six, which normally would have been the time he would be stepping off the train out at Fairlawn. Actually, of course, the station wasn't at Fairlawn; it was at Hicksville, but Hicksville was the nearest station on the Long Island Rail Road and Len preferred to think of the station as Fairlawn rather than Hicksville. Fairlawn sounded better, somehow.

In any case, Len telephoned his wife at six-five on the spot. It was the first opportunity he'd had since George Randolph called him upstairs shortly after four o'clock that afternoon. Naturally enough, he'd wanted to call Allie right off, the very first minute he heard the news. But he could hardly make the call from Mr. Randolph's private office and so he had been forced to wait, barely able to contain himself, until he returned to his own small cubicle on the third floor of the building. He was impatient with the delay as the operator put the call through, knowing that any second Mr. Randolph would be down to pick him up. He neither wanted to have George Randolph overhear what he had to say, nor did he want to keep Mr. Randolph waiting.

The operator apparently had to wait a few seconds for a circuit and Len nervously tapped his long tapered fingers on his green desk blotter. A little twisted smile played around the corners of his wide, pleasant mouth and it was in strange contrast to the faint frown which marred his forehead, a frown brought on by his impatience.

It happened just as he had been afraid it would. Allie picked up the receiver out in the ranch house at Fairlawn, just as George Randolph walked into the office. He was buttoning up his gray tweed topcoat and adjusting his scarf.

Len looked up at him, a half apologetic smile on his face, as Allie said hello.

Embarrassed in the presence of the other man, Len quickly changed his mind about what he had planned to say.

"Allie," he said, "Allie, this is Len."

He heard the slight, hesitant sort of sound of a breath being sharply withdrawn from the other end of the line. He didn't give her a chance to ask any questions.

"I'm still at the office, honey," he said. "Just leaving. But I'll be a little late so don't wait dinner. You and Bill go on without me. I'm having dinner with Mr. Randolph."

He wondered why he should feel so self-conscious, almost guilty, as he said the words. He hardly heard Allie's surprised voice as she started to ask questions. Looking up again at George Randolph's solid figure as the older man stood looking out the window he desperately wanted to tell Allie the news; suspected that Mr. Randolph himself would expect him to. But somehow, he couldn't do it. It was something he wanted to share with her alone, something he didn't want to tell her in front of anyone, not even the man who was responsible for the news itself.

And so he cut in again and repeated himself, telling her once more that he'd be late and for her to go ahead and have dinner and not to worry. He hung up while she was still talking, not meaning to cut her off, but because he was nervous.

Five minutes later, Len Neilsen, traffic manager for Eastern Engineering Company—who next Monday morning would assume his new duties as general office manager—and George Randolph, senior vice-president of the firm, left the building on East Thirty-eighth street and turned uptown.

Len was sorry that he'd cut Allie off so short; he was also sorry that hadn't been able to tell her about it. Nevertheless he felt like ten million dollars.

A light snow was beginning to fall, the first of the season, although it was January. They didn't bother with a cab.

"It's only a few blocks," Randolph said, pulling up his coat collar to keep the wet snow from falling on the back of his neck, "so let's walk it. It's about the only chance I get for a breath of fresh air and exercise, walking from the hotel to the office and back each day."

Len agreed with him, enthusiastically.

Len was a little surprised that they were going to the hotel. He'd sort of half expected Randolph would take him to any one of the dozen or so places in the immediate neighborhood.

When they reached the lobby of the Waldorf, Randolph went immediately to the bank of elevators reserved for the Tower Apartments.

"We'll go up to my diggings and freshen up," he said. "We can order a drink and while we're waiting, I'll have a menu sent up."

After they had taken off their overcoats and hats, and dropped them over a chair in the dressing room, Randolph turned to him and asked what he'd like. Len was on the verge of saying Scotch and water, but before he had the chance, Randolph went on to say that he himself invariably had a Martini before dinner.

Len at once said that he, too, would like a Martini.

"I like them dry," Randolph said, "about eight to one."

He laughed and reached for the house phone. When he got room service, he gave his name and his room number first.

"Two Martinis," he ordered. "Very dry, you know, the way I like them. Tell William they are for me." He turned and looked at Len and smiled. "Better make them doubles," he added, and hung up.

Len smiled back at him.

"After all," Randolph said, "this calls for a little celebration."

Later, they ordered dinner from the menu which the bellboy had brought up to the room and after Randolph found out they would have a half hour wait for a table downstairs, he ordered two more Martinis.

Len had a little trouble finishing his second double. The older man hadn't been lying when he said he liked them dry. They tasted like straight gin. Len looked at his boss with new admiration. A couple of hours ago he would have sworn that George Randolph was a man who probably didn't take one drink in a month. It just showed—you never really knew.

They ate in the main dining room and the food was exceptional. The only trouble was, Randolph ordered a bottle of sparkling Burgundy with the dinner, and Len, not wishing to be impolite, drank drink for drink with his host. That, on top of the two double Martinis, was a lot more than Len Neilsen was used to. He plowed through the guinea hen and wild rice hardly appreciating the excellence of the cuisine.

He knew that the liquor was affecting him—his heavy, horn-rimmed glasses seemed to continually cloud up and he was having a little difficulty in focusing his eyes. Alcohol always seemed to affect his eyes the first thing.

He had expected the other man to talk about the work and possibly the new job, but for some reason Randolph avoided all shop talk and confined his conversation to a monologue about his earlier days with the firm, when he was an engineer out in the field.

While they were waiting for the brandy and coffee, Len looked at his wrist watch and was surprised to see that it was already a quarter to nine. He was amazed how swiftly the time had passed.

Taking advantage of a temporary lull in the conversation, he said, "I wonder if you would excuse me for a moment, Mr. Randolph. I'd like to call Allie—that is, Mrs. Neilsen—back. I'm afraid I'm going to be a little later than I thought."

Randolph looked at him, slightly amused.

"You do that, son," he said. "Never let the little lady start worrying. I did.

That's one reason I'm single today."

When Len stood up, he felt a bit dizzy, but he quickly gathered his wits and started for the lobby. He was conscious, however, that his steps were unsteady. Well, he'd have the brandy and coffee and that would be it.

He was amazed at the many unexpected facets to George Randolph's character—small, unimportant but interesting bits of information which had come out during the evening. Somehow or other he'd assumed that old Randolph had always been a pretty stolid, dull sort of character. Randolph, however, was turning out to be anything but dull.

Not only that, but apparently Randolph knew how to handle his liquor, and plenty of it. Len knew that he himself was definitely getting a little bit tight.

It wasn't until he was shut in the telephone booth down in the men's room, however, that he realized just how tight he really was.

Len couldn't remember his own telephone number. He had already found a dime and put it in to get the operator and give her the number, when for some ridiculous reason, his mind went completely blank.

He put the receiver back after she had twice asked what number he was calling. It was the silliest thing. Of course they had only lived out there in Fairlawn for a little over three months, being one of the last families who had moved into the development, but still and all, it was pretty damned silly, not remembering his own telephone number.

He had quite a time explaining to the operator that the number was not yet listed in the directory, but she finally gave him information and she in turn, after a long delay, got it for him. The toll charge was thirty cents.

Allie answered almost at once.

"Honey," Len said, "I'm sorry, but I'm still tied up. Looks like I'll be a little later than I thought."

"Is this you, Len?"

It was a bad connection, but he finally got through so that she understood him.

"Your voice sounds funny, Len," Allie said. "Are you..."

"I'm fine, honey," he said. "Never felt better in my life." And then, for some reason and without even planning it, he blurted out the good news.

"Baby," he said, "listen. This dinner is a sort of celebration. I have some great news. Got a new job!"

"Len," Allie said. "Why Len, what do you mean? What happened to the old job. Where are you anyway and..."

"You don't understand me," Len told her quickly. "I mean I got a promotion. I'm the new office manager. And at twelve thousand. Twelve thousand a year, honey."

He had to repeat it twice before he got her to understand and then she was as excited as he was and they were both talking at once for the next couple of minutes. At last he told her that he'd have to hang up, that his money was running out, and that the boss was waiting.

"You take care of yourself and don't worry," he said at last. "Bill in bed yet?" he asked.

"Of course, silly," Allie said. "And don't worry about me. Don't worry at all. Take your time. I'll wait up."

"If you're nervous," Len began.

"I'm not nervous a bit," Allie said. "Not one little bit. Anyway, they have a big party going on across the street and I'm just sitting here listening to their radio blasting away."

The operator told him that his time was up and so he yelled a quick good-by and told her once more not to worry.

Hanging up the receiver, he turned to open the door. "A darling," he said, half under his breath. "A real darling!"

Going back to the dining room, he determined to get away as soon as he could. He knew that in spite of what Allie had said, she might well be nervous out there all alone with young Bill. After all, until they were married, and in fact up until he had made the down payment on the house in Fairlawn, Allie had never in her life lived away from New York City or farther than three blocks from the nearest subway entrance.

Len smiled, amused, as he thought about it. When Allie had first seen the little six-room house and the less-than-quarter-acre plot, her eyes had opened wide and she'd squealed with pleasure. The developers had called it a ranch house, and to all intents and purposes, it was truly a ranch house to Allie, who in all of her life had never even lived in a place which could boast a back yard.

Allie had been pretty skeptical at first about moving out of the city, but she'd been forced to agree with Len when he'd argued that young Bill was almost six and that he didn't want any child of his being brought up in New York and going to the New York City schools. They'd managed to save several thousand dollars and had started looking around.

Len had been pretty discouraged at first. They'd started in Connecticut and Westchester County as they had to limit the area of their search to commuting distance.

Len had been amazed at the prices the brokers wanted for houses. He himself had been brought up out in Dayton, Ohio, but for the last dozen years, since he'd left home to go to college and then taken the job with Eastern Engineering, he'd been away from home. The places they'd looked at, smaller houses than the one he'd been brought up in himself, were going for around thirty and forty thousand dollars. Most of them were jerry-built at that.

They'd had to give up ideas about going north and began looking around

Long Island. The minute they'd seen the place out at Fairlawn Acres, Allie'd fallen in love with it. The fact that it was just one of some five or six hundred other houses, all of which were almost identical, hadn't seemed to phase her in the slightest. Of course, to Allie, who'd always lived in apartments, this didn't strike her as in any way unusual.

And she'd been fascinated with the newly planted lawn, with the half dozen small evergreen trees, the shrubbery and the tiny flower garden. Everything about the place pleased her—the modern, up-to-date kitchen with the dishwasher and the tiny service bar, the fresh new paint of the bedrooms and the vaulted, cathedral ceiling of the living room. Of course she didn't notice, or criticize, the phony, nonsupporting beams. The size of the room, which to Len seemed cramped, struck her as more than adequate. Compared to a New York apartment, it probably was.

The price of the place was $14,995 and they had more than enough money to make the down payment. Len drove around the neighborhood with Allie and they passed the newly constructed, modern schoolhouse, the playgrounds and the public swimming pool, designed exclusively for the use of the residents of Fairlawn. Allie was wild with enthusiasm and Len didn't have the heart to try to disillusion her.

After all, he reflected, it was a damned sight better than a New York apartment and young Bill would have other kids—his own type of kids—to play with. They'd have plenty of fresh air and they weren't too far from the beach.

So Len made his down payment and they moved in. They were among the last hundred families to take possession.

George Randolph was standing up, his napkin in his hand as he talked with a short, muscular man and a gray-haired woman, when Len returned to the table. He introduced them as Dr. and Mrs. Peatri, friends of his. He invited them to sit down to a drink.

"Len here," he said, "is our new office manager. We were just holding a sort of little private celebration."

Mrs. Peatri smiled at Len and her husband insisted the occasion called for a bottle of champagne. Randolph agreed, but insisted the party was on him and he called the wine steward.

Len sipped the brandy and coffee while the waiter brought the bottle to the table in a silver ice bucket. He carefully covered the neck with a towel and drew the cork after twisting the bottle for several minutes in the cracked ice. Dr. Peatri was busy talking with Randolph and his wife turned to Len.

"Are you new in New York?" she asked.

Len told her that he'd been with the company for several years, in fact since he'd graduated back in 1947 from M.I.T.

Mrs. Peatri said, "How nice for you."

The waiter poured and they lifted their glasses.

The conversation went on, but later, when Len tried to remember what they had talked about, he was unable to recall a single thing.

Somehow or other time passed and the next thing Len knew all of them were leaving the dining room. They ended up at a night club in the East Fifties, but Len never did have the slightest recollection of it.

There were, also, more drinks.

Somehow, he didn't remember leaving the night club and getting into the taxi. And then the next thing he knew; someone was shaking him by the shoulder.

His glasses had fallen off and he had to squint to see at all. He was in the back seat of a cab and the door was open so that the overhead light was on. A man in a peaked cap was half in the back of the car and was trying to get him awake.

"We're here," the man said. "Wake up, fellow, we're here."

Len looked up and tried to get the man in focus.

"Where's here?" he asked, his voice thick.

"Where you said to take you. Fairlawn Acres. Now tell me, which is your house? I'll drop you off."

He wanted to go back to sleep. His head was splitting and all he wanted to do was curl up in the seat and go back to sleep.

"Listen, Mister," the driver said, "tell me where to take you. I want to get home sometime tonight, myself."

Len made an effort and opened his eyes again. It took every bit of concentration possible, but finally he got the words out.

"Crescent Drive," he said. "Take me to Cres' Drive."

"You gotta number?"

"Yeah—ninety-six. Nine six Cres'."

Len closed his eyes again. He'd forgotten all about his glasses, which were lying on the floor at his feet.

It took the driver a half hour to find Crescent Drive. He cursed whoever it was who'd laid out the development as he drove around, straining his eyes to see street signs. He was tempted to drop his passenger at random and go on back to New York. But he remembered the twenty-dollar bill that the big gray-haired man had given him and he resisted the temptation. The man might have taken down his license number before he had piled his passenger aboard.

When he did find Crescent Drive he looked at the long row of houses in disgust. Each one was an exact replica of its neighbor and try as he might, he was unable to see a number.

"Goddamn 'em," he said, "you'd think they'd at least put the goddamned numbers where you could see 'em."

He stopped finally and took a flashlight from his pocket. He flashed it on the front of a house and still found no number. So he climbed down from his seat and walked toward the front door. Finally the light found what he was looking for. It was number eighty-two.

Going back to the cab, he drove in low gear for several hundred yards until he came to the seventh house down. He didn't bother to use the flashlight again, but got out and opened the back door of the cab.

"O.K. chum," he said. "You're home." Once more he reached in and shook Len by the shoulder.

Len Nielsen looked up blankly, squinting his eyes and finally closing one of them. He grunted unintelligibly and then staggered from the cab. The driver hesitated a moment before taking him by the arm. They walked up the path and to the front door of the house.

"You're all right now, bud," he said. He turned as Len fumbled in his pocket for his keys.

Back in the front seat of the taxi, the driver slipped the car into gear and then hesitated, his foot on the clutch. He watched as Len tried to fit his key into the front door lock.

When the door wouldn't open, Len started to reach for the bell, then hesitated. He was still pretty tight, but his mind was beginning to clear. He knew it was very late; the house was dark. Allie would have gone to bed. He didn't want to awaken her.

It was probably because he had lost his glasses, but somehow that damned door wouldn't open. Len knew the bedroom window would be half opened and he remembered that he himself had taken off the screen shortly after they had moved in.

Allie was a heavy sleeper. She would never hear him.

Still staggering slightly, and holding one hand out in front of himself, Len carefully felt his way around the side of the house. He stumbled once over a small bush, but didn't fall. He found the window and it was opened barely a crack. But he was able to put his hand in and wind the handle opening the casement wide.

He lifted one foot high and put it over the window sill. A moment later and he was in the room.

The taxi driver waited until Len had disappeared around the side of the house. Then he slipped the clutch and the car left the curb.

"Brother!" he said. "Some load. I wouldn't want to have his headache tomorrow morning!"

He never said a truer word in his life.

Chapter Three

Actually, it is surprising that anyone at the Swansons' heard the shots over the blare of the hi-fi phonograph and the general noises made by the party. And certainly it is even more surprising that of the more than a dozen persons crowded into the small living room and kitchen at 95 Crescent Drive, the one person who heard them was Myrtle McNally, Myrtle being, beyond any question of a doubt, the drunkest person at the Swansons' that evening.

Howard, Myrtle's husband, would have been the logical one to have caught the sharp double explosion, because Howard, at the time, was just closing the back door, having gone out into the yard in order to relieve himself. But Howard's mind was concentrating on something which had suddenly seemed very important to him and when Howard was concentrating, nothing in this world able to penetrate the orderly processes of his thinking.

Howard was thinking of girls; to be specific, one particular girl. A girl whom he had never seen up until some three hours ago, but a girl who interested him vastly.

The fact that this girl was not more than fifteen or sixteen years old, and was, at the very moment, home baby-sitting with Howard's own infant daughter, didn't prevent Howard from thinking about her.

At the very moment the two reports came to her ears, Myrtle, standing at the kitchen sink where she was attempting to get the cap off a fresh bottle of ginger ale, was watching Howard as he re-entered the house. Her mind was confused because of the drinking she had been doing, but still she was sober enough to wonder where Howard had been. Her lips moved slightly as she spoke under her breath.

"The son-of-a-bitch," she said. "The dirty, skirt-chasing son-of-a-bitch! I wonder who was out there with him this time."

And then she heard the shots and it seemed to her that they came from the direction of her own house, which was diagonally across the street. Her mind at once discarded all thoughts of her husband and went to her six-month-old daughter. She gave up trying to open the bottle and took a few faltering steps until she was facing her husband.

"Howard," she said, "Howard." She shook him by his arm, seeing the vague look on his face.

Howard twisted his head in annoyance and looked at her. He had to look up slightly as Myrtle was a tall woman and he himself was only five foot six. He weighed more than a hundred and ninety pounds and he had the round, guileless face of a newborn baby. His blond hair was thin and, within another two or three years, would be completely gone, although he was not yet thirty-five.

Staring into his pale-blue eyes, Myrtle suddenly thought, good God, what can any woman see in him? What did I ever see in him?

"Howard," she said, her voice thick, "I just heard noises coming from over our way. Sounded like shots."

Howard shook his arm free.

"Good Lord, Myrtle," he said, "Don't start that. Don't start imagining things. With all of the noise going on in this place, you couldn't have heard anything at all."

He stared at her, unblinkingly, annoyance marring the baby smoothness of his face.

"Are you drunk already?" he asked. "I warned you not to..."

"Not drunk," Myrtle said, sullenly. "Anyway, what did we come here for unless it was to drink?"

"Drink like the rest of the people do, then," Howard said. "Can't you have a few drinks and then stop? Do you always have to get slopped to the gills?"

"Where have you been?" Myrtle asked, quickly stepping back and changing the subject. She didn't want to discuss her drinking. Damn it, she thought, what's it to him if I do get drunk. If it wasn't for him I'd never have started...

"If it's any of your business," Howard interrupted her thoughts, "if it's any of your damned business, I've been outside taking a pee."

Myrtle stepped back, weaving slightly and braced herself against the sink.

"You may have had your pants undone," she said, "but..."

She stopped quickly as the kitchen door opened and Grace Swanson came in.

"Hey, where's that ginger ale," Grace said. "You been out here for . ." She suddenly saw Howard and stopped. "Well!" she said, "you two lovebirds doing a little private necking here all by yourselves? Married couples, you know. That's incest in this neck of the woods."

She laughed and quickly reached for the ginger ale bottle and snapped the cap off.

"Come on," she said, "join the company. We're going to choose up for charades."

Myrtle decided to follow her into the other room where the rest of the guests had just finished dancing. Myrtle wanted to check up and see if anyone's wife was missing.

Grace Swanson, who was throwing the party, had already gone through the door and Myrtle was about to follow her, when Howard spoke.

"What did you say, Myrtle?" he asked. "You heard something from over our way?"

Myrtle hesitated.

"I thought I heard a couple of shots," she said. "But don't let it worry you. Don't let anything worry you at all. Just go on having a nice time."

She hiccupped as she turned toward the other room.

"O.K." Howard said, suddenly. "O.K. I'll just run over and see if everything's all right. You tell them I'll be right back."

He left by the back door as Myrtle re-entered the living room.

Although he hadn't bothered to put on his coat and was hatless, Howard wasn't cold as he quickly started across the street heading toward the front door of his own house. The light snow had been falling for several hours now but it wasn't sticking to the streets.

Howard wasn't worrying about the weather. He was busy thinking about what had happened some three hours ago, before he and Myrtle had left the house to come over to the Swansons' party.

Howard himself had been late getting home. He'd taken the new girl at the office out for a drink, after work. The girl was directly under Howard's supervision and had not wanted to refuse a request from her boss. She was a rather plain girl, fresh out of business school and it was her first job. Unfortunately, Howard worked for one of the big insurance companies and didn't do his own hiring. A personnel director took care of that.

As a result, few of the girls in Howard's department would have qualified for beauty prizes, although in all fairness it must be admitted that without exception they were competent stenographers and typists.

The new girl—her name was Hazel Baumberg—interested Howard for three reasons. First, she was new and didn't know anything about Howard's reputation with the other girls in the office. Howard was referred to, in secret of course, as "Itchy Fingers," by most of the female employees.

Secondly the new girl was young, not more than nineteen or twenty, and although she was a plain girl whose features were too large for her pale, egg-shaped face, she had a very nice form. Howard, who had an eye like an X-ray machine, was perfectly able to visualize her overdeveloped breasts, fully appreciating their seductive contours despite the fact that Miss Baumberg had modestly enveloped herself in a rather severe tweed suit.

The third reason which made the girl interesting to Howard was probably the most important of all. She had acquiesced to his invitation and Howard never passed up any possible opportunities. One could never tell just what a drink might lead to.

Unfortunately, the drink had led to nothing except making Howard late in getting home. Miss Baumber had accepted the drink, carefully removed Howard's hand from her upper thigh, and in no uncertain manner had let Howard understand that if her job depended on submitting to passes from her boss, she was perfectly willing to look for a new job.

Howard had not asked her to have a second drink. He had held no resentment, however, but had merely shrugged the entire thing off. One thing about Howard, he tried them all and if he was snubbed and turned down, he merely went on to someone else. He worked on the theory that the law of averages would take care of him, and surprisingly enough, it usually did.

In spite of his wife and child and his own rather unfortunate physical appearance, an amazingly large number of women found something in him to appeal to them and willingly succumbed to seduction.

Howard arrived at number 100 Crescent Drive just after six-thirty. He knew that he and Myrtle were expected that evening over at the Swanson's and he also knew that he would have to hurry with his dinner in order get showered and dressed in time.

Myrtle was in the kitchen with Melanie, the baby, when Howard walked into the house. She was standing at the stove, a spoon in her right hand, as she stirred pablum into warm milk. In her left hand was a glass containing rye and soda. On the burner next to the pablum, a pot of spaghetti and meatballs slowly simmered.

As he entered the kitchen, pulling his arm from his coat sleeve, Howard had been about to say something, make some sort of excuse for being late. But when he looked at Myrtle and saw the drink in her hand, his face flushed with anger and he turned and removed his other arm from the coat and hung the garment on a hook in the closet.

He didn't speak as he turned back into the room and walked over to where the baby lay in her portable crib. His eyes, however, were on his wife.

Myrtle was about ten years younger than her husband, a large, handsome girl with very lovely azure eyes, long blond hair and a fine, slender body. She is, thought Howard, one hell of a lot better looking and more attractive sexually than that silly Baumberg female. On the other hand, Howard felt not the slightest desire for her. He hadn't, in fact, been aroused by her since long before the baby had been born.

Sometimes he couldn't understand it himself. This complete aloofness to his own wife, who was, by any standard, a lot more desirable than most of the women who so intrigued him. It never occurred to Howard that the fact she was always available, might have had anything to do with it. She merely seemed like another piece of furniture around the house.

Right now, however, Howard was feeling anything but indifferent.

"Jesus Christ, Myrtle," he said, "why in the name of God do you want to start drinking now? Can't you wait until we get to the party?"

Myrtle stopped stirring the pablum, laid the spoon down and carefully dipped her index finger into the mixture to test it for temperature. Then she looked up at him and spoke.

"I'm just having a cocktail before dinner," she said. "Why don't you make one for yourself while I feed Melanie. It might make you a little better natured."

"There's nothing wrong with my nature," Howard said, shortly. He leaned over the baby and spoke to her, using that strange gibberish which all adults employ in communicating with infants.

"Who's going to be there tonight?" he asked. He knew that it would be pointless to pick on Myrtle because of her nipping. It would only make her contrary and when she got contrary, she'd drink more than ever.

Myrtle splashed some whiskey and water in a glass, tossed in an ice cube and handed it to him before answering.

"Drink this," she said, her voice more friendly. She had detected the subtle change in his own voice, a change which let her know that he wanted to avoid an argument. "It's nasty out and it'll keep a cold away." She lifted her own glass and finished the drink. "Well, I don't know. I met Grace at the super market this morning and she said Tom was having some people from his office."

"He's with one of the plane companies, isn't he?" Howard asked. He didn't much care where Tom Swanson worked, but he wanted to keep the conversation going. He wanted to keep Myrtle in a good mood. If Myrtle felt all right, she would probably control her drinking and behave herself.

"Yes. I think Republic, but I'm not sure. Anyway, they're having the office people and maybe a few of the regulars from the neighborhood. By the way, I met the new neighbors."

Howard set his glass down and lighted a cigarette. 'People who moved in next door?" he asked.

"Yes. That is I met her. I think she's some sort of foreigner or something. They have a little girl. She, the mother, stopped by for a second this noon to ask about getting milk deliveries. Seemed a little strange and when I invited her in for a cup of coffee she hesitated for a second and just then somebody from her house called out. I guess it was her husband. Anyway, she acted sort of half frightened and said that she wouldn't be able to—that is, be able to stop in for coffee. She turned and hurried right back into her house."

Howard grunted.

"This goddamned neighborhood is filled with freaks," he said. "I guess one more or less won't make much difference."

"Most of the people are nice enough," Myrtle said.

Howard snickered.

"Yeah? Nice like the Neilsens, I suppose? The stuck up sons-of-bitches."

Myrtle looked at him, surprise on her face.

"They aren't stuck up," she said. "They just like to keep to themselves. I think Mrs. Neilsen is very nice. And that little boy of their's is a real doll."

"They're stuck up," Howard said. "I ran into Neilsen the other day down at the gas station. Asked him to drop by and see the fights on television and he told me he wasn't interested in fights. Stupid bastard."

"Well..." Myrtle reached for the bottle to pour another drink. She decided to let it go. She didn't want to start another argument. Certainly not about the Neilsens. "Well, anyway, the Swansons are good people and a lot of fun. Maybe we'll meet some other people who are fun tonight."

"You keep knocking off that goddamned rye and you won't be able to tell," Howard said.

Myrtle looked at him, not concealing the disgust on her face.

"And you'll make passes at their wives and you'll probably think they're stuck up, too."

Howard's face went red. He took a step toward Myrtle and for just the fraction of a second, felt an almost uncontrollable impulse to hit her. Unconsciously he closed his right fist, half raising his arm.

"Go ahead," Myrtle said. "Go right ahead, just try it. I'll smash this glass down your fat throat!"

Quickly Howard dropped his hand and stepped back. The fact was he knew that she actually would. The last time he had struck her, shortly after Melanie was born, Myrtle had put her hand to her bloody mouth and stared at him for a moment, saying nothing. He'd turned away and the next thing he knew, he was lying on the floor with blood pouring from the back of his head. She'd crashed a frying pan over his skull.

"For God's sake," he said, "let's not fight. Let's, just for once spend an evening without fighting."

"That's fine with me," Myrtle said. She slugged her drink in a single gulp.

They had the baby in bed by seven-fifteen and then sat down in the kitchen and had dinner. Myrtle ate very little. Later, while Myrtle cleaned up the dishes, Howard went into the living room and turned on television. He had decided not to change his clothes. He'd just run the electric shaver over his chin and change his shirt, after the baby sitter arrived.

The doorbell rang at ten minutes to eight.

"Get it," Myrtle called from the bathroom, where she was working over her face with cleansing cream. "It's probably Louisa, the sitter."

Howard went to the door.

Every now and then nature, usually a capricious and perverse minx, decides to give humanity a rare treat by creating an individual who is endowed with only the finest of the various physical features of each of his or her parents. In the case of Louisa Mary Julio she had seen fit to perform this unusual favor.

Louisa's father was a Spaniard, a small, wizened little man with narrow shoulders, an almost grotesque posture, but with large expressive dark eyes and fine, delicate bone structure. Louisa's mother, who had been Kathleen O'Hara before her completely baffling marriage to Louisa's father, had the full-blown, buxom beauty of a North Ireland lass. She possessed golden blond hair, a flawless, peachlike complexion and a body in perfect proportion and of the type to make sculptors go into a frenzy.

Louisa herself, her mother's third child and second daughter, was no larger than her father but she had a body which made her seem a miniature replica of her mother. She had her father's black eyes and long dark lashes, but her mother's fair skin and her mother's beautiful golden blond hair. She was a very beautiful girl and although she had just turned fifteen, she could easily have passed for two or three years older. Her breasts were fully developed, but she still had the tiny waist and hips of an immature girl. Her legs and arms were full and round.

She positively exuded sex. And she was well aware of this fact.

The light was on over the front door when Howard answered the bell and the second he saw the girl standing there, he was almost overwhelmed at her beauty. For one of the few times in his life, he was speechless in front of a member of the opposite sex.

Louisa looked up at him from under her long dark lashes.

"Mr. McNally?" she asked.

"Come in, come in," Howard said, stepping back, half in confusion. He held the door wide for her. "Well—I guess you must be the baby sitter," he said.

She smiled at him, saying nothing as she passed in front of him and entered the living room. It seemed as though she purposely brushed against the buttons of his jacket.

Howard closed the door. He turned as the girl cocked her head and removed the black beret, letting clouds of golden hair loose to swirl around her face.

"Better let me have your coat," Howard said.

She smiled at him again and took off the short, cloth coat she was wearing, to reveal a tight-fitting jersey sweater with a turtle neck. Instinctively and at once, Howard knew that in spite of her maturely developed body, she was not wearing a brassière.

She wore a short, plaid skirt which barely came to her knees. Her legs were bare but for half socks which showed a few inches above her low heeled red shoes.

"Sit down," Howard said. "Just sit down anywhere. Mrs. McNally will be right in."

Howard went over to the television set and turned down the volume.

"This is the television," he said, rather aimlessly. "I guess you know how to work it?"

The girl nodded, again smiling at him.

"And there are cookies and ginger ale in the icebox," Howard continued.

Suddenly he felt like a fool. Offering this girl cookies and ginger ale. Good God, he felt completely silly. He was talking to her as though she were a child. But she was no child. It didn't matter how old she was, she was not a child. If he had been asked to guess, Howard would have put her age at seventeen at the very most, possibly as little as sixteen.

But no matter what he might have guessed as to her age, he recognized immediately certain qualities in her make-up which automatically removed her from the status of adolescence.

Howard was still trying to find something to say when Myrtle entered the room from the hallway. Myrtle hardly looked at the girl.

"I'll show you the baby," she said. "She's asleep already and I don't think that she'll wake up until we get back. But if she does, there's a pan of water on the stove and the formula is already made up in a bottle in the icebox. You'll probably know..."

The girl left the room, following Myrtle, and Howard heard her giving the usual instructions. Howard went into the bathroom to get ready for the party.

They left the house at twenty after eight. Myrtle walked with a firm step and she looked fine. But Howard knew that already she was half drunk. He just hoped to God that she'd behave herself.

They passed in front of the home next door, the one in which the new neighbors had just moved, and both noticed that the lights in the living room were on. The Venetian blinds had been drawn and they were unable to see inside, however.

The Neilsens' house was also lighted up and the McNallys could see Mrs. Neilsen's silhouette where she sat under a reading lamp, with a book.

They were the first couple to arrive at the Swansons' and Tom Swanson greeted them with a drink in each hand.

Howard's mind, however, was still back in the living room of his own house and he hardly heard Tom Swanson's hearty greeting. Howard was thinking about the new baby sitter.

He was still thinking about the new baby sitter as he recrossed Crescent Drive some three and a half hours later, returning to his house for a moment to see if everything was all right.

When Howard reached his own front door, his breath was coming in short, hard gasps, in spite of the fact that he had only been walking. He noticed at once that the light was on in the front room, but he also saw that the window of the bedroom at the side of the house was also lighted up; the bedroom they had turned into a nursery.

Howard took the key from his pants' pocket, inserted it in the keyhole and was surprised to find that the door was unlocked. He twisted the knob and entered the living room. He wasn't surprised to find the room vacant.

Quickly he stepped across the room and entered the hallway. In a moment he was standing in the opened door of the nursery.

The girl was leaning over the crib, her back to him. She was cooing at the baby.

For no reason at all, Howard lifted his hand and rapped with his knuckles on the door. At the same time he spoke.

"Don't be alarmed," he said; trying to keep the tone of his voice normal. "Don't be alarmed, youngster, it's only me."

The girl quickly swung around, her eyes wide. But she didn't look in the least alarmed.

"Oh," she said. "Oh, are you back already?"

Howard smiled at her and stepped into the room.

"No—no," he said. "But Myrtle, Mrs. McNally, thought she heard some noises coming from here and I just thought I'd stop by and see if everything was all right. Did you hear..."

The girl suddenly put the fuzzy teddy bear which she was holding back in the crib. She looked up at Howard and smiled.

"They made some noise next door," she said. "I think it woke up the baby, but she's gone back to sleep already."

Howard stepped over next to her and looked down into the crib.

"Yes," he said, "Yes, she's gone back to sleep."

The girl just stood there, next to him, not moving and not saying anything.

Howard felt the sudden dryness in his throat. He couldn't keep his eyes away from her.

"I, well, I better turn off the light before she wakes up again," he said finally.

The light switch was within arm's distance and Howard reached over and clicked it. The girl still hadn't moved.

He was standing not more than two feet from the girl and he reached out and his hand found her arm.

"Come out to the kitchen," he said, "I'll find us a soft drink." He realized as he spoke that his voice was a little too high, that it reflected the tenseness and excitement he felt. He didn't want to frighten her, so he quickly released her arm.

She followed him into the kitchen, looking at him queerly, he thought. His laugh was a little false as he smiled at her.

"I'll bet you like coke," he said. "Or maybe you would rather have a glass of beer."

"I'm not supposed to drink beer," she said. "But I do like it."

He was reaching into the icebox now and he took out two bottles of beer.

"I'll bet that there are a lot of things you like that you're not supposed to do," Howard said. It was a pretty corny line and Howard knew it. But what the hell, this was just a kid; he wasn't sure exactly what line to take and he had to start somewhere.

Suddenly she reached over and took the bottle which he was beginning to uncap, from his hand. Her own hand touched his and he experienced a quick, breathless thrill at the contact with her flesh.

"Let me," she said. "I know how."

"No," Howard said, "I'll do it. Here, let me show you the best way."

It was pretty clumsy but he managed to encircle her waist with one arm as she still held the opener. She half turned and looked up at him with wide innocent eyes.

The girl was deliberately flirting with him, definitely playing up to his subtle pass. There was no doubt about it in Howard's mind. He'd had enough girls and women in his life to know.

"My," he said, "you're really a big girl."

"Oh, I'm big enough."

"You are," Howard said. The excitement had grown in him now until it had reached an almost unbearable pitch. His intelligence told him, that even if he were right about this child, this girl, he should play it carefully, take his time. But his intelligence was no longer controlling his actions.

Quickly, he spoke again.

"You are big enough," he said, his voice almost a whisper now. "Big enough to be kissed, I'll bet."

She didn't say a thing but just stood there in the circle of his arm and looked at him. There was a smug little half smile on her lips.

Howard suddenly drew his arm tight; at the same time dropping the beer bottle on the sink. He pulled her to him and as Louisa opened her mouth in sudden alarm, he leaned down and pressed his lips against hers.

She was like an eel, then, struggling to pull her face away, her small fists pushing against his chest.

The more she struggled, however, the more passionate and uncontrollable became his own desires. It was strange, that even then, one small rational fragment of his mind kept saying, "you fool! You insane fool. This girl is dynamite. She's a child. Even if she lets you, it can be serious trouble. It can be jail."

But the other and by far greater part of Howard's intelligence was completely paralyzed by his desire. The fact that she was struggling, meant nothing. A lot of them struggled, but sooner or later they came around. The ones who struggled, in fact, had been the most passionately acquiescent in the long run.

It only lasted for two or three minutes, minutes which found Howard tearing at her clothes, wild with a frenzy of uncontrolled desire. And then suddenly he dropped her and yelled. She had sunk her small white teeth into his lip and the blood was welling over his mouth.

For a split second, she just stood there, staring at him wild-eyed as he jumped back and put his hand to his face. Then, completely calm and collected, she spoke in a small, childish voice.

"I'm going to tell your wife," she said. "I'm going right over and tell her..."

Howard's hand dropped from his mouth and for a moment his eyes were insane as he looked at her.

"My God," he said. "My God, you can't. Listen. Listen, let me..."

But she had turned and already had the kitchen door open. She was running as she left the back porch.

Howard knew only one thing. He had to stop her. Had to reason with her. She had to listen to him and understand. God damn her, she couldn't tell Myrtle!

Even then, in that split second as he thought about it, the idea of Myrtle wasn't really what bothered Howard. But that child would run across to the Swansons' and in front of everyone, she'd make her accusation.

Howard knew only too well what it would sound like. A young girl, her clothes torn and disheveled. Himself with his lip all bloody. There wouldn't be any doubt about it at all. It would be attempted rape—the attempted rape of a child by a fat, middle-aged man.

Even as he thought about it, he turned and with amazing speed, darted for the living room. He would get out through the front door and intercept her as she rounded the house to cross the street. He had to intercept her. His home was at stake, his job was at stake—even his freedom was at stake.

It was at this very moment, the moment that Louisa Julio left the kitchen of the McNallys' house and Howard started to run for the front door, that Gerald Tomlinson was crossing his own back yard between his garage and his house.

He was half crouched over, moving slowly. Silhouetted in the moonlight, he looked like a man with a great hump on his back.

He had to move slowly because of the weight. Dan Arbuckle was a very heavy man.

Chapter Four

Len Neilson couldn't imagine why Allie had moved the chair. It wasn't, actually, a chair at all, but more of a chaise lounge. When he and Allie had been married it was the one thing Allie had taken along from her family's hotel apartment. She'd had the chaise in her own bedroom and she'd grown attached to it. As she said to Len, "I know it's pretty horrible, darling, but I've always liked it. We can have it done over in a corduroy, or one of those new crash materials, and it won't look too awful."

Len hadn't objected at all, in spite of the fact that the thing took up way too much space for the small bedroom. But Allie liked it and would spend a short time each afternoon cuddled up in it while little Bill had his nap and she caught up with her sewing. Len himself had to admit that it made a convenient catch-all on which to toss his clothes when he undressed before going to bed.

He didn't want to awaken Allie, so now, moving as carefully as he could, he fumbled around in the dark, brushing heavily against the end of the double bed, as he reached out blindly to find the chaise. He figured that he'd just lie down on it for a while and grab a catnap. He didn't want to climb into bed with Allie for fear he'd disturb her.

He knew he was still pretty tight, but he was beginning to come to a little. He felt pretty bad about getting as drunk as he had, but he wasn't used to heavy drinking and also, he couldn't honestly see how it could have been avoided. He just hoped to God that he hadn't made a complete fool of himself.

But he still couldn't understand what had happened that goddamned chaise.

He gave up trying after a minute or two, as, standing near the end of the bed, he carefully began undressing. Once or twice, while he bent over to untie his shoelaces, he almost lost his balance. When the knots failed to yield, he merely forced the shoes off his feet. He dropped one heavily to the floor, and then, remembering the old gag, stood with the other one in his hand and grinned foolishly in the dark.

He managed to get his coat and shirt off and he was beginning to feel pretty dizzy again. For a moment it occurred to him to go to the bathroom, but he was afraid he couldn't make it. He decided to just sit on the end of the bed for a minute and sort of catch his breath.

He reached around until he found the edge of the bed and sat down. A second later, he leaned back, his feet and legs hanging over the end of the bed. In a moment his eyes closed.

It was probably because of his unusual and cramped position that he woke up within less than a couple of hours.

The first thing he noticed was the slit of moon staring at him through the window. It took him a moment to remember where he was. That short sleep had done him a lot of good. He had a horrible taste in his mouth and every bone in his body ached, but he was just about sober. He suddenly realized he was lying there, half on and half off the bed and that he was still partly dressed. He felt like hell, but he was no longer drunk.

The moon, aiming her shafts of reflected light directly through the window, threw a sort of pale, purplish glare to the room. As Len sat up on the end of the bed, the first thing he noticed was the double dresser over against the wall. He suddenly remembered the missing chaise lounge.

The chaise was gone and in its stead was a double dresser. Dizzily he shook his head from side to side. He couldn't imagine what Allie had been doing with the place.

He decided that he'd better turn on the night light. The condition he was in, he doubted that he'd even be able to find the bathroom in the half dark, especially as Allie seemed to have booby-trapped the place with some new and odd pieces of furniture.

The night light, which had always been on the small end table at the side of the bed, was missing. In fact the table itself was missing.

Len pulled himself to his feet and staggered over to where the door of the room would be. Next to the door was the overhead light switch. By God, that couldn't be missing!

He stumbled over his shoes, but recovered himself. He found the light switch without trouble. He snapped on the light. His back was to the bed and so the first thing he saw was the wall of the room. Allie had not only changed the furniture, she'd repapered the damned walls!

By this time Len was almost completely sober.

He started to turn towards the bed. It suddenly had occurred to him that something was very, very wrong. Allie might change furniture around and she might, just possibly redecorate a room. But Allie, not even by the wildest stretch of the imagination, could ever have selected a purple wallpaper, decorated with mauve roses!

It was then that Len Neilsen saw the body on the bed.

Later on, when he would think about it, Len would silently congratulate himself for the rare presence of mind he showed during that next five minutes. It hadn't been easy.

The body was that of a bald-headed man; a man carelessly dressed in a leather jacket, a blue shirt and brown shoes with built-up heels. But it wasn't the man's clothes which attracted Len's horrified attention. It was the fact that the man had a small round hole in the exact center of his forehead and that from this hole, a small channel of blood had dripped out, making a narrow little river down the man's parchment face before forming a small pool on the white pillow case. The man's eyes were wide open and he was staring intently at the ceiling. But Len didn't need to have a medical degree to know that the man was not actually seeing the ceiling. He knew, instinctively and at once, that the man was very dead.

It was funny how his mind worked. The very first concrete thought he had was, my God, if I were a woman, I'd scream.

He felt an almost irresistible inclination to scream anyway, in spite of his sex.

Instinctively Len took a step or two toward the bed. At this precise moment the realization of what must have happened came to him.

He was not in his own bedroom; in fact, he was not even in his own house at all.

When the firm of Cohen and Mathews planned the development which they were to call Fairlawn Acres, they did an extremely competent and workmanlike job. They had started out finding what to them seemed an ideal location and a certain amount of credit must be given them for rare visionary powers.

Certainly the average layman looking at the bleak and treeless potato field, some forty miles out of Manhattan, would not have seen its possibilities. Oddly enough, Cohen was the visionary and designer and Mathews was the money man.

They had converted this two-hundred-acre field, purchased at a price of five hundred and ten dollars an acre, into some six hundred and fifty small plots. They also allowed for a shopping center, a school—the land for which they sold to the town for eight thousand dollars an acre—a couple of playgrounds and several other civic centers which helped to make their homes attractive buys.

The homes themselves were a good value for the slightly less than fifteen thousand dollars sales price. They were fairly roomy, not too badly constructed. There was only one thing wrong with them, from an aesthetic point of view.

Cohen had set up two master designs, one of which he called "colonial" and the other "ranch." Every house in the development fitted into the pattern of one or the other of these designs. And, as each house was located on an identically landscaped plot, coming with two dozen assorted shrubs, a few evergreen trees and a driveway, each house was identical to its neighbor. The total effect was one of deadly monotony.

Len Neilsen realized, that drunk as he had been, he had very obviously been delivered to the wrong house. Unfortunately, he had no sooner realized this than he heard the sound of a door slamming. Living as he did in a house with an identical layout, Len had no difficulty in identifying the source of the sound. Someone was leaving the adjacent bedroom.

Had he been given perhaps another three or four minutes to think the thing out, it is conceivable that he might have looked for a telephone and called the police. But Len was not permitted this essential period of grace.

He was in a strange house, in a strange bedroom, with a man who was very dead. The man had either recently committed suicide or been murdered. The fact that Len saw no gun, convinced him that the latter theory was probably the correct one.

He heard quick, soft steps outside in the hallway.

There was no time left at all. The killer had heard him or someone was going to enter that room and find him with the body. Either could well prove fatal.

Len had his shoes in his hand and his coat, overcoat and shirt under his arm as he reached the window. He didn't hesitate, but hit the ground in his stocking feet. He wasn't even conscious of the cold slush as he started to run. Nor did he look back as he hurried across the side yard and then ducked behind the garage of the house next door. If he had, he would have seen the dark silhouette of the figure in the bedroom window he had just vacated, staring into the night after him.

He guessed that it must be somewhere around four o'clock when he reached the street directly behind and running parallel to the street on which stood the house he had just left. He held his wrist up but he was unable to make out the face of his watch. He didn't bother to light a match. There was, at this moment, but one thought in his mind. He had to find his own house.

For a second or two he just stood still, desperately attempting to orient himself. He saw that he was standing on an icy cement sidewalk, in front of a ranch house which looked exactly like the one he had only a moment before vacated, and also exactly like the one in which he himself lived.

He felt no sense of cold, in spite of the fact he was naked from the waist up. He was too shocked; too frightened. Even the hang-over had, momentarily, faded from his immediate consciousness.

He was leaning down to try and get his shoes on when he heard the sound of the car. It came from the direction of the place he had just left. For a second he just stood there, frozen into immobility. And then he knew he would have to do something immediately. He realized the possible significance of that car's sudden muffled roar. Someone was looking for him. Someone must have seen him make his escape.

It could mean any one of several things—all of them bad. He had very likely witnessed a murder, or at least, the physical results of a murder. It was very possible that the murderer was aware of his presence in the house. At best, should anyone have seen him leaving by the window, he would be wanted for breaking and entering. But no matter who it was, or what had happened, he would have considerable difficulty in explaining his presence.

The best he could expect would be some bad publicity. The sort of publicity which would do him no good down at the office.

As he stood there, attempting to gather his wits, he suddenly became aware of the twin headlights sweeping around the corner at the far end of the block.

With no more hesitation, Len turned and started running.

Within seconds he could hear the sound of the rapidly approaching car. He knew that in no time at all it would be even with him.

Turning quickly, he darted into the nearest driveway. As he did, his shoeless right foot struck a large stone and he stumbled. The pain was overpowering. But it wasn't enough to stop him.

Once more he passed alongside of a house similar to his own and started through the back yard. This time, coming to the end of the yard, he found himself facing a four-foot, woven wood fence. As he hesitated, he suddenly drew a sharp breath of relief. He almost cried out as his hand found the top of the fence and he prepared to vault it.

He knew, at last, just where he was.

Len Neilsen himself had put this fence up at the rear of his property just a month ago, to divide his own small back yard from that of the property which adjoined it in the rear. There could be no mistake. Even in the semi-darkness, he recognized it.

A second later and he had climbed the fence and dropped to the ground on the far side. Yes, it looked like his house all right. But he took no chances. Carefully he crept to the small one-car garage. He found the side door and opened it. A moment later, as he shaded the tiny flame from his cigarette lighter, he was able to identify his own two-year-old Ford sedan.

By this time he was shaking so badly that he had difficulty in holding the lighter. He let the flame go out then and went back to the garage door, opening it a crack and listening. There was no sound on the still night air.

A moment later, he had found his door key and he began to circle the side of his house. The front door opened at once.

Len was in the bathroom, five minutes later, rubbing his face with lukewarm water, when he once more thought he heard the engine of a car. It seemed to come from the street in front of the house, but he couldn't be sure. Somehow, he felt a sense of relief, however, as he reflected that he had snapped the patented burglar catch on after slamming the front door.

He was reaching for a towel as the bathroom door softly opened.

"Len—Len, for God's sake what's happened!"

He swung around swiftly to face Allie, where she stood in the opened doorway. She looked, oddly enough, half asleep but thoroughly frightened.

He put his finger to his lips, reached for her and pulled her into the room. She was staring at him as though he had lost his senses as he closed the door behind her.

"Sit down," he said, "sit down and don't say a word. Something terrible has happened."

Her brown-flecked eyes wide now, Allie leaned against the glass door of the shower.

"Len," she said, "oh, darling! You're bleeding!"

"I think I broke my goddamned toe," Len said. And then began to laugh. He began to laugh and he tried to stop, but he couldn't to save his life. Couldn't stop until he was doubled over and the tears were coming out of his eyes. Couldn't stop until Allie had taken the glass of ice-cold water from the faucet and thrown it into his convulsed face.

Allie had realized that in spite of the smell of stale liquor which permeated the room, Len wasn't drunk. She had recognized the hysteria.

It wasn't until a half hour later, as they sat on opposite sides of the table in the dinette, with the Venetian blinds closed and the drapes carefully pulled shut—sat there having black coffee—that she understood the reason behind that sudden hysteria.

Allie had pulled on one of Len's bathrobes, the big terrycloth one which went almost twice around her slender figure, and her feet were warm in a pair of fluffy bedroom slippers. She managed to comb back the ash-blond hair from her eyes. She was talking as Len poured the last of the second cup of scorching hot coffee down his throat.

"But Len," Allie said, "I think you should. I think you should call the police and tell them everything."

For a moment he looked over at her and stared, a helpless lost sort of expression on his face. His head was splitting and he knew that he had a first-class hang-over. But his mind was clear and he was thinking very carefully.

"Len," Allie suddenly said, almost as though she were interrupting herself. "Len, where are your glasses? You haven't got your glasses."

Vaguely he shook his head, feeling instinctively with his right hand toward his face.

"No wonder everything seems a little fuzzy," he said.

"When did you have them last?"

He tried to remember, but he couldn't.

"I don't know," he said at last. "I honestly don't know. I don't think I had them while I was in that house. I couldn't have had them. That's why, probably, I was a little confused, why I didn't realize at first I was in the wrong place."

"Do you think you could have left them there?"

"I don't know."

For a moment she stared at him, sudden alarm on her face.

"What else have you lost, Len?" she asked at last.

Once more he shook his head, trying to remember. And quickly he looked up at her.

"My hat. I think I must have left my hat. I didn't have it when I got home."

Allie stood up.

"Len, call the police."

He started to get to his feet, but halfway up, changed his mind and sank back into the chair.

"No," he said. "No, Allie, I can't. Don't you see—I just can't. Good God, what can I tell them? How can I explain? Don't you understand, honey? I don't even know what house it was. It must have been on this block, but that's as near as I can come to it. I don't know what house, I'm not even sure of the street. And anyway, how in the name of God could I explain being there?"

For a second she looked at him closely.

"You're sure, honey?" she asked at last. "You're sure about the dead man? And the blood and all? Maybe... don't forget, Len, you say you were pretty tight still. Maybe it was just..."

"Listen Allie," Len said, "Of course I'm sure. I was tight all right. But not that tight. And anyway, if you have any doubt about it, look at my feet. Look at my clothes. I couldn't have dreamed them up. No, I'm sure."

"Then the only thing to do..."

Len put up his hand to stop her.

"Listen, baby," he said. "I don't think you quite understand. There was a dead man there, a man that I have every reason to believe was murdered. Someone murdered him. And someone saw me there in that house. I feel sure of it. Maybe they didn't recognize me, but they saw me.

"Don't you see what that means? Don't you understand about the car? Now if there was a man, and he was murdered, and someone did see me, then the chances are the body has been moved by this time. The body has been moved and the traces of the crime, if there was a crime, have also been removed."

"It doesn't matter," Allie said. "So you just tell the police that..."

"Allie," Len said, "Listen to me. I tell the police what? That I saw a dead man in a house that I had no right being in? That I don't even know what house it was? The police will think I'm crazy. They'll understand that I've been drinking and they'll think I'm nuts. They wouldn't even look. And even if they do look, what will they find?"

"It doesn't matter. You should still report it."

Len reached over for his wife's hand.

"There's something you're forgetting, darling," he said. "I don't want to frighten you, but there's something you are forgetting. Suppose I do tell the police and suppose they do believe me and start looking. And then they don't find anything. Then what? What about it if someone did kill someone else and they find out that I have gone to the police?"

For a moment he stopped and stared at her intently.

"Don't you see? The police won't believe me, but someone else will. A murderer will believe me. A man who has already committed one killing will understand that I know about it."

He was watching her closely as he spoke and he saw the blood suddenly leave her face. Her eyes were wide now as she gave a little gasp and her hand clinched and tightened on his.

"Don't be frightened," he said quickly. "Don't be frightened, Allie. But you have to understand. I must have time to think about it. I must have time to decide."

"Oh, Len," she said, "Oh Len, what are we going to do? What can we do?"

He hesitated a moment, trying to find something to say to reassure her. He hated himself for having frightened and alarmed her and he wanted to erase it. He forced a thin smile.

"Right now," he said, "we're going to bed and get some sleep. That's the best thing to do. Then, in the morning, we can..."

Suddenly she leaned across the table and her lips found his. Her hand went up and through his hair.

"Darling—darling," she said.

He started to get up again from the chair, but she pushed him back.

"You're right, honey," she said. "We're going to bed and get some rest. But first I'm going to get some Mercurochrome and fix up the cuts on your hand. Your hand and your cheek are both scratched up."

He nodded, looking down at his hand where it rested on the table.

"Must have done it when I was plowing through those damned bushes," he said. "It's nothing."

"And you're going to see a doctor about that foot in the morning," Allie said. "It's all swollen and you might have broken a bone."

Twenty minutes later, after they had looked in on young Bill, Allie and Len lay side by side in the big double bed. Allie was amazed how quickly Len fell asleep. She herself twisted and turned for almost an hour. She was trying to remember everything about the evening, trying to remember the sounds she had heard of people coming and going from the adjacent houses.

The trouble was, with the party across the street, over at the Swansons', and the usual traffic, heavy on a Friday night in the development, she couldn't remember anything which might have been particularly unusual or out of the way.

But she was convinced of one thing—Len had been telling her the truth and he had been in a house nearby. A house exactly like the house in which they themselves lived—except that it was a house which contained the body of a dead man.

The last thing Allie thought of before finally falling asleep was that no matter what, she would convince Len in the morning that the only thing to do was see the police. That's what the police were for—to handle things like dead men with bullet holes in the center of their foreheads.

Chapter Five

In her sixty-sixth year, Martha Kitteridge had, at long last, found peace and contentment. It is, in a sense, rather odd that of the more than six hundred families who had settled in Fairlawn, Martha and her husband, Reginald Parson Kitteridge, were happiest about their new home. We can dismiss Reginald's feelings and opinions with the one brief statement that he was a man who was bound to reflect whatever opinions his wife might hold. Reginald Kitteridge, during the forty years of his marriage, had been totally consistent in a major domestic attitude; whatever made Martha happy made him happy. Should Martha have decided she preferred to live in a lower East Side tenement, Reginald would have been satisfied.

But Martha had found the little development house out at Fairlawn and had fallen in love with it at once. The thing which made it so unusual was the fact that Martha Kitteridge—and her husband, of course—had lived in a score of widely different homes, in a dozen different countries. Kitteridge, a British citizen attached to the diplomatic services of his country, had never attained a particularly significant stature as a statesman. Now, in the twilight of his life, he was vice-consul for his government in New York. This, his last and probably final assignment, had followed long years of service in the Orient (where the Kitteridges had lived like minor royalty with many servants and no end of prestige); several years in Copenhagen (where there had been fewer servants and a much simpler economic plan of living, but where each had found a great deal of intellectual stimulus); a short tour of duty in the Near East, about which the less said the better.

When Kitteridge had been transferred to the States some years back, he had accepted the assignment gratuitously, but with a certain deep skepticism. The first two years, spent in a small apartment hotel in Manhattan, had done little to alleviate the skepticism. And then, when he had finally reached the conclusion that this American assignment would probably be permanent as well as final, they had decided to take a house. Martha had done the shopping; it was she who had discovered Fairlawn.

The price, which was certainly reasonable enough in view of the inflated value of money at the time, had been a little steep for the Kitteridges, who were limited by the still austere standards of their native land and salary, but Martha had a small inheritance of her own which she had never touched. She didn't hesitate to cash it in and use the money to buy the Fairlawn house.

A small-boned, delicate woman with fine tender white skin which never seemed to burn even in the hottest sun, she was to be seen, from the day she moved into the place, at almost any hour of the day, pottering around her tiny garden, her hands invariably encased in white canvas garden gloves and a wide-brimmed "African Veldt" hat shading her very alert, pale-blue eyes. Beyond doubt, Martha Kitteridge had a green thumb; there is no question but that her great passion in life was the nurturing and cultivation of flora and fauna. Of the hundreds of homes in Fairlawn, hers was outstanding as a result of the shrubs and flowers, the perennials and annuals with which she had landscaped the plot surrounding the house.

In spite of her rather strange and foreign British accent and a certain inherent shyness, she took almost as much interest in her new neighbors as she did in the garden upon which she devoted so much of her energy and her time. Martha Kitteridge loved people.

It is worth commenting that people in turn seemed to love and to trust her. She was probably the only woman in the whole of Fairlawn for whom everyone had a kind word. The MacSweeneys may have disliked the Piazzas, considering them little better than immigrants; McNally may have hated Neilsen because he thought him a snob; the Olsens could have looked down upon (and envied) the Cathcarts, because Mrs. Cathcart was obviously a drunkard and her husband came home with strange women, but no one, no one at all, disliked Mrs. Kitnitridge. She was so very obviously exactly what she appeared to be—a simple, sweet, little old lady who loved her garden and was very polite and very kind to everyone who passed her house. She was sweet to the dirty-faced children who ran across her newly planted flower beds; she went so far as to pet and surreptitiously feed the dogs who had excavated her recently planted bulbs.

Mrs. Kitteridge would, of course, run out and wave her apron at the dogs when she saw them doing it, usually with a bone in her hand to reward the treacherous animal for his trespass. In fact, that is precisely what she was doing on that Saturday morning at exactly ten o'clock when Len Neilsen, her neighbor from two doors up the street, drove by. She stopped waving at the dog just long enough to wave at Mr. Neilsen.

She was just a little surprised, and possibly a little hurt, when Mr. Neilsen passed hurriedly by, ignoring her completely. She could have sworn that he saw her, too. His car passed within less than a dozen yards.

The fact is, however, that Len Neilsen was completely unaware of the little white-haired woman with the large ham bone in one hand and an apron in her other. Len Neilsen was on his way to the police station.

The decision which had been so difficult to reach a few hours before, as Len and Allie had sat in the cold predawn, staring white-faced at each other, had seemed simplicity itself in the warm light of the morning. They hadn't discussed it at all, as, sleepy-eyed they had once more sat at the breakfast table with little Billy babbling away between them. Nothing had been said until the child had finished his own hearty breakfast of soft-boiled eggs and orange juice, toast and milk, and gone back to his room to play.

The moment the door closed behind young Bill, Len got up from his chair and walked around the table. He leaned over Allie, looking down into her upraised face.

"I'm getting dressed now," he said. "I'm going to the police station."

Allie's expression didn't change.

"I knew you would," she said.

There had been no need for further words. At nine fifty-five, Len went out to the garage, looking neither right nor left. He raised the overhead door, backed out the Ford, and stopped in the driveway long enough to get out and reclose the door. He finished backing into the street, swinging the car around so it faced north. And then he drove surely and quickly off.

The nearest police station, a branch of the Nassau County Police in whose jurisdiction Fairlawn lay, was some three miles off, at the edge of the next town. Len had looked up the address in the telephone book.

Allie watched him leave, standing in the front room and looking out of the window. For some reason, she instinctively stayed well off to one side, so that no one would observe her from the street. The moment the car was out of sight, she went back to Billy's room, where the youngster sat on the floor playing with a new collection of toy soldiers.

"Wanna get dressed and go out an' play," Billy said, looking up at his mother.

"I think you'd better stay in this morning, honey," Allie said. "I think you had..."

"I wanna go out an' play."

"This afternoon," Allie said. "Wait until Daddy comes home and then maybe we'll all go out."

"Can we go to the movies, Mommy?"

"When Daddy comes home," Allie said. "Yes, we can all go to the movies. Now you stay in and be a good boy and play with your soldiers. Mommy wants to get her work done."

Allie went back to the kitchen. She was tired, but she wasn't sleepy. She'd completely forgotten about Len's good news. Completely forgotten about the promotion down at the office, the additional salary. She just hoped...

Detective Lieutenant Clifford Giddeon was a man who looked forward to his week ends. One of the big advantages in working for a county organization, as opposed to a large metropolitan police force, lay in the fact that the hours—in the former—were comparatively civilized. He could, under normal circumstances, count on long week ends; week ends which usually stretched from sometime late Friday until Monday mornings.

This arrangement made it possible for Lieutenant Giddeon to pursue his favorite pastime and hobby, a diversion which in a good many ways made up for the normal domestic life so many of his contemporaries enjoyed. Lieutenant Giddeon had never married and had no family, that is, with the exception of his widowed mother with whom he lived and who kept house for him. Instead the lieutenant had a hobby which he pursued with a passionate and absorbing devotion. He was a yachtsman.

The word yachtsman, would, of course, have been slightly ludicrous had anyone used it in front of the Lieutenant. However, the fact remained that he did own a forty-foot ketch and he spent almost every waking hour thinking about it and certainly every free hour either sailing the small vessel or working on her.

During the long summers, when he took his usual two week vacation, Lieutenant Giddeon kept the ketch berthed on the North Shore and he spent every free hour sailing her up and down the Sound. In the cold winter months when it was no longer possible to use the boat, he'd have her hauled up in a yard not too far from his home in Hempstead and, because the owner of the yard was a long-time friend, he was allowed to do his own work on her. As a result he saw very little of his mother during his week ends off duty. (She didn't mind as she happened to have her own hobby which consisted of attending the funerals of her friends, who were rapidly dying off—and when there were no funerals of friends, she'd go to funerals of strangers). Giddeon spent these week ends assiduously working over his vessel, sanding down her smooth mahogany sides, repainting the hull, cleaning up his tackle and in general preparing for the summer months to come.

On this particular Saturday morning, however, the lieutenant was not working down in the yard on his sailboat. As the result of a particularly busy Friday night, during which two teenaged gangs had clashed (one fifteen-year-old boy was shot and not expected to live), a couple of estates had been burglarized, and half a dozen other assorted criminal activities had taken place, the department was shorthanded and Lieutenant Giddeon had been asked to hold down the desk for a fellow officer who was busy working on a case.

The knowledge that he would be given full credit for the extra time did little to erase the lieutenant's annoyance. He'd been planning a varnish job on this particular day, a chore he was particularly anxious to finish while the weather remained fairly dry. Once the first real cold spell came, it would no longer be possible to accomplish this task and he'd been anxious to get it out of the way. As a result, Lieutenant Giddeon was in an extremely bad mood when the desk sergeant directed Len Neilsen to his office, a tiny cubicle on the second floor of the precinct station house.

But irritated or not, Lieutenant Giddeon was an excellent cop. Even before Len opened his mouth to speak, the police officer, who'd looked up the moment the other man opened the door and entered the room, made two quick observations.

Nice-looking young fellow, he at once reflected; probably from one of the new developments around here. The second observation was slightly less complimentary. He's got a hangover; a bad one. Although Lieutenant Giddeon himself had never in his life suffered a hangover, he knew the signs only too well. He was a hard man to fool.

"What's your problem, young fellow?" he asked, consciously making an attempt to sound pleasant as he realized his own foul mood only too well and didn't want it to interfere with his business relationships with the public, who were, after all, his employers.

Len looked over at the straight-backed oak chair at the side of the desk at which the lieutenant sat. The other man nodded toward the chair and Len moved to it and sat down. He sat on the edge of the seat and for a moment just looked embarrassed. And then he spoke.

"I'm afraid, sir," he said, "I'm afraid this is going to sound crazy."

"I hear a lot of crazy things."

"I should imagine," Len said. He began to feel a little more at ease. This cop, sitting there in his civilian clothes and looking like anything but a police officer, seemed an understanding and intelligent sort. He couldn't be more than thirty-six or thirty-eight himself, but there was something very solid and very sure about him.

"Well, I hardly know where to begin. It seems..."

"Just begin at the beginning," the lieutenant said. "You can start with your name."

"Len Neilsen," Len said. "I live over in Fairlawn. And last night I saw a murder. Or at least I saw a man who had just been murdered."

Lieutenant Giddeon's expression didn't change. "That isn't the beginning," he said. "Where were you last night?"

"I was home."

"Is that where you saw the murder?"

Len shook his head quickly. "No—of course not. You see, I was a little drunk last night and..."

Giddeon waved his hand, shaking his head slightly. "Listen," he said. "Let's try it again. Start all over. Start, let's say, about the time you took the first drink. When and where was that?"

It took a long time, but the officer was extremely patient. He let Len tell it in his own way and rarely interrupted. This capacity of his for intelligent understanding and patience was probably one of the reasons he was a lieutenant of detectives instead of pounding a beat.

Len went through the entire thing, starting with the previous evening when he'd first been invited out to dinner by his boss. He told about getting the promotion and calling Allie and the whole thing. While he talked, he noticed that the lieutenant had taken a yellow, lined pad from a desk drawer and occasionally jotted down notes. Once or twice he nodded, in an understanding way and now and then he'd interrupt with a question in order to get things straight. But mostly he just listened. At no time did his expression change in the slightest; an expression of polite, interest and understanding. At no time did he show the faintest degree of skepticism. He didn't show anything.

Even when Len started talking about the dead man, he remained the same. He waited until Len was all through. Then he leaned back in his chair and stared for a full minute at the wall over Len's head.

"And you say," he said at last, "you say you had never seen this man before, never seen the room before, haven't the faintest idea in which house you'd gotten by mistake?"

Len nodded.

"And you're sure the man was dead?"

"He certainly looked dead."

Giddeon slowly nodded.

"Just how drunk were you?"

"I've told you. Damned drunk. That is, until I came to, turned on the light and saw the dead man. After that, well, after that I'd never been more sober in my life."

Giddeon tapped the end of his pencil on the table for several seconds. At last he stood up and walked over by the window, turning and looking back at Len.

"You get drunk very often?"

Len blushed.

"About as often as I get a promotion," he said, his voice slightly defensive. "That's about once every five years."

Giddeon nodded.

"Ever pass out—draw a blank—anything like that, before?"

Len stood up then himself.

"Look, officer," he said. "I'm not nuts, I haven't been dreaming or seeing things or making this up. I'm telling you exactly what happened. I got in the wrong house by mistake, I saw a man with what certainly looked like a bullet hole through his head. I think the man was murdered. And I think someone knows that I saw him."

"All right. All right, I believe you. The only thing is, we want to be pretty sure. After all, no one reported any disturbance out that way last night. No one reported hearing a shot or seeing anything suspicious. That doesn't mean, of course, that something couldn't have happened."

"Well, what do you intend doing about it?"

"We'll investigate it, naturally. Thing is, though, in a case like this, we have to move a little cautiously. Can't just go bursting in on every place in the neighborhood. Another thing—say you're right and you did see this man and he was murdered. We don't want to tip our hand and alarm whoever did it by screaming up with sirens open. I think the best thing is for you to go on home now. Chances are, your missus will be a little nervous and upset, particularly as you seem to have told her all about it. Be best if you get back and stay with her. I don't have to tell you not to mention anything about this."

Len nodded. "Of course," he said. "And you will..."

"We'll start looking into it at once," Giddeon said. "Just you go on back. Stay around the house for the next day or so. We'll have someone nearby. We'll be looking into it."

Len nodded, again, a half-skeptical expression on his face.

My God, he thought, I wonder if he thinks I'm really nuts. I wonder if he thinks I just dreamed the whole damned thing up. Maybe he's just getting rid of me in a nice way—figures I had too much to drink or something. He turned, hesitantly, toward the door.

"We don't pass up things like this," Lieutenant Giddeon said quietly, as Len started to open the door. "No matter how crazy they sound, we look into them."

Len felt better as he walked down the stairs to the street floor. He'd done the right thing after all, he figured.

Passing through the information room on the ground floor on his way to the street, he was vaguely aware that the sergeant on the desk was speaking rapidly into the telephone. It was the same sergeant to whom he had first told his story, less than an hour ago. The sergeant was talking in a tight, urgent voice over the phone, at the same time beckoning to a man in plain clothes sitting tipped back on a chair at the side of the room. He didn't notice Len at all.

Had Len not been so busy with his own thoughts, the chances are he would have heard something of what the sergeant was saying. He would have recognized the name, perhaps. As it was, he passed by and went out into the street and got into his car and didn't hear a word of it.

What the sergeant was saying, and what might possibly have attracted Len's interest, were a few simple words, but words spoken in a quick and urgent fashion.

"... yes, yes, Mrs. Kitteridge. Just don't worry—don't let yourself get excited or frightened. We'll have a man out there in less time than it takes to tell you about it. Just don't become hysterical..."

Chapter Six

The newspapers, and especially the tabloids, made a big to do about the fact that it was little Mrs. Kitteridge who found the body. But actually they were wrong; it wasn't really Mrs. Kitteridge at all. Instead, the nameless dog whom Mrs. Kitteridge had rewarded with a bone for trampling across her shrubbery, made the discovery. Completely unappreciative of the little old lady's kindness, this dog, a multicolored mutt of dubious ancestry, had at once taken his unearned reward from her hand and pranced off to the side yard and lost himself beneath the foliage of a low, spreading juniper bush. He was in the process of looking for a likely soft spot in which to bury his treasure when some atavistic instinct warned him of the sinister presence of death. Penetrating the tangled leafy cavern another foot or so, his yellow eyes took in the prone body lying on its face.

He began the series of dismal howls even as he slowly backed out and into sight once more.

Mrs. Kitteridge, who had followed his progress around the side of the house, stood silently watching him for several minutes. The dog seemed in some sort of agony, and she spoke to him gently. He ignored her and continued his weird wailing.

The first thought which occurred to Mrs. Kitteridge was that, in attempting to bury the bone, he had encountered some broken glass, or perhaps a rusty tin can, and injured himself. She attempted to approach him, but as she did, he turned and galloped off, still howling. Mrs. Kitteridge noticed that he no longer had the bone. With a thought of possibly retrieving it, and also investigating to see what might have caused the dog's strange behavior, Mrs.

Kitteridge went at once to her garage to get a rake. She would lift the branches of the juniper and see what might be beneath them. Passing out of the garage she noticed one of her rose bushes needed attention—it was a yellow climber and had fallen away from the trellis next to the garage on which it was supposed to climb—and so she attended to that. Thus, it wasn't until almost an hour had passed that she took the rake and lifted the profuse foliage of the low-growing evergreen.

What she saw affected her almost in the same way as that grisly sight had affected the multicolored animal. Mrs. Kitteridge, looking down on the prone and slightly twisted body lying on its face with the long blond hair stained red with blood, did not, however, howl. A more civilized member of the animal kingdom, she merely gasped and for several frozen seconds, stood there staring with her mouth wide open and the color slowly draining from her face.

It is an index to Mrs. Kitteridge's character, and a compliment to her breeding, that she didn't scream. Several things were at once apparent as her gentle eyes took in the scene. The body was that of a young girl and the girl was dead. The killer, whoever he or she might be, had apparently slain the girl somewhere else and dragged the body to this spot in an attempt to conceal it. Mrs. Kitteridge could see that one small slipper was half off and that there were two distinct marks where the feet had dragged across the soft earth. That part of the face which lay exposed beneath the flare of long blond hair, indicated that this girl had been extremely attractive. The purple red blood, already dried and caked, on that hair, showed all too clearly that her attacker had crushed the thin shell of her cranium with a "blunt instrument." And the disheveled appearance of the clothes—the child's skirt was torn and lay creased and rumpled almost up to her waist and her bare legs above the bobby socks were badly scratched and bruised—would indicate that she had been violently and criminally attacked, just previous to her death.

Mrs. Kitteridge backed out from under the bush and turned and entered her house. There was a certain amount of confusion in reaching the proper people at the police station, but within three minutes Mrs. Kitteridge was telling her story. Within five minutes of the time that Lieutenant Giddeon had finished listening to Len Neilsen's strange tale concerning *his* discovery of a murdered man out at Fairlawn Acres, he was hearing the details of Mrs. Kitteridge's grim discovery. The lieutenant arrived at Fairlawn less than eight minutes after the nearest radio patrol car had drawn up in front of Mrs. Kitteridge's neatly kept home.

Under normal circumstances, Len himself would have returned in time to have witnessed the convergence of police vehicles on the street in front of his and his immediate neighbors' residences. As it was, however, Len had the distinction of being just about the only resident of that particular section of Fairlawn who was not present during the first hysterical hour as the neighborhood turned out en masse to wallow in the sensationalism of the gruesome find.

There were two other persons conspicuous by their absence. Reginald Parson Kitteridge was in the basement of a friend's home in Great Neck playing darts. It is a significant comment on his wife's character that although she knew where he was and what he was doing at the time, it never occurred to her to call him up and tell him the news. She was appreciative of the fact that the weekly dart games were almost his only hobby and pleasure and she could see no reason for interfering with the regularity of his pastime.

The other person absent was the newest resident of the street—Gerald Tomlinson. Mr. Tomlinson's failure to be present was for a far more significant reason than that of Mr. Kitteridge. Tomlinson, at the exact moment when Lieutenant Giddeon was parting the juniper bush to lean over the dead girl's body, was busily occupied with a dead body of his own. To be exact, he was removing his particular cadaver from the trunk of his car in a lonely spot in upper Putnam County and preparing to lower it into a fresh dug, shallow grave.

In spite of the chill and winter weather, Tomlinson was sweating profusely. He had just finished digging the grave in the frozen earth with a mattock he had carried alongside the body in the trunk of the car. The absence of Kitteridge and Tomlinson during that first grim hour was neither noticed at the time by their neighbors and police, or commented upon later. The absence of Len Neilsen, however, was a far different matter.

To the very last, Len found it extremely difficult to explain this absence of his, both to Allie, his wife, and to Lieutenant Giddeon. Afterward, when Len did attempt an explanation, Giddeon would remind him that he, Len, had said he was returning directly home from the police station. So why did Len go to a saloon instead?

But to Allie, the idea of Len's going to a saloon made even less sense than it did to Giddeon. As Allie herself reminded Len each time the subject would come up, Len had never in his life been in a saloon in the morning. And that morning of all mornings! She simply couldn't understand it. In Allie's favor one thing must be said; in discussing Len's visit to a saloon on that fatal Saturday morning, she never once brought up the fact that it had been Len's drinking the previous evening which had involved him in the tragedy in the first place.

The strange part of it all lay in Len's complete inability to explain exactly what had driven him on a direct route from Lieutenant Giddeon's office to the tavern out on Jericho Turnpike, halfway between the police station and Fairlawn. How could he explain that he merely wanted a quiet secluded spot to sit and think? And how could he explain that the thing he was thinking about, the thing he was trying to figure out, was whether or not the Lieutenant may have been right after all; that maybe he had been merely drunk or crazy or something and just imagined the whole thing?

No, he couldn't explain that—not after finally getting home a couple of hours later that afternoon, a little tipsy as a result of the several beers on top of last night's drinking, and finding out about the murdered girl.

The absence of Len, as well as the Messrs. Tomlinson and Kitteridge, was more than offset by the number of Fairlawn residents who did find time that Saturday morning to crowd and jostle around as Lieutenant Giddeon and his more than a dozen police associates converged on the spot where a ruthless and brutal murderer had discarded the slender young body of Louisa Mary Julio beneath Mrs. Kitteridge's private juniper bush.

That it was Louisa's body was established beyond the faintest shadow of a doubt within three minutes of the time the first police car arrived on the scene and one husky patrolman hurried to question Mrs. Kitteridge while his partner stood guard in the driveway to hold back those curious and macabre neighbors who were so soon to gather.

Kathleen Julio, her large handsome face red with anger, was just leaving the front door of the McNally home, several houses down the street on Crescent Drive, when the police car arrived. Mrs. Julio was both angry and worried. Only an hour before she had discovered for the first time that Louisa had failed to return home the previous evening after her baby-sitting chore. The fact that there was so long a delay in her discovery of the girl's absence is not as unusual as it might seem.

Mrs. Julio was the mother of six children and she was also a very careless and possibly even inattentive mother. On the other hand, six children, ranging in age from seven to nineteen, combined with a highly temperamental husband, had, over a period of years, given Mrs. Julio a certain aloofness to the irregularities of her life and her sprawling, brawling household. She was used to Louisa's being out late at night when the girl would baby-sit for the neighbors' children and she never worried as Louisa had her own key and it was the custom for the man of whatever family Louisa sat for, to see the girl to her home at the end of the evening.

When Mrs. Julio had gotten up on Saturday morning, she followed her usual routine. She fed first her husband and then the younger children. Then she opened the morning newspaper and read it in the kitchen as the older children prepared their own breakfasts. The fact that Louisa had not been among the others hadn't particularly worried her. She always let the child sleep late after being out on a baby-sitting job the previous evening. Thus it wasn't until Mrs. Julio happened to go into the room shared by Louisa and one of her younger sisters, sometime around midmorning, and noticed Louisa's unslept-in bed, that she first realized the girl was missing. A quick and high-pitched questioning of the other children soon revealed that no one had seen Louisa since the previous evening.

Louisa's father had left for work by this time—he was a musician and had to go to New York for a practice session each Saturday morning—and so Mrs. Julio had at once thrust her thick arms into the sleeves of her mouton fur coat and, not bothering with a covering for her head, had started for the McNally house. Mrs. McNally, eyes red and last night's blurred make-up still on her face, had answered the door, her feet in broken slippers and a faded, rather soiled bathrobe tied around her waist. It had been an extremely unsatisfactory interview.

Mrs. McNally was only able to tell Louisa's mother that the girl had left for her home sometime after midnight the previous evening. No, Mr. McNally had not walked the girl home. Why not? Mr. McNally had been drunk. And why hadn't Mrs. McNally taken the girl home? Because Mrs. McNally didn't want to leave her baby alone and for Mrs. Julio's information, being in the house with Mr. McNally when he was drunk was exactly like being alone.

Furthermore, Mrs. McNally could see no reason in the world why the girl shouldn't be perfectly safe walking the three or four blocks to her home, no matter what the hour.

Mrs. Julio began to say something about the criminality of permitting a young girl, a mere child...

Mrs. McNally interrupted to tell Mrs. Julio that anyone who demanded a dollar and twenty-five cents an hour for baby-sitting was not to be considered a mere child.

It was at this point that Mrs. Julio told Mrs. McNally exactly what she thought of her and turned to leave, yelling that she would report the whole thing to the police at once. The words were hardly out of her mouth, when, the door of the McNally place having slammed behind her furious back, Mrs. Julio started down the steps and spotted the police car at the curb several hundred yards away. She made for it at once.

At that moment the patrolman, who had been talking with Mrs. Kitteridge, quickly came out of the house and spoke to his fellow officer, at the same time pointing toward the juniper bush at the side of the drive. This second patrolman, a kind-looking elderly man whose amazing girth around the middle would have kept him off any metropolitan police force, at once turned and went toward the bush. He raised its branches from the ground and leaned down to peer under them as his partner hurried back into the house.

A moment later and Mrs. Julio was looking over his shoulder.

Mrs. Julio screamed.

The confusion of the next few minutes, as the patrolman attempted to pull Mrs. Julio away from her daughter's dead body and later as his partner came to his aid, served to hopelessly erase whatever footprints there might have been in the immediate vicinity of the body and which had not already been obliterated by the mongrel dog and by Mrs. Kitteridge.

It was also unfortunate that the hot early morning sun had already melted the last traces of the previous evening's snow.

Mrs. Julio was still screaming by the time Lieutenant Giddeon reached the scene, accompanied by his partner, Sergeant Dan Finnerty. But somewhere during the course of her hysterical crying and sobbing, she had firmly established that the dead girl was her missing daughter. Her piercing shrieks had also attracted more than a hundred men, women and children from nearby houses.

Allie Neilsen's awareness of the commotion came at the sound of Mrs. Julio's first scream. She turned and listened for a moment, not quite sure, and then as the cries continued to penetrate her living room, where she sat nervously on the couch watching young Bill playing with his trains, Allie stood up and went to the window. She could see nothing.

It was while she was pulling on a light tweed coat and preparing to go to the front door that she heard the sirens of the approaching ambulance, which had been called immediately after Mrs. Kitteridge had first notified the police.

One thought and one thought alone came to Allie Neilsen. Len had been right. Len had not been dreaming. There had been a dead man and now not only Len knew about it but the police knew as well. It was with almost a sense of relief that Allie opened the front door of her house, turning at the same time to tell Billy to keep on playing and that she would be right back.

Allie walked swiftly down the flagstone path to the sidewalk and immediately saw the crowd gathering in front of Mrs. Kitteridge's home, several hundred feet down the street.

Ten minutes later Allie Neilsen returned to her own home. Her cheeks were drained of color and there was a dazed, unbelieving look on her pretty, heart-shaped face. She held one small hand to her partly opened mouth as she once more entered her living room. Almost aimlessly, she half slouched on the couch, not bothering to remove her coat. She didn't even hear young Billy as he repeatedly tugged at her skirt and asked questions.

She was thinking of Len. Thinking of Len and of a dead man with a bullet hole in the center of his forehead. She was thinking of Len sitting across the table from her less than a dozen hours ago with his scratched and bloody face and his wild eyes, telling her... telling her about...

She stopped thinking then for a second and when next she was conscious of the workings of her mind she was thinking of the slender body of a murdered fifteen-year-old girl lying in her own blood under a juniper bush a few doors down the street.

Suddenly the tears welled in Allie's large blue eyes and her throat contracted and she fell half sidewise on the couch and there was no sound at all as her shoulders convulsively shook.

Billy Neilsen looked at his mother with wide, uncomprehensive eyes for a full minute. And then his arms went around her knees and he hugged her tightly and he too began to cry. His crying, however, was anything but silent.

McNally came to only after the full impact of the pitcher of ice-cold water struck him in the face. He was swinging his arms like a channel swimmer and sputtering as he pulled himself to a sitting position on the bed. It took him a full minute to clear his head sufficiently to look up to where Myrtle stood staring at him.

"Jesus," Howard said. "Jesus Christ on a mountain top. What the hell kind of a way is that to..."

"Howard, for God's sake, Howard, wake up."

Even in his half-sleepy, half-hung-over condition, Howard McNally somehow realized that this was not just one of Myrtle's usual capricious angers, not one of her all too often violent exercises of temper in arousing him from a sound sleep. He sensed at once, without even being conscious of her chalk-like face and hollow, half-hysterical eyes, that something was wrong. Something was terribly, terribly wrong.

"Howard, for God's sake get up. Get up at once!"

"What—what in the name..."

"Howard, listen to me!"

"Yeah, all right. I'm listening. But what the hell is the..."

"Howard, for God's sake shut up and listen. Are you awake? Can you understand..."

"I'm half drowned, but I'm awake. Go ahead and..."

"Howard—it's the girl. Louisa."

For a second Howard stared meaninglessly at his wife. A slow blush began to spread over his face.

"Yeah. Well. So..."

"Louisa. The baby-sitter. She's been murdered. They found her body over in the Kitteridges' yard just now. Oh God..."

Howard's mouth suddenly fell wide and the blood left his face even faster than it had started to fill it a moment before.

"What in the name of Christ are you saying, Myrtle! My God, are you still drunk? What..."

"Murdered, Howard. Her head all beaten in and her clothes torn and... oh my God!"

Myrtle sank down on the side of the bed and Howard quickly turned and got out on the opposite side. He was stark naked, but he didn't bother to reach for the dressing gown lying on the chair next to the bed, or the leather slippers under it. He walked to the kitchen and reached for the whiskey bottle and poured a juice glass a third of the way full. He drank it straight without a chaser and then refilled it, this time halfway. A moment later and he was back in the bedroom handing it to Myrtle.

She downed it in a single gulp and then, for several minutes, the two of them just sat there, Myrtle on the bed and Howard in a chair a couple of feet away, and stared at each other.

"Tell me about it," Howard said at last, his voice hollow and barely above a whisper.

Myrtle continued to stare at him and her head moved almost imperceptibly from side to side. She barely opened her lips when at last she spoke.

"Maybe you better tell me about it," she said at last.

Howard reached over and slapped her hard across the face, several times, and Myrtle merely sat there. Then she began to cry.

It took a full twenty-five minutes for her natural female curiosity to overcome her fear. But ultimately and inevitably Marian Tomlinson, Gerald Tomlinson's sister-in-law, succumbed to the stronger of her two emotions. The curiosity was aroused by the commotion that was going on down the street. The fear, of course, was of Gerald, her dead husband's brother. Gerald's last instructions, upon leaving the house, had been clear and concise.

"Under no conditions, none whatsoever, are you to go outside. Anyone comes to the door, answer. But let no one in and don't go out. And don't let the kid out. I'll be back later."

Marian Tomlinson knew what she could expect if she were to disobey those instructions. Gerald was not a gentle man and he was a man who tolerated no disobedience.

But curiosity finally grew too much for her and so, warning the child to be quiet and not answer the door if anyone should ring, she finally put on her heavy coat and tied a shawl over her head; then thrust her feet into over-shoes and opened the front door. She made no attempt to penetrate the crowd being pushed back by the police, which surrounded the house down the street. She asked no questions, but then she didn't really have to. A dozen excited conversations going on around her quickly informed her of what was happening.

A strange, almost relieved smile seemed to twist the corners of her hard, bitter mouth when she learned that it was the body of a young girl which had been found.

Quickly she turned away and once more entered her own house. When the child, Patsy, asked her what was happening, she merely smiled thinly and half shook her head.

"Nothing—nothing important," she said. "Just some kid down the street got hurt. It's nothing—you go on an' play."

"What should I play with?"

"I don't care what you play with. Only stay out a the bedroom and the bathroom and play in your own room. Now go on, get. Go in an' play."

A few minutes later, making herself a cup of tea in the kitchen, she muttered under her breath.

"Gerald wouldn't like all those cops around, that's for sure," she said.

The Swansons, who had thrown the party the night before, like Marian Tomlinson, stayed only long enough to get the bare outlines of the tragedy and then returned to their half-eaten breakfast.

"A terrible thing," Grace Swanson said, spreading marmalade carefully on a toasted English muffin.

Tom Swanson didn't bother to look up from his eggs and Canadian bacon.

"God damn it all," he said, "a thing like this can stink up a decent neighborhood. You'd think..." the words died in a mumble as his new set of six-hundred-dollar false teeth closed over a mouthful of food.

Chapter Seven

It was fortunate for Howard McNally that Lieutenant Giddeon believed the first and most important stage in the investigation of the Julio murder—once he had assigned a certain number of technical assistants to routine work at the spot where the body was found—would be a visit to the Nielsens. As a result, Sergeant Finnerty was delegated to stop by the McNallys', theoretically the last known persons to see the dead girl alive. Finnerty was a good cop, but in this type of work, he was a little over his depth; until a week before the tragic death of the Julio girl, he had specialized on larceny and burglary cases.

Finnerty had observed both of the McNallys on the Kitteridge lawn, but had paid them little heed. By the time he got around to paying them a visit, they had already returned home and McNally had had a chance to shave and shower and drink several cups of black coffee. Myrtle McNally, realizing the police would soon be around, substituted a double Bromo Seltzer for the coffee, but was presentable in fresh make-up and a newly pressed house dress. She had a raging headache, but it was almost of secondary consideration to the extreme emotional fatigue she was suffering when Finnerty arrived.

Finnerty established his identity and authority by exposing his gold badge and was at once invited into the living room. He sat, a little uncomfortably, in a low butterfly chair and the two McNallys were several feet across the room, side by side on the imitation leather couch. Finnerty sensed at once that Mrs. McNally was boss in the family and he addressed most of his questions to her. One look at the pudgy figure of Howard had failed to impress the detective and he felt a vague sort of sorrow for Myrtle McNally, fine figure of a woman that she was, being yoked in wedlock to so insignificant a man.

It was Finnerty's mild enchantment with Myrtle which probably, more than anything else, blunted the sharpness of his mentality as he talked to the two of them. In no time at all he learned the Julio girl had arrived at their home in the early hours of the previous evening and that the McNallys had left shortly afterward to attend the party across the street at the Swansons.

Finnerty questioned them carefully as to whether the girl had been expecting anyone to drop in on her and received a negative reply.

"Perhaps your youngster might know if she had a visitor," Finnerty said.

Myrtle forced a smile.

"The youngster is six months old," she said.

Finnerty nodded sagely.

"Would it be that one of your friends, perhaps, may have dropped by?"

Both the McNallys spoke up to deny any such possibility.

"Well, these baby sitters," Finnerty said, "you know how they are. Sometimes a boy friend you know..." He rubbed a lean, bony finger down the side of his long nose. "Don't suppose you noticed if there were any dirty dishes or empty soda bottles or anything when you returned?"

Myrtle shook her head.

"And what time did you return?"

McNally opened his mouth to speak, but Myrtle quickly cut in.

"We came back, oh, let's see." She frowned for a moment, concentrating and out of the corner of her eye saw that Howard was again about to say something.

"After midnight," she said quickly. "Maybe around two o'clock or maybe even a little later."

"And the girl seemed all right then—nothing unusual or anything?"

"The girl was fine. Everything was quiet and we paid her and she left to go home."

"How much does she get an hour?" Finnerty asked.

Without hesitancy, Myrtle replied.

"A dollar and a quarter—an outrageous price. But around here, it's almost impossible to get anyone on a Saturday night. These kids—they all seem to want nothing but to go out with their boy friends and..."

Finnerty interrupted quickly. "Well," he said, and there was the note of pride in his voice at his own astuteness, "in that case we can determine exactly when the girl left. You say she came just before eight and you know how much you paid, so if it was a dollar and a quarter an hour, then..."

He looked brightly at Myrtle McNally, probably expecting to see some appreciation of his acute reasoning reflected on her face. What he saw was a sudden half-frightened, half-bewildered look. Unfortunately, Finnerty at the time was so busy doing mental problems involving multiplying one and one quarter by various digits, that he failed to interpret the significance of her expression.

"I didn't have change," Howard interrupted. "She was coming back today and we were going to straighten it out."

Finnerty looked over at him, disappointment heavy on his face. Myrtle eyed her husband at the same time with an expression almost approaching admiration.

"You didn't drive the girl home?" Finnerty asked, now turning his attention to Howard.

"Well you see, I was a little under the weather—tight you know," Howard said. "Quite a party across the street!" He laughed a little hollowly.

"Then she..."

Myrtle cut in quickly.

"I offered to take her home," she said. "But she lives only a few minutes away and she told us she was perfectly willing to go home by herself. After all, Louisa's a big girl..." Myrtle's voice, which had contained a defensive inflection as she had started to speak, seemed to fade into nothingness at the mention of the dead girl's name.

Finnerty went on to ask a number of routine questions—how often the girl had sat for them, how well they knew her, did they know of any boy friends and so forth. He obtained no information of value. They had never used the girl before the fatal night and Myrtle explained they'd gotten her name from another girl they had once employed. Finnerty was on the verge of asking more questions about the party across the street. He knew that it might be important to know who had been there and what time each person had left, but he hesitated a moment and then decided to pass it up. He knew Giddeon would have that angle checked and right now Mrs. McNally was asking him if he wouldn't like a cup of coffee.

"Come on into the kitchen," she was saying, "and I'll pour. It's all made and hot."

As Finnerty was hesitating, Howard spoke up.

"Go right ahead," he said. "I'll just skip it myself; want to look in on the baby for a moment."

Finnerty decided to have the coffee and to all intents and purposes that terminated his interview with the McNallys. He was still wondering what a fine figure of a woman like Myrtle McNally could see in that sad excuse for a husband as he followed her well-curved figure down the hallway to the kitchen.

Lieutenant Giddeon wasted little time at the Kitteridges'. A word or so with Mrs. Kitteridge assured him that she was beyond guile and he quickly assigned a man to take down her statement. He learned of Mr. Kitteridge's whereabouts and dispatched a car to pick him up. There were a few other routine matters he handled and then he left. He was anxious to talk with the Neilsens.

Allie, her eyes red and swollen, answered the doorbell's first ring. Young Billy stood directly behind his mother and peered around her at the visitor with wide-eyed curiosity.

"Mrs. Neilsen?"

Allie nodded.

"I'd like to see your husband."

"My daddy's gone to the police station," Billy said, proudly.

Allie turned and said, "Hush."

"Mr. Neilsen's not here just now," she said, looking back at Giddeon.

The lieutenant concealed his quick surprise.

"Well, may I come in a moment? You see, I'm an officer"—he showed her his shield—"and I'd like to ask you a question or two."

Allie nodded wordlessly and stepped to one side. Giddeon walked past her and into the neat living room. He waited until Allie came in and sat down and then he too found a seat, leaning forward and with his soft felt hat in his hands.

"Billy," Allie said, "you go into your room and play."

Billy started to protest, but then, detecting a note of unexpected sternness in his mother's voice, he turned and silently left the room.

"Just where is your husband, Mrs. Neilsen?"

Allie looked over at him and she found it hard to keep her chin from quivering. She wanted to cry.

"As Billy said," she started at last, "he went..."

Giddeon interrupted her.

"I know," he said. "He went to the police station. As a matter of fact, he came to see me. But that was some time ago. He left my office more than an hour ago and told me he was coming directly home. Do you know why he came to see me?"

Allie nodded.

"It was about the murder."

"About what murder, Mrs. Neilsen?"

Allie stared at him for a moment and in spite of herself she blushed.

"Not that poor girl down the street;" she said. "No, it wasn't about that. Len didn't know anything about that. It was..."

"Your husband told me that you knew all about the thing he had to tell me about," Giddeon interrupted. "He said that he told you about it last night, or rather early this morning. Now Mrs. Neilsen, I want you to tell me exactly what your husband did tell you."

"But if he has told you already..."

"I still want you to tell me in your own words."

Allie hesitated a moment, and then she started talking in a low, almost motionless voice. Even as she spoke the words she realized how insane they must sound; how silly and ridiculous the whole story was. Only it hadn't sounded at all silly, or ridiculous, when Len had told it to her in the early hours of the morning. But of course that was before this other thing—this terrible thing which had happened almost next door to their very house.

God knows, she'd been affected enough when Len had told her the story about the dead man; it had seemed terribly frightening and tragic. But somehow or other this other thing, this actually seeing for herself the dead body of a ruthlessly and brutally murdered young girl—seemed to make Len's tale fade into insignificance. It made it appear too utterly absurd to have ever happened at all.

As Allie talked she cursed herself for ever having convinced Len that he should go to the police in the first place. She began to wonder if perhaps he hadn't dreamed up the entire thing; that it was all a part of some mental fantasy brought on as a result of his unaccustomed drinking. She was mouthing the words, repeating what Len had told her, almost automatically. And as she talked she was thinking more and more of Len. She finished speaking in a rush.

"And I don't understand it—I don't understand it at all," she ended. Suddenly, quite beyond her control, the tears welled up in her eyes and then she was crying openly.

Lieutenant Giddeon felt very sorry for her. But he was smart enough to just sit there and say nothing. After a few minutes, Allie looked up at him and wiping her eyes with the back of her hand, faltered, "I'm sorry, really. It's just that..."

"I understand, Mrs. Neilsen."

"And I don't know where Len is. I can't understand it; I thought he'd be home now for sure. I just can't seem to understand anything. I..."

"You haven't any idea where he might have stopped off?"

Allie shook her head.

"Well, I wouldn't worry," Giddeon said, "he'll be along soon, I should imagine. I'll tell you what, why don't you go and sort of dry those tears now and maybe freshen up. I'll want to ask a few more questions. Just routine things. While you're doing it, I'd like to use your phone if you don't mind."

Allie stood up and looked at him gratefully for a moment.

"The telephone's in the hallway there," she said. "I'll just look in on Billy and I'll be back in a few moments."

She left the room and Giddeon watched her go with a curious expression on his face. He felt sorry for her; he believed that she had been telling him the truth. He believed that Len Neilsen had told her exactly the story she had repeated to him and which he himself had heard from the man's own lips less than a couple of hours back. But he didn't necessarily believe that the story itself was the truth.

Waiting until he heard the door of the bedroom close, he stood up and walked over to the telephone which sat on a small table in the hallway just off the living room. He dialed headquarters and spoke for several moments in a low, barely audible voice.

"And get it on the teletype at once," he ended. "I want him picked up and picked up quick. He can't be too far away."

He was back in the living room, again sitting in the chair and with his hat in his hands, when Allie Neilsen returned.

"Mrs. Neilsen," Lieutenant Giddeon said, "I wonder if I might ask a slight favor of you?"

Allie looked at him with faint surprise.

"Why certainly."

"I have a splitting headache and it's been a rough morning. You couldn't let me have a small drink of whiskey, perhaps?"

Allie started to speak and then blushed.

"I'm sorry," she said, "really sorry. I could give you a glass of sherry. You see neither Len nor I drink much and we don't bother to keep..."

"The sherry will be fine," Giddeon said.

While Allie was getting the wine, Giddeon looked around the room. He'd been right about Neilsen, he reflected. The man wasn't a drinker and he'd probably been telling the truth when he'd said his overindulging of the previous night was highly unusual. It didn't really prove anything, of course, but at least he'd been telling the truth.

The detective shook his head. He was doing what he had so often done in the past, making the same old mistake. He was forming opinions about people based on his personal liking or disliking of them. Mrs. Neilsen seemed to be a fine young woman and completely honest and aboveboard. Her husband had also seemed a likable enough chap. They weren't at all the sort of...

His eyes took on a colder expression. The hell, he thought, with whether they were likable or not. It was entirely beside the point. Hell's bells, hadn't

Lipski, the arsonist, been likable? Didn't Watson, the notorious procurer, have one of the most charming personalities he'd ever encountered? And even Blackmere, the rapist...

But the hell with that. Giddeon was a detective and he was investigating a murder. It didn't matter about the personal characteristics or qualities of the people involved. He was out to find the truth and to trace down a killer.

At this point, Lieutenant Giddeon was no longer considering the possibility that he might be investigating two murders. There was only one crime in his mind—the brutal slaying of a fifteen-year-old child whose body was even now being removed to the police morgue where an autopsy would be performed.

The Nassau County Police Department is probably as efficient an organization as most similar groups in the country. Certainly, when it is considered that the department works in close cooperation with the New York City Police, the State Police and local town and village officers within the county, it can be said to lack nothing in either physical and technical equipment, or in manpower. The intelligence quota of that manpower is probably even a bit above the average of the country in general.

However, in the case of Len Neilsen, something somewhere must have fouled up.

Len Neilsen was in no sense a crook and he had none of the cunning or knowledge of a criminal who was on the lam. As a matter of fact, Len didn't even realize, on that particular Saturday, that he was on the lam. Or at least, on the lam in the minds of the thousand or so police officers who were frantically searching for him. If he had been, it is highly doubtful that even with his total lack of criminal experience, he would be sitting drinking beer in a public tavern on what was probably one of the most traveled roads in the county and a tavern not more than a mile and a half away from the very police headquarters from which orders had been dispatched for his immediate arrest.

The fact that he was in a tavern and drinking beer on a Saturday morning, and especially this particular Saturday morning, was in itself completely contrary to Len's usual habits and character. Why he had suddenly decided to stop, while driving past the place, was very easy to understand. He had reached for a cigarette and discovered he was carrying an empty pack. Although far from a slave to the habit, Len felt an urgent need for a smoke. The talk with Lieutenant Giddeon had not been easy and his already frayed nerves were jumpy. No sooner had he discovered his lack of cigarettes than he noticed the tavern sign. Without a second thought, he pulled the car off the highway and parked in front of the place.

The beer was like the cigarette. It wasn't alcohol so much that he craved—

he merely had the usual hangover thirst and sighting the seductive beer sign hanging over the bar—it was one of those fantastic electrical contraptions which showed a foamy stream of amber liquid being perpetually poured into a slender goblet from a never-ending mechanical tap, he had suddenly decided it was just what he needed.

He plunged the button on the cigarette machine and retrieved the pack of cigarettes from the hidden compartment beneath the device and as he tore the cellophane wrapper to get at its contents, he walked to the deserted bar and climbed on a stool. The place was warm and pleasant and for a moment he relaxed. When the bartender approached, he ordered a beer.

It was really amazing. That one beer seemed at once to clear away the cobwebs from his head, alleviate the pain from behind his eyes and completely relax him. He ordered a second beer. It would only take a few additional minutes and he wanted a chance to think.

To begin with, he was beginning to wonder if he hadn't really made an ass out of himself. That detective had certainly seemed friendly enough and had even pretended to believe his story. But now, in thinking the entire thing over, it seemed to Len that the story itself was utterly fantastic. Fantastic even to him, Len Neilsen, who had, so to speak, been the victim of its circumstances. Not of course—and Len smiled at himself in the mirror behind the bar—quite the victim that the dead man had been. But certainly a victim, if only in a minor capacity. Len started reliving the previous evening.

He ordered a third glass of beer.

Yes, by God it had all been true. Even if that fellow Giddeon thought he was out-and-out crazy, it had all been exactly as he remembered it and exactly as he had explained it. But still, he'd probably been wrong about going to the police. What was there to be gained, after all?

Now, in the cold light of day, things seemed vastly different than they had the night before. Now that he was cold sober—he was ordering his fourth glass of beer as this idea crossed his mind—now that he was cold sober and no longer under the strain of a terrible hangover and shock, well, how, could he actually expect anyone to believe the story? Anyone of course with the exception of Allie. Allie knew him; Allie knew he didn't imagine things or have strange and unreal illusions. Allie knew anything he said had happened, actually and in all truth, *had* happened.

But the police? The police were another matter. What he had done, he suddenly realized, was to put himself into a stupid and completely untenable position. Just suppose it all was true? Suppose they—the police—did actually discover that a murder had taken place? Then he, Len, was going to be right in the middle. Not of course in the middle of the murder, but in the middle of some damned unpleasant publicity. And it would come at the worst possible time.

Oh, it would be great all right! They'd have him up to testify and his name would be in all the papers. He, Len Neilsen. The guy who got so drunk he couldn't even find his own house. Real nice. Randolph would like that! Sure, Randolph drank himself; had even helped Len get drunk. But Randolph knew how to hold his liquor and he would expect as much from his assistants. Particularly from a man he'd just promoted into a really important job.

Len sighed with disgust. He'd been a fool. A first-class, grade A, goddamned fool.

He ordered another beer.

Had Len Neilsen a little more experience with hangovers, he would have understood the insidious influence of a few beers following on the heels of a siege of heavy drinking. He would have realized that it only took four or five of them to blend in with the alcohol still in his blood stream and get him drunk all over again. But this was the sort of knowledge that Len did not have. The two or three times in his life when he had taken too much to drink had been signal and unusual occasions and they had been followed by week ends of remorse and headache—and solemn vows never to do it again.

By the time Len had finished his fifth beer he was beyond realizing his condition—he merely felt pretty good. In fact he felt fine. The only thing which bothered him was a slight tendency toward double vision and this he laid to the fact that he was not wearing his glasses. He had even forgotten when and how he had misplaced them.

The tavern began to fill with customers and Len had to knock on the side of his glass with a coin to attract the attention of the suddenly busy bartender. The man drew a beer without waiting for the order and put it in front of him.

Shortly after one-thirty, Len left the bar. He noticed a nursery next door and saw that there were vases of cut flowers in the window. Pleased with himself, he staggered over and entered. He purchased a dozen roses. Allie deserved something after all the trouble he had put her to.

Being without glasses, Len drove very carefully. He found the entrance to Fairlawn without difficulty and turned in. Once on Crescent Drive, he became aware of the hundreds of people still gathered in front of the Kitteridge home. The crowd was so great, in fact, that a few stragglers were even standing in groups and talking on his own front lawn.

Len had to honk his horn several times in order to get through. He left the car in the drive and started for his front door. Knowing that something unusual was going on, he stopped for a moment to ask a man whom he'd never seen before, what all the confusion was about. For a moment the man stared at him, then spoke.

"My God man, where've you been? Don't you know there's been a murder a couple of doors down the street? Why they just now got through taking the body away."

"A murder?"

"Yep, a bloody goddamn murder."

Len rushed up the front steps of his house. He threw the door open and the first person he saw was Allie. She stood in the center of the living room staring at him as he entered.

"Baby," he said. "Gees, baby! So I was right. See, I was right all along. They've found the body!"

Len failed to notice the glassy look in Allie's eyes as he moved toward her.

"I brought you some roses," he said.

Lieutenant Giddeon, who had been standing at one side of the living room entrance, reached Allie Neilsen just before she slumped to the floor in a dead faint. He reached her in time to keep her head from crashing into the side of a mahogany end table as she fell.

Ten minutes later Allie lay on the couch, her feet high on piled-up pillows and a wet towel on her forehead. Young Billy, looking frightened, stood a few feet off watching his mother. Detective Lieutenant Giddeon stood beside Len Neilsen near the door leading into the hall. He was watching Allie as he spoke.

"Now you're sure you will be all right?" he asked. "You're sure you don't want me to call somebody and ask them to stay with you?"

Allie's voice was weak, but clear and collected when she answered.

"No," she said. "No. I'll be all right. Only, well, only I don't know why you have to take Len back to the police station with you. Haven't you asked him enough questions already? Haven't you..."

"I'm not taking him back to ask him questions," Lieutenant Giddeon said. "I'm taking him to book on charges of suspicion of murder."

This time Allie didn't faint. She didn't even gasp. She just lay there and stared at the two of them.

For a moment Len stood stock-still and then he swung quickly to the detective. He no longer felt woozy, no longer had that vague, pleasant sensation which had suffused him when he'd entered the room.

"My God man," he said, "are you nuts? So I found a dead man; I came to the police station and told you about it. You think if I'd killed some guy I'd come and tell you? Why..."

"I'm not interested in a dead man," Lieutenant Giddeon said. His eyes were on the scratches on Len's face as he spoke and his voice was a dull monotone.

"I don't know anything about any dead man. I'm talking about the murder of a young girl with dark eyes and blond hair. You must have got the sex wrong, mister. The time, and I guess the place, were right. But you got the sex wrong."

Chapter Eight

The tragic and brutal murder of Louisa Mary Julio was to have a vital effect on the lives of a good many widely different people, many of whom had never ever heard of her, or in fact, had as much as heard of Fairlawn Acres.

Martin Saunders, correspondent for the Long Island edition of a New York tabloid, did such an excellent job in covering the story that he was at once taken on the staff as a full-time newspaperman. He immediately married the girl he had been engaged to for some six years, thus condemning her to a lifetime of poverty as the wife of a working reporter. On the other hand, a man named Peters, who was supposed to be covering the story for a metropolitan morning newspaper, got drunk at a bar across from the police station while he was waiting for a news break. He was fired. Later he became an electrical appliance salesman and ended up as the millionaire owner of a chain of cut-rate stores.

A Mrs. Chiofski, one of the newer residents of the development, who had been for weeks seeking an excuse to open a conversation and perhaps develop a friendship with Mrs. Cathwright, her next-door neighbor, discovered a suitable subject in the widely discussed local crime and the two became intimate companions, a relationship which beyond question of doubt led to the forming of a business partnership between their husbands some time later.

Possibly the person most affected by the murder, with the exception of Allie and Len Neilsen—and of course the victim herself—was young Peter Doyle. Peter was the only son of Patrick and Ann Doyle and he was twelve years old at the time the murder took place. He had a fine Irish imagination and a more or less poetic turn of mind, so much so that he was rapidly developing into a chronic dreamer and storyteller. Peter's mother found nothing charming in this particular facet of his character and was more inclined to think of her child as a dedicated liar.

One result of the murder on Peter was that soon after Louisa Julio's sudden death, he never again told a lie as long as he lived. In a way, it was unfortunate that this metamorphosis didn't take place in Peter's character just before the murder rather than shortly after it. Peter's final flight of fancy—or lie, as his mother would have had it—was directly responsible for the crystallizing of an opinion in the mind of Detective Lieutenant Clifford Giddeon. It was a lie which did much to propel Len Neilsen in the direction of that narrow, green hallway leading to the electrically wired chair in a small, square room on that dismal island in the Hudson River.

In a great many ways, Peter Doyle was an unusual child. Long after other children of his age had been disillusioned by the legend of Santa Claus, he continued to address annual letters to the North Pole. Later on he learned about leprechauns and fairies and elfs and he believed in them completely. He was a lonely boy and he didn't play much with the other children in the neighborhood, preferring to spend his idle hours poring over books.

From fairy tales he graduated to comic magazines and from them to detective stories. Peter was always the hero, always the keen-eyed cop who solved the terrible crimes and came up with the brilliant solutions which so shocked and amazed his fellow sleuths at Scotland Yard or the Sûreté, as the case might be.

Immediately following his breakfast on the morning of the murder, Peter had retired to his bedroom and at once became deeply involved in the construction of a stage-set. He was planning the production of a play and was busily cutting out cardboard figures when his mother rudely interrupted him. She ordered him out of the room and out of the house. She felt that he needed fresh air and exercise and didn't believe that sitting around in his bedroom on a Saturday morning was a healthy activity for a boy of his age.

Reluctantly Peter had pulled on his leather jacket and left the house. He picked up a long stick as he passed by the garage and then started down the street. Instead of walking on the sidewalk, he at once stepped into the gutter and as he strolled along, his mind still on the play which he was planning to produce in his bedroom theater, he idly swung the stick.

He was not satisfied with his cardboard set and about the time he turned into Crescent Drive, he suddenly changed his mind about the entire plan. Peter decided that he would enlist the aid of several other children in the neighborhood and stage a real live show. They could have it in the garage in back of his house and he would manage the entire thing himself. He could rummage up in the attic and find some discarded clothes and...

At this point in his meditations, Peter passed in front of number 98 Crescent Drive. He stopped for a moment to concentrate on his thoughts. His stick was still swinging carelessly and he suddenly became aware that one end had encountered an obstruction. Peter looked down at the ground with a frown and suddenly his eyes focused and he saw the felt hat. Instinctively reaching to retrieve it, he observed the pair of glasses with one broken lens lying next to the hat. Without thinking, he picked up both objects and stuffed them into the wide pocket of his jacket. The hat made a tight fit, but he managed by rolling it up. The two finds would make excellent props for his newly planned play.

Less than an hour later, Peter had completely forgotten about his play. Peter, like a hundred other children who lived in Fairlawn, had something much more fabulous, and much more tangible, on his mind. Peter was a member of that large and curious crowd which had gathered around the Kitteridge house while police officials removed the body of Louisa Julio.

Among that curiously morbid crowd were many who were honestly horrified by the murder; there were others who merely absorbed a vicarious thrill by being in proximity to what would without doubt develop into a sensational news story. A few were revolted and frightened and decided to assume sudden and strict control over the destiny of their own children to insure their future safety.

The children present were thrilled beyond measure. Peter's reaction was exceptional in that almost at once he seemed to feel himself a vital part of the drama which was taking place. He immediately examined the men who were busily occupied in and about the place, deciding which were detectives and which were police laboratory experts. He looked around at his neighbors almost ghoulishly, trying to decide in his own mind if any of them looked guilty and if one could be the killer.

This was really something; not a storybook crime, but the real honest-to-God legitimate thing.

When Sergeant Finnerty left the Kitteridges' and went to the McNallys' house to seek information, Peter at once spotted him as a detective. It really wasn't too difficult. Finnerty *looked* like a detective. Peter, fascinated, followed in Finnerty's footsteps. While Finnerty was in the McNally residence, questioning Howard and Myrtle McNally, Peter was half hidden in the bushes beside the living room window and straining his ears to overhear what was going on. His face was alive with excitement and his nervous hands kept scratching in and out of the pockets of his leather jacket. It was when his right hand suddenly came into contact with the broken glasses that Peter got his great inspiration.

Finnerty almost missed the boat. He was halfway down the pathway from the McNally's front door to the sidewalk, when he felt the tug at the sleeve of his blue serge suit. Not changing his stride, he looked down into the freckled face of a boy whose large blue eyes were wide with excitement. The boy's wild red hair was crew cut and uncovered. He held a soft felt hat in his free hand.

"Go away, sonny," Finnerty said. "Can't you see that I'm busy?"

"You're a detective," Peter Doyle said. He made it a statement and not a question.

"I haven't any time now to..."

"Listen, Mister, you *are* a detective, aren't you?"

As the youngster apparently had no intention of detaching himself from his sleeve, and as Finnerty observed that several people were watching him, he felt disinclined to rudely jerk his arm away. He hesitated for a moment.

"I said I'm busy, lad," he said. "Now go on—run along and..."

"Listen, Mister," Peter said, and in spite of his excitement, he managed to keep his high-pitched voice barely audible. "Listen, you are working on the murder, aren't you? You..."

"I'm a detective and I'm working on the murder," Finnerty said. "Now go on with you and don't bother me. I got things to do."

"Well if you're working on the murder," Peter said, "You'd better talk to me."

"Oh yeah? So I better talk to you had I? Well, listen here, sonny," and Finnerty carefully detached Peter's clutching fingers from the sleeve of his coat. "You don't want to be turned over my knee and get a paddling, you better..."

"Listen to me," Peter said. "Listen. I got a clue. I got something right here that will lead you right to the killer!"

"So you got a clue, have you?" Finnerty permitted himself an indulgent smile.

"Yes, I got a clue," Peter said. He suddenly thrust the hat and the glasses in front of Finnerty's eyes.

For a moment the detective looked at the objects blankly. When he spoke, his voice was kindly, but a little patronizing. It was the tone of Finnerty's voice, rather than the actual words he spoke, which caused the damage. The quality of Finnerty's voice was indirectly responsible for Peter Doyle's greatest lie and his last lie.

"A hat and glasses," Finnerty said. "So what son—so what?"

Up until that very second, Peter had merely meant to tell the detective he had only that morning found the objects in the street near the scene of the crime. Even up until the very second he opened his mouth to speak, he still intended to explain the event just as it had happened. But there was something about the smug, arrogant manner of Dan Finnerty's voice as he said that "So what..."

"Listen," Peter said, "I found these over there this morning. In the yard where the dead body was. Right next to the bush. I was playing and I found them right there beside..."

"Well for Christ sake!"

Ten minutes later, Peter Doyle, twelve-year-old sleuth who baffled the finest brains of Scotland Yard and the French Sûreté with his amazing criminal deductive powers, was being ushered into the information room at the sub-police station from which Len Neilsen had departed an hour or so previously.

It was the most thrilling moment of his life; it made those silly plays of his seem like nothing, nothing at all. Peter was a central figure in a real, true-to-life murder investigation.

By this time, Peter had completely convinced himself that he *really had* found the hat and the glasses next to the juniper bush in Martha Kitteridge's side yard.

A couple of hours later, Lieutenant Giddeon, looking down on the table where that hat lay next to the glasses—the hat containing the initials L.N.—reached two conclusions. The first was that perhaps Sergeant Finnerty was not as big an idiot as he had first thought him to be; the second was that he'd never again let his sense of logic be influenced by his liking or disliking of a criminal suspect. He was probably wrong in both conclusions.

If Peter Doyle can be said to have served fate as the carpenter who sawed the pine boards for what was certainly planned to be Len Neilsen's coffin, Tom Swanson was, in his own way, no mean assistant. Swanson, however, was forced to resort to a lie, not because of an unusually vivid imagination, but as an instinct toward self-protection.

The first of the several times that the Swansons were questioned was around three o'clock on Saturday afternoon. The questioning was done by a young, ambitious traffic patrolman, who during the manpower shortage at the precinct station, was temporarily serving as a substitute detective. His name was Farraday, Fred Farraday, and he was assigned to question the Swansons because, in the first stages of the investigation, they were not considered key witnesses.

The Swansons had finished their delayed breakfast without further conversation. Each was busy with his thoughts and the tragedy which had been enacted across the street meant little to them. After all, it was none of their concern and they had plenty enough to worry about without borrowing trouble. It didn't even occur to Tom or Grace Swanson that they could have the remotest connection with the crime; that is up until the time when Tom turned the radio on late that forenoon and they heard a report of the case over the air. That's when they learned that the victim was the young girl who had been baby-sitting with the infant daughter of one of their guests of the previous evening.

It just happened that both Grace and Tom heard the news at the same moment and that each of them was, at that very minute, thinking of the McNallys. Grace was remembering how Myrtle McNally had disappeared sometime late during the previous evening. She was remembering that soon after realizing her neighbor from across the street was no longer at the party, she'd started looking for Tom. And Tom was nowhere to be found.

Grace Swanson didn't need a blueprint; there had been other parties and there had been other big blond girls who drank too much. Grace remembered only too well that time a couple of years ago when she'd found Tom and that horrible Schwartz woman sitting out in the front seat of the car in the garage. It was funny, but Myrtle McNally even looked like Helen Schwartz. And Helen, like Myrtle, had been married to a little, fat, bald man whom she had loathed in pretty much the same way that Myrtle seemed to loathe her husband.

The Swanson party had gotten a little out of hand as the evening wore on and Grace was having a little trouble remembering the exact sequence of events. Myrtle had disappeared and then she'd noticed Tom was nowhere around. Grace had been too proud to go outside and start looking for him. But she had been aware of Myrtle's return; Myrtle looking disheveled and a little hysterical.

That must have been well past midnight as near as she could time it. By then, Tom was already back in the house, preparing a final batch of drinks for the guests who were getting ready to leave.

Grace had not intended to say anything about it. She probably never would have, either, if it hadn't been for this new development.

Tom himself was thinking of Myrtle McNally. It wasn't exactly that she'd flirted with him, but there had been something about her manner. Some little gesture or other which he had detected and which told him that she was the sort—well, that she probably wouldn't object too much if he were to make a pass at her.

Tom had seen Myrtle leave the house. And he had, as Grace suspected, left himself a minute or two later. Tom had stood in his own front yard as he watched Myrtle McNally cross the street. He had it all figured out. She was going over to check up on the baby and then she'd return. Tom planned to intercept her on her way back. He'd lighted a cigarette and just stood there waiting. Some ten or fifteen minutes passed and he was getting restless. And then he had heard the door slam across the street and a moment later someone had run from the house. It could have been Myrtle; Tom was not sure. What he was sure of, however, was that a moment later, a second figure had left the McNallys' place.

Tom ducked back out of sight. He'd overheard Myrtle's low tense voice as the two of them passed within a few feet of him.

"You fool! You stupid, fat, gross fool," Myrtle was saying. "What did you do—scare the girl out of her wits? It would serve you right if..." The words were lost as the two of them circled to the rear of the house to re-enter the back door.

Tom had shrugged and flipped his cigarette onto the lawn.

Grace herself had been in the kitchen when Myrtle and Howard returned. It was obvious to her that the two had been fighting.

Grace strongly suspected that McNally had found his wife outside with

Tom, but she said nothing. Grace didn't like scenes.

By the time Farraday questioned them, later that Saturday about the party, Grace and Tom each had his story ready.

When the detective asked if they had noticed anyone leaving the party during the evening, Tom was the first one to answer.

"No," he said. "Everyone was here until the party broke up." Tom wasn't going to admit in front of Grace that he had followed Myrtle out of the house. He wasn't going to give her a chance to start anything, and anyway, he didn't really consider it important.

Grace looked at her husband for a moment, barely concealing the surprise on her face. She was on the verge of saying something when Farraday again spoke.

"Thought maybe," he said, "someone might have left early; maybe seen something which would be helpful."

Grace suddenly realized that it would be foolish to mention the temporary disappearance of the McNallys. It would only lead to further questions and further involvement. And there was no reason they should be mixed up in the thing. She realized full well that Tom was lying and she believed she understood why. He didn't want to admit in front of her that he had gone out after the McNally woman. It really didn't mean anything anyway, as far as the crime itself was concerned.

Certainly Tom, if he had seen anything of significance, would speak up. At that moment, Tom did speak up.

"The fact is, officer," he said, "although I don't remember anyone leaving the party, I did, myself, happen to step out for a minute or so sometime after midnight. I wanted to get a breath of air."

Both Grace and Farraday looked at him with surprise.

"Yes," Tom said, "I went out the front door for a cigarette and I did see something which might be important. There was a man and a woman across the street and they seemed to be having an argument of some sort."

Tom figured it was a pretty smart touch. Now, if the McNallys did admit leaving the house, and if by any chance they happened to have seen him watching them, he'd be covered.

"An argument, you say? And was it anyone you knew or..."

"Too dark to really see them," Tom said. "All I can say is that it looked like a man and a woman and they were in front of the McNally place. But it wasn't anyone from this house, I'm sure of that."

"Why do you think they were having an argument?"

Tom hesitated, and then said, rather weakly, "Well, that was sort of the impression I had. Anyway, I didn't think it was any of my business and while they were still there, I turned and came back into the house."

"Can you tell me what they looked like, anything about them? Maybe..."

"Nothing. The only thing I could see was that it was a man and either a girl or a woman. And, oh yes, they were both bareheaded. That's all I can remember."

Grace waited until the detective was through asking questions and had left, before she turned to her husband. "It was the McNallys you saw, wasn't it?"

Tom stared at her for a moment before answering. When he spoke his voice was cold and sharp.

"Don't be a damned fool," he said. "I don't know who it was. All I know is that I saw two people. And for God's sake, let's not get ourselves involved in this thing. There's going to be enough trouble, without our getting mixed up in it. Anyway, you yourself told the detective that none of our guests left the house, as far as we know. Let's just stick to that."

Grace looked at her husband for a long moment and then nodded.

"All right, I guess there's no point in getting mixed up in the thing. We'll stick to it."

Late that Saturday afternoon, when questioned by Lieutenant Giddeon, both Myrtle and Howard McNally denied leaving the Swanson party until the time they had returned home together and dismissed the Julio girl. Howard lied to the detective for a very simple reason; he didn't want to go to the electric chair and he knew that if the slightest hint of what went on in the kitchen of his home the previous evening should ever come out, they'd probably condemn him without so much as a trial.

Myrtle lied because, no matter how much she might hate her husband, she wasn't going to have the father of her child tried as a murderer.

Even gentle little Mrs. Kitteridge, in her own quiet way, contributed to the picture which had rapidly crystallized in Lieutenant Giddeon's mind of Len Neilsen as a killer. She did it in complete innocence and quite by accident. It was while she was talking to the lieutenant of her own activities shortly before the discovery of the body that she made her damaging statement and a statement which made a considerable impression upon the policeman.

At the time she made it, she hadn't the slightest idea that Neilsen was a suspect in the case. She would, in fact, have been the last person in the world to do or say anything to hurt anyone.

"Oh yes," Mrs. Kitteridge said, in answer to a question by the lieutenant. "I know the Neilsens, although not well, of course. Why Mr. Neilsen passed my house just a few minutes before I called you. It was funny, too. He didn't even seem to hear me or see me when I spoke to him. He's usually such a nice young man, too. I guess he must have had something on his mind."

"I guess he must have," the lieutenant said dryly. "I think I know what it was, too."

Dominic Spagan was perhaps the one person who might have come forward and told his story and by so doing have offset, in some small part, the damage being done to Len Neilsen by the testimony of those other witnesses. The fact that Dominic failed to come forward, was, ironically enough, the result of a desire on his part to help Len rather than to hurt him.

Dominic was the cab driver who had taken Len home early that Saturday morning. It had been his last fare of the night and he had returned from Long Island, put his cab up in the lot over on the West Side and at once taken a subway to his own small apartment in the Bronx. It wasn't until late the next day, just before going back on duty, that he learned of the murder out at Fairlawn Acres. By that time the newspapers were carrying the story of Len's arrest as a possible suspect. They also had a picture of him, as well as a very glamourized picture of Louisa Julio and several shots of the scene where her body had been discovered. Dominic read the story avidly.

He had recognized Len's picture at once and he remembered the address from the previous night. His first inclination had been to immediately contact the police with the information which he had. And then he began to think it over.

The young guy, this Len Neilsen, had sure been drunk. So drunk he hadn't even been able to open his own front door. For a moment, stopping and trying to remember the details of the previous evening, Dominic for the first time wondered if it *had* been his own front door. He remembered watching as Len staggered around to the side of the house and started to crawl into a window.

That was something the police would probably be pretty interested in. But because a man was so stinking drunk that he couldn't find a keyhole—well it didn't necessarily make him a murderer. But Dominic knew how the police worked—or at least he thought he did. Tell them the guy was drunk and probably breaking into a house and that would be just about all they'd need. They'd be sure he could be guilty of anything.

There was the other thing; they'd probably raise hell with him, Dominic, for not putting in a report on it. They might even pick up his medallion.

Yeah, Dominic knew how the cops worked all right. Let 'em get just the littlest thing on a guy, and hell, they were ready to believe almost anything. Hadn't it been less than two months ago they'd fined him, those cops down at the hack bureau? And for what? A simple little infraction of the traffic rules. It had cost him a week's pay.

"The hell with the cops," Dominic said, under his breath. Why should he help them? The poor guy is in enough trouble already. There was no point in stirring up more for him. Telling the cops that the guy had been blind drunk, hadn't hardly known where he lived... well it wouldn't help anything and it might get him into even worse trouble. The best thing to do was to stay away from the cops.

Thus, the one possible person who could have even begun to verify Len's story of the night before, remained silent in the mistaken belief that he was doing the kindest possible thing to a poor drunk who'd got himself jammed up with the law.

Chapter Nine

At five minutes to six on Saturday afternoon, Gerald Tomlinson was approximately seventy miles north of Albany. He was driving the sedan at a conservative fifty miles an hour and expected to reach the border within a couple of hours. Tomlinson was acting on a snap decision and the fact that he had been forced to make that decision on the spur of the moment as it were, had put him in an evil mood. The single consolation which, when he periodically thought about it as he carefully drove north, served to lighten his dark and brooding mind, was the thought of the $48,000 which he had painstakingly sewed into the upholstery of the back seat of the car.

Aside from that, everything had gone wrong. Everything. First that damned woman and her screaming; next Arbuckle. Not that he had any particular regrets as far as Arbuckle was concerned. But the man, in letting himself become wounded, had set up a terrific problem. A problem which had called for a sudden and radical switch in plans; plans which involved the firing of two bullets into a dying man in the middle of the night.

And then lastly there was that business back at the house a dozen hours ago. The business of that goddamned drunk wandering in just as he was beginning to get things straightened out again.

Tomlinson still didn't know just how much the man may have seen or understood. But he couldn't take chances. Not now, after what had happened about Arbuckle, he couldn't.

The fact that he knew who the man was didn't alter the situation. He'd been forced to act and to act swiftly and surely. Thinking about it, he cursed under his breath. Jesus, the beautiful way he had figured this thing. Right now he should have been safely back at the house out at Fairlawn Acres and that stupid sister-in-law of his should be getting dinner ready. He was tired and worn out and a good hot meal would have been welcome. He should be looking forward to a nice rest during the next few weeks in a comfortable hideout—without danger and without risk. In time he would have been able to have made a foolproof getaway. He would have left the woman and the child enough money to hold them for a while and he could have gone. Gone where he wanted to, without fear of leaving a trail.

As it was, God only knows what might be happening. He'd never seen so perfect a plan, so badly fouled up. And by nothing but the damnedest possible string of bad luck.

He didn't worry too much about the woman and the child. The child herself knew almost nothing, and, like her mother, was so thoroughly frightened that she'd never dare talk. The danger didn't lie there. It didn't lie in the house itself. Thank God, he'd had enough time to clean up in the garage; to see that there were no telltale stains left in the bedroom. Even if the police were to make a search of the place, they'd find nothing.

No, the danger lay elsewhere. The danger lay with that drunken damned idiot who had wandered and fumbled around and ended up in the wrong place at the wrong time. There was no telling just what he had seen; no telling what he'd remember once he sobered up. Well, there was nothing to do now but run for it.

Tomlinson stopped thinking about it for a while and once more began to think about his sister-in-law. In a way, he was actually glad that he wouldn't have to put up with her and the brat any more. All except for one thing; she was a damned good cook.

Thinking of Marian's cooking, suddenly reminded Gerald Tomlinson that he was hungry. He'd been all day with nothing to eat and it had been a hard day, both mentally and physically. Digging in that frozen ground hadn't been easy work.

Up ahead and to the right of the road, he noticed a string of neon lights and he began to slow the car as he approached. A moment later and he saw that the lights circled a long, low diner. There were two trucks and an old sedan parked in front of the place. For a moment he hesitated, his foot light on the throttle. He would have preferred a more deserted spot. But then he took his foot off the throttle and pressed lightly on the brake, at the same time turning the wheel. He parked next to one of the trucks. Carefully he took the key out of the ignition switch and climbed from the car. He locked the doors before entering the diner.

The moment the combined warmth and the thick odors of cooking struck him after closing the door, he was glad he had stopped. There was a light snow outside and it had been cold, in spite of his keeping the heater going.

Tomlinson walked past the cash register on the end of the counter and headed for a Formica-topped table. Three men were sitting on stools at the counter itself, leaning over plates of food. Behind the counter was a girl in a starched uniform and a man in an apron and chef's cap. The girl came at once to the table where Tomlinson sat, feeling for the first time a sense of complete exhaustion. She had a typed menu in her hands and gave it to him wordlessly. He didn't look at it.

"Hot roast beef sandwich," he said. "And a cup of coffee—I'll take the coffee now. Then some pie and some more coffee."

"What kind of pie?"

"Apple, if you have it."

The girl said she did and left. Passing around the end of the counter, she stopped momentarily and reaching up to a shelf over her head, adjusted the television set, which was turned on but which, until she turned the knob, was soundless.

"See if you can get the race results, sis," one of the men at the counter called out.

"They'll be on right after the six-fifteen news," the girl said.

Tomlinson was listening closely as an unctuous-voiced announcer finished a commercial extolling the health-giving qualities of a certain cigarette, which seemed, because of its extra length and amount of tobacco, superior in every sense to the normal-size smoke.

A moment later the news commentator of a chain program originating in New York, took the air. His first few minutes were devoted to world-wide and national news events and then he was interrupted by another commercial. When he returned to the air, he gave the latest news of metropolitan New York. The first item had to do with the sensational murder of a young school girl out on Long Island; the murder of Louisa Mary Julio and the discovery of her brutally violated body in the quiet, peaceful suburb of Fairlawn Acres.

Tomlinson, his face studiously blank, looked up as a picture of the scene in front of the Kitteridges' house was flashed on the screen. A moment later the picture shifted and it showed several men walking up the front steps of a police station.

"Late this afternoon," the announcer's voice said, "a man named Leonard Neilsen, who lives with his wife and one child at 96 Crescent Drive in Fairlawn, two houses away from where the child's body was found, was taken into custody by Nassau County Police and is being held for questioning in connection with the crime. It has been learned that Nielsen had deep scratches on his hands and face."

Gerald Tomlinson quickly dropped his eyes and reached for the cup of coffee on the table in front of him. The sense of relief he suddenly felt was so overpowering that he had difficulty in controlling his expression and his emotions.

"Neilsen!"

Yes, there could be no doubt of it. That was the name all right. That was the man. The man whose presence had so completely upset his own plans.

God, what a break! The thing seemed almost too good to be true. Here he,

Tomlinson, was gambling everything on sudden flight and all because some drunk had accidentally stumbled on him while...

He drew a long breath and took another sip of the coffee. So—the police had Neilsen and they were holding him for the girl's murder. It was almost too much of a coincidence. It was the one break he had needed.

Tomlinson was thoroughly familiar with the workings of police departments. He understood the mentality of a detective; knew exactly how they operated. They had a nice sensational murder on their hands; they had the body of the victim and they had a prime suspect. What in the hell had he, Tomlinson, been worrying about anyway? Those cops wouldn't be thinking of a robbery which had happened twenty miles away and which was out of their district in any case. They wouldn't be thinking of a dead man with a bullet hole in the center of his forehead. A dead man they didn't even know existed. They'd be thinking of only one thing: getting enough evidence to send a man named Leonard Neilsen to the electric chair.

When Tomlinson left the diner some ten minutes later, he deliberately headed the sedan's nose south. He started back for New York; for Long Island and Fairlawn Acres. He was safe; he'd continue to be safe. All he had to do was sit tight and let events take their course. Gerald Tomlinson was, after a number of bad breaks and detours, back on his original schedule.

It was shortly after midnight when Tomlinson reached Crescent Drive and slowed down to make the turn into his garage. He noticed that although his own house was dark, there were lights on in the living room of the house next door; the house in which the Neilsens lived. He had also observed the two cars parked in front of the place. He smiled thinly as he entered his house by the back door.

Each Saturday afternoon for the last two decades, Martin Swazy, senior member of Swazy, Steele, Caldwalder and Kohn, had played nine holes of golf on the links of the Westchester Country Club. When the weather made this impossible, he played bridge in the clubhouse. The routine had never varied, with the exception of two tragic occasions; the first being the sudden death of his wife in a car accident on the Taconic Parkway, and the second when he received notice that his only son was missing in action over North Korea.

Martin Swazy was not a man to let trifling matters interfere with the routine pattern of his ways. This characteristic was both admirable and appropriate, in view of the fact that Martin Swazy was widely recognized as one of the most astute attorneys in New York, and, in fact, the entire country. The firm of Swazy, Steele, Caldwalder and Kohn specialized in corporation law. Among their more important clients was the Eastern Engineering Company and they had handled the firm's work for a good many years. Swazy himself devoted a large part of his time to the company's business and he was a close friend, as well, of George Randolph, the senior vice-president.

It was probably more because of this personal friendship than the actual business relationship that Martin Swazy permitted an interruption to his usual plans for Saturday afternoon and evening.

The message from Randolph reached the lawyer as he was about to deal, from the south position, the first hand in the second rubber. It was brought to him by one of the bellboys and the wording of the message was sufficiently dramatic to cause an interruption in Swazy's deal. The message was very short. It read: "Call me at my hotel at once. A matter of absolute and vital necessity. I shall wait to hear from you." It was signed, "George Randolph."

The use of such strong language on the part of George Randolph had been inspired by an overwhelming sense of guilt. The vice-president of Eastern Engineering had learned of Len Neilsen's trouble only a few minutes before he called the attorney; word had come to him from that same Dr. Peatri with whom he and Len had been drinking the previous evening. The doctor's wife had seen the story in the late afternoon editions of the newspapers and had at once recognized Len's name as that of the rather nice young man she had met with George Randolph. She couldn't quite believe, for a moment or so, that it really was the same young man, but then as she had read further in the story, and encountered Len's address and the name of his wife, Allie, there had no longer been room for doubt. She remembered only too well of Len's talking to her, in a rather maudlin fashion it must be admitted, of his place out at Fairlawn Acres and his wife and his little boy.

Mrs. Peatri was shocked beyond words and at once called her husband's attention to the thing. He had called Randolph.

George Randolph had, of course, in turn called the police and verified the facts. The police had been signally uncommunicative, but at least he'd been able to learn that it really was Len Neilsen they were holding and that he was being detained at headquarters in Mineola.

Randolph didn't for one moment consider the possibility of Len being guilty of the heinous crime. He considered himself an excellent judge of character—which is the principal reason he had detected in Len those sterling qualities which had inspired him to promote him to office manager of the firm. Randolph figured only one thing; it had been obvious to him the previous evening that Len had not been used to drinking and that the liquor had had an unusually violent effect upon him. At the time this had merely amused Randolph, but now he found it hard to forgive himself for having encouraged, in fact, almost forced, the boy to overindulge. Somehow or other, Len had managed to get himself into this terrible thing and it was beyond doubt merely a result of his having been drunk and probably unable to explain the facts of the case to the police.

There was only one thing for Randolph to do; he must get hold of Swazy, the firm's attorney and his own good friend, and get Len out of it as soon as possible, before there was any further unfavorable publicity. It was not only a matter of a responsibility which Randolph felt fell squarely on his shoulders—there was also the matter of the firm's reputation.

Even as Randolph reached for the phone to get in touch with Martin Swazy, he smiled just slightly and stopped worrying temporarily. A damned unfortunate thing all around, but hell, he'd have it all straightened out in no time at all.

But it wasn't quite that simple.

Swazy had had very little experience with criminal law, but even he realized it wasn't going to be a simple matter of calling the Nassau County Police and explaining things to them over the telephone. He tried to convince Randolph that the best course would be to let things develop over the week end and get started on Monday morning, when they'd know a little more about the matter. George was having none of that.

"O.K. Martin," Randolph told the attorney, "if you can't do it over the phone, the only thing then is for you to get right out and I'll take a cab out from here. Save time all around. I'll meet you at police headquarters, wherever that may be."

Swazy, with considerable reluctance, agreed to do just that. It was a damned nuisance, but after all, Eastern Engineering was just about the most important client Swazy, Steele, Caldwalder and Kohn carried on their books.

Things didn't go at all as Randolph had planned. In the first place, Martin Swazy was late in arriving and Randolph spent a full three-quarters of an hour pacing back and forth in front of police headquarters waiting for him, which did little to improve his frame of mind. And then when the attorney did finally show up and they went inside and asked to see Len Neilsen, they were ushered into the presence of a lieutenant of detectives who, although very polite, was completely uncooperative.

"You don't seem to understand," he told them after the preliminary skirmishing, "this man, Leonard Neilsen, is being held on a homicide charge. The fact is, we expect to have him indicted for first degree murder. He has only been in custody a matter of hours; he's still being questioned. I'd like to be able to oblige you, gentlemen, but there isn't the slightest chance in the world of letting him out on bail."

Swazy, in spite of his lack of criminal experience, was willing to let it go at that; he could see the complete impossibility of their position. But Randolph was made of sterner stuff.

"All right," Randolph said. "All right. So you feel you have the right man.

You're entitled to do your job the way you see it. On the other hand, I insist the prisoner has some rights. Mr. Swazy here is his attorney. Neilsen has a right to see his attorney. I believe that is the privilege of any prisoner. If you won't let me talk to Len, then at least let Mr. Swazy see him."

Lieutenant Giddeon hesitated. He had never heard of Martin Swazy or even the firm of Swazy, Steele, Caldwalder and Kohn and had no idea of that firm's importance. Swazy himself had hardly opened his mouth during the interview. On the other hand, this man Randolph was, without a doubt, a big shot of some sort. He seemed like a man who would have connections and important ones. There was no point in antagonizing him. Not that Lieutenant Giddeon was going to let anyone, big shot or not, tell him how to run his business. But the prisoner did have certain rights and it wouldn't really matter whether the attorney talked to him now or later.

After all, the police weren't beating the man or misusing him. They were merely questioning him and could be interrupted for a few minutes. Giddeon, by this time, was convinced in his own mind that he had an open-and-shut case.

He called a plain-clothes man and gave him instructions to permit Swazy to see Neilsen.

"He can have a half an hour," he said.

While Swazy was gone, Giddeon talked with George Randolph. He explained exactly what had happened. "It isn't a matter of whether you, or I, think Neilsen is guilty," he said. "It doesn't matter what anyone thinks. Certainly it is unimportant that you—or I—believe he is not the sort of man to commit this particular type of crime. We have to go on the facts. And the facts are beginning to look pretty conclusive."

He went on then, for the next few minutes, enumerating a number of the facts.

"So you see," he ended up, "we do have quite a bit of evidence. And then, to top it all off, there's that story Neilsen came in and told us. You must admit that it was pretty incredible. A little too fantastic. The thing might just possibly have had some substance to it—if it hadn't been for this other thing. This business of the girl.

"I'm not even saying that Neilsen may not, in his drunken condition, have believed the story. That's possible. I can see how it might have happened. He was drunk and he didn't remember a lot of things. Just that there was a dead body and that he was running through back yards and so on. Except—and this is giving him all the best of it—he didn't really remember what happened. It could be that way. I don't really know. But I do know this; the police can't work on the premise of completely fantastic coincidences. Particularly when we have a file of concrete evidence stacking up against a man. And that we have."

By the time Swazy had returned from seeing Len Neilsen, Randolph realized this was one matter which he "wouldn't straighten out right away."

The two men stopped at a nearby restaurant for coffee after leaving the station house. Martin Swazy seemed very uneasy.

"Well," Randolph said, as soon as they were seated and ordered sandwiches and coffee, "well, what did he have to say?"

For a long moment, Martin Swazy looked at the other man. When he finally spoke, he avoided the question.

"George," Swazy said, "George, you know this sort of thing is really out of my field. After all, Swazy, Steele, Caldwalder and Kohn..."

"Goddamn it, I know all about Swazy, Steele, Caldwalder and Kohn. I also know all about your 'field.' Haven't we been paying you around a hundred thousand a year now for the last fifteen years? Just tell me what he had to say."

Swazy was unruffled by the other's words and he continued to look at him with half-closed, but unperturbed eyes.

"That's just the point," he said. "What he had to say."

"Stop being a damned lawyer," Randolph barked. "Don't go beating about the bush, Martin. Just tell me."

Swazy nodded and changed his tone. If Randolph wanted it between the eyes, that's the way he'd give it to him.

"The damndest silly story I ever heard in my life," Swazy said. "In fact, I could swear the man must still be drunk. He even smelled like it. Smelled like a stale brewery. Anyway, all he did was to completely deny ever having seen the girl or ever having heard about her. But when I asked him what he was doing last night, that is last night after you'd put him in the cab and sent him home, he gave me a completely fantastic story. Something about getting into the wrong house, which he cannot identify, and finding a dead man, and..."

"I know, I know," Randolph interrupted. "The lieutenant told me about it. I must admit that it sounds just a little bit strange."

"Strange! Why it's..."

"Yes, I understand. But tell me, Martin, do you think Neilsen may have become temporarily, well say, perhaps have lost his mind or something?"

"If he expects anyone to believe that story of his, he's certainly..."

"All right, Martin," Randolph again interrupted. "We'll skip the story for the time being. Now tell me this. Do you think Neilsen is guilty—that he killed the girl?"

Swazy looked at Randolph and his expression was slightly shocked.

"Now George," he said, "that's hardly the sort of..."

"For Christ's sake, stop equivocating," Randolph said. "Stop being a goddamned lawyer. Just answer my question. Do you think he's guilty?"

Swazy hesitated for another moment or two and then spoke in a low voice.

"Frankly, I do," he said.

"Let's go out and see Mrs. Neilsen," Randolph said. He reached for the check.

George Randolph and Martin Swazy were still at the Neilsen house at the time Gerald Tomlinson passed on his way home, late Saturday night. They had been joined by a third man, one I. Oscar Leavy. I. Oscar Leavy was, like Martin Swazy, an attorney. Although he was considered by a number of persons, including several judges and a good many fellow lawyers, the top man in his particular field, he and Swazy had never before met and the chances are, had it not been for the Julio case, they never would have met. Leavy was probably the best criminal lawyer in the East and very possibly the best anywhere.

It was while Allie Neilsen was in the kitchen, making a pot of coffee, that the decision had been made. The two men had already talked with her for better than a half an hour and Randolph had suddenly come to the conclusion that what Martin had told him in the car on the way to the house had been right. It wasn't at all the sort of case for a firm like Swazy, Steele, Caldwalder and Kohn. It wasn't a matter of whether Neilsen was guilty or not guilty. That was beside the point. What was needed was a smart criminal lawyer, a man who knew his way around in matters of this sort. The fact Randolph had become convinced that Neilsen probably was guilty, made it all the more apparent.

George Randolph created an opportunity for a quick few words with Swazy, by suggesting coffee to Mrs. Neilsen, right after she had finished repeating the very story Len had told the lawyer and that the lieutenant had told Randolph himself. The moment she was out of the room, Randolph turned to Swazy and spoke in a low voice.

"All right, Martin," he said. "I guess you're right. We're going to need a specialist. Who would you suggest?"

"Well, Monday morning I'll get together with..."

"The hell with Monday morning," Randolph said. His jaw was very square and Swazy recognized the hard, aggressive expression on his face which was so familiar from past experiences when Randolph had insisted on taking the immediate, though possibly more risky, course when it might have been safer to have been a little more cautious in making decisions.

"The hell with Monday. Who's the best criminal lawyer available?"

"Well, I guess you'd say that Leavy is, I. Oscar Leavy. Used to be a magistrate and before that was an assistant district attorney. Doesn't have the most savory reputation, possibly, but he's..."

"I don't give a damn about the man's reputation," Randolph said. "I just want to know if he handles this sort of thing—and if he gets his clients off."

"He gets them off," Swazy said. There was faint disapproval in his tone.

"Then get him on the phone and get him over here." Swazy looked at Randolph in surprise.

"Now George," he said. "I don't know. After all, this man Leavy is pretty expensive. And after all, Saturday night and..."

"I don't give a goddamn how expensive he is," Randolph said. "And as far as Saturday night and so forth, that's probably why he's expensive. He's undoubtedly used to working at all sorts of hours—if he's the kind of fellow you say he is and the kind that we're looking for. You see if you can get hold of him and have him get out here. I'll go in and talk with Mrs. Neilsen."

Leavy, fortunately, lived in Old Westbury. Also, fortunately, he was home when Martin Swazy telephoned. I. Oscar Leavy was, as Swazy had said, a top criminal lawyer. Not only that, but he had an almost psychic insight into the private assets of a potential client.

He knew the firm of Swazy, Steele, Caldwalder and Kohn, by reputation. He knew the type of client in which a firm of this sort would be interested. He didn't hesitate to call his chauffeur and come running the minute he hung up the receiver.

The thing which Swazy never did realize is that Leavy would have probably taken the Neilsen case even if it was not for the fabulous fee which George Randolph privately agreed to pay him for handling the matter. It was the sort of case on which Leavy thrived.

A young, beautiful girl murdered, possibly a sex attack. Headlines. It was right down his alley. The publicity alone, especially when the client was ready-made for the tabloids, would be well worth it. The fact that the client, as Leavy determined a few moments after his arrival at the Neilsen home, was probably guilty as hell, just made it that much the better.

Allie Neilsen was crying when George Randolph went into the kitchen while Swazy got busy on the phone.

An odd thought crossed Randolph's mind as he looked at her standing near the stove, the tears falling gently down her pale cheeks. If Len killed that girl—and Randolph was pretty much convinced that he had—it couldn't be any simple sex crime. The liquor must have driven him temporarily insane. No young fellow of Len's caliber, with a wife like this, would go around raping and murdering young girls if he were in his right mind.

Once more Randolph experienced a sense of deep guilt. He'd gotten the boy drunk. Well, he'd get him out of this mess, no matter how much it cost or what he had to do.

He walked over and patted Allie Neilsen on the shoulder.

"Now stop that," he said. "You don't have to cry. We'll get your boy out of this."

Allie looked up at him.

"He didn't do it," she said. "Len didn't do it. I don't care how drunk he was or anything else, Len didn't do it."

Randolph knew that she really believed this; knew there was no question at all in her mind.

"It doesn't matter," he said. "Doesn't matter. We'll get him off all right."

A moment later and he felt like biting his tongue off. Seeing the look in her eyes, as she stared at him, understanding—understanding that she knew what he thought, he cursed himself for being the world's biggest idiot. Yes, she knew what he was thinking. There was no mistaking the gradual look of horror which came into her face as she stepped back to stare up at him.

Chapter Ten

It is an established fact that all too frequently violence seems to set off a sort of chain reaction; as though the very fact of an initial act of violence were to spark a veritable epidemic which travels from one person to another, in greater or lesser forms, so that before long people who have had no connection with the first event are involved in all sorts of odd situations which could not be foreseen and to which they react in various fashions.

In a way, that is what happened when Gerald Tomlinson first lifted his arm to bring a revolver butt down on the skull of Angelo Bertolli as that unfortunate man was about to make a deposit of the horse-parlor money in the South Shore Bank.

By Tuesday of the following week, this strange epidemic seemed to reach its climax, so far as its widespreading aspects were concerned, although the intensity of the disease had thinned out and grown comparatively anemic by this time.

Tuesday was a significant day in the lives of a number of people, none of whom had ever as much as heard of Bertolli, the private detective.

First there was young Peter Doyle. Peter received the first real thrashing he had ever had in his life and although he was completely innocent of any wrong doing at that time, it was without doubt a licking he'd had coming for a number of years.

Howard McNally, who usually never took a drink before sundown, managed to get drunk before noon and the sudden Dutch courage inspired by the liquor misled him into striking his wife, Myrtle, who in turn gave him a beating with a leather belt.

Grace and Tom Swanson had an equally bitter domestic scene, although no physical violence was involved.

Marian Tomlinson lost her head completely when her brother-in-law struck her daughter after the child admitted having left the house the previous Saturday. In losing her head, she also, for the first time, temporarily lost her fear and dared to talk back to Gerald, who in turn beat her so badly that she was unable to see out of one eye for a week and carried a broken nose on her already plain face for the rest of her life.

Mrs. Julio, the dead child's mother, missed her daughter's funeral when she suddenly became hysterical, a condition which swiftly developed into a state of temporary insanity and was responsible for her being taken to a hospital and placed under sedatives.

Even gentle little Mrs. Kitteridge and her husband had sharp words for the only time in their lives.

It was almost as though an evil curse had fallen over the residents of Fairlawn Acres. The thing which made it so strange, of course, was that with the exception of one of these cases, each particular act of violence followed immediately upon the heels of a visit from Allie Neilsen, who, suffering her own particular brand of grief, certainly hadn't the slightest intention of triggering difficulty for anyone else.

But that was on Tuesday.

Monday was something else. Monday, the day during which Allie went through enough emotional tension and violence—as far as her feelings were concerned—to serve the entire population of the suburb. On Monday Allie was permitted to see Len for the first time since his arrest. She saw Len but only after she had talked with the man who had been selected to defend her husband, I. Oscar Leavy.

Leavy telephoned Allie while she was still having breakfast. It wasn't really breakfast, merely a cup of black coffee and a cigarette. She hadn't even cared about the coffee, but little Billy was having his breakfast and she wanted to sit with him. She knew the child was restless and upset; Billy sensed that something was going on and the fact that no one was able to explain it to him, made things very difficult.

Billy had been asking for his daddy ever since Lieutenant Giddeon had taken Len away. Allie had tried to explain that Daddy was "away on business," but it had been a thin explanation at best and this combined with the comings and goings in the house, as well as the additional fact that he'd not been allowed out to play as usual, had been enough to throw his emotional balance completely off center. Billy knew something was very wrong and he wanted to know what it was all about.

So Allie had sat down at the table with him while he had his cereal and milk and tried to pretend everything was normal. She didn't fool him at all.

Allie was still stalling, still avoiding his curious eyes and his questions, when the telephone rang. She recognized Leavy's high-pitched voice at once.

"Has the press been around?" was his first question after he had told her who it was that was calling.

"Not this morning," Allie said. "But yesterday, all day..."

"I know." The attorney spoke quickly and wasted no time. Whatever was on his mind, Allie realized, must be urgent. "You'll be seeing a lot of them before they are through, I'm afraid. I was just worried that they had already arrived."

"Why? Why, has something else..." There was sudden alarm in her voice.

"Now there's nothing to get upset about," Leavy quickly said. "It's just that I'm afraid there is going to be an indictment the first thing this morning. And I don't want you to see anyone or talk with anyone."

"I want to talk to Len," Allie said. She found it hard to keep her tone level. She suddenly wanted to start crying all over again. "They've got to let me see..."

"Now listen, Mrs. Neilsen," Leavy spoke quickly. "Listen, I'm going to try and arrange it today. I'm sure that I can. But right now this is more important. If any reporters come around, or anyone else for that matter, I don't want you to admit them. I don't want you to even answer the phone again after I hang up. Understand? Don't see or talk with anyone."

"What..."

"I'll explain when I see you. I'm coming right out. Just do as I say. Don't answer the phone or the doorbell. I'll be there in less than an hour."

The doorbell began to ring as the lawyer hung up on her. For a moment Allie sat there and then she suddenly jumped to her feet. She had become aware of Billy going into the hallway to answer the doorbell.

"Billy," she said, "Billy, come here dear. Mother will get it."

Billy stopped and looked at her.

"Go back and finish your breakfast," Allie said. "I'll take care of it dear."

A moment later, as Allie stood in the hallway and looked through the diamond shaped small pane of glass in the center of the front door, she realized how right the attorney had been. Outside stood two men and a woman. One of the men wore a camera strapped over his shoulder and carried a leather case which she guessed must contain his photographic equipment. The second man she recognized as a newspaper reporter she had talked with the previous day. The woman, little more than a girl, was dressed in a severe tweed suit and wore a small black hat on her short blond curls.

The bell stopped ringing and Allie quickly shook her head back and forth. She could just make out the words as one of the men called her name.

Again Allie shook her head and turned to leave. The doorbell again began ringing.

For a moment she hesitated, and then, trying her best to ignore the shrill sound of the bell, she started for the kitchen. This time she was unable to keep the tears back.

Twice within the next hour the phone rang for long intervals, but each time Allie steadfastly refused to answer. Once again the doorbell rang and for a while, Allie ignored it. And then it occurred to her that it might be the attorney and so she got up from the table and again went down the hallway. By this time Billy was crying. He didn't quite know why, but he just felt like crying.

It was Leavy and there was a middle-aged woman with him. As Allie opened the door to let them in, she saw a man leap from a car parked down the street. It was one of the newspaper people.

Leavy himself locked the door after them when they had entered.

"We'd better go into the living room," he said. "Oh, by the way, this is Mrs. Manning. She's a nurse. I've brought her to look after the youngster."

Allie automatically turned and said hello, then quickly turned back to the lawyer, who was busy removing his neatly pressed topcoat.

"A nurse?" she said, surprised. "But I don't need a nurse. I can take care of Billy all right myself. I didn't ask..."

Leavy interrupted her in a kind, but determined tone.

"Please don't ask any questions just now," he said. "You will need someone here. If you are to see your husband, someone will have to stay..."

"But I've already planned to have my aunt come in from..."

"Please listen, Mrs. Neilsen. Let Mrs. Manning go in with the child for the time being and explain everything to you."

Allie nodded in an almost half-conscious way, as though none of it was quite clear to her.

"Billy's in the kitchen," she said, almost listlessly.

"Take Mrs. Manning in and introduce them to each other and then come to the living room."

Allie obeyed. Five minutes later she was back in the living room talking with the attorney. Billy, finding someone to talk with him for a change, had quickly dried his tears. He took to the woman at once, especially after she had told him that she'd *like* to see his electric train.

"It's like this, Mrs. Neilsen," Leavy was explaining. "I don't want you sending the child away while all this is going on. It's much better that you stay here together. And you should have someone..."

"But I've already explained," Allie said. "My aunt is coming and anyway, we can't afford a nurse. Especially now..." Once more she felt the tears coming to her eyes.

Leavy again interrupted.

"It isn't a case of not affording," he explained. "It's what's best. You must let me handle things in my own. Everything has been arranged by Mr. Randolph. He's taking care of..."

"Mr. Randolph?"

"Yes. You see, he is determined to see this thing through. To stand by your husband. He's turned the defense over to me and has instructed me to take complete charge. Now..."

"But what has Len's defense got to do with..."

The lawyer reached out and sort of half patted Allie on the shoulder.

"A thing like this is very complicated. You want to see your husband go free, now don't you Mrs. Neilsen?"

"Why of course. Of course I want to see..."

"Then you must let me do things my own way. In this type of case it is frequently more important what takes place before the trial than during the trial. The general impression the public has of the prisoner and his family..." he went on talking and suddenly Allie was no longer listening to the smooth, unctuous phrases.

"This type of case."

My God, Allie thought, can this really be me? Can this thing actually be happening to Len and myself and even to Billy? This odd little fat man with his immaculate clothes, his precise high-pitched voice with the Brooklyn accent and his white, pudgy manicured fingers—can he actually be sitting here talking as though Len...

But once more the voice came through and she was aware of the words.

"So you see that it is vitally important the press learn only what we want them to learn. That, as much as possible, we try to form a sympathetic picture of Neilsen and Neilsen's family. That you be protected, by competent people, from questions which might be embarrassing. Which reminds me, about the story your husband first told. The business of getting into some wrong house and finding a dead man and all of that. I can't..."

Allie looked up quickly. "Len's story?" she said. "What about Len's story? It's the truth, Mr. Leavy. Len would no more tell a lie than..."

The attorney nodded his small round head.

"Of course, Mrs. Neilsen," he said. "Of course. I'm not questioning the story. It isn't a case of whether it's true or it isn't true. It doesn't matter even whether it actually happened or your husband, in his condition, just imagined it happened. The point is..."

"But if Len says it happened, it did," Allie spoke almost sharply. "I can assure you..."

Once more Leavy interrupted.

"You must try to understand me, Mrs. Neilsen. And please let me finish.

Let me explain."

He was being very patient; Allie could see that he was taking her emotional condition into consideration and being patient. She bit back the words she was about to say and nodded, dumbly.

"The one thing we have all got to do is to forget that story. If I am to defend your husband—and to have him cleared—above all else, we must forget any story about his being drunk and wandering into the wrong house and finding dead men lying around. There are several lines of defense which I may or may not use. It will depend largely on developments and the way things turn out. But no matter what method of procedure I shall take, we certainly cannot depend on anything as fragile and nebulous as Mr. Neilsen's original story of what happened on Friday night—or Saturday morning to be exact.

"It is possible, that as a last resort I might have to use a temporary insanity approach, although I..."

In spite of herself, Allie once more interrupted.

"Do you for one moment think that my husband actually had anything to do with killing..."

Leavy stood up this time and reaching out put both hands on Allie's shoulders, almost as though to hold her back in the chair.

"No—no, nothing at all like that, Mrs. Neilsen," he said. "You simply have to try to understand me. At this point, the police have a good case, a very good case. It doesn't matter in the slightest what we think. It doesn't matter that Mr. Neilsen can be completely without guilt. He looks guilty and the police feel that he is guilty and they have a great deal of substantial facts to back up their theory. We have to try to set up an equally strong set of facts to disprove it."

"But then I should think learning the truth, what really happened that night, would..."

Leavy shook his head, fighting to keep the irritation out of his voice and his expression.

"The truth is meaningless unless you can get someone to believe it," he said. "In order to believe Mr. Neilsen's story, you'll first have to produce a body. The body of a dead *man*. At the moment, the body the police are concerned with is that of a dead girl."

Allie sank back in the chair. She didn't interrupt again, but just sat and stared at him, her face white and her eyes wide as he continued to talk.

"No. The story is out. If it should come up in court, and it probably will, we shall have to figure some answer for it at the time. But in the meantime, the less that it is mentioned, the better. Our best bet, at this moment, is to firmly establish in the minds of the public—and don't forget that the jury will be selected from that public—that your husband *couldn't* have done the murder. That he just isn't that sort of person. That you and he are happily married, a normal young couple with a healthy, happy child. That he could have no possible motive for committing such a crime. As to his alibi and his activities at the time—well, we'll work that out as the case develops."

He hesitated and taking a white linen handkerchief from his breast pocket, carefully patted the bulging brow under his neatly parted white hair.

"And now, if you'd like, I suggest we leave the child with Mrs. Manning and you come with me. I shall try and arrange for you to see your husband. Will you be able to reach that aunt you talked about and cancel her visit?"

"I guess I can reach her," Allie said.

Twenty minutes later they left the house together. A couple of the reporters waiting outside immediately climbed into a cab to trail Leavy's chauffeur-driven limousine. The others remained outside the house.

Leavy would have to leave after taking her to the police station, but would arrange for a cab to take her back home.

Her conversation with the attorney had been difficult; the one she had with Len an hour later almost completely broke up Allie's determined desire to maintain her control and not go to pieces.

They didn't even let her kiss him.

The entire thing only lasted a few short minutes and perhaps it was just as well that it did. Sitting across from him and watching his face—the two of them were on opposite sides of a wide table and there was a glass partition between them so that they were unable to have any physical contact—Allie at once observed the dark blotches beneath Len's bloodshot eyes and saw the tired, beaten look on his face. It took all of her control to keep from crying, but she managed a little half smile. His voice came to her through a small screened opening in the glass partition and it didn't even sound like Len when he spoke.

For the first half of the interview, all they seemed to do was reassure each other that there was nothing to worry about. Nothing at all. Len kept asking after Billy and telling her, Allie, not to worry, that everything would be straightened out. And Allie kept telling him that she and Billy were fine and that there was nothing for *him* to worry about. But each was lying and each knew that the other was lying.

Each was aware that Len had already been indicted on a charge of first degree murder.

There was a guard in the room and he could hear every word each of them spoke, although he had an indifferent and disinterested look on his stolid face. Finally, after nervously looking over at the guard, Allie changed the tenor of her conversation.

"Len," she said, "Len, they don't believe your story. You know, about the wrong house and the dead man and all."

He nodded at her through the glass, his eyes somber.

"I know," he said. "Nobody believes. No one at all, Allie. Not even my own lawyer or anyone."

"If we could only prove it," Allie said. "If there was only some way..."

Len shook his head.

"There's no way," he said. "As far as everyone but myself is concerned, it just didn't happen."

Allie looked up at him.

"I believe it, darling," she said. "I believe anything and everything you have ever told me. I believe you and I love you."

This time the tears did come and in spite of every ounce of will power she could exert, they trickled slowly down her cheeks.

"Baby," Len said quickly. "Baby, don't cry. Don't—please don't honey."

"I'm not crying," Allie said. She wiped at her face with a tiny handkerchief.

"As long as you believe in me," Len said, "nothing can happen. Everything will be all right. Somehow or other..."

They talked for another five or six minutes and then the guard told them their time was up.

Allie sat there while they led him out of the room. It wasn't until the door closed behind him that she really cried.

Her eyes were red and swollen when Lieutenant Giddeon passed her in the hallway as she was leaving. She was hurrying, but he had enough time to see her and to recognize her. He followed her out of the building, catching up with her as she reached the sidewalk.

"One minute," he said, quickly stepping to her side. "Just one minute, if you don't mind, Mrs. Neilsen. I'd like to talk with you."

Allie hesitated, looking up half blindly and not recognizing the policeman at first.

Moments later they were sitting alone in his private office. He'd sent down for containers of coffee and Allie was having coffee and a slice of toast, which he had also ordered and which he insisted that she eat.

Lieutenant Giddeon waited until she had finished with the toast and coffee before he spoke.

"Mrs. Neilsen," he said, at last, "I don't want you to think of me as an enemy."

Allie looked up at him and in spite of herself, her lips formed a bitter smile.

"No?" she said. "No, Lieutenant? You are trying to put my husband into the electric chair, aren't you, Lieutenant? Should I think of you as a friend?"

"Now Mrs. Neilsen," the lieutenant said. "Now Mrs. Neilsen, that's not quite true. I'm trying to put the man who killed the Julio girl in the electric chair. I'm sure that even you, Mrs. Neilsen, are willing to admit the child was slain—brutally slain. And I think you will agree that the killer should be made to pay for his crime."

"Then why don't you find the killer?"

"That's what we are trying to do," the lieutenant said. "At the moment we are holding your husband. We are holding him because he is unable to establish an alibi for the time of the crime, because we found him with his hands and face scratched and with blood on them. Because his hat and his glasses were found beside the body. Because he admittedly was drinking on the night of the murder and can give us no clear explanation of these various circumstances."

Allie nodded, not in agreement, but merely as an indication that she was following him.

"I can't explain about the hat and the glasses," she said. "Neither can Len. He only knows that he lost them. And had been drinking. He even came in and told you about it. As for his alibi, he explained. He explained everything."

"He told us a story. The same story he told you. But I am asking you, Mrs. Neilsen, what proof has he offered? For the moment, we may overlook the completely fantastic quality of that story. We can even overlook the unbelievable coincidence of two murders in the same place on the same night and so forth. But where is the proof? What house *was* your husband in? Don't forget—it could have been the McNally house, assuming he went to the wrong place. And if he saw a dead man—where is that man now? No, Mrs. Neilsen, he'll have to do better than merely have a story. He'll have to have some facts to back up that story."

"But you are not giving him a chance to get those facts!" Allie said. "You've already had him indicted for murder. You're locking him in jail and keeping him there."

"He has an attorney," the lieutenant said. "One of the best in the country, as a matter of fact. I don't like to say this, but your husband's attorney is a man who has a reputation for getting his clients off; clients who all too often are actually guilty. In any case, I am sure that if your husband's story is true, certainly I. Oscar Leavy will be able to find substantiation for it."

"But... but Mr. Leavy doesn't..." Suddenly Allie stopped and bit back the words. What was she saying? Dear Lord, what was she about to say? That not even Len's lawyer believed the story? How could she expect the policeman to believe it if Len's own lawyer didn't. How could she expect anyone to believe it?

"You were about to say, Mrs. Neilsen?"

"I was about to say that Mr. Leavy is doing everything he can."

"I'm sure he is. Frankly, I'll tell you, Mrs. Neilsen. When I first met your husband, I liked him. He still seemed a little hungover at the time and he wasn't quite clear about things, but I liked him. I like you. You seem like an ideal couple. But right after your husband came and told me that story of being drunk and finding a dead man and all, right after, he went out and at once got drunk all over again. You tell me he almost never drinks. It just doesn't make sense. Something had to be wrong."

Allie looked at him and there was a frown on her face.

"What is it you want from me?" she asked. "What do you want, anyway? Haven't you done enough? Haven't you..."

"I want to help you if I can," the lieutenant said. "You'll be talking to your husband now and then. I want you to ask him to tell us the truth." He hesitated for a minute and looked at Allie with a curious and almost paternal expression.

"Perhaps I shouldn't tell you this," he said, "but an autopsy has been performed on the dead girl. She died of a vicious blow on the back of her head. There were finger marks on her throat and she had been partially choked. Her mouth was bruised and her clothes badly torn. But she hadn't been raped and apparently no attempt had been made to abuse her—if you know what I mean?"

Allie looked at him and nodded.

"Obviously the motive wasn't robbery. It couldn't very well have been revenge or anything of that sort. She was merely attacked and killed. A silly, insane sort of crime. What I am getting at is this. Isn't it just possible that your husband may have, in a temporary insane drunken condition..."

"No!" Allie almost screamed it. "No, no and no! Not ever. You don't know Len, you don't understand him. Len is completely sane. No matter how much he may have been drinking, he couldn't possibly, ever, do anything like that."

Lieutenant Giddeon still looked sympathetic, but he half shrugged.

"In that case," he said, and then stopped. He didn't quite know what to say. He started again.

"In that case, you must try to make him remember a little more about what he said really did happen. He must explain about the hat and the glasses and all the rest of it. He must remember and explain—and get some sort of concrete proof."

Allie stood up.

"I think I'll leave now," she said.

"I'll have a car take you home," Lieutenant Giddeon said. "Mr. Leavy arranged for a cab, but I'll have a police car take you back home so you won't be annoyed by reporters or anyone."

Chapter Eleven

Sometime during the lonely, bitter hours of that Monday night, as Allie lay wide-eyed and sleepless in the very center of the large double bed, the transition took place within her. Monday night was the worst one yet. The initial stages of shock had receded and she was at last awake to the ultimate tragedy of the situation.

The sense of lostness, inspired to a certain extent by the mere physical absence of Len, from whom she had never been separated since the night of their wedding, gradually began to be replaced by something else. Even that vague, undefinable fear which had so paralyzed her, began to fade, overshadowed by the full realization of the scope of the tragedy which had suddenly blighted her home and her life.

In short, from a little girl who had been playing house with a nice young husband and a pretty baby boy, Allie Neilsen that night developed into a mature and grown woman, ready to bare her claws and fight for that which was her own.

Calmly and collectedly and without tears, Allie lay in her lonely bed, unable to sleep in spite of her bone-weary body, and carefully reviewed everything which had happened. Several significant facts began to make themselves obvious at once.

Len was not guilty. Of that there was no doubt in her mind.

Len was in deep and serious trouble and she, Allie herself, was in a large part responsible. If she hadn't convinced Len to go to the police with the story about getting into the wrong house and finding the dead man, the police probably never would have picked him up as a suspect in the murder of Louisa Julio.

Len's story was true. There had been another house, another bedroom and a man lying on a double bed with a bullet hole through the center of his forehead.

This, at least, was clear in Allie's mind. And from these facts, her thoughts progressed in a logical fashion.

The police, and even Len's own lawyer, disbelieved Len's story of what had taken place that night. They also believed he was guilty of the girl's murder. Consequently, neither the police nor Len's defense attorney would make any particular effort to either verify his story or seek the actual killer.

Verifying Len's story seemed almost impossible, but of that she could not be sure. No one was trying to verify the story.

Finding the real killer seemed equally impossible; but there again, how could anyone expect to find the killer if they were satisfied they already had their man?

Allie alone was the one person who believed in Len. It was up to her, then, to prove his innocence.

Long after midnight, Allie at last found sleep. By no stretch of the imagination could it be said that she had found peace. But the mere fact that she had decided to act, to play a definite part and take a definite stand, did much to relieve the terrible emotional tension under which she had been living these last few days. That—and the natural fatigue which resulted from missed meals and almost no sleep, did it. For Allie Neilsen was, after all, a normal, healthy young animal and the moment she had made up her mind to fight, her subconscious mind went along and agreed to give her the strength for the battle.

Allie slept until daybreak and then quickly got up and showered and prepared breakfast before Billy and Mrs. Manning were awake. As she ate alone in the dinette, she gradually mapped a campaign. She had to start somewhere and it seemed to her that the logical place would be at the scene of the crime—the crime that everyone knew about. Allie decided she would wait until eight o'clock and then pay the Kitteridges a visit.

Martha and Reginald Kitteridge were having tea and scones in the dining room—which had been converted from a bedroom that they didn't need—shortly after eight o'clock when the back doorbell rang. For the first time in as long as either of them could remember, there was a trace of tension in the air. The Kitteridges had gone through many things together and, in their fashion, faced minor and major crises. But never before had there been tension. Another couple might argue, might bicker and nag or occasionally plague each other with recriminations—but not the Kitteridges. Their emotional life had been uniformly serene.

The unfortunate truth was, however, this morning, although no words had been spoken, there was a disturbance in the atmosphere. Martha Kitteridge knew, knew in her heart, that in some odd way her husband held her partly responsible for the terrible thing which had taken place. He had said nothing, but Martha knew. Martha, as always when it came to her husband, was quite right.

It can honestly be said that Reginald Parson Kitteridge, had, in his own way, been completely in love with and completely loyal to his wife during the many years of their marriage. To him, her every desire and wish had been law.

But the fact remains that over and above his feelings for his wife, one greater loyalty and passion ruled Reginald's life. Like almost every other Englishman who was a member of his empire's official family and represented that empire in the far outposts of the world, Reginald Kitteridge had an all-abiding and overwhelming respect for the dignity and position of the great country which he had served so long and faithfully. He may not have represented his nation with extraordinary brilliance, but there could never be any question about his loyalty and his exquisite sense of propriety.

Her Majesty's Government was Reginald's first mistress. Martha Kitteridge ran a close second, but a second. At the very moment the doorbell rang, Reginald was speaking.

"Simply can't understand it, my dear," he said. "Absolutely confounds me. A paper like the *New York Times* mentioning the thing. And mentioning my name and official position in connection with it. Leaves me fairly appalled, it does. Terrible mistake taking the place out here."

He means, thought Martha, it was a terrible mistake in my taking the place out here. Of course Reginald was right so far as the *New York Times* was concerned. But after all...

"There's someone at the back door," Martha said. "I'd better get it, dear."

"If it's one of those damnable journalists..."

But Martha was already on her way to the kitchen.

To Allie, it was obvious at once that the Kitteridges found her presence annoying, although it was equally obvious that the couple were far too well-mannered to do anything but invite her to share their breakfast and treat her with the utmost kindness. Allie had a fleeting moment of regret as Martha Kitteridge insisted she sit down and take a cup of tea with them.

"So good for you, my dear," she said. "Much better than coffee, don't you know."

After a few slightly embarrassed remarks—how was the little boy and so forth—Allie realized that the old couple were much too reserved to ever bring up the subject of the murder. If she was going to find anything out, she'd have to start the ball rolling herself.

Politely, refusing a scone, she looked directly at Mrs. Kitteridge.

"You know that Len, my husband, has been arrested and is going to be held for the girl's murder," she said.

Reginald Kitteridge coughed and half covered his face with his linen napkin. Mrs. Kitteridge put her tea cup down quickly.

"A terrible thing," Martha Kitteridge said. "A really terrible thing. I am sure that Mr. Neilsen had nothing to do with it at all."

"Police make some awfully stupid blunders, you know," Mr. Kitteridge said. "Really, quite stupid."

They continued to protest and Allie had the sudden realization that finally she had found two persons who were not thoroughly convinced that Len was guilty. On the other hand, she quickly reflected, they didn't necessarily think he was innocent, either. It was just that the entire thing was out of their realm of comprehension. A murder which had nothing in the world to do with them and about which they knew nothing. They didn't know who did it; they didn't want to know. They probably didn't even care—just so long as that sort of thing didn't happen again.

"I'm talking to people," Allie quickly said. "Talking and trying to find out anything I can which may help to find who really did commit the crime."

Reginald Kitteridge was first to speak up.

"There's nothing," he said, "nothing at all we can tell you. Like to help of course, and all that, but we know nothing. Told the police as much already."

"I was just wondering if perhaps, the night that the girl was killed, you may have heard anything. You know, noises of people walking around, or anything at all."

"Nothing, my dear," Kitteridge said. There was a note of finality in his voice. "Like to help, but we heard or saw not a thing."

"Not until I saw that poor unfortunate child's body," Mrs. Kitteridge began, but her husband cut her off shortly.

"No point in covering all that again," he said. "None at all. Frankly," he turned to Allie and tried to speak in a kind and understanding manner, "frankly, my dear, we would much prefer to keep out of the limelight."

Allie nodded. She started to rise, and then, once more settled back in her seat.

"There's just one thing," she said. "The hat and the glasses which were found by the juniper bush. The papers said a little boy found them. They must have been there when you looked under the bush."

"I have already said," Reginald began, only to be interrupted by his wife.

"Now that is an odd thing," Martha Kitteridge said. "The fact is, I didn't see them. I'm sure I would have if they had been there, but I certainly didn't see them."

Reginald looked at his wife with the faintest trace of irritation on his normally shy and polite face.

"Nonsense," he said. "Sheer nonsense. The child must have come by early in the morning and found them. And then you came out later and found the body after he had already taken them."

Martha Kitteridge looked relieved and Allie Neilsen looked disappointed.

"Yes—yes, of course. That must have been it."

"May I ask just one more question?" Allie said. "What time did you first go out on Saturday morning?"

Mrs. Kitteridge thought for a moment.

"Well, I was in the yard at around nine o'clock. Yes, just about nine, right after Mr. Kitteridge had left the house. I remember quite clearly."

"And the boy couldn't have come and taken them after that without your having seen him, could he?" Allie asked.

"No, he couldn't."

Allie got up then and thanked both of them. Martha Kitteridge took her to the door.

"Anything I can do, my dear," she said. "Anything at all. Just let me know."

Allie thanked her.

Two minutes later and for the first time in the forty married years of his life, Reginald Parson Kitteridge spoke harshly to his wife.

"You're a damned busybody, Martha," he said. "I told you to stay out of this matter. I have already had more than enough publicity."

Martha Kitteridge stared at her husband wordlessly for a full minute. Her face suddenly took on a firm and defiant expression.

"Reginald," she said, "if there is anything I can do to help those poor children, I'll gladly do it. They are more important than your privacy or the dignity of the entire British Government."

Mr. Kitteridge looked at his wife with shocked disbelief. He couldn't have been more amazed if she had thrown a cup of tea in his face.

Mrs. Patrick Doyle, standing at the sink in the kitchen and peeling the potatoes which would go into the Irish stew which she planned for that evening's dinner, had a sour expression about her usually good-natured mouth. She was thinking of the difficulty a parent encountered who faced the problem of raising an only child. The fact that Peter was an only child was not a biologically planned phenomenon; it was simply the result of an unfortunate physical inability on her own part to bear more children after the birth of her first-born. But Mrs. Doyle, unfairly enough, seemed to blame Peter rather than herself or sheer caprice. Peter was an easy child to blame for almost anything. Especially was this so during these last few days. Peter's sudden overnight elevation to a pinnacle of fame since the discovery of his prominent part in the Julio case by the tabloid papers had so affected the boy that he'd become almost unbearable.

Not only did he seem to live in more of a fog than ever, but the whole thing had so gone to his head that he was no longer manageable.

"Peter, you are already late for school. You'll miss that bus for sure," Ann Doyle suddenly said, turning to where her offspring sat engrossed in the pages of the morning newspaper, his elbows resting on the kitchen table and the bowl of cereal untouched in front of him. "Eat that food and eat it now."

Peter looked up blankly at his mother.

"The *News*," he said, "says right here that me, Peter Doyle, has probably supplied the one most significant clue in the entire case."

"Drop that paper and eat your breakfast!"

Peter turned back to the cereal, but continued to read as he tentatively dipped his spoon in the bowl.

The cereal was still unfinished several moments later when the doorbell rang and Ann Doyle quickly reached for the dish towel to dry her hands before going to answer it. A moment later and she returned to the kitchen, Allie Neilsen walking in front of her. Allie was talking.

"And I really do hate to bother you, but you see I must find out everything I can," she was saying.

Mrs. Doyle had never met Allie, but she knew all about her as a result of the stories in the papers. She was extremely embarrassed, but, basically a kindly woman, she felt sorry for the girl. After all, Mrs. Neilsen was little more than a girl. This morning, even with the dark shadows under her eyes and the pale, drawn face which all too plainly showed the strain of the last few days, she still looked young enough to be Mrs. Doyle's own daughter, had she ever had one. Mrs. Doyle felt very sorry for her.

"Please do have a cup of coffee," she said. "I do understand what you must be going through and..." her voice faded away and Allie smiled weakly at her.

"Thank you," she said. "But I've already had too much coffee. But may I smoke?"

"I'll sit right here and have a cigarette with you," Mrs. Doyle said. "Move a chair up for the lady, Peter."

Peter, somewhat grudgingly, did as he was told; his mother at the same time surreptitiously reached over and took the newspaper from the table.

"This is Mrs. Neilsen, Peter," Mrs. Doyle said.

For a moment it didn't penetrate. Then the boy quickly looked up and openly stared at Allie.

"Gee," he said. "'You're—why it's your old man who's..."

Mrs. Doyle's hand darted out and boxed him on the ear.

"Shut up and finish that breakfast," she said.

Allie sat down and was reaching for a pack of cigarettes in her bag when the other woman offered her own.

"Take one of these, dear," she said.

Allie took one and lighted it.

"I wanted to ask about Saturday morning," Allie said.

Mrs. Doyle looked just the slightest bit defensive. "Yes?"

"Well, about Peter here. He found the hat and glasses you know."

"I know all right," Mrs. Doyle said.

"Would you mind if I asked Peter to tell me about it?"

Mrs. Doyle nodded. "Certainly not," she said. "Peter, tell the lady what she wants to know."

Peter looked up and blushed.

"Aw, I already told the cops. I tol' 'em everything." Quickly he looked down again, avoiding Allie's eyes. He began furiously attacking the cereal.

"You tell Mrs. Neilsen what she wants to know."

Peter half shook his head.

"The cops told me not to talk to anyone. No one at all."

Mrs. Doyle's mouth drew in sharply.

"Peter," she said. Her arm reached out and she half shook the boy. "Peter, you just stop that now. My gawd, all you've done is talk about it. For three days, that's all you have talked about. I don't care what the cops told you. You answer Mrs. Neilsen's questions."

Peter looked stubborn and unhappy, but he turned and faced Allie.

"What you want to know?"

"I want you to tell me just how you happened to find the hat and glasses. What were you doing? When was it? Just the way it happened, if you will."

"I was just walkin' along and there they were and I saw 'em and picked 'em up. That's all there was to it."

"All there was to it!" Mrs. Doyle was indignant and again reached over and shook her son. "You explain now the way you been telling us for the last three days. Go on, explain."

Allie interrupted.

"You found them on Mrs. Kitteridge's lawn, by the bush in the side yard?"

Peter looked her straight in the face. His voice was defiant.

"My gosh," he said, "sure I found 'em there. Everybody knows that. You can read all about it in the papers."

"What were you doing in Mrs. Kitteridge's yard, Peter?" Allie asked.

For a moment the boy looked startled, but quickly recovered himself.

"I was chasin' a ball," he said.

His mother suddenly looked at him in surprise and started to speak, but then thought better of it and closed her mouth sharply. But she continued to stare at her son.

"Peter," Allie said, "just what time did you find them? What time were you in Mrs. Kitteridge's yard?"

"I don't know. Sometime Saturday morning. After the murder, that's all I know."

"Was it before nine o'clock?" Allie asked.

Peter shook his head.

"I don't know, I told you," he said.

Mrs. Doyle suddenly looked at Allie.

"It couldn't very well have been," she said suddenly. "You see, that was Saturday morning. We let Peter sleep late because he's allowed to stay up on Friday nights for the television. No school the next day so we let the boy stay up. Then he sleeps late on Saturday because Pat, that's Mr. Doyle, and myself, we like to sleep late too. We get up around nine and have breakfast and then Peter goes out to play. That is," she added, "when I can get him out of the house. He don't like..."

"Are you sure he wasn't out before nine?" Allie said.

"I'm sure. I remember he was playing in the house and I made him go out. All he ever wants to do..."

Again Allie cut in. This time she turned directly to face the child.

"Peter," Allie said, "I talked with Mrs. Kitteridge. She was in her yard from nine o'clock on. She remembers it very definitely. And she is quite sure that she didn't see you. She also has no memory of seeing the hat or the glasses."

Mrs. Doyle turned to stare at her son.

Peter stood up suddenly and stamped his foot. His face was a fiery red and his voice was pitched inordinately high when he spoke. The words came out in a childish sort of half scream.

"I don't care what that old woman says. I tell you I found them in her yard, right next to the body."

"Next to the body?" Allie said quietly. "I thought you said..."

Peter turned and ran from the room.

Mrs. Doyle started to get up.

Allie also stood up.

"I'm afraid I've..." her voice was apologetic.

"Don't you worry," Mrs. Doyle said. "Don't you worry, dear. If Peter has been lying, I'll find out about it. Don't you worry a bit. I'm his mother and I'll be able to tell." She hesitated a moment, as though to get her breath. When she spoke again, her voice was controlled.

"He isn't a bad boy, understand, Mrs. Neilsen. He just has that crazy imagination. I think it comes from all these comic books and detective stories and what not. He isn't really a bad boy and I know he doesn't mean to hurt anyone. I'll talk to him."

"Thank you, Mrs. Doyle," Allie said. "I think I had better go now. Perhaps later..."

"I'll talk to him. I'll tell you if there is anything. Don't you worry. I'll tell you."

Allie found her own way to the door as Mrs. Doyle went in search of her son.

That morning Peter Doyle received the worst thrashing he had ever had in his life. In a sense, it was a little unfair. The thrashing came after Peter had already confessed to his mother that he hadn't really found the hat and the glasses under the juniper bush in Mrs. Kitteridge's yard.

But by this time Mrs. Doyle, a rather imaginative woman herself, was so completely shocked and upset to learn of the possible damage her son had caused, and the possible repercussions, that she went ahead and gave him the licking anyway. After it was all over and Peter was left in his room alternately crying and feeling the sore places on his bottom, Mrs. Doyle called the police. She thought vaguely of calling her husband at his office first, but finally decided against it. Patrick Doyle had an ungovernable temper and she was really afraid of what he might do to his son and heir.

Allie Neilsen went home. She wanted to think. Think what to do next.

One thing she was sure of. The child had been lying. But did it really matter? Did it make a great deal of difference?

Chapter Twelve

The thought of deceit, of concealing her true identity, never occurred to Allie Neilsen until the very moment Kathleen Julio opened the front door of her home and spoke the words. The words came even before Allie herself could make the little speech which she had so painfully prepared.

"Thank God—oh thank God you have come!" Mrs. Julio said. "The agency said you wouldn't be here before noon but I am so glad you could get here early."

Mrs. Julio reached out and took Allie by the arm and almost literally pulled her into the front hallway.

The next two or three minutes were so totally confusing that later, when Allie tried to remember them and put the various incidents in any sort of order, the only thing she was able to recall was a sort of mad, insane kaleidoscope of hysteria and general confusion, punctuated by Kathleen Julio's screaming voice and the sounds of what seemed to be dozens of children yelling back and forth.

Mrs. Julio was a large woman and greeting Allie as she did, faded bathrobe thrown across her shoulders and open down the front so that it exposed huge breasts covered only by a torn brassiere, her face flushed and eyes streaked with mascara and deeply shadowed, she seemed almost monstrous.

Allie remembered being rushed through a room filled with half-dressed, yelling children. There was a small, immaculate, dark-complexioned man standing somewhere in the room and he was busy knotting a bow tie around the neck of a ten-year-old boy who was a smaller image of himself. And then in a moment they were through the room and Allie had been propelled into a bedroom which looked as though a cyclone had struck it.

"Come in here with me while I finish dressing and I'll give you your instructions," Mrs. Julio was saying. She hadn't lowered her voice and Allie could detect the hysteria in back of the high-pitched tones.

"God, oh God, what I've had to go through!" Mrs. Julio slumped at a cluttered dressing table.

"You know, of course. You know about my poor baby, my poor murdered baby. Today's the funeral. That's why I had to have the agency send someone. We are leaving the smaller children home and someone has to stay with them. And everything is so confused. Poor Mister Julio has gone all to pieces. And we're moving—we only rented this place, thank God! We're getting out of this terrible neighborhood. Murderers—that's what they are—murderers!"

She turned and stared at Allie. Her eyes looked insane and Allie was glad that she had not introduced herself, as she had originally intended. She sensed at once that this woman, ridden by grief and bitterness, would never answer her questions. Already she was figuring a way of getting out of the house—regretting that she had come in the first place.

"You know about my poor baby?" Mrs. Julio said. She didn't wait for an answer.

"They killed her. A poor defenseless baby. They all got together and killed her. Those McNallys, they were the ones. They should have brought her home. A young girl like Louisa, they should have seen that she got home safely. But no. Why that McNally slut! She even told me her husband was too drunk to bring the child home. It's this neighborhood. Drunken parties, goings-on..."

Allie had backed to the door and her hand had reached for the knob. Suddenly she hesitated.

"I read about it in the papers," she said. "You say that the McNallys were drunk? I didn't read about that."

Mrs. Julio turned to her and stared for a moment wildly.

"Didn't read about it? No, the papers didn't have that. They didn't write about what really goes on out here. But we should have known. A man like that Neilsen allowed to move into a decent neighborhood. A sex fiend and a killer!"

"He's not a killer!"

Allie put her hand to her mouth even as the words left it. She had spoken instinctively and without thinking. She knew that it would be of no use to argue with this woman in her present condition. Any sensible conversation would be futile.

But Mrs. Julio had not even heard the words. She was in the middle of a tirade about the neighborhood and her dead daughter and nothing would stop her.

Suddenly, in the very midst of her outburst, she turned from the dressing table and stopped speaking and stared silently for a moment at Allie.

"You," she said. "Why aren't you out helping with the children? That's what the agency sent you here for, didn't they? That's what we have to pay for. Get out and help..."

Allie opened the door and started to slip through it. As she did she saw that the other woman had reached for a half-filled bottle which had been sitting on the floor at the side of the dressing table and had raised its uncorked neck to her lips. Allie could have made her exit without trouble if at just that moment someone hadn't approached the door and started to open it from the other side. As it was, the two of them collided and jammed together in the narrow space between the doorjambs.

The girl was as tall as Allie and only a few years younger. She had Mrs. Julio's hair and features, but had dark, somber eyes. She was talking as she pushed into the room.

"Mother," she said, "for God's sake Mother get hold of yourself. They can hear you yelling all over the neighborhood." Suddenly she spotted the bottle in the older woman's hands.

"I told you to lay off that juice," she said.

Mrs. Julio looked up at her and there was a pout on her heavy lips.

"I was just talking to this woman here," she said. "I had to tell her what to do while we're at the funeral. About taking care of the kids while we bury poor Louisa." The tears came to her eyes as she spoke her daughter's name.

The girl turned from her mother and looked at Allie, who still stood in the doorway. Suddenly her eyes went wide. She turned quickly to her mother.

"Mother, you fool," she said. "This isn't the woman who is to take care of the children. This is Mrs. Neilsen. Mrs. Neilsen, don't you understand? You've seen her picture in the paper." She swung back toward Allie "What do you think..."

But she never finished the sentence.

Mrs. Julio had staggered to her feet. Her clawlike fingers reached out and she started to lurch across the room as she began to scream.

"Murderer! Murderer! You killed my..."

Allie didn't hear the rest of it. In one confused headlong rush, she turned and ran. She half stumbled over a child and almost fell, but quickly reached her feet and continued on. A moment later she flung open the front door and ran down the flagstone path to the street. It wasn't until she was a block from the house, breathless and shaking, that she slowed down.

Allie was so shaken by her experience that she decided for the time being she would call off her investigation and return home. She wanted a chance to rest and to think, a chance to recuperate. Turning into Crescent Drive a few minutes later, she hurried toward her house. She was walking fast and with her eyes straight ahead, hardly seeing where she was going and oblivious to anything but her own churning thoughts. Instinctively, she turned in when she came to the front of her house. It was only in the nick of time that she saw a child standing there, leaning over and tying a shoelace. As it was she brushed against the little girl.

Allie stepped quickly to one side.

"Oh—I'm sorry," she said. She'd pushed the youngster and almost upset her.

Patsy Tomlinson looked up, her eyes frightened. She reached with one slender hand and pushed the lock of dark brown hair from in front of her face, and then quickly smiled.

"Hello," she said.

Allie smiled back.

"Hello."

"Can I play with your little boy?"

Allie hesitated for a moment. She recognized the youngster as belonging to the people who had recently moved into the house next door. She was an attractive little thing, in spite of the large frightened eyes and the plain clothes she wore.

Allie slowly shook her head.

"I'm sorry," she said, "but I'm afraid not." She hesitated, seeing the quick hurt look on the little girl's face. "You see my little boy has to stay inside. He has, well, he has a bad cold."

She hesitated again for a second, on the verge of turning away, and then asked, not wishing to sound abrupt, "Shouldn't you be in school, honey?"

The girl opened her mouth to answer when the call came from the house next door.

"Patsy—Patsy, you come home. Come here right now!"

As Allie hurried to her front door, her eyes slid sidewise and she saw the tall, thin figure of the dark-haired woman standing in the doorway. A moment later and she was in her own house. She wanted to take a few minutes to have something to eat; to plan her campaign for the afternoon.

Gerald Tomlinson stood at the end of the hallway, knuckled fists on his hips, as the child entered the house and the mother closed the door quickly and locked it from the inside. He had been shaving and one side of his face was still covered with lather. His thin hair was uncombed and there was a vicious expression on his dour face. His feet were bare and he wore only a pair of canvas trousers. He was naked from the waist up.

The mother said, "Go to your room, Patsy."

The child had to pass him and she cowered instinctively as she went by.

Tomlinson's open hand reached out and struck the girl a sharp blow across the face. He waited then until the door had closed behind the child. Almost casually, he unthreaded the wide leather belt from around his waist.

"I told you," he said. "I told you not to let her out. I warned you about it. She had to talk, eh? Had to get gabby with the neighbors, eh? Well all right. I'll give her a lesson she won't forget."

Marian Tomlinson put her hand to her mouth, fear glowing in her eyes.

"No, Jerry," she said. "No. You can't do it. It wasn't the child's fault. She didn't mean anything. Please don't..."

"Shut up. Shut up right now. I told you. I warned you. You had to let her out. Well I'll see to it..."

Marian rushed up and put out her hands imploringly.

"For God sake's Jerry, don't. You've already misused her enough. I just can't take any more." She was half crying and looked pleadingly at him.

"Oh God, I never bargained for anything like this," she said. "I just can't stand any more. You said you'd take care of us, after Bill died. You said..."

Tomlinson lifted his hand and struck her across the mouth.

"I said shut up. You want a lesson, too? You want a beating?"

He turned toward the door of the bedroom which the child had closed softly behind herself.

Marian again reached out, half throwing her arms around him to stop him. There were tears in her eyes from the blow and her face felt numb, but her voice had a deadly calmness.

"You touch that child," she said, "you touch her and I swear to God I'll call the police. I don't care what you do to me. It doesn't matter any longer. But if you touch that..."

She never got to finish the sentence. Tomlinson's fist caught her full in the face. He felt the soft crunch as the bridge of her nose shattered.

He made no effort to touch her then, after she fell to the floor.

Walking into the kitchen, he tossed the belt on the sinkboard and reached for the bottle of whiskey. He poured a water glass a third of the way full and downed it in a single swallow. Then he took a pitcher from the shelf above the sink and filled it from the cold water tap. Returning to the hallway he went to the fallen woman and poured it over her face.

He lifted her from the floor as she moaned and carried her to the couch. He waited until her eyes had opened and he was sure that she was fully conscious. He spoke in a voice without passion; almost without feeling.

"You'll do as I say," he said. "From now on you'll do as I say. Otherwise I'll kill that kid of yours. You know I'm not fooling. I'll kill that kid."

Marian Tomlinson began to cry softly.

Allie Neilsen, sitting across the dinette table from Billy—Mrs. Manning was in the other room on the telephone—was thinking what a shame it was she hadn't been able to have the little girl in to play. But there was no telling what the child may have heard and might say. She had to protect Billy at all costs. She hated to keep him in the house, hated to see the puzzled, unhappy look on his face as he asked her questions which she was unable to answer. But she didn't dare let him out and she didn't dare have any children from the neighborhood in the house.

They were eating lunch of sandwiches and milk and Allie was hurrying. She had a lot to do.

Already she felt she had learned a lot. Learned a lot but it didn't really mean too much. Not unless she could find a good many other pieces of the puzzle to fit in the vacant places. The thing to do was try and get a complete picture of that Friday night. Find out what each and every person who might have been involved or might even have been near the neighborhood, had been doing. There was no telling who may have seen Len, or may have seen the Julio child after she had left the McNallys'.

An odd thought occurred to her then. Had the child actually ever left the McNallys'?

She shook her head and dismissed it. Obviously she had. But, again, obviously she had been murdered within minutes, or even seconds of leaving that house where she had been baby-sitting.

Mrs. Manning returned to the kitchen.

"I've been talking with Mr. Leavy," she said. Her voice was just the slightest bit sharp. "He doesn't think you should be going out."

Allie looked at the older woman.

"Have you been reporting my movements, Mrs. Manning?" she asked.

"No. Only he called while you were gone and I..."

"It doesn't matter. I'm sorry if I was abrupt. But my understanding was that you are here to take care of the child. I'm going out again, in fact. And if Mr. Leavy calls you can tell him I'll be back later in the day."

She walked around and kissed Billy, and then quickly left the room. A moment later Mrs. Manning heard the outside door slam. Immediately she went back to the telephone. Little Billy reached for the piece of cake which his mother had left uneaten on her plate.

One of the principal reasons that the Swansons had chosen Fairlawn as an ideal place to settle was that fact that Tom worked for an aircraft company which was located not more than a mile and a half away. Getting back and forth in the mornings and evenings was such a simple matter that he figured it gave him an extra hour of leisure each day. In fact, should he feel like it, he could even make it home for lunch. Being a sort of junior executive, it didn't matter if he stretched the lunch hour a little now and then. Of course it wouldn't do to abuse the privilege, but then Tom Swanson wasn't a man to abuse any privilege. On this particular Tuesday, however, he felt justified in taking an hour extra.

Grace had been feeling nervous, what with all of the excitement going on in the neighborhood and so he'd driven home at twelve-thirty to have lunch with her. It was now after one, but Tom was in no rush to get back. They'd understand over at the plant and anyway, it was nice to sit around and have a couple of beers. God knows he could use them; things had been just a bit tense ever since that party.

He was still on the first beer when the doorbell rang and Grace got up to answer it. She came back to the room—the Swansons like the Kitteridges, not having children, were able to convert one of the bedrooms into a dining room—a moment later with Allie Nielsen. Grace sounded embarrassed as she made the introduction.

"This is Mrs. Neilsen, Tom. From across the street, you know," she said.

Swanson stood up. He was, after all, a gentleman.

"Glad to..." he began.

"I'm awfully sorry to bother you," Allie said quickly, "but you see, I thought maybe I could ask you a few questions."

Both of the Swansons looked at her a little vaguely. They felt extremely uncomfortable, knowing who she was and all. They couldn't imagine why she had called. Tom's first thought was that she must want help of some kind. But when she mentioned asking questions, he quickly spoke up.

"Really," he said. "Really Mrs. Neilsen, we'd be glad to help in any way we can, but there isn't anything..."

"Do sit down," Grace Swanson said. "I'm sure that if there's anything..."

Tom glared at his wife and reluctantly pulled a chair out for Allie. She sat down and started fumbling for her package of cigarettes. Quickly Grace leaned across the table and handed her her own pack. She smiled sympathetically as she did.

Grace Swanson felt terribly sorry for little Mrs. Neilsen. She wasn't even thinking of whether her husband had committed the murder or hadn't committed it. All she knew was that this woman, who looked little more than a school girl, was in deep and serious trouble and Grace felt a certain kinship for any woman who was in trouble. She felt this way especially if the trouble was caused by a man. She determined to do anything she could to help her.

"You had a party over here on Friday night?" Allie said. "There must have been a lot of people and I..."

"Mrs. Neilsen," Tom said, "the police have been all over that with us.

They've questioned us several times. They've also questioned all of our guests. I'm sure that if there's anything..."

"We did tell the police," Grace interrupted, not looking at her husband, "but we'll be glad to tell you anything you might want to know."

Once more Tom glared at his wife.

Allie drew a couple of quick, nervous puffs on the cigarette and turned toward the woman.

"Well, you see, because the girl, the Julio girl was baby-sitting for one of your guests, I just thought that maybe..."

"But we've been all through that," Swanson said. "It can't possibly have anything to do with us."

"I didn't think it had anything to do with us either," Allie said bitterly, "but now my husband..."

Grace stood up and walked around the table.

"Now dear," she said, "don't you let yourself get upset. You go ahead and ask anything you want."

This time she glared at Tom. He in turn sank back with a resigned expression and reached for his beer.

Allie waited a second and then again spoke. It was more difficult than she'd realized. She really didn't know where to start, what to ask. Didn't quite know what she was even looking for.

"I thought maybe when the party broke up and people were leaving," she began.

"They left at the same time. Long after midnight. After the girl was killed, according to the way the police figured it," Tom said.

"Did anyone leave earlier, or maybe arrive very late?" Allie asked.

"No one."

Once more Allie hesitated before continuing. She looked lost and helpless and Grace Swanson, watching her little pointed face and seeing how pale she was, felt a surge of compassion. She wanted to do something—anything—to help and comfort her.

"Then perhaps," Allie said, "one of the guests may have gone out at some time or another—you know, for a breath of air or something."

Grace looked up quickly.

"There was Myrtle, remember..."

"No one left this house," Tom quickly interrupted. He looked at Grace as though he would have liked to have killed her on the spot.

Allie ignored him. She looked directly at Grace.

"Myrtle?" she asked. "You say..."

Grace glared at her husband as she spoke up.

"Yes, Myrtle McNally. From across the street. I know that she went out once late in the evening. I think it was to go over and see if the baby was all right. But I'm not sure. Maybe it was to look for Howard. Howard's her husband. He was out in back a couple of times. You know we only have one bathroom," she added, almost coyly.

"Goddam it all, Grace," Tom said, "what's the matter with you, anyway? No one left this house. I'm damned sure no one did. That's what we've told the police and that's what we're going to stick by. I'd like to help you, Mrs. Neilsen," he added, turning, to Allie, "but there's no point in digging up a lot of stuff that just doesn't have any possible bearing on the matter."

Allie might even have agreed with him, if she'd had time to think it over, but Grace didn't give her time.

"Don't you tell me, Tom Swanson," she said. "That bitch was out of this house for a good fifteen minutes. And you know it. So was her husband, although from the looks of her, it would have been more likely to have been someone else's husband. And another thing, with all the people running around and half of them soused, how the hell can anyone say who was where or when."

Tom banged the empty beer bottle down on the table.

"Grace," he said, "Grace, you are a bigger goddamned fool than even I thought you could be." He turned to Allie. "All right, Mrs. Neilsen, maybe someone did go out at one time or other. It could have happened that way. Maybe it was Myrtle McNally or maybe it was Howard McNally. I don't know. But as far as I'm concerned, I'm still sticking to my story. I didn't see anyone leave."

He stood up and went to the icebox for another glass of beer. Allie left while he was out of the room. She thanked Grace Swanson for her help and Grace patted her on the shoulder and told her she could call on her any time. She'd do anything she could, she said.

At the front door, she said, "Men! My God, there isn't a damned one of them that's worth a spot in hell. They're all double-crossers."

She meant well, but it was an unfortunate remark.

Allie never did realize it, but if it hadn't been for Lieutenant Clifford Giddeon every effort that she was to make in seeking a solution to the murder of Louisa Julio would have been completely futile. The odd thing was that the lieutenant himself never realized the very vital and significant part he played in the drama which was about to unfold. In fact, even when the whole thing was over and forgotten, the lieutenant still had no idea that he was, completely by caprice and accident, the direct cause of Allie's finding the solution to the strange enigma which had engulfed the residents of Fairlawn Acres.

At the time this happened, this completely accidental incident which in itself was without meaning, Allie was furious with the lieutenant. The very thing he did convinced her that the sinister man was intent only on sending her husband to the electric chair.

Upon leaving the Swansons', Allie simply couldn't wait to rush across the street and pay a visit to Myrtle McNally. She knew, knew deep down inside of herself, that somehow or other the McNallys were the key to the whole thing. The McNallys knew something or had seen something that would give her the one essential clue that she needed.

The thing which Lieutenant Giddeon did was to stand directly in front of the Swansons' house when Allie left its front door.

The lieutenant hadn't even known Allie was in the house; he'd wanted to see her, having stopped across the street and discovered she wasn't home, but he hadn't known she was visiting the Swansons. The reason he was standing there was because, not finding Allie at home, he'd decided to take a walk around the block while he waited for her. He'd crossed the street, having seen a boat in the driveway of the house next to the Swansons'. The boat was sitting on a trailer and the lieutenant, with time to kill and being extremely interested in boats of all sorts, had crossed over to look at it. And then Allie had come out of the Swansons' house and was walking down the path.

He recognized her immediately.

The sight of Allie Neilsen, almost without fail, brought a happy feeling to those persons who encountered her. Even casual strangers, seeing her for the first time, sensed a pleasant reaction.

On this occasion, however, Lieutenant Giddeon was anything but happy; he was distinctly and definitely annoyed.

"Mrs. Neilsen," he said. "Well, I was looking for you."

Allie drew up shortly. Intent as she had been on crossing the street and talking with Myrtle McNally, the encounter with Lieutenant Giddeon served merely to disconcert her. It took her a moment to recognize him.

"Why, Lieutenant," she said.

"I just left your house, Mrs. Neilsen," the lieutenant said. "I wanted to talk with you."

Allie was about to say that she was busy, in a hurry; that she'd be glad to talk with him later. But something about his manner arrested her.

"Yes?"

"Yes. Mrs. Neilsen, I don't like to say this, but you're causing a lot of trouble. This going around and seeing people and upsetting them—well, it's making a lot of trouble. I don't think you should do it."

Allie stared at him. Her cheeks suddenly flushed and she felt a sense of anger coming over her.

"You don't, Lieutenant?" she said. "You really don't?"

"No, I don't," Giddeon said, stolidly. "You saw Mrs. Julio and now she's under the care of a nurse with a case of hysteria."

Allie blushed, but quickly recovered.

"I saw the little Doyle boy," she said. "Perhaps..."

"Mrs. Neilsen," the lieutenant said. "Let me explain something to you. I'm a cop, a dumb cop. But I'm not stupid, irrespective of what you may think. I've known for a long time that the Doyle youngster was lying. But don't you see? It doesn't matter. Sure, he lied about where he found the hat and glasses. But the fact remains that he found them. And he found them somewhere in this immediate vicinity. I don't want to upset you, Mrs. Neilsen, but the girl was not killed on the Kitteridge's lawn. The body was carried there and hidden under the bush. So it doesn't really matter where the hat was found—so long as it was found *outside* of Mr. Neilsen's home."

The lieutenant stopped for a moment to catch his breath. Allie just stared at him.

"I'm not trying to frame your husband, Mrs. Neilsen," he said. "Believe me, the police don't work that way. But for God sakes, let us have a chance to work. Don't interfere. If your husband is innocent, we'll find out about it. Now I want you to go home and stay there. The only thing you can do is confuse things."

And so, Allie Neilsen, instead of going to the McNallys' as she had planned, went home. Not that she had the slightest intention of ignoring the McNallys. It was only that she didn't want the police to know that she was seeing them.

As a result, she didn't see Myrtle McNally that afternoon, when Myrtle was home alone. Instead she waited dark, when she was sure no one, especially the police, would be watching her. Then she left the house and crossed the yard to the McNallys' back door.

By this time Howard McNally was also home.

It almost cost Allie her life.

Chapter Thirteen

The one person involved in the Louisa Julio murder who never once gave a thought to the possible guilt or innocence of Len Neilsen was Howard McNally. Howard, during those first few days following discovery of the brutal crime, was far too occupied in considering his own status in the matter to think of anyone else.

The thing which served most to upset Howard was the uncertainty about the case; he couldn't tell if the police were merely holding Neilsen in order to throw the real killer off guard. He didn't know just what his own wife, Myrtle, knew or suspected about the events of that terrible night. He wasn't sure what the Swansons might have observed. He wasn't sure whether he had been seen or not during those last tragic moments in the girl's life, after she had run from the kitchen of his house, frightened and hysterical, only to find death beneath the maniacal attack of a ruthless killer.

It was this not knowing which gradually tore down the fabric of his mind and served to disintegrate his will power and self-control. Myrtle herself, with her accusing eyes and her tight-lipped, bitter mouth, which she only opened to release cynical remarks, did more than anything else to bring about his collapse. God, he hated to even think about it.

He had only done what any normal man would have done; he'd seen a sensuous, attractive girl who had looked at him with flirtatious eyes and he had been entranced by her. He had made a pass at her—which of course he was unwilling to admit most normal men would not have done. He had, inadvertently, frightened her.

And now this.

It was fantastic how one thing could lead to another until suddenly...

Howard had gone to work as usual on Monday morning, but it had been a mistake. He'd been unable to concentrate on anything; his mind kept returning to the Julio girl and the events of that Friday night. By noon time he was suffering from a raging headache and he decided to plead sickness and return home. The office was understanding about it.

But returning home had failed to bring him peace. Myrtle was home and from the minute he walked into the house, complaining of not feeling well, she had stared at him with her accusing, unsympathetic eyes and avoided speaking except in monosyllables. It suddenly occurred to Howard that his wife not only despised him; she hated him.

He had slept fitfully on Monday night and by Tuesday morning was feeling so bad that he called the office and explained he wouldn't be in. But he didn't stay around the house. He left at his usual hour and drove to the station; there he parked his car where he usually parked it. But instead of getting on the train, he went to a small restaurant and took a table well to the back. He'd purchased the morning newspapers and while he waited for the breakfast he knew he would not be able to eat, he began to read every word in them concerning the Julio case.

Although he merely picked at the food and managed to swallow less than half the cup of coffee the waitress brought him, he managed to kill better than an hour loitering over the meal. At last he realized he wouldn't be able to stay in the place forever and so, reluctantly, he called for his check and paid it. He left the restaurant with a lost sort of feeling; he wasn't going to the office and he didn't want to return home. Vaguely he thought of going to a movie and killing a few hours, but then he realized there would be no picture house open so early in the day.

That's when he decided that he'd go to a bar. The bars were always open. He had the added thought that although he had been unable to eat, he might be able to get a drink down. He ordered a whiskey sour, and after the bartender put it in front of him, he reopened the papers to finish his reading.

The first whiskey sour went down pretty hard, but he managed it. The second one went a little easier and with the third, he almost felt human. At least the nervous jerking of his hands had stopped and there was a warm, pleasant glow in his stomach. Even his restless mind seemed to find some surcease from the thoughts which had been rampaging through it for the last few days.

He began to think then of Myrtle and the way Myrtle had acted. She had been unfair; bitterly, stupidly unfair. After all, what did she know, really? She was guessing and she was perfectly willing to suspect him of the worst. Why she had already condemned him, condemned him without a hearing, without evidence, without anything but her rotten, suspicious mind.

Howard began to lose his sense of fear and terror and replace it with a feeling of indignation.

By God, here he was, forced to hang out in a damned barroom, when he should be home resting and recovering. He wasn't well and terrible things had happened, and instead of being able to find peace and refuge in his own home, she had driven him out with her damned accusing looks and her bitter words.

Howard ordered his fourth sour and when the bartender put it on the bar in front of him, Howard looked up.

"Women," he said. "Wives! Jesus Christ, why does a man ever get mixed up with them in the first place?"

The bartender returned his look, his eyes bored.

"I wouldn't know, buddy," he said, "I wouldn't know."

Howard nodded sagely.

By one o'clock Howard was thoroughly drunk. He was also, conversely, famished. He staggered from the tavern and found a steak and chop house down the street. While he waited for a table, he stood at the bar and had another drink. By this time he had switched to straight Scotch.

He had no difficulty in eating a tremendous sirloin steak and although he skipped the vegetables, he had a shot of brandy with his coffee. Then he went out and found a movie. He fell asleep almost the second he slumped into the seat, well in the back of the theater. He didn't awaken until around six o'clock.

It took him a little while to realize where he was. Once more he had the splitting headache, but still, he didn't feel as bad as he had that morning. It was already dark when he reached the street and he started back to where he had parked the car. He had to pass a tavern on the way and instinctively he turned in. He went back to the whiskey sours which had done so much for him that morning.

By the time Howard McNally returned home it was almost seven-thirty. He was drunk all over again. He was drunk and he was feeling very much abused. It was all Myrtle's fault. If she had just been a different sort of wife—well, he wouldn't have to be always looking around for other women. He wouldn't have made that initial fatal pass at the Julio girl. He wouldn't be in all this trouble.

Myrtle had just put the baby to bed and was sitting alone in the kitchen, staring at the floor, when Howard slammed in through the front door. She looked up and stared at him. There was something about the look—an expression of supreme disgust, even hatred on her face, which at once served only to infuriate him.

Wordlessly he passed through the room. He was taking off his hat and coat when the doorbell rang. Myrtle and Howard reached the back of the house at the same time, It was Myrtle who opened the door. She recognized Allie Neilsen at once.

Half reluctantly, she invited her in.

The moment she entered the place, Allie could sense the tension. It was almost like a physical thing. She knew that McNally was drunk. She could tell from the sickening odor of stale whiskey which emanated from him as she was forced to pass him to enter the room. His bloodshot eyes, the manner in which he staggered as he went to the couch and half fell on it—everything indicated his condition. When he spoke, his voice was blurred and barely understandable.

But Mrs. McNally was cold sober. Sober and obviously in a state of nervous tension, bordering on hysteria. It was very difficult for Allie to start the conversation. But she managed to explain, finally, that she was trying to trace the Julio child's activities on the night of the murder. She wanted to find out anything she could and she felt that because the girl had been baby-sitting at the McNallys' they might be able to help her.

"We don't know nothing about it—nothing," Howard said. He glared at her and Allie was momentarily taken back by the violence of his manner. Somehow or other, this little fat man seemed sinister and dangerous in spite of his innocuous and even ridiculous appearance.

"The girl was here while we were at the party," Myrtle said in a flat voice. "She was here and then we came home and she left. That's all there was to it."

"And no one called for her?" Allie asked.

"No one," Myrtle said.

"Listen," Howard interrupted, "there is nothing you can find out here. Police already..." his voice trailed off.

"I was wondering," Allie said, "wondering if perhaps, sometime during the evening, you didn't look out from the Swansons' and perhaps see someone around the house? Or perhaps run across and check on the baby and perhaps notice..."

"Well," Myrtle began, "we did..."

"Shut up! Shut your stupid big mouth." Howard lurched to his feet. "Why are you asking these questions?" he demanded, turning to glare at Allie. "What is it you want, anyway? Are you trying to make trouble for us? Is that your idea in sneaking over here? Is that..."

"You shut up, Howard," Myrtle suddenly interrupted. She turned back to Allie. "Pay no attention to him," she said. "He's stupidly drunk and doesn't know what he's saying." She hesitated then for a second before continuing. "I'd really like to help you, Mrs. Neilsen, but there really is nothing I can say. We hardly knew the child—it was the first time she had been here."

Allie nodded, the feeling of helplessness and futility once more coming over her. She sat and stared straight ahead for a full minute and then looked up. It was at that moment she noticed the large goldfish bowl sitting on the mantel. There was a handprinted cardboard sign hung around the bowl with the words "baby's bank" printed on it. The bowl was half filled with copper and silver coins and amongst them she could see the fragments of several pieces of paper money. Quickly she dropped her eyes.

"When the girl left," she said, "her mother told the police that she didn't receive her money for baby-sitting. She didn't leave before you returned did she?"

Howard looked up quickly, but Myrtle spoke first.

"She left after we returned," she said. "You see, we didn't have change and we intended to pay her the next day."

Howard's face went very red.

"You fool," he yelled. "Myrtle you fool! Don't you see she's trying to trap us? Don't you see..."

"I'm not trying to trap anyone," Allie said. "I'm only trying to find the truth—to find out what really happened. I'm..."

"Get out of this house. Goddamn you, get out right now!"

Howard was screaming and he lurched across the room towards Allie. Myrtle jumped up and intercepted him, but his arm shot out with a vicious blow. It caught his wife on the side of her face and for a moment she stood motionless, and then slowly sank to her knees. Howard again drew back his fist.

But by this time Allie was already at the door. It slammed behind her a moment later.

Even in the confusion of the moment, her mind was racing. Two things were very obvious. The McNallys were lying; they had not paid the girl—but it wasn't because of a lack of change. And they had returned to the house sometime before the child had left.

The Julio girl must have departed suddenly and unexpectedly. Otherwise why wouldn't she have waited for her money? And why were McNally and his wife lying to her?

Hurrying down the front lawn toward the street, Allie turned to go back to her own house. She noticed the lights on in the living room of the house which separated her home from McNallys'; the house where the new people, Thomas or Thompson or something like that, had moved in recently.

On a sudden instinct, Allie hesitated and then went to their front door. Someone had been at the house on that Friday night. Allie had seen the lights. And if someone had been home, there was just a slender chance they may have either heard something or seen something. They were the McNallys' closest neighbors.

Howard McNally didn't strike his wife a second time. Instead he stared at her for a brief moment and then turned and staggered to the front window. He was standing there, staring out, as Allie knocked on the Tomlinsons' front door.

He was still there five minutes later when the leather belt struck him across the side of his face.

Myrtle McNally held the belt by the end and used it so that the belt buckle caught Howard across one corner of his mouth. The first blow sent him to his knees.

She didn't stop raising and lowering the belt until he had fallen prone on the floor, his arms and legs outstretched as the heavy strap fell again and again across his back.

Myrtle McNally, the baby in her arms and tears streaking down her face, left the house while her husband still lay in a quivering heap. She was muttering under her breath as she hurried past his fallen figure.

"The bastard," she was half crying. "The dirty bastard. I'll teach him to hit me. I'll tell the police just what I know."

The strangest part of the whole thing was that Howard, when he staggered into the bedroom a few minutes later, his face streaked with blood and the taste of blood and tears in his cut mouth, wasn't even thinking of Myrtle at all. Wasn't even thinking of what she had done to him.

As he searched frantically in the top bureau drawer for the twenty-two cal. target pistol he had brought some years back and never used, or even fired, a single idea kept going through his mind.

"She's trying to pin it on me," he repeated over and over to himself. "That sweet-faced bitch is trying to pin the murder on me. She must have seen something, must know something. And now she's over next door, trying to find out more. She's going to put me in the electric chair."

He didn't bother to bandage the cuts or clean up before sneaking out of the back door and starting for the rear of the Tomlinsons' house, across the shadowy back yard.

Chapter Fourteen

The thought kept going through her mind.

These people, they simply can't be as strange and unreal as they seem. The Swansons, the Doyles, the Julios and the McNallys. And now the Tomlinsons. It must be that she, herself, Allie Neilsen, was seeing things out of perspective. The events of the last few days had probably been too much for her.

But still, no matter how she turned it around or analyzed it, they had all seemed so completely strange and weird. They had all been evasive and there had been that constant undercurrent of tension. It was almost as though they had contracted some fantastic emotional disease.

The fact that each of their houses had been identical, yes, even identical to her own house where she and Len had hoped to find so much happiness, made it all even more unreal. How could people all live in the same house with the same design and the same rooms and almost the identical furniture and drapes, and still be so completely different from each other? So different from Len and Billy and herself.

Even these last two, the Tomlinsons, were in their own way very odd. Not like the others. They had been friendly and had greeted her kindly. Tomlinson himself, sitting over there in his shirt sleeves and smoking a curved pipe, had been almost gentle as he'd answered her questions.

And yet she sensed something strange and intangible in the very atmosphere of the house and its occupants. She felt it first when she asked about the little girl.

"Your daughter," she had said. "She wanted to play with Billy today and I am afraid I was a bit discourteous. The way things are, I didn't feel that he should be seeing other children for a while yet. I hope she didn't mind."

Allie couldn't help but notice the quick look which flashed between the two of them. Tomlinson's expression, as his eyes went to the woman, seemed to carry a sort of subtle threat. But then again the man's voice was friendly when he spoke.

"Patsy, that's our little girl, shouldn't be playing with anyone these days," he said. "She's had a very bad cold and we've been keeping her home from school. Might be very catching, that sort of thing."

The woman said nothing. Allie was just a little surprised. The child certainly hadn't appeared to be sick when Allie had spoken to her.

The talk went on for a while then and suddenly Allie had the most peculiar sensation that everything which was being said was somehow studied and designed to deceive her. There was, for instance, his wife, whom he'd introduced as Marian. That great bandage over one side of her face and her frightened, whisper of a voice. He explained the bandage of course.

"The missus had a little accident," he'd said. "Fell against a fixture in the bathroom. Pretty bad blow she got, but it's going to be all right."

Allie looked at the woman sympathetically. "It's really a shame," she said. "I'm so sorry. When did..."

"Couple of days ago," Tomlinson interrupted. "But it'll be all right. Just a black eye and a busted nose."

Allie remembered then that she'd seen Mrs. Tomlinson sometime within the last two days; this very morning, in fact. She hadn't been wearing a bandage then. But Tomlinson was still talking in his rather high-pitched sympathetic voice. Once more she concentrated on what she was saying.

"And we'd really like to help you, Mrs. Neilsen," the man said, "but the fact is we neither saw nor heard a thing. It we do remember anything, we'll be very glad to tell you about it."

He stood up then and went to a side table. Reaching down he lifted a wine bottle and took a pair of thin-stemmed glasses and filled them. He carried one over to Allie.

"Take a little of this," he said. "It will relax you, make you feel a little more easy, perhaps."

He held on to the other glass and went back to his chair. He didn't offer any to his wife or comment on the fact that he didn't. The woman sat like a statue in her chair. She had said less than a dozen words since Allie had entered the house. There had been only that shy, half nod and greeting as Tomlinson had introduced her.

"Yes, it was a terrible thing," Tomlinson said. "But the police will get to the bottom of it. Never fear, they'll get to the bottom of it all right."

Allie opened her mouth to speak then, at the same time preparing to put the almost full wine glass on the table at her side. She wasn't really watching as, almost instinctively, she reached for the table she knew to be there and that is why, as she set the glass down, she didn't see the ash tray. The glass, leaving her hand, half sat on the edge of the tray for a split second and then tipped and spilled. Some of the wine splashed to the floor, but a good part of it spilled across Allie's lap.

Instinctively she gave a little cry and leaped to her feet. Tomlinson was on his feet at the same instant.

Allie flushed and turned to him.

"Oh," she said, "I'm sorry. I'm so sorry. Really, I don't know what in the world..."

Tomlinson smiled.

"Please," he said. "Please. It was an accident. Could happen to anyone. But I'm afraid you have spoiled your dress." He turned to the silent woman with the bandaged face.

"Marian," he said. "Get a rag out of the kitchen."

As Allie stood there, feeling the liquid soak through the fabric of her skirt, he moved toward her.

"You'll find a towel in the bathroom," he said. "I'd suggest..."

Allie nodded weakly.

"Oh the dress will be all right," she said, "but I'm afraid that I've..."

"The bathroom is right down the hall. Go through the bedroom at the left."

Allie started for the hallway as the other woman hurried into the kitchen. She heard Tomlinson call directions about finding the bedroom light switch. But Allie didn't have to be told. It would be in the same place as the switch in her bedroom.

It took Allie two or three minutes to rinse out the red stain and she didn't get it all out. She was really a mess and she gave a sort of half sad little laugh as she finished trying to dry the dress with tissue paper. Then she turned and started out of the bathroom.

It was when she had walked halfway across the bedroom that she came to a dead stop and her eyes slowly widened.

Allie was staring at the wallpaper.

It was purple wallpaper, decorated with mauve roses!

For a stunned moment she just stood there as the blood drained from her face. In spite of herself then, the small little cry forced itself from her constricted throat. She turned slowly and surveyed the room. The large double dresser sat opposite the bed.

There couldn't be the slightest possible doubt about it. Not one possible lingering question of a doubt. It was the room which Len had so adequately described. The room in which a dead man had lain on a bed with a small bullet hole neatly drilled through the center of his forehead.

She was still standing there staring down at the neatly made-up double-bed, when the voice spoke.

"Were you looking for something, Mrs. Neilsen?"

Allie gasped and swung around.

Gerald Tomlinson's gaunt, rangy frame filled the doorway. There was a not unpleasant smile on his face, but the eyes were cold and searching as he stared at her. The smile did nothing to erase a peculiarly sinister tone which went with the man's words.

Standing there, not ten feet away from him, Allie felt the fear begin to rise in her. Her soft mouth fell half open and her eyes were wide and staring. Her hands made feeble, clutching gestures behind her back as her fingers opened and closed. She knew that in a moment the scream would come.

Tomlinson took a couple of steps into the room. The scream was very close now; she could feel the cords in her throat as they tightened and her mouth opened wider. The smile left the man's face.

"I think Mrs. Neilsen," Tomlinson said, "that if you have finished you had better go. There really isn't anything more that we can tell you. Nothing we can do to help you." He stepped a little to one side and half turned, making a very slight bow as though to usher her out of the room. His eyes never left her face.

He knows. It was the first conscious thought to penetrate her sudden terrible fear. Yes, he knows. He understands that I have discovered something. He's standing there, staring at me, and I'm unable to conceal it.

It took every ounce of effort to take the few steps which carried her past him and through the doorway of the room. She was unable to utter a word. Even if her life had depended on it, Allie couldn't have sounded a single word. She was still pale and shaking as she reached the front door of the house and the man stepped beside her and wordlessly opened it for her. The woman was no longer in sight.

Only by the greatest exertion of will power was she able to avoid running the few steps to her own front door. It was probably her keyed-up emotional condition which prevented her from observing the silhouetted figure of Howard McNally as he stepped from the driveway at the side of Tomlinsons' and followed after her.

It was only after she had locked the door of her bedroom that the fear began to fade and to be replaced by the peculiar sense of exaltation which the discovery she had made in the bedroom of the house next door created within her.

Oh, God, he had been right. Len had been right all along. But the question now was what to do about it. Should she call the police at once? The temptation was great, but Allie took time to think about it. Surely, when the police saw that room they would understand. They would know Len had been in it.

For a moment, then, her face fell. Yes, she could prove he had been in the room. But what about the dead man? Was the dead man still there in the house?

Allie sat on the edge of her bed and her mind raced as she tried to figure it out. If Tomlinson had killed a man, certainly he wouldn't leave the body lying around. And Len had thought someone had seen him in the room with the dead man. That person must have been Tomlinson. Tomlinson, knowing he had been discovered, would hardly keep a piece of evidence like that in his house.

No, the first thing he would have done was to have gotten rid of the corpse. There wouldn't have been time to bury the body, no time for digging a hole in the basement or anything like that. The only thing he could have done was to have put it in his car and taken it some place. Or perhaps, just possibly, the body was still in the car.

Allie shuddered as she thought about it. And then she thought about Len. Suddenly she knew what she had to do.

Mrs. Manning was in the living room watching television and she was so involved in following one of her favorite programs that she barely nodded as Allie looked in on her. A minute later and Allie was in her kitchen. She didn't turn on the light but she needed no light to find her way to the drawer under the sink counter and find the flashlight. Quickly she opened the back door and slipped outside.

The moon was behind a cloud and there were no stars in the black, overcast sky. It only took her a minute or two to circle around until she was in the back of the Tomlinsons' garage. She had to be very careful, but she knew her yard well and was able to avoid obstructions.

Trying the rear window of the garage, she found it securely locked. She walked around to the side of the garage. From here she could see the Tomlinsons' house. There were no lights in the rear windows.

With a silent prayer on her lips, she found the knob on the side door. It turned under her hand and she gently pushed. And then she was inside of the garage.

She was still shaken from her experience in the house and it was only the knowledge that at last she was on the verge of accomplishment which gave her courage to go on.

Shielding the beam as best she could with the palm of her hand, she switched on the flash. At once she noticed several things. Heavy canvas tarpaulins had been hung over the rear window as well as the window in the side door of the building. The Tomlinsons' car was standing directly in front of her. The double, overhung door was tightly shut.

At once she breathed a sigh of relief, knowing that no one would be able to see the reflection of the flashlight from outside the building. At the same time, however, she experienced an odd, macabre sensation, almost as though she were locked in a tomb.

Her chin quivering in spite of an iron effort at self-control, Allie went to the car. It took almost superhuman effort for her to force herself to open the trunk. A quick look as the searchlight swung around and illuminated the cavernous space, showed nothing but a spare tire, a few tools and a strange looking implement which somewhat resembled a gardener's spade or hoe.

Allie quickly dropped the cover. She stepped to the side of the car and opened the rear door. Once more her fingers pressed the button and the light flashed into the interior of the car. The relief at not seeing a body was only offset by her sudden sharp disappointment.

Carefully she lifted the flash up and down, examining the upholstery.

The dead man had had a bullet in his forehead. Len had told her a trickle of blood was flowing from the wound. Perhaps, if Tomlinson had carried the body in the back of the car in order to get rid of it...

But Allie saw no signs of blood. She was about to once more douse the light in disappointment, when she did see something else. Quickly she reached down and from the floor, just under the edge of the seat, she picked up the piece of paper. The light from the flash fell full on it. Allie was holding a fifty dollar bill in her hand.

She was still staring at it, a perplexed look on her face, when it happened.

The voice spoke as the overhead garage light flashed on. Allie didn't need the light, however, to identify the owner of that soft, almost gentle voice.

"Nosy—just like your husband, aren't you Mrs. Neilson?"

Allie gasped and swung around.

Gerald Tomlinson stood with his back to the closed side door. There was a bitter smile on his long face.

Allie stared wordlessly as he moved. He held a narrow red plaid scarf in his long-fingered, sinewy hands.

"Yes," he said, "nosy. Just like your old man."

It was like a dream, some horrible nightmare when you were drowning and a hundred people were standing around and you tried to cry out and attract attention and for the life of you, you couldn't bring out a sound. Your mouth was open and you were screaming, but there wasn't a sound.

She could see the look in his eyes as he came toward her. She knew what he was going to do.

And then at last the sound came, but it wasn't a scream. It was barely a whisper.

"No," she said. "No. You can't... can't just..."

"But yes, I can. I can, Mrs. Neilsen," Tomlinson said. "You are trying to say I can't kill you, but I can. The same way that I killed Arbuckle. The same way I killed that foolish girl who saw me as I was carrying his body in from the car, early Saturday morning. The same way I will kill anyone who interferes with me or who gets in my way."

Allie at last found the scream which she had been unable to utter. But the sound of that scream never passed her lips.

By then the scarf was around her neck and Tomlinson was leaning far over her, twisting the ends tightly together.

It was then that Howard McNally, that little, fat, rather ridiculous man, did the one thing which went far to make up for many of the shoddy acts of his monotonous and uninteresting life; performed the single heroic deed of his entire thirty-odd years of selfish, self-centered living.

Upon leaving his back yard, McNally had sneaked around the side of the Tomlinsons' and had peered through the slit left where the curtain failed to meet the sill in the living room window. He had seen the Tomlinsons sitting there and he had seen Allie, leaning forward and talking with them. He had watched as she spilled the glass of wine down her dress. And he had seen her leave the room for the rear of the house.

He'd watched as the light came on in the bedroom, and he'd gone to that window.

What had happened in the bedroom and the words he'd overheard, meant nothing to him. But he had waited and watched and then later, as Allie left the house, he'd again followed her.

He was still trying to make up his mind what to do when once more she had left her house. This time following had been harder, but his ears had replaced his eyes and he knew when she went to the rear of Tomlinsons' garage and then circled to the side to open the door.

McNally was on the verge of following her into the garage when his keen ears had heard Tomlinson's footsteps. He barely managed to duck in time as the other man approached. The moment Tomlinson silently slid into the garage, McNally was back with his ear to the door.

He still had the target pistol in his hand. It wasn't that he was actually going to use it. He didn't even think about that. No, there was just the one single thought in his mind. This woman, Mrs. Neilsen, was trying to frame him for a murder. He must find out what she was saying, find out what she was doing. And he must stop her from doing it at all costs.

By this time Howard McNally was cold sober. Perhaps not quite sane, but certainly cold sober.

The moment Tomlinson snapped on the overhead light, Howard dropped to his knees so that the keyhole was within an inch from his eye. He had a clear view of Allie, blocked only by the silhouetted shoulder of Tomlinson. He heard Tomlinson's words, which didn't at first mean anything to him.

But then he heard Tomlinson mention the murdered girl. He saw Tomlinson reach out for Allie Neilsen and twist the scarf around her neck.

There was no mistaking what Tomlinson was about to do.

The gun wasn't even loaded: The target gun which Howard McNally still clutched in his hand.

He didn't even think as he crashed through the door. He didn't even realize that he was holding the gun by the barrel and pointing the butt of the gun at Tomlinson in a completely ridiculous fashion, as he yelled the words.

"Drop her," McNally yelled. "Let her go!"

To do what he had to do then, Tomlinson was forced to take his hands from the scarf.

As the gun in Gerald Tomlinson's fist, the gun he'd jerked from his rear pocket, quickly leaped in his hands and the impact of the shots blasted in the small rectangular room, the sirens screaming a block away reached the killer's ears.

Howard McNally never heard the sirens, although it was his own wife who had called the police to the scene. He was already dead as he slowly dropped across the doorsill half in and half out of the room. He never knew that it was Myrtle who had called the police to arrest him for the Julio girl's murder; the same police who within minutes were to capture Gerald Tomlinson as Tomlinson tried to shoot it out with them on the lawn of his home in Fairlawn Acres.

Chapter Fifteen

Now and then Lieutenant Clifford Giddeon will think about Fairlawn Acres; not long ago he drove through the place, passing along Crescent Drive. He was on his way from his home over to a new yard out near Northport, where he keeps his ketch. He turned in at Fairlawn on a whim; he sort of felt sentimental about the neighborhood.

Things haven't changed a great deal in Fairlawn, although Mathews and Cohen did add a couple of hundred additional homes. A few of the older residents have moved away and their houses have been purchased and occupied by new young couples, most of whom have children.

The Tomlinsons, of course, are no longer there. Tomlinson himself is in the death cell up in Sing Sing—they never did try him for the Julio murder, but a hunter accidentally discovered Arbuckle's body when his beagle began digging around for a rabbit and uncovered a swollen hand. The bullet in Arbuckle's skull matched Tomlinson's gun and a conviction was easily obtained, in spite of the brilliant defense by I. Oscar Leavy, who took on Tomlinson's case immediately upon losing Len Neilsen as a client.

It happened only two weeks after Tomlinson's capture and was very convenient all the way around. Marian Tomlinson and Patsy just disappeared and no one knows what has become of them.

The Swansons are still there, but the Kitteridges have sold their place and moved into a residential hotel in upper Manhattan.

Oddly enough, Myrtle McNally also still lives in Fairlawn. It turned out, much to her surprise as well as everyone else's, that Howard had taken out a double indemnity policy for fifty thousand dollars less than a month before he was killed. The money makes it possible for her to keep her house and bring up little Melanie.

The Julio family have long since departed but the Doyle youngster, Peter, still lives around the corner with his mother and father. He has turned into a very normal boy and is wildly enthusiastic over baseball and football and has given up most of his childish fancies. He is no longer interested in play acting.

Of course the Neilsens are no longer around; they sold the house and took a place up in Westchester, where, finally, they were able to uncover a good "buy" within their means. Len is doing fine as the office manager at Eastern Engineering and is in line for an assistant vice-presidency any day now. He drinks nothing stronger than root beer.

Perhaps the strangest thing is, that of all the people whose lives were to be so vitally affected by that rather miraculous incident mentioned in the very beginning of this story—the incident of Mrs. Manheimer's scream when Tomlinson was about to bring his gun down on the skull of Angelo Bertolli—only Mrs. Manheimer herself really benefited.

During the course of the Julio murder investigation and the subsequent trial of Gerald Tomlinson, Mrs. Manheimer sold an extra hundred papers over the counter of her newsstand each day.

It couldn't have happened to a more deserving person.

THE END